Nocturnus, Book One

The Wisdom of Blood

By A.G. Howard

A.G. Howard is the #1 NYT & International Bestselling author of young adult retellings/spinoff novels and adult gothic paranormal romances. Her dark Alice in Wonderland inspired Splintered series has been published in over a dozen languages and has hit bestselling lists both internationally and domestically. You can find all her titles and connect with her online at aghoward.com.

PART I: FAIRYTALE

"Art, like Nature, has her monsters …
Things of bestial shape and with hideous voices."
~Oscar Wilde

CHAPTER 1

Tatabury, Southern England
June 30, 1832

She wanted a fairytale.

Seated on the edge of the bed, Mordecai Dureance ceased working at the fastenings of his trousers. He didn't know much about honeymoons, this being his first, but he suspected *that* wasn't something a man often heard from his new wife only moments away from consummation.

"I know I'm being a nervous ninny, but . . ." Lynora's voice trembled.

He looked into his bride's eyes—the green-amber of rich liquor. They were clouded with tears.

"No, no." He knelt to the floor, nuzzling her hand as she propped up on her elbow. "Not at all."

Her chemise clung in a dewy film across her body after the bath she'd taken. Only five minutes earlier, he'd been standing with his arms around her. He'd pressed his lips along her skin, tasting lavender soap and innocence. His hands glided over her body, the curves once foreign and forbidden soon to become a book well read . . . the pages suppler and more enchanting with each new turn. She'd responded— a haven of delicate trembles as he carried her to the bed and placed her atop a sprinkling of rose petals.

He clenched his jaw in an effort to tame the desire still lapping at the lower edges of his gut. "Perhaps another sip of port will do the trick?"

She caressed his cheek and he leaned into her soft touch. "I want my mind and body sound. That fairytale you told Isaac before he left . . . the one with the prince and his lady love. It was so romantic and soothing. I simply need a momentary distraction."

Mordecai pushed aside his body's own uncomfortable distractions. She was nineteen—five years younger than him, sheltered and inexperienced. He wouldn't rush this, regardless that Isaac, his seven-year-old half-brother, was staying with trusted acquaintances to give them this time alone, and they had barely a few hours before his return.

In the past, Mordecai had enjoyed living in such a tiny cottage. Less housework and upkeep. Tonight however, the one-room abode no longer felt cozy. It felt inadequate. Another blatant reminder of how little he had to offer his debutante bride who had grown up in a townhouse with servants, four flights of rooms, and several acreages to tromp upon.

The candlelight dipped and turned, illuminating her flushed cheeks and kiss-swollen lips. He'd barely managed to remove his boots and peel off his shirt before her untimely request for a bedtime story. Surely, he could get things back on task without resorting to fables and folklore.

"I thought you'd had enough of story-telling after our trip to the Egyptian Hall this morning." He took her left hand in his.

"That was history, not fanciful tales."

"A bit of both, I would say. And we left that exhibit determined to write our own history, did we not?" He tapped the ring on her finger—woven of thread and promises—that he'd placed upon her scant hours earlier. Seated once more on the bed's edge, he coaxed his bride into a sitting position, fingertips finding that dip in her lower back which drew a purr from her throat each time he touched it. "Sweet Lynora . . ."

"Lady Dureance." She sighed against his neck. Her arms eased around his nape.

"*Wife,*" he teased, finding her mouth. Before his tongue could breech her lips, she drew back again.

"Just one telling, Mordecai. Then I promise, I'll be ready."

Damn, but she was persistent. Of course, considering all she'd given up for him, she deserved nothing less than her heart's every whim.

He kissed her cheek in surrender. "I'll do better than recite a fairytale. I will *enact* one."

She answered with a breathtaking smile.

He grinned and slid to the floor, kneeling before her. "Fair princess, I would wander the barbaric wilds for treasure, just to prove my love for you."

Lynora curled her legs beneath her chemise—all but the provocative curve of a bared ankle. "That would never do, my prince. Lest you tread barefoot through the sky. And dare not return without a star in hand for me to wish upon."

"Done and done." Mordecai stood, shrugged into his shirt, and strode to the door where he lifted a leather necklace off its hook beside the frame.

Throwing her legs over the bed's edge, Lynora gaped. "I thought we were playing make believe! You're not to actually go out, are you? Barefoot . . . to your cellar lab?"

Mordecai held up the key dangling from the necklace. "I told you. I'm to enact the fairytale. All the way down to the happily ever after." He looped the necklace over his head. With a wink, he opened the door and stepped over the threshold.

She leapt from the bed to meet him at the opening, a coy slant to her chin as she looked up at him. "You'll walk through the sky and bring me a star, then?"

He grasped her hand, lifting it to kiss the pulse point of her inner wrist. Her heartbeat escalated beneath his lips. "A scant compromise. Through the briars, for a star-*flower*."

"You're going to bring it here? Your hybrid that glows?" Her enthralled expression pleased him.

"Much like your eyes, it blinks with the tenderness of a firefly," he answered with a tap to her dainty nose.

A cool breeze swirled her long midnight hair and her gown's hem. Her expression faded to worry again. "But the trail is dark. And what of the bats? They're haunted creatures . . ."

He smiled. "I should've tossed out Isaac's collection of dreadful sketches before you saw them. We don't live within a horror-scape, sweet love, and we've nothing to fear of bats."

Her frown deepened. "Isaac's drawings are never to be tossed out as rubbish, scary or no. And you should at least take a lantern."

He kissed her wrist again, following a thin blue vein with his tongue to the bend of her elbow. "I grew up in this forest. I can walk it blindfolded." Pressing his lips against her pulse once more, he released her and stepped off the porch.

She shivered in the night air, hanging on the door frame. "Your courage inspires me. When you return, I'll have no more reservations. So please hurry."

He walked backwards, admiring how the light splayed behind her head, as if it were a halo. "Nothing in this world could keep me from returning to you tonight."

They held gazes until the door shut and the light whittled away to a thin stream at the edge of the porch. Mordecai waited to hear the lock click, then turned to follow the darkened path. He dodged an archway of wild roses and honeysuckle on his trek. It had been his wedding gift to her. He'd trained them to grow across the latticework over the months he'd come to know her, and earlier this eve, in the presence of Isaac and a judge, it had become their floral cathedral beneath the open skies. Now, the moon and stars glistened across the leaves and petals, lighting them up like ice sculptures. He took a deep breath of the perfumed fragrance to staunch a rush of bitter shame. He'd wanted to offer his bride a true cathedral for their marriage, but her family didn't approve and would've done all they could to stop it. Like everything else in his life, this momentous event had to be enacted in secrecy.

He turned away, and his feet plodded onward. He knew this trail, knew its winding slant through the brush and trees—inasmuch as he knew the veins that crawled through his own wrists. A fallen twig jabbed the vulnerable skin between his toes. Whispering an oath, he nudged it aside and continued on the path.

Less than a quarter of a mile away, a carriage scuttled along the dirt road leading from the cemetery. Merchants carrying freight often took the road parallel to this thicket. However, tonight the scrape of hooves sounded strange—a rattle of metallic clangs. Alongside, a whirring squeak whistled on the air like gears being turned. Squinting at the resulting swarm of dust in the distance, Mordecai couldn't make out anything other than shadows, trees, and the occasional pipistrelle swooping down for a meal of insects.

Unlike Lynora, the bats didn't unsettle him. Instead, they pained him, stirring memories of his past—a jagged looking glass which sliced him to bleed each time he glanced within. A small part of him despised the flighty creatures for stealing his father's attention for so much of his childhood, but Mordecai still respected their graceful descent into gluttony and self-preservation each night. There was also the added benefit that their presence deterred outsiders from venturing into the forest. The rumors surrounding the bats enabled him to live in solitude, away from the condescending eyes of his town.

Tatabury . . . a cornucopia of manor-houses made up of mellow stones and sparkling stucco which overflowed with earls, viscounts, and barons alike. Hard to believe, not so many years ago, he had been one of their own.

Cool night wind rattled the grasses. He glanced up through the shuddering leaves overhead, his footsteps slower as discontent stirred within his chest. He traced the leather strand at his neck and squeezed the brass key at the end, tight enough to leave its imprint in his fingers. A moth landed on his shirt. He tweaked its feather-soft wings to send it back into flight. Sedge, thick like feathers, tickled his ankles from both sides of the trail.

Coming to a juncture in the path, he veered left and plunged through some brush. He disregarded the clatter of carriage wheels seemingly growing closer. They'd soon pass with no knowledge of his presence. Having brought no light, he had nothing to give him away. After counting five steps, he crouched beside the dense blanket of barbed stems and leaves concealing the trapdoor to his cellar lab.

"Hello, my lovely." At the sound of his voice, the leaves rattled and serpentine stems disentangled from one another to reveal glimpses of wood beneath. They continued their slithering momentum until they bordered the frame, leaving the door bared and accessible. Satisfaction curled through Mordecai. Though he cherished all of his hybrids, the stinging-creeper vines were his pride.

He traced his fingertip along the door's rusted padlock. Inside, his bride's gift waited: his most recent horticultural coup. He couldn't contest the nervous chill within his core. Showing Lynora his luminous perennial was the smallest of steps. Tomorrow, he would allow her into his lab for the first time and reveal all the byproducts of his visions. Up till now, not even his little brother had seen them. To cross-breed plants with any other species would be construed by some as a form of sacrilege—by others the fetish of a hedonistic madman. But Lynora didn't bend to such prejudice, for she knew his heart.

He tugged the leather cord off of his head and leaned over to unfasten the padlock. Before he could insert the key, the thunder of clanging hooves and the grind of mechanics surged all around him.

Gripping the key, he whirled around as a post chaise and four brightly shimmering steeds charged off of the road and into his grove of ash trees. The gust, combined with the shock of their arrival, almost knocked him over.

He stepped back and stared—mouth agape—at the horses, piecing together what made them shine so strangely. Starlight reflected off of brass hides as the quartet settled in place just like living counterparts might, flicking tails of silvery aluminum threads and shaking manes of the same. A metallic jingle followed every movement. From each of their noses burst a puff of steam that blended with the clouds of dust on the air. His own breath clung inside him, trapped between rapt horror and admiration for the ingenuity of such a creation.

The carriage's door opened and its occupants descended onto the path. Five men wearing dark, hooded cloaks surrounded him, each standing at least one hand taller than his own shoulders, and their frames wider by no less than a hand's span as well. In all of his twenty-four years of life, he had never been looked down upon by anyone, at least physically. Tasked daily with pruning large-branched trees and planting hefty shrubs, his musculature was far from slight. Yet he felt akin to a bug next to these strangers. How could so many men of such stature fit into a standard equipage? Yet again, there was nothing standard about this carriage, was there?

His throat dried. "Who . . . what . . ."

From beneath their hooded cloaks, they glanced at one another as Mordecai struggled to frame a coherent thought.

"Are . . . you lost?" he finally sputtered.

"We believe you are the one lost, Lord Dureance," one of the strangers answered. "But we have reserved a place for you, in our carriage." The man gestured to the post chaise, his hand glistening and milky like cobwebs in moonlight.

Mordecai tottered back, as much at hearing his name as at the man's unnatural complexion. His elbow brushed one of the horse's wiry tails. Had the beast been real, the proximity would surely have spooked it. "Do I know you . . . have we met?"

"Please, Your Lordship." A second man spoke up. "We aren't asking for your soul. Simply for a carriage ride."

"One midnight jaunt around the forest." A third speaker stepped in front of the other four. This one's complexion appeared dark as night, yet still aglow—a storm cloud with the moon behind it. His voice sparkled with melody, richly sonorous and seductive. The cadence of consonants and vowels wrapped around Mordecai's consciousness like soft summer rain, until he could no longer remember why he had come to stand at the door of his cellar lab with key in hand; until he could no longer recall the events of the night leading up to this; until mechanical horses and spectral skin seemed like something from a child's lullaby, not a nightmare.

"We have a proposition for you," the lyrical stranger continued. "We shall return you to this very locale unharmed, should you decide to stay here in your colorless, common world. You'll remember nothing but a sweet dream of wine, women, and song." As the others held the carriage door open, the third man drew off his hood with slender, darkly luminous fingers.

From beneath a mane of lustrous black hair, a face emerged . . . young like Mordecai's, yet European in its symmetry with an austere slant: full, burgundy lips and strong jaw. His lashes—as thick as a raven's plumage—emphasized piercing amber eyes that flashed against the leafy backdrop behind him with the glint of gold coins.

He was beautiful. Too beautiful.

Ashamed of his own disarray, Mordecai shifted to hide his naked feet behind some sedge. Spurred by his movement, the creeper vines squirmed and knotted around one another until they camouflaged the cellar door again.

"Magnificent." The dulcet stranger stared at the blanket of leaves, not the least unnerved by the plant's activity. "So . . . you spliced a serpentine constrictor with a genus of invasive nettle weeds. What was the purpose?"

"H-how could you know that?" Mordecai's tongue seemed to swell on the query.

"Oh, we know everything about you, Lord Dureance." The stranger knelt down next to the ivy and the leaves trembled. He brushed his hand across the plant without touching it, then stood. "Were you hoping to give it flexibility to maneuver at will? You must have been so pleased at the result. To have her gain percipience so she responds to her caregiver's voice . . . well, that is beyond any miracle of science I've yet to see."

A thousand questions pounded behind Mordecai's temples; but he couldn't voice a single one for the shuddering race of his heart. He shifted his feet, stirring a swarm of gnats to rise from the sedge. Mordecai started to shoo them off but stiffened as the stranger lifted a hand toward him. A cloying perfume emanated from his flesh—like wet flowers mildewed in the sun. When his fingers came within inches of the gnats, the bugs scattered without even a wave or a touch, as if the man's mere proximity repelled them. Come to think of it, even the cricket songs had vanished upon the chaise's arrival.

Panic grated along Mordecai's spine, splitting a trail though the hairs on his neck. He needed a weapon. His dagger waited below in the cellar, but he could never release the padlock in time. He wedged the jagged copper key between his index and middle finger, holding it behind him, ready to gouge the stranger's queer flashing eyes should the need arise to defend himself. "Who the hell are you?"

Without releasing his gaze, the exquisite man bowed with all the grace of a noble. "I am Augustus Vallance of Nocturnus. Your humble servant." He swept out his arm. "Here to serve, Your Lordship."

Mordecai cinched the key tighter, wincing at the title. Could they not deduce his status from his attire? His faded trousers, his worn shirt—open and bereft of a cravat. "I fear you have me confused with another. I am no member of the elite. And Nocturnus . . . I've never heard of such a province. In all rightness, perhaps I should be bowing to you."

Augustus straightened. He glanced at his companions behind him with an amused smirk, then back to Mordecai. "Are you not the Honorable Earl of Nottingham? Lord Mordecai Dureance . . . son of Cornelius. Born by blood to the title?"

Mordecai felt a tangle bind his gut. Yes, he had been born to it; and he would have been proud to share it with Isaac—despite the child's illegitimacy. Until their widowed deuce of a father squandered the earldom and all of the estates with trips to Egypt years before Isaac was even born. Once Cornelius finally returned, he delved into card games and gambling, hoping to finance his erratic scientific schemes. In the end, just one step away from debtor's prison, Mordecai's father had simply disappeared.

Now, Mordecai and his brother lived in a humble weaver's cottage on a patch of land no bigger than five square yards, isolated here in the forest. The property had been bequeathed to them by a deceased aunt who had kept it for a servants' abode, but that was none of this stranger's concern. Unless . . . perhaps they had met Cornelius abroad. In which case, he no doubt owed them money and they'd come seeking it through his sons. They were to be sorely disappointed. Blood never flowed freely from a stone.

Mordecai divided his attention between one stranger and the next, sizing the four of them up. He had been raised a gentleman, refined in the arts of boxing and pistol duels. After being snubbed by the *ton* for so long, his walk amongst the less savory of society had also enlightened him to the finer points of street fighting. Yet even he couldn't take five such sturdy assailants at once.

He cut a glance to his creeper vines. The best plan would be to lure two or three of the men closer to the plant so its constrictive instinct would overtake and snatch them off their feet, stinging them with its stickers. He had once watched the vines immobilize a deer in such a way.

As if Mordecai's thoughts reflected in his face, Augustus cocked his head. "Perchance there are too many of us for comfortable negotiations." Without looking away, he gestured to his four companions.

In an instant, the other men vanished—cloaks, vestments, shoes . . . everything. In their place, clouds of mist twined around one another and filtered like smoky snakes into the open carriage.

Mordecai squelched a groan. He had finally gone mad like his father . . . fair dues for following in the old man's footsteps—keeping late hours in the lab, experimenting with things better left undiscovered.

Playing God.

Could these be demons, sent from the Devil himself to carry him to Hell's gate? That would explain the metal steeds. The steam from their nostrils must be drifting up from the flaming pits of hell itself.

Mordecai scanned the beaten path beside him. He considered racing for the cottage, but that would merely lead these creatures to. . .

Lynora.

Warmth drained from his face as memory came flooding in; she was alone at the cottage unprotected, waiting for him. Behind his back, he laced his hands together with the copper key between his palms. The circle of twine pinched his left ring-finger.

"Your Lordship," Augustus crooned again, melting Mordecai with his harmonious voice. "I do hope you aren't anticipating an escape. Can any mere mortal evade a cloud?"

Fog billowed within the windows of the carriage where the men had siphoned in as mist, ready to break out at any moment and overtake him. Mordecai faltered, swayed by the breeze, almost too weak to stand against it. Only one explanation could suffice for this madness. The cheap port he earlier shared with Lynora had gone to his head and he was out cold. This was all a delusion.

Within the next few minutes he would awaken on the ground with a bruised brow from stumbling. He would stagger back to the cottage and Lynora's tender lips would soothe his frazzled nerves and pounding head.

A slight pressure on his elbow roused Mordecai from his mental reverie. Dazed, he dropped his brass key into the midst of his creepers, entranced by Augustus's flashing eyes.

Mordecai didn't feel his bare feet make the carriage steps offered by a coachman—a sixth cloaked stranger not visible before. Nor did he feel himself climb onto the squabs within the compartment. Instead, he floated, drifted, until he was simply there, nestled amidst the mist and velvet. And just as effortlessly, Augustus took the backward seat across from him and closed the door, his physique almost filling the opposite side.

At the crack of a whip and the clatter of hooves, Mordecai started to relax, even as the dusky landscape danced to life in his peripheral. He no longer felt afraid, for he was dreaming . . . none of this could possibly be real.

The chaise bounced over the terrain, rattling a cage above his head where a queer bird the size of a wren hung upside down by its clawed feet. A flash of moonlight blinked in the window through the passing trees, revealing the featherless state of its wings.

"It is a carrier." Augustus answered the query before Mordecai could ask it.

Mordecai squinted. "It is a pipistrelle bat."

His host grinned at his rebuttal, even more alluring with white teeth bared and framed by dark lips. "So it would appear. To a commonplace man. But we would like to lift you above all that."

"Ah." Mordecai propped his feet on the squab next to Augustus, wriggled his dusty toes, and crossed his arms behind his neck. If he was to be treated as royalty in this dream, he would happily play along. "And how do you intend to lift me from the dregs of banality? Are you to give me back my lost inheritance?"

Regarding Mordecai's naked feet where they dented the cushion next to his thigh, Augustus ran his tongue along his teeth. "A *new* inheritance. Via conversion, my lord." From beneath the seat, he drew out a corked bottle and a pewter mug. He worked off the seal and poured the fragrant drink, so deeply red it appeared black. "Have some fruited ale. One of the many luxuries Nocturnus has to offer you."

Mordecai took the mug, and holding it steady against the jostle of the carriage, drained the drink in one gulp. The taste was seductive—warming, sweet and bright—as if he sipped liquid sunshine off of a woman's bared breasts. Aside from a familiar tang he couldn't quite place, he'd never tasted anything like it. He nodded his gratitude and swiped some droplets from the stubble around his lips. His fingers curled through the mug's handle, perching it on his knee.

Augustus gestured to the twine around his ring finger. "The significance?"

Mordecai held up his hand to the passing moonlight. "I was wed tonight. My bride has one to match it." Embarrassment simmered hot behind his cheeks and ears. Even while walking through an unconscious delusion he felt obliged to justify his frugality. "It is only meant to be a symbol—until I can acquire a ring worthy of her."

"Yes, of course." His imaginary host appeared intrigued as he tucked away the bottle of ale. "And what kind of ring would be worthy of such a lady as your Lynora?"

"Well, she is accustomed to the finer things . . ." Mordecai paused, realizing his host had spoken his wife's name with intimate accuracy. In a knee-jerk reaction, nerves shook his abdomen—and this surprised him, to suffer nausea in a dream.

He smacked his lips. The syrupy backwash of the ale still coated his tongue.

Shoulders tensing, he glanced at the moving scenery again. He could taste things, feel things. No mere dream could be as vivid as this, could it?

15

The alternative shook him to the core. If he was awake, these strange men . . . or beings . . . were taking him farther and farther from his bride. Fear sliced his lungs, cutting his breath into rasps. Trees blurred outside the window. No chance of jumping out at this brisk pace. Even if he hit the dirt road instead of a trunk, his neck would snap on impact. Aside from that, confusion began to rime his brain—a frosty dizziness indicating he'd been drugged.

Dragging his heels from the squab, Mordecai slammed his feet to the floor and the pewter mug toppled next to him with a clang. Breaking up the mist, he grabbed the stranger by the neck of his cloak and dragged him forward. "What did you put in my drink?"

Augustus looked him square in the eye. "Only blood, my lord."

CHAPTER 2

"Blood?" Mordecai swiped his tongue with his sleeve while fighting a gagging sensation. The familiar tang he'd tasted . . .

Augustus laughed—a sound that sparkled. "I should clarify. 'Tis the blood of a fruit. A pomegranate."

Nose-to-nose with his host again, Mordecai glared. "And you tainted it with some hallucinogen. How else could your friends have performed such a vanishing act?"

"Ah." His host held up a long finger. "But you drank it *after* the vanishing act, yes?"

Mordecai clenched his hand around Augustus's cold throat. "Then you're paid illusionists. Lynora's uncle sent you, didn't he? That bastard. Well he's too late. She's mine. In the eyes of God. In the eyes of man. No one, and nothing, can change that. Return me to my cottage *now*," he seethed through his teeth. "If they've taken her anywhere . . ."

The stranger's eyes flashed twice and the nerves in Mordecai's hand cramped. His fingers released, as if an unseen force pried his grasp open.

"Your Lynora is safe where you left her. If it comforts you to discount the mist as an illusion, then so be it. However, if you've courage enough to see the truth as it is, we've much more to show you." Augustus rubbed the place where Mordecai had grasped his

17

neck. The bruising marks faded in a blink. "We are acting on no one's behalf but ours. Tonight, we've come for you only. Should you later decide to bring your bride down, we can take it before the Agnate." His perfect features were as serene as a midnight sky.

Mordecai shook out his hand to ease the residual tingle in his fingers. "Bring her down? The Agnate? Your magician's vernacular is lost on me. I demand you use colloquialisms I can understand."

"Demand? Ah, it does warm the blood, to see you've retained your pride despite the blow the *ton* has dealt you. Despite your lowly vocation as a barefoot husbandman."

Mordecai pressed his spine to the cushion behind him and covered one foot with the other on the floor. His fingers strummed his thigh. "There is no dishonor in honest work. I'm a gardener, and therein is my pride."

"But your hands were meant for so much more, Your Lordship."

Mordecai stared at the hands in question, at the dirt gathered beneath his fingernails and caked on his callused palms—dirt that no amount of scrubbing ever dissolved. He loved gardening: the scent of the earth, the warmth of the sun on his bare back and a breeze through his hair, the brush of petals and cool leaves against his feet as he worked. He only wished it could be all about the pleasure, and not the meager wages and low status he earned.

Augustus sighed. "Is it not time you receive notoriety for your *true* accomplishments? Why do you hide your genius under lock and key beneath a cellar door?"

Mordecai clutched his knees, shocked again by the stranger's insight into the private details of his life. "Because the world is ruled by sanctimonious fools." He grimaced, unable to hold his tongue. Surely this crafty illusionist had drugged him with a truth-telling serum. "I don't wish to bring shame to my bride or brother through my unconventional enterprises."

Augustus lifted his hand, studying the glistening gold circle on his own left ring finger. "She must be a remarkable lady to accept your peculiarities without question. Most people in your society would never understand such vision. They would think you mad, or worse, possessed."

Feeling more alone than ever, Mordecai looked at the dirt on his hands again.

"What if I told you," Augustus said, leaning closer, "there is a kindredship who would understand . . . who in fact would revere you for such daring farsightedness?"

Augustus laced his immaculately preened fingers through Mordecai's. So taken aback by the chilled softness of his flesh, Mordecai didn't attempt to pull away.

"You have a strong pulse, my lord. A pulse inspired to Providence." Augustus turned Mordecai's palm up. A wave of numbing ice skimmed Mordecai's blood as his host ran a finger from his palm to his wrist, tracing the veins. Mordecai inhaled the musk of his captor's arctic breath and fell prey to an intense fascination—as if their spirits were connected on some level deepened by this minute intimacy.

His heart banged against his sternum. He should be in bed with his lovely bride. Yet here he was, being seduced by a beautiful trickster. Denial surged through him—chased away by the indomitable pull of feral magnetism. He wanted to draw back, but couldn't. Staring from beneath his lashes, Augustus traced Mordecai's veins to a smudged callus on his palm. When the stranger lifted his finger, the dirt was gone. *Another magic trick.*

"Do not let the vanities of the gentry taint your view of the world as a whole." Augustus's command was a serenade. "Dandies and greenhorns, all of them too beef-witted to even water their own hollyhocks. The elite's idea of industry is to sit in a premier club with their snifters of brandy until they are corned and pickled. Then they rally to attend galas with paper cards touting their worth. But you need no calling card. You are above them, Lord Dureance. Zeus to their Olympus. They are merely too ignorant to bow to your intellect. So, abdicate the throne."

Augustus freed Mordecai's hand and from his cloak withdrew a silk bag filled to the size and shape of a lumpy apple. Untying the grosgrain ribbon from its mouth, he emptied the contents into Mordecai's lap.

Mordecai gasped. Never had he seen such a pile of gold coins. He sifted them through his fingers, enthralled by the cold, metallic jingle as they slipped between his legs onto the cushion beneath. Raising his left knee, he gathered the coins into a glossy heap on the squab bedside him. "Are they real, or is this another illusion? Perhaps I'll blink, and they become seashells."

Augustus met his gaze. "They are as real as the lambent blossoms you have lighting up your cellar."

Mordecai balked. "How do you know of those—"

Augustus shushed him, took a coin between two fingers, flipped it, and caught it on his iridescent palm. He then arched a regal eyebrow. "We are prepared to give you one of these for each such flower you can successfully harvest in Nocturnus. You see, our location presents us with some rather—unique—lighting and atmospheric challenges. And your plant hybrid is the perfect solution."

Raking the gold from Augustus's palm back into the pile on the squab, Mordecai again noticed his host's lack of body heat. His flesh was every bit as cold as the coin. "So, all I need to do is plant some luminary flowers, and you'll remit payment fit for a king?"

With such a generous income, he could acquire his bride a ruby ring and choker to match, in just a matter of months. He could give her the lifestyle she deserved, the life he had taken from her. Not to mention the toys, clothes, and education he could provide for his growing brother.

"There is *one* other condition." Backed against the seat, Augustus rubbed his nape, thoughtful. "You must be willing to live in

Nocturnus. You shall be our gardener . . . yet so much more. We want you to continue your experimentation. We will finance your endeavors, anything you wish to pursue in your horticultural ventures. So long as you share your findings with us. The title for your position would be: *Master of Botany.* How does that suit you?"

Mordecai smoothed his trousers. A title. And an honorable one at that. Not one of petty heritage bequeathed through no merit of his own. One of respect and prestige, earned by God-given talents he had honed all of his life. Even as a youth, he had never agreed with the mindset of this society, never understood their one-sided view of the world. Wealth and peerage acquired by birth instead of intellect and ability—so unjust and infantine.

Mordecai's chest warmed. Had he finally found a place to belong, a people who were discerning and deep instead of shallow and trite?

His host had indicated that Lynora could live in Nocturnus as well. And Isaac, of course, would complete their trio. There was no downside . . . apart from the oddities of this man and his companions. Surely his family could adjust to living among such a progressive, intriguing society of magicians. For he was convinced now that's what they were—a traveling band of mages. Were he to join them, perhaps they would teach him their vanishing trick. Why shouldn't he embrace their artifice as a logical way of life, considering his own affinity for stretching nature beyond the natural?

Hands clasped on his lap, Mordecai tried not to appear too eager. "A change in domicile might be appealing. Where is this grand city of yours?"

Augustus's broad shoulders stiffened. The serenity of his countenance passed beneath a disturbed cloud for an instant then brightened again. "All in good time. But first . . ." He gathered the coins back into the bag and tied it off. "I need to be certain you grasp what I am asking of you. To live there, you must be a true citizen— you must *become* one of us. Tis the only way."

Mordecai narrowed his eyes, suspicious again. "And what does that entail? You want I should sign an oath of loyalty with my blood?"

Augustus smiled. Mordecai recoiled at the sharpened edge to his host's canine teeth— a monstrous mirage formed by the shifting moonlight.

Augustus tweaked the cage overhead, causing the captive to flap its wings for balance. The wire frame creaked eerily. "You know of bats, do you, Lord Dureance?"

Mordecai muscled his lips to an expressionless line. "In my youth, my father studied them. The forest is teaming with pipistrelles each night."

"But what of their legacy, their lore? Do you know of this?"

"Only oral narratives and handwritten tales of horror and misfortune passed from generation to generation. I wouldn't consider those worthy of a legacy; the tales are cheaper than the rags they're scripted upon."

"Hmm. I assumed you were above such narrowmindedness. To walk as one of us, you must be willing to see the purest amber-grain of truth fossilized within the fiction."

Augustus's mouth had caught Mordecai's attention again. Though sealed shut, a slight protrusion on either side of his lips gave a bestial quality to his mien, as if he were hiding fangs. It wasn't an error of light, or a mirage. A cold sweat formed on Mordecai's forehead.

Augustus turned his profile to the window's passing scenery and lifted his hood back over his hair, hiding his face as he spoke. "In Ancient Egypt, bats were long revered as the death-eaters born in the wilds of Necropolis, city of the dead—a restful world of wilted flowers and moonlit skies. The creatures were brought forth as a curse to Osiris, god of fertility, in the climax to a bout of sibling rivalry between him and his brother, Seth, god of chaos. After Seth killed and dismembered his brother, ensuring that Osiris became god of the underworld, Osiris's secret son, Horus, stepped forward to take his father's earthly throne back. His uncle Seth released a plague to torment Horus's father even in the afterlife, flying beasts that could slip through windows of dark gloom between Necropolis and this world. Creatures that would imbibe the essence of the departed souls and return them to their fallen bodies on earth by way of biting them. With their spirits intact, the dead would rise and walk again as though never gone, thus wreaking havoc on Osiris' efforts to maintain the border between life and death."

Mordecai wriggled on the squab, trying to assuage the unease crimping his gut. "I was at the museum on Piccadilly just this morning. I saw no mention of such a grotesque fable in the Egyptian exhibit." Yet even as he said the words, he remembered the screen he'd stood behind with Lynora. He'd been so intent on her, his gaze had barely skimmed the bats interspersed with mummies, scarab beetles, dismembered arms and legs, and other symbols—such a swift glide it didn't even register. Until now.

Augustus turned full around, eyes glimmering beneath his hood. "Perhaps you didn't look hard enough. And it is more than a fable, Lord Dureance. It is *history*. And there is more to the story yet. As the undead not only retained physical markers from their time in Necropolis—a moonlit aura to their flesh, a faint scent of decomposing flowers, eyes that could see in darkness—but they were altered internally by the bats that carried their souls over. These unusual characteristics forced them to hide from typical humans."

The hair on Mordecai's arms lifted beneath his shirt. He glanced at the cage above, remembering Augustus's strange reference to the creature earlier. *A carrier.*

Augustus lowered his voice to a pulse as hypnotic as a lullaby. "Horus attempted to seal the boundary, instructing his father Osiris's priests to build tombs of brick and stone, giant triangular mazes with no discernable way out, to hold the resurrected imprisoned. But Seth appointed his own priests to engrave directions for his revived subjects in the form of hieroglyphics on the walls. They were shown how to find others of their kind. Furious, Horus ordered Osiris's followers to embalm any and all deceased thereafter, removing the crucial organs and stuffing the cavities with linen or sand to render restoration impossible. Then, as an extra precaution, they wrapped the prepared bodies tightly in bindings—impenetrable to the bats' teeth."

Mordecai's jaw tightened. "Pyramids and mummies."

Augustus laughed, the chimes within his throat tinkling. "Indeed. And Horus assumed his stratagem had worked, as the bats—unable to carry out their duties—abandoned the underworld forever, learning to survive among the living by sipping the blood of humans, animals, or insects. But it was too late. A new breed of undead beings had already been spawned, able to walk the earth in spirit or solid form, and they were shaping subcultures of their own. Seeing the special gifts Seth had lent them, Horus drew upon his own powers of fertility—bequeathed by his father—to curse the race so they could never procreate."

Mordecai fidgeted as if scarabs crawled beneath his very flesh. He wanted to go back to believing his host was an illusionist, but they were beyond that now. He struggled to stop listening, concentrated instead on flickers of moonlight breaking through the trees as they swept by, but Augustus leaned into his line of sight, determined to be heard.

"You must bear the conclusion, Lord Dureance, if you wish to rise above your humble existence. I am required by our laws to tell you all of it. The god of chaos enabled his unearthly breed to convert common mortals in a ritual exchange of blood, ensuring the race could still multiply. But there was a third player in this act . . . Isis— goddess of the sun—looking down from the heavens, watching it all. She was more powerful than any of the gods, and she loved Osiris above Seth—as they shared their son Horus. Thus, she intervened to make conversion a complicated process, offering only one way to fully crossover. The blood exchange itself would alter the human somewhat, but without taking the final appointed step—experiencing the *Wisdom* of the blood—they would not be full Desmodai."

"*Desmodai?*" Inching back in his seat, Mordecai balked. It was apparent that this fool believed everything he said to be true. And try as he might, Mordecai couldn't escape Augustus's web of persuasion; the more he tried to resist, the tighter the threads bound. He'd seen many oddities tonight. Oddities that begged outlandish explanations.

Augustus steepled his fingers beneath his chin. "The kindredship adopted the title Desmodai, in honor of the Desmodontidae—the vampire bats that taught them to feed and live in the dark of night. The race was a hearty lot, ageless and nigh impossible to kill, as Osiris had forbidden them to enter Necropolis for rest and peace ever again with few exceptions. They flourished, sending out ambassadors two to three at a time to recruit others they deemed worthy of their kindredship. In a matter of centuries, they had founded clandestine cities all around the world."

To alleviate a sudden chill, Mordecai clasped the open collar at his neck. "So, your Nocturnus . . ."

"Is such a city, albeit a young one. Our founders came here in the late seventeenth century."

"Here? As in England?"

"Tatabury, in fact."

Mist thickened around Mordecai, a reminder of Augustus's vanishing companions, a mirror of his own obscured thoughts. Mordecai pointed to the haze. "Am I to believe your benefactors traveled like this?" His voice sounded ragged and tremulous, even to his own ears. Something inside of him yearned to accept it all, even hungered to hear more.

"Some took their spirit form. Others had belongings to carry, heirlooms, livestock, a heritage to preserve just like any other race. Those traveled in typical fashion though only at night, posing as foreigners with queer customs. The world's span is microscopic—every province, every continent, joined by the blood of mother earth. Her deepest veins reach around the globe a thousand times over, intersecting to provide opportunities for concealed pilgrimage."

Mordecai raked his fingers through his hair, growing more fascinated by the minute. "Oceans and rivers. They sail at night to conceal their differences in the shadows."

"At one time. But our scientists have developed fleets that now enable us the advantage of subaquatic navigations, so we can travel by day or night. The Desmodai had successful submersibles two full centuries before that mortal in France ever drew up his blueprints on the Nautilus." Augustus beamed with pride.

Mordecai slammed his shoulders against the cushion at the sight of three-inch fangs glimmering from within the hood.

Augustus shrugged back his cloak to expose his monstrous beauty in the moonlight. "Do not be afraid. You see, what sets us apart from other beings, is we select who we are to bring into our circle. 'Tis an honor to be approached, as we don't make the choice lightly. We want only those who can further our society, who have something unique to contribute. This carriage, these mechanical stallions so realistic in their appearance and movements—are such an example. Animals can sense the change in us . . . the internal, instinctual differences. They become skittish and unruly. A problematic quality for a mount. The mechanic who conceived of our robotic counterparts was a former clockmaker, and is now one of our most respected citizens. We give our postulates the choice of whether or not they want to join. You shan't be forced into anything, I assure you."

Before he could catch a breath to respond, Mordecai heard the aforementioned mechanical horses snort while slowing from a gallop to a trot. Headstones, draped by moving shadows with flashing eyes, peppered the midnight landscape outside. He stiffened. There looked to be at least six more of the Desmodai creatures lurking without.

"Why have you brought me to the cemetery?"

"As death is the way in, Your Lordship. To Nocturnus."

Terror spread through Mordecai like wildfire. Making a break for the door, he forced the latch open and leapt from the advancing carriage. Two solid forms broke his fall as the mist surrounding him transmuted back to Augustus's companions. They rolled with him in a tangle of legs and arms until a large tombstone stopped their momentum. Mordecai's body ached from the jolt. The taste of powdered granite coating his lips mingled with their sickening perfume as they steadied him upright and held him clutched beneath his arms.

"Easy there," one murmured as Mordecai attempted to jerk free. "Are you sure he is worth all this fuss, Augustus? I propose we pour the rest of the valerian down his throat and entrance him to forget."

Valerian . . . of course. That was the familiar flavor he couldn't place in the drink. Mordecai struggled to escape, growling as his captors' fingernails clamped into his arms like vicious talons.

"He seems to lack etiquette," another one snarled. "Isn't even properly shod." He glanced at Mordecai's feet.

As they gathered around him, Mordecai counted eleven Desmodai—not including his host.

Augustus slid from the carriage in an elegant sweep of dark fabric. "Surely you realize that a scientist of his caliber doesn't need shoes to prove his worth. At the age of seventeen, he spliced a living sea sponge with English Ivy to make a groundcover for his gardens that would retain moisture for weeks on end. Anyone with such a transcendent mind will see the boundless opportunities our proposition can afford him."

The previous objector tightened his grip on Mordecai. "I am not contesting his brilliance. But mayhap we miscalculated his readiness. Could be he's not seasoned enough to accept our lifestyle with grace. I propose we wait a few more years—"

"No. We are bound by law. This is the one and only time he will be approached. He is at his peak in this moment. He has been on the Desirable list since the age of fourteen, a pet project of the Brotherhood for close to eight years now. So, we give him time to make the choice. Unless you wish to question Regent Ezra's foresight in the matter."

The other man grew silent, his grip loosening. Taking advantage of the pause, Mordecai lunged. He fell to his knees, dragging two other captors with him. Augustus stepped forward and brushed the back of his cool hand across Mordecai's cheek.

Mordecai stilled and looked up. "You drugged me," he accused.

"A precise measurement. Merely enough to calm you for the ride here." Augustus tilted Mordecai's chin upward. "As you can see, it's already worn off. I want your mind clear; I want you to fathom what we're offering." He grasped both of Mordecai's shoulders and urged him to stand. "Escape from this petty drudgery. From the curdled cream of a society that sees you at worst a common laborer, and at best, an eccentric dreamer. You belong among us, Mordecai. An aristocracy ruled by virtuosos. Others like you who will understand and appreciate your most curious aspirations. In Nocturnus, you'll be respected above any mere Earl or Duke. You will have status and wealth and power to shame the peerage. And above all, you will experience life in its purest design . . . without any of this in your future." His long sleeve rippled as he gestured to the crumbling tombstones behind him. "Once you cross the boundary, your days and nights can be free of death and the ravages of time. You can be locked in the form you have at this very moment; forever at the peak of your genius, youth, and vigor . . . eternally virile and seductive. And above all—even five-hundred-years from now—retain a mind as keen and hungry for knowledge as it is today. Imagine all you can accomplish outside the limits of mortality."

Adrift on the mellifluous stream of words, Mordecai wrestled his waning doubt.

Augustus drew back. "That is good, my brother. Consider your options. For we'll respect whatever choice you make as final. There are many who have skills, but very few have ambition enough for such a venture. Should you decline, you will never be approached again. We'll leave you with no memory of our interlude." Augustus nodded to his companions. "Release him now. He has no desire to run." Upon his command, the other Desmodai loosed their hold.

Mordecai dusted off his trousers and straightened his shirt.

Augustus offered his palm as the other Desmodai distanced themselves. "What say you? Are you to be Mordecai, Master of Botany in Nocturnus? Or are to you to drowse away a limited existence here amongst the mortals: an unrequited Earl . . . a gardener whose back bends beneath the weight of a forgotten regret . . . who sloughs behind the shadow of a dream he almost grasped, but instead, let slip through decaying fingertips?"

Mordecai's eyes met his host's. Augustus averted his hypnotic gaze, his long lashes fanning down to cover the flashing lights; when he looked up again, the irises were no longer that of a creature's but of a man's—an equal. Mordecai felt a snap inside, a release from Augustus's entrancing persuasion. His own clarity returned: a moment of utter self-possession and certainty as to his identity, as to his place in the world. A place he wished to elevate.

Without another word between them, he took Augustus's silken hand. They strode into a thicket of trees bordering the cemetery with five other Desmodai flanking them on all sides—out of sight of the carriage, and into the gaping maw of death.

CHAPTER 3

"See my monster?"

Lynora glanced up from packing to look at Isaac's latest masterpiece. He stretched it between uplifted hands like a banner. Even from across the cottage, his seven-year-old smile, complete with dimples and missing teeth, lit up the darkness like a glint of summer sun. Upon his parchment, he had scribbled a charcoal creature with long, bald wings—similar to a bat yet humanlike.

Lynora shivered. "It is a fine picture, Isaac." She attempted to hide her aversion to the creature, managing a smile before she turned her back to fold a small shirt to be tucked atop the others piled upon his bed. She would pack everything at the opportune moment when Isaac wasn't looking. Blocking her actions with her body, she held the shirt to her nose so the scent of dust and outdoors—the essence of childhood—could ease her nerves.

Earlier, she'd made a small bag by folding and stitching together the edges of a rug once laid by the door. It had been her first attempt at sewing anything bigger than a patch over a frayed pant leg. She'd pricked her thumb, yet that sting was nothing compared to the internal barbs gouging her for the betrayal she was about to enact.

"What're you doing?" Isaac looked up again from his sketches, the right side of his face and his golden hair—so like his brother's—awash with flickering light from the candle in the table's midst.

Lynora laid the shirt in its stack. She had remained on the darkest side of the cottage in the hopes he wouldn't see her movements. Her throat tightened. Back turned, she answered, "I'm folding the wash." She whisked some tears away with her frock's sleeve. "Tell me of your picture there. What's the name of your monster?"

Her ruse worked, for she could hear him scribbling again. "Haven't yet thought of a name." His plump hands thrummed either side of the parchment where it laid on the table. "He's from the slums. Y'know . . . one of the batfolk."

Lynora gripped her wrist, allowing her fingernails to pinch the tender skin in an effort to quell the unease within her. She hadn't realized Isaac knew of the rumors. When murderers, thieves, and harlots went missing from the Tatabury slums with only a few drops of blood or torn clothing left behind, townspeople claimed the sinners fell to soul-sickness and became the pipistrelles. Someone had fashioned the ludicrous tale to explain the growing population of the species . . . to rationalize their strange flight patterns from the cemetery during broad daylight.

A few days ago, she'd heard rumors a man of Mordecai's build and hair color was seen at the edge of the slums—his face stuffed into the bosom of a whore as if he were feasting on her. The thought made Lynora ill, and for the first time, she hoped the tales of the pipistrelles were true. Mordecai deserved to be transformed into an ugly bat for abandoning their vows. Even more so for abandoning his brother.

She toyed with the circle of braided twine around her ring finger that had weighed her down for the past six weeks; tonight she would take it off and bury it. She'd worn the lie long enough. In the beginning, she had felt partially responsible for her husband's disappearance. He left their honeymoon bed to appease her nervous whimpering, after all. But she was no longer the anxious nit she'd been then.

That first month of Mordecai's absence, she'd cried herself to sleep each night, fearing the worst. She ventured out on her own to explore his cellar lab but couldn't get past the creeper vines. Triggered by her proximity, the plant moved and twisted, knotting its stickery leaves and stems until they formed an impenetrable sheath over the trapdoor's entrance.

During Mordecai's courting, there had been three different occasions Lynora managed to talk her lady's maid into accompanying her to Tatabury so she could have secret picnics with Mordecai and Isaac upon the cottage grounds. Mordecai had tried to coax Lynora into befriending the creeper at the time, but the serpentine movements made her squeamish. He finally gave up and warned her that since the creeper didn't know her, she should never provoke it.

However, with Mordecai gone—when her efforts to charm the hybrid failed—she went against his advice and her squeamish nature to get answers. She borrowed a scythe from a neighboring farmer and for three hours, thinned out the squirming groundcover using extreme caution and muscles she didn't know she possessed. Her palms blistered and her heart broke as she massacred her husband's beloved hybrids. However, vindication replaced guilt when she realized the padlock had been taken along with everything worth protecting within. Tables had been wiped clean, the floor swept and dusted. And there, sitting upon an empty table, a note addressed to her in Mordecai's handwriting.

"I must leave for a time, but worry not. I'm well. Take care of Isaac, and keep my heart safe for me. I will hold fast to memories of you both until I see you again."

There was no other explanation in those loops and coils of unfeeling ink. He'd simply left his bride and his brother without any real means to survive. So, Lynora, whether right or wrong, allowed Isaac to grieve. She told him Mordecai died, because he had in fact, to her.

She clenched her jaw and fingered the twine ring again. Despair no longer resided within her. Hatred blossomed in its place—as venomous and binding as the creeper plants themselves.

A knock on the door brought Isaac to his feet. He rushed to the oval window beside her and pushed aside the sheer drapes. His forehead pressed against the lower curve of the glass. "Tis Viscount Cummings' carriage." Isaac turned to look up at her. "What do you s'pose he wants?"

In the short time it took for Lynora to cross to the door and open it, Isaac found the carpet bag beside the bed and his clothes in piles ready to pack. Discernment iced his blue eyes to the color of frost on a lake—a desolation that left Lynora's every emotion suspended in the freeze.

"No!" Isaac scrambled into the far corner of the room, fitting his spine along the seam where the two walls met as if he wished to slide within. "I'll not go!"

Lynora glanced at the elderly viscount where he stood on the threshold. He tipped his hat and his tender smile bolstered her courage.

"It's only for a time, Isaac," she said. *The exact vow Mordecai had given her.* She forced her gaze to hold on the child's, willing him to believe the words that soured her tongue. "When I have a way to care for you properly, I'll bring you back home—" Her cracking voice betrayed her.

Isaac's face flushed to a red as deep as an opened wound. "You lied!" Launching himself from the corner, he raked his folded clothes onto the floor. Then he sprinted to the dining table and picked up a kaleidoscope—the gift Mordecai purchased from the Egyptian Hall on the morning of his and Lynora's marriage. "You said you'd never leave again! At the museum, you said it!" He sobbed, holding up the brass toy. "You lied!"

The viscount stepped within, picking up the clothes to stuff into the carpet bag. "It will be all right, son."

"I'm not your bloody son!"

Lynora caught Isaac before he could spring for the door. With a catch in her throat, she knelt to the floor to level their gazes. "Nor are you mine . . . however much I long for you to be."

He buried his face into her shoulder, moistening the muslin sleeve with his sobs. "You were to be the queen. Remember?" His muffled voice tapped her conscience like a brittle branch scraping a windowpane. He looped his arm around her neck and the kaleidoscope's cold stiffness grazed her bared nape. Isaac used to pretend the toy was a telescope through which he could see worlds even a map couldn't contain. Night after night, Lynora would sit by the window and let him charm her with his tales of adventure and exploration. He swore that one day he would sail her away somewhere undiscovered, kill all the monsters in the land, and she would be queen.

Lynora nuzzled her face into his soft hair to breathe him in. "I haven't forgotten. I will never forget." Being his caregiver had kept her feet grounded and her heart afloat all these weeks. How would she survive without his tiny voice, his toothless smiles? Tears streamed her face. "Be brave." She spoke the command more for herself than the child. "You will like it there. The viscount and his wife are very kind."

Isaac shook his head against her. "I want to stay with you."

Lynora stroked his shoulder blade. "It will be grand fun. You'll make friends your age." She winced at this thought, hoping his peculiarities didn't surface. She had always accepted Isaac's physical differences as part of him. But what would other people think were they to notice? "Try to be careful when you play. Don't get any scrapes or scratches . . ." Catching the viscount's questioning glance, Lynora added, "And keep your chamber picked up."

With a sympathetic grin, the elderly man resumed packing. Satisfied he'd construed her words as maternal ramblings, Lynora hugged Isaac tighter.

THE WISDOM OF BLOOD

"Why must I be orderly?" Isaac asked.

"Other children might be sharing your chamber, so you'll have to keep your things put away, or they might trip over them."

"I don't want to share a room. I want my bed . . . and our cottage."

The viscount had moved to the door now. From across Isaac's shoulder, Lynora caught a glimpse of the child's bed. Without the stacks of clothes, one could see the parchment maps strewn across the sheets. Chunks of graphite smudged the floor—dropped in a dash to mark some favorite locale. Her life would be barren in the absence of his clutter. In the midst of such precise order, everything would feel so out of place. But she couldn't keep him. Not for such selfish reasons.

"I can't care for you as I should," she whispered in his ear. She had tried for six weeks and barely managed. She'd cut her waist-length locks and sold them to a wig maker after a month. The proceeds bought only enough for two weeks' worth of food. Lately, they'd been eating what was left of Mordecai's dying garden out back; but Isaac needed more than cucumber preserves, boiled artichokes, and stewed carrots spooned over bread, and he was outgrowing his pants faster than she could patch them. "You need sustenance. Apparel."

"I'll eat grass and weeds like a goat," he answered in childhood innocence. "I can make clothes of leaves. Like in the garden of Eden." With each desperate plea, his breath burned hotter against her tear-dampened shoulder.

"But you deserve so much more, Isaac. I'll find real work. *Lasting* work. And then I will come for you. I promise."

Neither she nor Isaac wanted to turn loose. It took Viscount Cummings' gentle prying to break them apart.

"I'll visit you on the morrow." Lynora stared at the floor, unable to look at the child's face just yet. "I'll bring your maps and your toys."

When she made herself meet his gaze—wet and glistening—he handed her the kaleidoscope. "Not this one," he said with a strength

35

beyond his years. "I want it here when I come home." He sniffed and wiped his nose with a sleeve.

She took the brass cylinder, knowing how much he loved it, being his only tie to Mordecai. For him to leave it with her was a gesture of good faith that he would be back. His collateral against her promise.

"I love you, Isaac." She tightened her grasp on the kaleidoscope and kissed his hairline where the fringe of his cowlick stood tall and rigid.

Taking his bag, the viscount gently pulled the child away and led him outside. He drew the door shut behind them. In spite of the heaviness in her chest, Lynora stood, locked the latch, then watched them leave from the window, holding in her sobs. She heard a faint call—"*Lynora*"—as the carriage wheeled away.

Tracing the smudge left on the glass from Isaac's forehead, she opened the window's sash . . . hanging on to the last syllable of her name . . . the final reverberation of a child's broken heart.

She leaned against the cold window frame so it supported her temple. The rolling hills vanished into the dark sky—draped in mist creamed by moonlight. Tiny flying shadows swooped through the haze, pulling holes that closed again before she could blink, a colony of pipistrelles on their nightly flight to the boneyard. The sight unnerved her.

Lifting Isaac's kaleidoscope, she aimed the wide lens toward the moon and peered through the peephole, trying to remember one of his delightful stories. Silver light caressed the jagged bits of sea glass in the other end. The view torched to an explosive collage of color. Then, with an incidental turn of her wrist, the kaleidoscope's prisms merged to a liquidized red as if the lens were bleeding. Cringing, she placed the toy on Isaac's bed.

Her mind was playing tricks. Her uncle and aunt had disowned her when she abandoned their desire for her to marry for wealth. And marrying a man ostracized by society removed her from the peers' favor, as well. Now without Isaac, she had no family. She was truly alone in the world—and that frightened her more than any monster could.

She had to get Isaac back. Tomorrow she would find gainful employment—no matter how daunting or humiliating. She'd seen a sign in the window of the Counterpoint Inn, bidding for a professional laundress. Granted, she held little knowledge of household management, littler yet of the inner-workings of a washing-house or their drying-closets heated by furnaces. But she had recently learned to mend patches, scrub clothes, and hang them dry. Throughout her youth, she'd watched her lady's maid enough to pick up the skill of ironing. Perhaps she could flimflam her way through the rest until she figured it out. She would succeed. She would be strong for Isaac, where his brother had not been.

"*Lynora.*"

She whirled around at the whisper. Her gaze roved the door for any sign of intrusion, but the lock remained intact.

Backed against the open window, she fought to steady her breathing. Her nape chilled from the night breeze behind her. At the tripod table beside her bed, a lit candle animated the evening's shadows to eerie proportions. She caught her image in the mirror on the opposite wall. No one in the room but her and her reflection.

The crickets hushed as a gust of air stirred the gauzy drapes and a thick mist rushed through the opened panel to settle along the floor at her ankles like an affectionate cat. Drawing back from the cold, she latched the glass shut and stepped through the fog toward the candle on her tripod table. Before she could reach it, the flame extinguished, along with the one on the dining table, leaving her in complete darkness.

She scolded herself for trembling, then drew up her frock's long skirt and propped her knee on the mattress to feel her way toward the tripod.

Something rustled behind her and she froze, perched on the bed's edge.

"You cut your hair."

This was spoken aloud, and the voice drizzled into her soul like an opiate cordial. A swift spread of gooseflesh prickled her arms and neck. She wanted to glance over her shoulder but couldn't move.

"Your bared nape is tempting, sweet love. But I've waited too long to see your face. Turn for me."

Her chest tightened and she spun to her feet. In the far corner between Isaac's bed and the window, a silhouette leaned against the wall, just out of moonlight's reach. She knew that body, even drenched in shadows. Her hands had traced those muscled shoulders and arms countless times.

"Mordecai," she murmured—his name a serrated blade carving trenches in her throat.

He shoved himself to stand free of the wall. He'd always stood a head above her, but appeared taller than she remembered . . . his build even larger. Yet his mannerisms remained true. His fingers strummed his thigh in nervous anticipation, the same fingers that on her wedding night trailed her curves over her gown as if she were made of petals. That was before he'd left her aching for his touch—alone and unfulfilled.

She fisted her hands at her sides. "How dare you come back?"

"I've come to reclaim my heart. I trust you kept it safe for me, Lynora."

"You've no heart to keep, blackguard." She winced at the quiver in her voice. He started toward her but she held out her palm, cutting through a strand of moonlight. "Stop."

"You have . . . calluses," he murmured.

Lynora frowned, curious how he could've seen her marred skin in the darkness from across the room. "I've been struggling to keep your garden alive. Oh wait . . . no, these are the battle-scars I earned by murdering your creepers." She savored the pained growl that followed.

"I assumed you would ask the local jurisprudence to investigate. They could've sent a foot patrol to dig up the cellar. That was no task for a tender lady."

"You made me promise to keep your cellar a secret. It appears tender ladies are more versed at keeping their vows than strong, powerful men."

Another growl. "I never wanted to leave you for so long. I didn't know the way out until today. You'll forgive me once you understand."

"The way out? Of what, our marriage? I'll not ever forgive you. Not until the day I see you dead. As dead as the rose petals you sprinkled upon our empty nuptial bed." Her fingernails gouged the blisters in her palms.

Mordecai took another step. "Ah, then today fortune has smiled upon me. For today I merit your forgiveness."

Pulse pounding, she tried to make sense of his words, to make sense of his entry to the cottage. The door remained locked. The window and the fireplace were both too small for even a child of Isaac's size to infiltrate.

Mordecai must've been hidden inside, waiting to reveal himself. But where would a man of his stature hide? Two short beds, a tripod, a miniature dining table and armchairs offered the only options, yet none would've sufficed. He must have used his key . . . snuck in the door silently while she watched Isaac leave through the window.

"How long have you been here?" she pressed.

"Long enough to watch Isaac leave with the custodian of the orphan asylum. Long enough to know I've broken both of your hearts. And that's the last thing I ever intended, my swan." As he inched closer, a spindly line of moonlight fell across his shapely mouth and brightened his square chin and jaw for an instant. The characteristic, clean-edged shadow still graced his face, and a part of her ached to touch the dark golden bur on his chin. Then she noticed his lips—as dark and rich as a rose's heart.

"You lie," she whispered. "You lie through a mouth stained by another woman's kiss."

His hand, encased in a nobleman's pale linen gloves, swiped at his lips. When he drew his palm from his mouth, the color remained unaltered. "This is no cosmetic stain. It's a result of the conversion." The moonlight reflected a strange glint off his teeth.

"Conversion." Lynora clenched her skirt to pleats. "Is that what they're calling adultery now? Do you even care that Isaac is at a charity home? Living amongst strangers, Mordecai. You left us naught but a cottage and a dying vegetable garden." She paused. Behind the wall of her anger, a fragile niggle of hope unfurled. "Did you bring funds? A means so I may keep him?"

Mordecai's clothes rustled in the darkness as he shifted positions. "I did have some gold coins saved. They were lost."

"Oh? Let me guess where you lost them . . . within your prostitute's bountiful cleavage."

Mordecai crooked his head toward the closed window, paused as if listening to something outside. All Lynora could hear was the piercing silence of his neglect to deny her allegation.

"Lynora, I have broken their laws to come to you."

"Abandonment of one's wedding vows is hardly considered a clergyable offense, although it should be."

"I've not abandoned our vows!" The force of his outburst roared through her flesh and rattled her bones. His fingers thrummed his thigh in a calming motion. "I know I left you little explanation . . . and you had nothing for company but dark notions and misconstrued fancies."

She clenched her jaw. "You're wrong. I had Isaac. Before I was forced to deposit him directly into the carriage of Viscount Cummings." Her gaze flitted to the dining table next to Mordecai where Isaac had left his latest drawing. "In his eyes, I'm every bit the monster you are to me now."

A pained expression on his mouth, Mordecai turned to the sketch on the table. "Things are never so black and white, Lynora. You must know I've missed Isaac terribly." With his thumb, he flipped the parchment around to view it. A moan caught in his throat, as if something in the lines disturbed him. "What made him imagine such a creature?"

"Did you forget how much he loves his tales of the macabre? I suppose it's well enough we never tossed them out. They were the only reading materials we could afford with you gone."

Mordecai shifted his attention back to her. "Isaac should find a more productive venue for his flights of fancy. Paying homage to demons is a dangerous pastime."

"Huh. Spoken like a man intimately acquainted with demons of his own. You made your choice."

Mordecai slapped the picture to the floor. "Yes. And I can't undo what has been done. Isaac is lost to me now." His voice grew husky with emotion. "But there's no way in hell I'm losing you, too. Pack your things. We've little time before they find me gone."

CHAPTER 4

"Pack my things?" Lynora huffed in disbelief. After all her sacrifices to hold onto Isaac, her absentee groom expected her to let the boy be raised by strangers. "Whomever you're running from has no bearing on me. I refuse to share my life with a man who cares so little for his brother." Her teeth gritted tight, words burbling forth like seething oil. "You made me break my promise to him. You left him with naught but toys and tainted memories. Nothing is keeping you here. Save your feckless neck, and don't look back on us. Take your empty sentiments and go!"

She grabbed Isaac's kaleidoscope from the bed and flung it at Mordecai's dark mouth, waiting, hoping, for the break of glass. Instead, she heard the slap of metal on skin. From the shadows, Mordecai's left hand eased into the moonlight with the kaleidoscope clamped firmly in his palm. Somehow, he'd caught it in the darkness.

Lynora balked, seeing the lines in his palm taking shape. He wasn't wearing gloves at all. His skin looked as if it had been dusted in fine, white flour. Noting the twine ring upon his finger, she thought upon her matching braided circle and tried to hide it in her skirt's pleats. "W-what has happened to you?"

He dropped the toy onto a chair with a clang. "You will soon see."

Something in his voice affected her like a devil's caress, as if it reached inside and pulled her heartstrings in two different directions:

passion at war with revulsion. Perhaps he was pale from lack of sunlight. "Have you been in the pillory?"

A low laugh rumbled in his chest but there was no mirth behind it. "No, although being away from you felt enough like prison to last me an eternity." Mordecai took several more steps forward, making an obvious effort to avoid the moon's tendrils where they floated in the air.

Lynora's panicked pulse pounded loud in her ears, magnified by the absence of his footsteps scraping the floor. He appeared to glide, free of gravity. Tears of dread weighed heavy on her lashes. "You told me nothing in this world could keep you from returning to me. And then you never came back . . . ."

"What kept me away was *not* of this world. I'm back now. Please, no more crying." He was almost on her side of the room, mere feet away from where she stood. "What I did was for the three of us. Or so I intended." His tone tendered. "The men who came for me—"

"Men . . . what men? The same ones you run from now?"

"They were strangers that night. They offered me more than wealth . . . they offered acceptance. And something far more precious. Something you can never imagine unless you experience it."

Lynora slapped her tears away. "The only thing I wanted to experience was a passionate honeymoon with a loyal husband who cared for his family. I believe he is out there somewhere for me. A real man . . . not a thoughtless *beast* like you."

A guttural snarl erupted from Mordecai's mouth then a cold gust of wind caught her breath and forced her eyes shut. When she opened them, she found herself alone. She inched away from the wall, studying the room. A morbid premonition beat in time with the frantic drum of her heart. This was not Mordecai. At least not the Mordecai she remembered.

Her eyes locked on Isaac's drawing again. Was she losing her mind to macabre tales of fantasy? Or had something truly happened to her husband in his absence? Something evil . . .

A whimper wedged in her throat. Before she could release the sound, the air took form behind her as if part of the darkness dropped down and sluffed into place, close but not touching. Every hair stood like icicles along her skin.

A cold breath brushed her nape—a stir of frost along exposed flesh. Arctic fingers stroked her temple then eased down to tilt her head back, rooting her ear to his lips. "If you were ever to offer yourself to another man, he would be a corpse before your naked body hit the bed linens."

He smelled thick and heady, like blossoms soaked in rain and withered by the sun. The scent permeated her muscles, relaxed her against her will. He squeezed her left arm gently, moved his fingers in a languorous line down her inner wrist, following her veins. Her thighs jittered as he nudged the twine on her ring finger.

"You belong to me." He matched his hand to hers so their rings touched.

Lynora shoved at his arm. "Let go!"

He turned her loose yet she still felt ensnared, as if his gaze cast a net over her back to contain her. Her mouth drained of moisture. She had to escape this nightmare. She needed a weapon for leverage, to buy time to escape the cottage. She must break the spell of his voice, of his touch, then she could lose him in the hills.

In one corner, the harp-like strings of her lyre caught the moonlight and glistened. If she could get to the instrument, she could—

"Oh, how I've missed you playing." His comment jolted her. In the darkness, he had followed her line of sight . . . or had he read her mind? "Your melodies used to melt my blood to tears. You must bring your lyre to our new home."

She lurched forward. With an inhuman swiftness and grace, he caught her elbow in a frigid clasp before she could reach her instrument. He aligned her shoulder blades with his chest.

"What are you to do with it, my swan? Serenade me . . . or pummel me? Would you flog a dead horse?"

His hands clenched around her abdomen, allowing no space between them. Everything he said was madness, yet her panic paled to the lust his hold evoked within her.

"Leave . . ." The request left her lips on a half-hearted whisper. She closed her eyes and held her breath, knowing he wouldn't go—excited by the knowledge. She anticipated his body heat, waited for it to penetrate her thin frock. But instead she felt cold and hardness. In his muscles, in his desire for her that pressed against her lower back like granite stroking silk. Lynora shivered. "Please, Mordecai . . . "

"Tell me you don't want me. That you haven't missed my touch. Only then will I release you." He leaned in so his frozen lips could find her nape, nuzzling, nibbling, as his fingers unbuttoned her frock and shoved it off of her shoulders. She made a half-hearted attempt to hold it in place before the warm muslin sunk around her feet in a puddle.

"I *hate* you." Lynora quivered, pressing her hips against him as she forgot her fear.

Looking down across her shoulder, Mordecai tugged at the ties on the front of her chemise. "Your body speaks with more conviction than your tongue." Her underclothes glided down her shoulders, held in place only by his hands at her sternum. An answering rush of chill bumps swept over her arms and chest.

A moan, pained and primal, dampened her bared shoulder beneath his mouth. His stubbled beard scraped her skin and roused her nerves to titillated awareness. "Flesh, blood, and bones, you welcome me." His palms cupped her breasts over her chemise, causing her to arch into him again—a begrudging appeal for more. Everywhere he touched stimulated her flesh like a plunge in a winter stream. "Deny that you still want our life together. Deny that you've dreamt of lying naked in my arms. If you can deny either of these, I'll leave and never return."

His dare coursed through her, ignited her nerves with a throbbing ache. Unable to answer, she used the last reserves of her strength to wrench his fingers free where they held the chemise to her chest. She twisted to face him. The fabric pooled at her ankles with her frock, leaving her in only her pantlets. Hearing her groom's sigh of approval, her cheeks blazed with fire.

He stepped toward her. "Heaven's light," he whispered, breathless. "I don't remember even the sun being so radiant."

Empowered by his reaction, Lynora took one step backward, forcing her arms to her sides in spite of her modesty. "If you wish to share my bed, first you must get Isaac back. Go out, earn funding. Provide a home for us."

Mordecai's upper half remained veiled in darkness as he caught her hands and held them, admiring her bared breasts. He hissed through his teeth. "*You* are my home. Leaving you *once* killed me. I'll never do it again."

Clenching her eyes shut, Lynora felt the weight of his resolve in every limb. Then his words began to take shape in her mind. It had *killed* him to leave her? What of her own pain, so close to death upon losing him and Isaac both? She wouldn't forgive and forget unless he offered a way to reunite their family. She slipped from his grasp, inching closer to the door. "You know nothing of death." A snarl choked her words.

There was something in his answering groan—a dry rattle of despair. "But I do," he rasped. "For I *am* death. See for yourself. Look upon your groom in the moonlight."

He stepped into the silvery strands that filtered through the window. At first, she only noticed the fineries he wore: Wellington boots buffed to a high sheen; form-fitting breeches containing the ripples of muscular thighs; an open velvet coat, the cuffs and lapels embellished with jeweled buttons which glinted like broken bits of stars. An embroidered silken vest was cinched across his linen shirt. He hadn't owned such elegant things in all their time together.

Fury burned in her, for the obvious life of luxury he'd been living as she and Isaac languished on rotting vegetables and threadbare clothes. But before she could voice any outrage, her regard reached his face and she gasped.

Yes, they were the features she had fallen in love with, but behind them, a spectral light shone from somewhere deep within. He was pale, his flesh the bluish white of shadows on snow, his lips as plump and delectable as winterberries, ripe and kissed with frost. Only his hair remained the same, thick and golden as always.

She remembered her terror then—and she couldn't move.

A cold forefinger tipped her chin toward him. "Find my eyes, Lynora." Stroking her cheek with the back of his hand, he leaned down to press a cool kiss to her lips, leaving them numb yet hungry for more. "Find my eyes."

As if tied to his command, she lifted her lashes. His once-blue irises reflected the moon, casting silver chinks of light upon her breasts and abdomen, and lower yet. She could see everywhere he looked upon her, simply by following the luminous trail.

Isaac's drawing shadowed her memory. Her husband had returned as a preternatural creature. A demon. Self-preservation almost coaxed her feet to move, almost yanked her arm free from his grasp. But in that instant, his eyes shifted back to the laughing blue she once remembered. The eyes of a gentle and brilliant gardener—a humble man. The familiarity blinded her, stripped away her willpower, fed the desire he always awakened within. All she wanted was him—her husband—beneath the covers with her, loving her, eternally at her side.

His lips found hers again and his fingertips circled her nipple. "Come to bed with me."

Yes. She couldn't answer aloud, so she leaned into him, allowed her knees to give. He caught her with the same otherworldly swiftness with which he'd caught the kaleidoscope. That grace now seemed natural, even necessary. Her arms looped around his neck. The discarded clothes slid from her toes as he lifted her. She drank from his chilled lips. His kisses had always left her breathless. Now they sent a quiver through her chest and limbs. She couldn't stop shaking. His whiskers pricked her face to add another delicious level of sensation.

It was torture. It was bliss.

She wouldn't release him when he bent to lay her atop the covers. Her arms tightened around his nape, fingers curled in his hair, demanding more. At last his tongue penetrated, finding hers. Upon contact, his mouth was no longer cold. He shared her heat, and their unity tasted like nectar—rich, warm, and tickling to her throat.

His hands discovered every inch of her hot, exposed flesh— soothing her like ice vanquishing a fire. He moaned into her mouth as he straddled her, his clothes an unwanted barrier. She moved her hands to tug at the buttons on his vest, but he restrained her wrists over her head and settled atop her, the heaviness a comfort she had craved for weeks.

His lips broke free of hers to trail her chin, nuzzle her neck.

"Forgive me, Lynora." She almost couldn't decipher his words for the growl in his voice. "Forgive me for loving you."

She heard and felt a pop simultaneously. Pressure drilled into her neck as if someone punctured her with frozen nails. She arched her back, screamed at the excruciating sensation. She wrestled his hold on her wrists, her body numbing.

"Shhh . . . it's all right . . . trust me."

Even as she realized that Mordecai drank from her between whispers, even as she felt the pull of life ebbing beneath his eager, lapping tongue, she couldn't cry out again. Her heart pounded as if it would burst from her chest, her breath erratic, her lungs ached from the effort to meet her body's demands.

Vision tunneling, teetering upon death, she watched her demon groom draw back, lips glazed with her blood, fangs dripping crimson beads. "Surrender to it."

Eyes wide, she cried out in agony. Her heart burst into flames within her chest. The taste of ash coated her tongue. She gasped for air, lungs shriveling. Dizziness spun the room around her as if the ceiling balanced on a wheel.

Mordecai shifted to lie beside her, his top leg closed over her thigh. "Hold on now. Hold on . . . " He lifted his left arm, pushed up his cuff, and pierced a hole in the thin skin of his wrist. Finding her lips, he drizzled his chilled blood into her gaping mouth. With each gulp, the dizziness slowed. Her lungs enlarged on a rush of air. It felt like heaven: the pressure easing, the swollen surge as her throat opened, as the coolness seeped into her heart to soothe it. Nothing compared to this flavor . . . sweet and bitter. A new hunger awakened, and with a power she didn't know she possessed, Lynora clamped her hands and lips around his wrist and drank, consumed by greed and ecstasy. Mordecai groaned. With his free hand, he caught a fistful of her chin-length hair.

"I need to be one with you. Help me remember sunlight and warmth." His lips caressed her neck, crossed his bite marks to her collarbones then her breasts. "Make me feel human again," he murmured against her.

He lifted his head to meet her gaze. Once more, she saw his laughing blue irises break through the silver glare of his eyes. She released his wrist and licked residual droplets from her lips while she searched for the clasp on his breeches. So intent on undressing him, she failed to notice his attention shift to the door. She barely heard his hiss before he vanished in a clouded haze to filter up through the fireplace and out the chimney. Somewhere in her mind she questioned how anyone could become a puff of mist, but the absence of his body over hers—her veins still humming with the fusion of their blood—diluted the intrusion of logic.

She cried out in protest when the door slammed open and someone jerked her to a sitting position. Hands came from all directions to wrap her in sheets, wipe the blood from her chin, dab at the wounds throbbing on her neck. Unfamiliar voices dragged slow, garbled in her ears as if she listened from beneath water.

"Damn. She's been altered."

"What of her Mentor?"

"We've had no requests for a sanctioned conversion. He was acting on his own."

"We should go after him."

"No need. He circled back and brood runners captured him. They've already taken him underground."

Though the intruders' words and treatment were far from comforting, Lynora floated upon a strange, untenable peace. Her entire body felt airy and light—still held within the frangible boundaries of ecstasy from her exchange with Mordecai, still tasting him on her tongue.

"Break the mirror," someone commanded. "Careful not to look in it." The shatter of glass rang out. "Destroy everything. This woman's life is forfeit."

"But the toys . . . they belong to a child. Do you think it's hers?"

"There is no child here. And this woman presents a danger to both the living and to us. Whatever her story, it ends tonight."

Through blurred eyes, Lynora watched the cottage walls shift and buckle beneath orange sparks. Inhaling curls of black smoke, she coughed. The sight of Isaac's drawing upon the floor brought clarity back to her mind. The charcoal monster crackled and curled beneath a spread of scintillant flame and on the chair above, the kaleidoscope's lens reflected the growing holocaust. A talon of terror clenched her heart. Too late, she attempted to stand, but a smothering, dizzy pressure chained her in place. She choked on her final breath, then darkness snuffed the light.

CHAPTER 5

"Welcome back from the grave, Mordecai."

Regent Ezra, the Agnate's most respected official, faced Mordecai's seat several feet away. Black marble tiles and red wall hangings added a lush aura to the background and floor, giving the domed room an air of royalty. Onyx columns—rich with scrollwork—supported the windowless round chamber.

Having been locked in utter darkness for weeks, Mordecai squinted against the glowing, tulip-shaped plants that drooped from bronze planters in the wall and frothed the room in a misty haze. *His* plants. Ironic that it was he who had lit this miserable realm, considering how dark his actions toward his bride had been.

"I trust you enjoyed your stay in solitaire," Ezra continued. The patriarch crossed his legs in his council chair and smoothed his velvet breeches. A gold band studded with a honeycomb opal clung to his right ring finger. A talented Desmodai artisan had carved the gem into the shape of a scarab beetle in honor of Nocturnus's sigil—a symbol for regeneration and eternity. The gem's hexagonal facets shimmered a deep violet-blue with every move of Ezra's hand.

Mordecai wriggled on the plush settee at the regent's sarcastic quip. What was enjoyable about being sealed within a tomb for a month? The tight space had wreaked havoc on his muscles and joints, but that was nothing compared to the spasms in his mind and heart while conjecturing what had happened to Lynora. That night seemed such a blur now. Upon hearing a carriage, he'd been spooked, transmuted to his spiritual form in an instinctual reaction. He'd left her a halfling, incomplete, unable to make the same escape via mist. Before he could circle back for her, Nocturnus's brood runners captured him and dragged him underground, sealing him within a tomb.

When the undead first flourished upon the earth, they'd had no laws. Careless Desmodai men would alter women in fits of passion then leave them as neophites—halflings trapped between humanness and Desmodai. These victims had to fend for themselves until they killed a human and experienced the *Wisdom* which brought them to full realization of what they were, and in turn triggered their metamorphosis. However, many caught sight of their mirrored reflection before tasting human blood and lost their minds to madness. Danger abounded in the form of those mad neophites wandering the streets and countryside, for they jeopardized the race's anonymity. To counteract this, every undead society around the world converted strong men, leaders who formed Agnate Brotherhoods to enforce Mentorship laws and thereby curbing such outbreaks.

In the eyes of the Agnate seated around him, Mordecai had resurrected the ancient crime with his impulsive, unsanctioned induction of Lynora. Perhaps he had, but only because he couldn't imagine a life without her, even more so an eternity.

"Well, did you find the sarcophagus accommodating?" Ezra pressed, relentless.

The other eight Regents sneered, pale as statues in their row of chairs—kings on their red plush cushions. Each man had a plain gold ring upon his right forefinger, and dark robes hung like wings from their shoulders.

Mordecai touched his own humble twine ring, still in place on his left hand. He'd been in torment worrying all this time, unable to see

Augustus or any of his friends—the only ones he would trust to tell him of Lynora's whereabouts. Every man in this room knew of his crime, of his remorse and terror, and they were playing on it. He wasn't about to give the elder the benefit of gloating.

"Oh, it was a dandy holiday," Mordecai answered at last. "Though the climate wasn't quite to suit . . . a bit dry and dense for my liking." He attempted a cocky smirk, but lost momentum when Ezra's eyes narrowed to slits.

Mordecai laced his fingers to keep from tapping a nervous rhythm along his thigh. He'd been exhumed from the grave for only ten minutes—long enough to clean up, don a dress suit, and smooth the perpetual stubble at his chin.

Like every citizen of this underworld, his physical appearance, including his facial hair, were locked forever in the state they'd been at the moment of his full metamorphosis. The only difference was his muscles became more pronounced, his height more considerable—his masculinity magnified, in much the way females became curvier, their skin softer.

As a result, looks were deceiving in this realm. He considered Regent Ezra's stern features. With parchment skin and waist-length silky white hair, the regent appeared to be one of the eldest Desmodai in all of Nocturnus. Ezra had peaked in his intellect and talents at a ripe age, and was now forever sealed in his upper fifties. Even though some of the other regents looked younger because they had peaked in their youth, they were older than Ezra, in Desmodai years.

Still, Ezra was the political superior to them all, apparent by the respect and reverence displayed as they sat quietly beside him, giving him the floor.

Scrutinizing Mordecai, Ezra slid his boot along a glossy black tile to a more comfortable position. "You're looking a bit thirsty."

A sharp pang shattered Mordecai's gut at the reminder. He hadn't fed once during his imprisonment. In this new form he could fast up to one month without starvation, but today he had reached that limit. He propped an elbow across his arm rest and plucked at the ruffles on his shirt's cuff, avoiding eye contact with the regent. Somewhere in the room was the scent of fresh blood—salty, sweet, and corrosive. Every muscle in his body tensed in anticipation. He searched for the source, mouth filling with saliva.

"Before we allow you to drink, you must account for your actions." Ezra's throat rumbled, bringing Mordecai's attention back to him. "What did you intend to do once you brought her here, *nursling* Dureance?"

Mordecai flinched at being compared to a suckling child. "I intended to hide her in my sanctuary, until I could get your approval."

Ezra snorted—a sound at odds with his regal air. "Hide her?" The regent ran his gaze over the other members of the Agnate, gesturing to Mordecai. "Brothers, I give you your genius."

Mordecai managed a wry smirk. "It is a well-known fact, Your Regent, that recklessness is a bedmate to brilliance."

Slapping aside the cape draped across his leg, Ezra leaned forward and glared at him. "Insolent fool! You've no idea the trouble you have stirred. Not only did you break the Decretum of Sanctioned Conversion, but you endangered our treaty with the Gwyndolaire Sisterhood." His pasty hands clenched two gold-plated lions that served as arm rests on his council chair. "As one of us, you represent Nocturnus and our standards in everything you do topside. Lady Nenet attributes any individual's actions to us as a whole. She might very well turn her back on our city now. Then where will we be?"

Mordecai's fingers clenched his thigh. The Sisterhood had caught wind of his actions? This was worse than he thought.

He had once believed—along with everyone in the town of Tatabury—that the Gwyndolaire Sisters were a sect of sisters and cousins who spun silk, carved wooden trinkets, and threw sensual masquerades for elite gentlemen to raise funding. It was rumored they'd come from the other side of the world almost a century earlier and bought the castle and grounds, bringing in younger family members as needed for upkeep throughout the years. As they were foreigners, they were held to different standards. Their questionable morals and peculiar habitudes were overlooked.

Now Mordecai knew what secrets the women were hiding behind their exotic clothing, matching hairstyles, and makeup. The Sisterhood was wary partners with Nocturnus, the true home of the thriving silkworm community known as the sericulture where a mill for twisting the silk was managed by underground canals that flowed through a large water wheel. Desmodai artisans—chosen to citizenship for their expertise in dyeing, spinning, or weaving the silk into lavish accoutrements for the home or body—were responsible for the masterpieces. Since full-blooded Desmodai couldn't go topside to sell their ware among common humans for obvious reasons, the Sisterhood served as the go-between. It was their contribution above ground that had made Nocturnus one of the wealthiest undead societies in the world. Without Lady Nenet's representation, Nocturnus would have no means for commerce other than making trade with other subterranean cities.

Unfortunately, the Gwyndolaire treaty with Nocturnus was fragile at best—contingent on no fraternization between Desmodai citizens and mortals. Mordecai had crossed that line. Though technically, Lynora was no longer a mortal now. One might think that would put her in less danger, but she was actually in more than ever before.

He wanted to scream . . . demand answers as to his bride's whereabouts, but the aroma of blood again circled his nostrils, reminding him of a present and more pressing need.

He clutched his knees to keep from leaping up and ripping the room apart in search of the origin. If he could just translate to a spirit mist under all their noses, he'd gorge himself, even if meant emptying the veins of his first living mortal victim.

Mordecai tugged at the thick metal ring encircling his neck—crafted of a mixture of brass and iron with cloves of dried garlic strung about the circumference. Since Desmodai lived off of blood rich in iron, the metal at its purest impaired their mental and physical faculties—mimicking inebriation. But diluted with brass, the binding-collars served only to neutralize spiritual transcendence . . . the equivalent of shackles and cuffs on a mortal man. The garlic—an irritant to the nostrils and skin—added a more benign level of torment.

For the past four weeks the collar had pinched Mordecai's neck, and he wanted to be rid of it. At this point he might be willing to behead himself were someone to offer an ax.

Regent Ezra's hands fell slack in his lap. "Throughout your seclusion, the Agnate has considered your irresponsible choices, and unless you can rationalize your misdeeds to our satisfaction, you will drink from the sacred vessel and become a diminutive . . . tonight."

Mordecai's hair bristled. That explained the scent of blood.

His fingers plowed ruts through his hair. What could he give them as explanation? Did the regents listen to their hearts beating in simulation beneath their perfect flesh? If so, passion and love were reason enough. They had to be.

Ezra sighed. "I take your silence as indication of your guilt. It pains us to lose such a promising mind. We assigned high hopes to you. But you must be made an example, lest others mimic this disregard for our laws."

The scent from the sacred vessel called to Mordecai: a silver chalice half-filled with water imported from Egypt—drawn from an isolated hot spring far beneath the Great Sphinx near Cairo. Said to be cursed by Bisu, the Dwarf god, it held microscopic contagions which ill-affected their kind when drank or injected into their system. Under normal circumstances, no Desmodai in his right mind would touch Bisu water. But, if it were topped off with fresh mortal blood and offered to an undead soul deprived to near starving, instinct would overtake and the victim could not resist.

Mordecai knew, once presented with the blood-mix, he wouldn't hesitate to drink . . . would drink it all, even as every razor-sharp swallow slashed his glorious form to shreds.

The regent cast a glance over his shoulder. "Let the gargoyles bring the sacred vessel forward."

Movement stirred behind the patriarch in the farthest throes of the room. So distracted by his thirst, Mordecai hadn't noticed the trembling grotesques cowering beneath drapes of red silk along the walls, or the chalice they held between them. These were not the winged, stony protectors of churches and tabernacles in religious lore. In Nocturnus, the sobriquet "gargoyle" was assigned to the diminutives of the Desmodai race—those who were condemned and mutated by the self-same drink about to be poured into Mordecai's mouth.

Upon Ezra's command, the small creatures slinked forward on legs much too gangly for their pot-bellied bodies. The elder Regent shifted in his chair and glared at them. "Make haste!"

Ears drooping, they froze. Their scaled flesh blended with the wall behind them until they appeared to vanish. The chalice seemed to float in midair.

Ezra sweetened his tone, his voice tight with the effort. "Come now, my devilings," he crooned. "Serve the drink and you shall have a new pair of hands to soften your toils. You will rule over this new brother come next feeding. Yours will be first pick of the drained mortals."

A greenish color bled back into the gargoyles' scales until they glistened like fresh caught fish. Two sets of serpentine eyes—the size of goose eggs and wide with idiocy—blinked at Mordecai. Tufts of grassy hair wafted on the tops of their heads.

Whispering to one another, they gimped forward like peddler's monkeys.

Some of the toxic mixture sloshed down the sides of the chalice. Two of the regents hissed and whisked their robes away from the puddles on the floor. Mordecai slammed his eyes shut. The scent of blood called to him. It took all of his control not to fall to his knees and lap up the mixture, to ease the flame within. He gripped the settee's armrest.

Were he to give in, within twelve hours, the change would be complete. His spine would curl like a used candlewick and shrink his stature to three feet or less. Then his glowing, glorious flesh would harden and split to resemble a trout. His Desmodai powers would warp—the ability to become mist degenerating to a trick of blending into the surroundings—no better than a chameleon.

Lastly, his intellect would fade to that of a simpleton. This terrified him most of all.

Fight the urge, you fool! He screamed in his head, even as the barbed tips of his fangs lengthened to escape the cover of his lips. He must think of Lynora. She needed him. He was to be her Mentor . . . the one to guide her through the final change.

He'd left her topside—a neophite halfling. She must be so terrified. Already, so much time was lost to them. Where was she? What would become of her if he fell to this fate? Who would help her reach metamorphosis, or would she be forever left to teeter on the edge of the in-between?

Doubled over by a spasm in his gut, Mordecai found himself inches from the chalice between the gargoyles' hands. His tongue trembled. His mouth watered.

He wanted it.

Needed it.

Just as his lips opened to embrace the chalice's brim, the double doors swept open across the marble floor from behind, breaking his trance. Mordecai jerked back, putting distance between himself and the vessel. Stirs of silk and the creak of parlor chairs followed. He turned to see Augustus seating his bloodmate, the striking and regal Florentia.

"What is this all about, Augustus?" Regent Ezra's bright lips curved down, but his demeanor softened as he regarded Florentia. He offered her a nod.

Augustus cleared his throat, recouping Ezra's attention. "I have come to address the sparing of Mordecai Dureance's body and mind, Your Regents." His mellifluous voice cut through the tension. "I've a compromise that should satisfy everyone. He will become a Reaper."

CHAPTER 6

Murmurs exploded amongst the Agnate, matching the nervous jitters along Mordecai's gut.

"A *Reaper*?" One of the regents echoed Augustus's proposition in disbelief.

Mordecai glared at his friend, shaking his head on a refusal.

"Let me understand your proposition." Ezra snarled as he spoke to Augustus over the cacophony of voices. "You expect us to send this lit-up powder-keg topside once a month to bring down food for the others . . . when we cannot even trust him to tend his gardens in the under-realm and stay out of trouble?"

Mordecai's entire body shuddered now. He couldn't do it. Going to the slums of all the nearest towns including Tatabury, seeking victims whose names were approved by the Agnate to be on the Feed List. Hunting never waned, for there was no shortage of the scourge of society. But he was a gardener at heart . . . a planter of seeds, a nurturer and obeisant of life. Sedating people for living sacrifices disturbed him, whether they be scourge or not.

"This is outrageous!" One of the regents snarled. "He has yet to drink deeply of undiluted blood. How do we know he can withstand the effects?"

Mordecai dug his fingernails into his knees. At last, someone made sense. Like every other Desmodai, he had come to metamorphosis by drinking a cocktail made up of the combined essence of several victims—the same drink the common populous supped upon during their monthly feedings. Fresh blood from a single mortal presented unique challenges. It took intensive training and a strong inner-will to withstand the flavor of sins. Most especially the sins of murderers and degenerates.

Mordecai caught Augustus's attention to assure him his answer was no.

His friend winked an amber eye.

Ezra's features melted to piqued interest and he focused solely on Augustus. "You are aware of the decrements he has broken."

A waft of air crossed Mordecai's back as Augustus came to stand beside him. "I am." Augustus squeezed Mordecai's shoulder. His Roman profile firmed with resolve. "But I'm also aware of the great strides Mordecai has made lighting up Nocturnus. If not for his hybrid bioluminescent plants," Augustus motioned to the droopy white, glowing blossoms in the planters on the wall, "we would still be struggling with fire and the havoc it wreaks on our limited oxygen supply. It makes no difference that the atmosphere doesn't affect our race as a whole; our plant life requires it, as does our livestock." He cast a pointed glance toward the gargoyles. "Not to mention, our confused little diminutives would still be burning their hands trying to capture the shiny lights were it not for the luminescent flowers that took the place of flame."

As if embarrassed, the gargoyles blended with the red panels behind them. The chalice appeared to float again and stirred Mordecai's thirst anew. He lunged for the sacred vessel.

"Please, Regent Ezra." Augustus shifted his stance to maintain his hold on Mordecai's shoulder. "Could we be rid of the vessel? And clean up the spills on the floor. It's cruel to torture him so, at least until his fate is decided."

With a reluctant nod, Ezra directed the gargoyles to blot the puddles from the marble tiles. Their mouths opened on stupid, snarled grins that cracked their faces from one pointed ear to the other. Chalice in hand, they crossed toward the door, shutting it behind them.

"Consider this, gentleman . . ." Augustus patted Mordecai's back as he stepped up beside him again. "Mordecai came without question on the night of his wedding, in answer to our need for a replacement gardener. He accepted our proposition, left his young, beautiful wife topside—untouched. We didn't even allow him to go to her with a reason for his absence. Then we held him here for a full six weeks so he could establish a thriving subculture of luminescent seedlings to prove his worth. Can anyone refute his sacrifice? Did he not prove his loyalty in this? Of course, the first thing on his mind when released topside would be to find his innocent bride. Of course, he would break every decrement to bring her back with him. Yes, he neglected jurisdiction, wandering outside of the fallows to go to her. Yes, he nigh cost us our concealment and exposed himself and our lifestyle to the mortals in an effort to turn her. But can any of us, in that part of our heart that still mimics a human's, say that we would not have done the same?" Augustus paused and glanced back, meeting the gaze of Florentia. "I for one, cannot. As I would go to any length to be with my mate."

Florentia's thick-lashed violet eyes glinted in acknowledgement of their shared commitment, although her smile seemed somewhat sad.

"Yes, true love might have been a worthy defense," Ezra said, "had he come to us with a request for her citizenship. Allowed us time to vote and appoint a Mentor."

Mordecai shot to his feet. "You said it could take years for you to decide her worth, after I had already signed my life away to your city of the damned! And let us be clear, it's *my* place to change her, not a Mentor's. I have heard the exceptions to the law. As her husband . . . I am to be her bloodmate!" He held up his left hand so all could see his wedding ring.

"Only with our permission," Ezra added without pause.

Mordecai strained against Augustus to get to the patriarch, to give him just one good shake.

"I take partial blame, your Regents." Augustus coaxed Mordecai to sit again. "On the night of his conversion, I was captivated by his genius, so unusual in one his age; I was beguiled by his ingenuity, far surpassing what I had seen in most mortal men. I explained to him all he'd gain as a citizen—but failed to entail the losses he would incur. However, I'm not alone in my negligence. Even you were so desperate to have him, you missed that he was the sole guardian to a child. Some could argue we have broken the Custodian Decretum that prevents us from courting a father or mother into our society and removing them from their dependents."

Ezra stood, his shoulders rigid and looming beneath his cape. "You need not define the laws for me, Augustus. I have been enforcing them for centuries. It was that very law that kept us from courting his own father, Cornelius."

Mordecai's ears perked. Had he heard right? They had considered recruiting his father at some point? Seeking clarification would only earn him another reprimand, so he remained silent.

"Yes." There was a smug lilt to Augustus's response. "I submit we owe Mordecai at the very least another chance. And do we not owe it to ourselves, with all he has to offer? His full talent for plant and animal amalgams has not even been tapped. What one of us here would think to take a cave flower that required no sun and graft it with a sundew plant? Regent Ezra . . . had you even come up with such an idea, would you have had the foresight to feed that carnivorous hybrid with phosphorous insects, such as glow worms and fire flies, to give it illumination?"

Ezra resumed sitting in his chair, snuffing in annoyance.

"You yourself observed him from the night shadows for years," Augustus continued, "when he worked within his lab. You wrung your hands for his talents to pique, so he would be ready to convert. Are we willing now to lay waste such untapped potential with the barbaric ritual of the vessel?"

The regents studied one another in silence.

Augustus straightened the lapels on his brocade dress coat. "Would it not appear unjust for us to punish him with such severity when we are to blame in some part? Humble yourselves, acknowledge your mistakes with a compromise. Do this, and you'll gain the respect and faith of our people. Otherwise, you will earn the reputation of merciless dictators."

The regents leaned back in their chairs, thoughtful. Mordecai steeled his nerves. No one could spellbind an audience like the great orator, Augustus. Mordecai knew that first hand.

He wasn't sure if he should feel hopeful or doomed. If Augustus managed to influence their choice, he would end up a Reaper. But if he failed, Mordecai would be a gargoyle. The line between the lesser of two evils had never been more blurred.

As his friend gripped his shoulder once more, Mordecai noted the residual sickening sweet of wilted flowers. He would never get used to the aroma, even though he radiated it himself. It was a marker born in all of them after metamorphosis. Only in that moment of completion, when they tasted the cocktail of human blood, did they inherit their full powers. Along with the hypnotic glittering eyes, the scent aided in the hunt. Seduction at its most base form, revolting and enticing all at once.

Ezra crossed his arms. "He still must be chastised. I held his identity anonymous from Lady Nenet by vowing to punish him severely—publicly to our citizens. She wants details of how I'm to do it. That was the only way I could appease her."

Ezra's rationale rallied a debate among the regents.

Augustus stepped forward. "Gentlemen, please . . ." His voice rustled beneath the regents' chatter. The group hushed to listen. "I propose this: Mordecai will wear the grounding collar during his five-week Reaper training. You can appoint a brood runner to watch him. The other citizens will see his penitence through his willingness to bow to such shame. And he will earn our trust again through his compliance."

Mordecai's spine stiffened. He couldn't have a brood runner watching his every move. He'd had enough of those guards on the night of Lynora's alteration, when they captured him and brought him below before he could finish her conversion.

He needed to go topside to find his bride before something terrible—irreversible—happened to her. And the one way to traverse covertly on the surface was in spirit form. He refused to wait another five weeks to be free of the collar.

"No. I will not agree to this," he said.

"You have not been given permission to speak, Lord Dureance." Ezra clasped his hands beneath his chin. "Go on, Augustus."

Augustus motioned to the Agnate. "What of you, Drakkarh?" He glanced at a burgundy-haired regent. "You were a Reaper in the past. Do you not concur that being adept in seduction is a preferred quality, if not necessary for reasons of stealth, in those we send to round up our quarry?"

Drakkarh—a good three centuries old, had only served on the Agnate for eight years. He was one of the oldest Desmodai, yet one of the newest regents. "I do." He tossed back a strand of hair to expose charcoal smudged eyes. "And what makes Mordecai a purveyor of such talent?" His elbow rested on his chair's arm and his ring flashed gold.

Augustus beamed. "He has an irrefutable charm. It's his eyes. The color of his humanness breaks through despite the glimmer of immortality, even when he's thirsty. He can appear trustworthy. Most of us lose that in our conversions. But he managed to retain it—perhaps due to his work with plants, a calm composure and patience that most of us lack. Less struggle from the victim means less evidence left in the wake. Less blood spills, less torn articles of clothing. He could bring us our quarry, intact and whole. He would be a great asset to the Feeding Faction."

Silence wreathed the chamber, magnifying the roar within Mordecai's head. He couldn't deny the truth. Persuasion came easily for him. So much so that he managed to cajole the one person who had always been able to see into his heart. He persuaded Lynora to consent to his bite by reminding her of his humanness. It had been easy to justify the deception—being in a hurry to evade the brood runners the Agnate had sent in search of him. He was determined not to leave without his bride again. But in spite of his good intentions, he surrendered to a desire to make love to her first and failed to complete the conversion. Then everything fell to rot.

"No bloody way will I do it," Mordecai blurted out. "It is my choice to make."

"You want a choice, nursling?" One corner of Ezra's lip trembled as if fighting a smile. "You shall abide our decision—whatever it may be—or drink from the vessel. Therein is your choice."

Mordecai raked his hands through his hair and left his fingers clenched on either side of his head. It had been easier to remove himself from the guilt of drinking blood as a citizen . . . sipping of a cocktail so diluted it was difficult to home in on any one sin. It was easier when he never had to see the bodies or take part in the capturing process. If they assigned him this position, he'd no longer have the bliss of ignorance to hide behind. And he would have the flavor of the damned to contend with.

"I say we give him a place with the Reapers." Drakkarh crossed his legs. "T'would do him good to walk amongst them. Perhaps a taste of the foulest sins will show him how debase our quarry is . . . instill the pride in his new kindredship that he lacks. Let him experience the *Wisdom*—at full potency." His darkly powdered eyes narrowed.

Horror crimped Mordecai's gut.

With a stir of robes, Ezra stood. "Thank you, Augustus. You have moved us to reconsider. Please take a seat."

Bowing his dark head, Augustus found a chair next to Florentia.

Ezra conferred quietly with the other regents then turned. "Mordecai Dureance, kneel at my feet for our verdict."

Swallowing the burn of humiliation in his throat, Mordecai knelt.

"You have heard the compromise." Ezra rested his hand on Mordecai's brow. "You will begin your Reaper training today after you are fed. Are you willing to agree to the terms?"

Mordecai's chest tightened against a refusal. "*Yes*, Your Regent." He ground out the expected answer, having every intention of finding a way around this judgement.

"Understand that the grounding collar will be irremovable during the five-week indoctrination, only to be taken off when you are practicing your captures in the Miseria Chambers. And at those times, there will be a regent assigned to stand over you. Elsewise, you will wear the collar everywhere. A guard will escort you to feedings, to social affairs, during your gardening stints—any time you leave your sanctuary. As your powers of spiritual transcendence will be inhibited, you will not journey topside for any reason until after you have taken the vows of the Reaper. Only then will you regain your freedom to come and go. Understood?"

Mordecai hesitated, taken off-guard by the last specification.

"Should you refuse this condition, you can drink of the sacred vessel tonight. And should you break your word once given, you will be locked in the solarium to face the sunlight on the morrow of your betrayal."

Gritting his teeth, Mordecai winced. Lose his mind tonight, or die tomorrow. What difference did it make? His immortality and sanity meant nothing without his bride. "But what of Lynora? You must tell me about her . . . where she is. How she fares . . ."

Ezra tilted Mordecai's head back by clenching the hair at his nape. "Sweet sanctum, Mordecai. It's as if your mind is a sundial, and this woman is the sun. Can you not turn a thought outside of her?" The patriarch's fingers released and he shook his head in pity. "We're not obligated to tell you anything."

Several other Regents snickered. A low growl rumbled in Mordecai's throat, held stillborn by his tongue.

Ezra shrugged from his robe. "You should have put your Lynora on the Desirable List to be considered for citizenship, if she'd had any worthy talents to offer us. Alas, now it is too late."

Knees pressed against the cold marble floor, Mordecai refused to be silenced. "No. It is not too late. She's already a neophite. Dangling between their world and ours. She's only one step away . . . it's my responsibility to bring her over. I'm her husband!"

His plea appeared to go unheard as everyone began to stand.

"We must consider what could become of her while she awaits acceptance by you!" Mordecai yelled this time, determined to be heard. "She could expose our kind!" Though they cared nothing for her, surely they'd take precautions for their own welfare.

The Agnate dismissed and filed out the door. Ezra paused only long enough to ask Florentia if he might have a word. Augustus nodded to them and stood aside as Ezra looped an arm through hers and escorted her out.

"What is wrong with all of you? What if she looks within a mirror and loses her mind?" Mordecai tried once more as the attendees trailed out the door. "Have you not considered any of this?"

Drakkarh paused and loomed over Mordecai. Catching his wrist, he forced him to stand. "You wish to conjecture what might become of your bride? What you should be considering is what became of her the night you made this mess." The Regent's dusky lashes lowered, and his ring cut into Mordecai's flesh through his ruffled cuff. "From what the Gwyndolaire Sisterhood reported, a fire started at your cottage after you were captured. Your home burned to the ground with your little virgin inside." Sporting a beastly grin, Drakkarh turned on his heel and strolled through the door.

Mordecai's legs went out from under him. His skeleton jolted as he hit the floor. He had been in solitaire since the night of the incident. No one had told him of any consequences topside. No one had told him . . . his bride was *dead*.

His hands went numb. He couldn't speak. Couldn't move. He swayed on his knees, unaware that Augustus stood behind him until he felt a firm grip on his elbow, drawing him upward.

"Come, Mordecai. You need to quench your thirst. Tis time to feed."

CHAPTER 7

When Lynora first woke after the fire, every part of her body ached with a thirst so intense, it felt as if parched snakes slithered through the dust in her veins. Yet she could keep nothing down—everything tasted of soot and rot—and the drought in her soul made her wild.

Emitting inhuman snarls and howls, she struggled to untie the knots that fastened her ankles and wrists to an unfamiliar iron bedframe in an unfamiliar room. There, she fell prey to madness—bound in a perverse unmaking as her mortality withered away. She was a captured butterfly, wings pinned to a corkboard . . . cocoon being forced back into place. The walls spun and tumbled around her, and the sunlight shook as if on an earthquake.

Her three attendants, coming in and out, appeared stilted in her convulsive state—time breaking in increments with their jittery steps. Yet their clothes rustled, graceful and liquescent: sleeveless tunics flowing down to cover hips, and full legged trousers that hovered like clouds to conceal the curves of thighs and calves before gathering snug at the ankles. Shimmery metallic cuffs embellished with gemstones graced their wrists and necks.

In rare moments of lucidity, Lynora conjectured they must be a family, triplets even, for they were remarkable in their likenesses. Each one shared the same ebony hair, braided with beads that clacked softly as they moved. They smelled of lilies, myrrh, and cinnamon. Their faces were at once beautiful and horrible, glittering metallic complexions with black paint stretched to feline lengths around their eyes. It was if the hieroglyphics Lynora had seen in exhibits—painted goddesses born of one's most sensuous and repulsive dreams—had peeled their outlines off of ancient, Egyptian walls and morphed into golden statues that served as her caretakers.

Much later, she would come to realize they were ordinary girls who shared her fate. Each with differing origins, ages, skin tones, hair color and body shapes, all of them orphaned and imprisoned by a tormenting hunger for blood. Their metallic makeup, called maquillage, alongside the exotic costuming and wigs, served as the cocoon within which their own wings of individuality stayed trapped, to keep their true identities hidden from the populous of Tatabury.

On the third day, Lynora kept down the water her caretakers gave her to drink, but still balked at the rice they offered. Each time they released her bindings, she lunged at them like a rabid animal. It was then she understood the binds were to protect her keepers as much as herself.

On day four, Mother Nenet—the matron of the castle wearing the same disguise as the nurses—brought in some sliced pudding, such a deep red it resembled clotted ink. This she fed to Lynora with alternate spoonfuls of rice. Though it lacked flavor, the diet soothed her hunger and thirst, and along with the kindness and tolerance of her newfound Sisterhood, Lynora survived her torturous transformation.

Now, a month later, Lynora still had cravings. Yet this hunger was sentimental, caused by a deprivation of things she would never feel again. The crumbs she followed in her mind always led back to that last afternoon with Mordecai and Isaac, their final moment of pure happiness before that cursed wedding night. What she craved was the delusion of bliss, when all that lay ahead of them were new beginnings founded on forgiveness and trust.

In the evenings she'd lie awake in her castle chamber, and stifle her anger so the memory could bloom in vivid color. There, behind the safety of closed eyes, time reverted. She became human once more, before she knew of blood-lust or the reality of monsters.

She had felt as small as a bug standing on the stairs outside the Piccadilly Museum that day, months ago. The four-year-old façade was carved with Egyptian motifs in tribute to the Napoleonic era. Two sphinx statues kept guard on the fourth and highest floor's balcony, crouched on their paws and nestled beneath the roof. Over the entry, two Egyptian monuments stood tall upon a stone platform held up by wide pillars on either side of the door. As if playing their foils, two skinny English constables had stood blocking the doorway to keep a watch for improprieties.

Single men, couples, and groups of people sauntered in and out— expensive perfumes and colognes overpowering the stench of dust stirring from hansom cabs and horses that passed on the street. Women were forbidden to enter unescorted. That had been the one crimp in Lynora's plan. After stopping at Mordecai's cottage, she'd been told by the housekeeper that he and Isaac were visiting the museum. She'd taken her uncle's hansom cab and tried to hurry, hoping to arrive simultaneously so she might catch them before they entered; but even if she had, it's likely Mordecai would've been too angry to hear her apology.

She clutched her reticule tight. Inside the pouch, she had a gift both *from* him, and *for* him. Proof that her love was true, despite what he'd come to believe.

Already, she'd been waiting by the entrance for a half hour, and still no sign of them. Seeking a means to search inside, she ducked back into the space provided by a neighboring building as a group of four men brushed by, one glaring at her and another appearing more interested than she would like. He turned off from the others.

"Aye there, little wee one. Would ye be lookin' for a man's

company? I be happy to take ye inside—fer a fair price." A harshness edged his Irish lilt, but it was the way his gaze chased up and down her body from neck to ankle that flipped her stomach. She may as well have been naked instead of properly clad in a demure day-dress draped with a shawl, bonnet, and gloves. She considered her escape, but before she could venture a step, another man appeared. Dark hair, matching hers in color, turned a thick fringe around the priestly collar which protruded from his cloak. His olive complexion was smooth and his features—although stern at the moment—radiated an almost angelic inner light.

"Good day. May my secretary or I be of service?" the priest asked the Irishman, encompassing Lynora in the question with a wave of his cane. The stick flashed beneath a slice of sunlight, appearing to be made entirely of metal instead of wood.

"Oh—erm, didn't realize ye was with the church, M'lady." Lynora's would-be-assailant mumbled it like an apology, and bristling his shoulders, strode into the museum.

Lynora breathed a sigh of relief. "Thank you, Father."

"It's my calling. To protect the innocent lambs of the world from rabid wolves." Full lips, as intricately shaped as any woman's, slanted to a one-sided grin. He tapped his unusual cane on the ground—as if in thought—eliciting a metallic clack. He appeared young for a priest, surely not much older than herself. She wondered why he needed aid in walking, or perhaps the cane was indeed his shepherd's crook.

"Well, if ever I needed a herd to disappear within," she said, "it is today."

The priest's gaze, a luminous gray like moonlit pebbles in a shallow creek, bounced from her to the entrance where the two constables stood. "Do you know either of the guards?"

"I don't."

"Then we maintain the pretense. You're my secretary, Sister Agatha . . . and we're here to visit the natural history exhibit, to assure the curator is giving due honor and respect to God's creation."

Surprised by his penchant for white lies, Lynora brightened her smile. She followed him to the doorway, noting he did have a limp after all. Once her escort introduced himself as Father Lucien Tanden and explained their mission, the constables nodded in veneration and allowed them entrance. As Lynora and the priest milled through the crowds, she kept her gaze trained on the surroundings lest Mordecai and Isaac should slip by. Giant candelabras dangled from the domed ceilings in each room, painting light upon tapestried walls. The addition of opened windows made the rooms feel warm and fresh, like the outdoors.

"So, is that truly why you're here?" Lynora asked her holy companion once they'd adjusted their voices to carry over the shuffle of feet while blending into the hum of multiple conversations.

"To herd sheep?" he asked, eyebrows raised.

Lynora felt her lips quirk. "To see the natural history exhibit."

"Oh, no. I'm here for something most *un*natural." His chin tightened, as if the admission troubled him.

Lynora frowned. She was considering asking what he meant when he turned the inquiry onto her.

"And you? What brings you here alone?"

Refocused on the crowd, Lynora bit her inner cheek. She debated whether to be honest or lie, then settled on something in between. "I'm not alone exactly. I have two escorts. They should be here already."

"They couldn't wait for you out front?"

"Well, I'm . . . surprising them."

The corners of his eyes crinkled in a smile. "I hope they like surprises."

A weight tugged on Lynora's chest. "I hope they still like *me*," she whispered the response, but her companion heard.

He slowed his pace and looked at her pointedly, an expression that promised understanding. She thought perhaps he wouldn't judge; he seemed different than any priest she'd met . . . teasing, quick to smile and slow to censure. Considering his age, it was possible he hadn't seen enough of the world's debasement to grow cynical quite yet. But it was the fact that he *was* a man-of-the-cloth—youthfulness notwithstanding—that persuaded her. Only a priest would have the answers she needed about the laws of matrimony. Thus, she broke down and told him the real reason she'd come—who she sought and why.

A hushed, somber conversation ensued between them, then they both grew silent upon approaching the Egyptian exhibit heralded by an imitation sarcophagus of Nefertiti inlaid with faux gold. Preserved insects and animals native to the land nestled in cases designed to draw the eye. A forest of imported tropical plants and native abodes sat alongside plaques filled with Egyptian mythology and folklore. White columns supported the rounded chamber, each one wrapped with leafy vines the color of summer moss. Purple velvet panels draped from one column to the next, giving the domed ceiling an air of royalty. The perfect setting for an Egyptian queen and her relics.

Noticing how intense and quiet the priest had grown in his observation of the décor, Lynora considered nudging him, but stopped short when she saw the back of two familiar blonde heads: one attached to a small boy and the other to a pair of broad shoulders that she'd laid her cheek upon countless times. The two stood behind a bust, listening to a spindly man with a waxed moustache and silver spectacles.

"Ah, I take it you've found your escorts?" Father Lucien had noticed her again and tilted his head toward Isaac and Mordecai, following Lynora's gaze.

Lynora smiled. "I'm in your debt."

"Not at all. I wish you every blessing, *Sister Agatha*. It's my prayer that you secure your happiness today, along with a herd you can call your own." He grinned again, and a strand of dark hair flopped across his forehead as he bowed goodbye, taking him from angelic to boyish in an instant. She watched him, once more musing over his fascination with the Egyptian hall and his earlier reference to the 'unnatural' as he limped into the midst of the exhibit.

Once he was swallowed by the crowd, Lynora wove her way toward the opposite side of the spacious chamber where Isaac and Mordecai stood by an Egyptian woman's bust alongside clusters of strangers. Lynora remained unseen, as everyone listened intently to the scholar hired to speak.

"All told, in Egyptian lore, Sekhmet was a goddess whose breath formed the desert sands." The speaker's wiry moustache twitched in an itchy fit. "However, there are those who conjecture this bust isn't so much a tribute to lore, but to a real heroine of Egypt—a simple mortal *named* after the goddess. She was a huntress who followed the desert warriors, dancing for them at night in exchange for lessons in weaponry and warfare. In her nocturnal travels, she stumbled upon a group of wayward young women subsisting in desert caves and took them under her wings. The huntress trained them not only to fight, but to dance and perform as means to earn funds for clothing and other necessities. Barbaric as her tactics were by our standards, her guidance gave the women hope and direction. Her troupe became one of the most powerful warrior companies, attacking only at night with the furtiveness and skill of panthers. This earned her the reputation of a desert goddess, and later she took the name Sekhmet in tribute."

There was a thoughtful silence wherein sniffles, cleared throats, and popping candles overtook.

"So . . . what became of her?" a man in the audience broke the quell.

"It was rumored she retired from her warring to seek peace in her elder years," the scholar answered. "Unfortunately, there's no record of her death nor any style of marked grave attributed to her. It's as if she disappeared altogether."

History lesson ended, Isaac and Mordecai withdrew from the group. The two headed toward the farthest side of the room where one of the curators spoke of a gift given to Nefertiti by a Greek prince who once courted the queen. As the curator lifted a curtain from the glass to unveil a jeweled cylinder of gold perched upon a velvet pillow, Lynora noted a tall, long screen along the wall that hedged the display. A canvas stretched across the woven frame to showcase hieroglyphics in bold relief—mummies, pyramids, bodiless legs and arms, and bats interspersed among other various symbols.

An idea struck Lynora, eclipsing the images on the screen. The few feet of space between the wall and the back of the divider would provide a perfect sanctuary until she was ready to be seen. Encouraged, Lynora cut through three groups of people and slipped behind the screen. She removed her gloves and peered out from a hinged opening to wait for Isaac's and Mordecai's arrival.

The child clung to his brother's hand, despondent. He seemed a shattered hull of the lively boy she knew him to be. Before she and Mordecai had lost all contact, Isaac had been anticipating this one-room tribute to Egyptian history and mythology honoring Napoleon's conquest of Egypt. It made sense Mordecai would bring him here on the day of its opening to cheer him. Yet even as they looked at several displays, moving ever closer to her screen, Isaac still remained uninterested . . . distant. Judging by the hunched set of Mordecai's shoulders and the frown upon his face, his mind was elsewhere, too. Lynora's eyes stung. She could only hope to set things right. She could only pray they would forgive her.

She nudged one hand into her reticule and felt the silken petals waiting there, tracing a fingertip across the slick stem. Swallowing hard, she watched through the divider's hinges as Isaac's voice carried over.

"What's that, Mord?" the child asked, stopping inches from where she stood.

Lynora took a breath, worried Isaac had spotted her. Instead, he pointed to the glass case surrounded by people off to the right.

Mordecai knelt next to his brother, arm cinched around Isaac's waist. "That is a kaleidoscope. It has colors and shapes within. It is a plaything."

Isaac appeared deflated, obviously having thought it something much more exciting. Lynora couldn't help but smile in the shadows, taken back to the afternoon picnics she'd spent listening to the child's tales. How she'd missed his unquenchable imagination.

She watched Mordecai grow thoughtful then draw his brother closer. "I've heard rumors, though," he said quietly as people passed behind them, "that when you look inside a kaleidoscope deep enough, you can see your dreams. And by turning the cylinder, it frees them so they might come true."

Lynora bit her lip. This was what had drawn her to her gardener more than anything . . . his endless commitment to making his brother's life happy.

Isaac leaned against Mordecai—blue eyes glistening with a light Lynora had been missing for weeks. "Do you think Lynora's inside one?"

A tender spot behind her sternum pricked at the innocent question, as if his tongue wielded a barb aimed at her heart.

Mordecai's jaw clenched, indicating he felt the same needle-sharp twinge. "Were I to look within, she would be, without a doubt."

Lynora drew the orchid from her reticule, holding it over her aching chest.

"Can we get closer?" Isaac asked his brother. "I want to see."

Mordecai stood and sought a path through the ring of spectators. Observing the child clutched to his hand, people smiled and allowed passage—bringing Mordecai and Isaac against the furthest edge of Lynora's woven sanctuary. Mordecai knelt again. Slippers making barely a sound, she moved close enough that she could reach from behind the screen and touch Mordecai's shoulder should she dare. She took a breath to steel her resolve. Her fingers tensed around the orchid's stem and she thrust it forward, slipping discreetly into that place beneath the curtain of blonde hair that covered Mordecai's left ear and fringed his shoulder—careful that no one else would see.

He slapped his neck—at first thinking it a bug—then upon feeling the petals and smelling the scent, went rigid from spine to ankles. It was why Lynora had chosen this hybrid from her uncle's gardens in Bath. Having been the one who planted it, Mordecai would know it as he would his own child. She withdrew the orchid and backed deeper behind the screen.

"Isaac," Mordecai's voice rattled, husky with emotion. "Stay here. Ask the curator any questions you have about the kaleidoscope. I'll return in a moment."

His brother complied, transfixed by the golden cylinder.

Lynora listened to the familiar stride crossing the floor at the front of the screen as Mordecai made his way to the other opening—an obvious move to distract observers from his intended destination. Keeping their meetings clandestine had become second nature to both of them, having played such games for months to hide their courtship from her uncle.

She adjusted her bonnet, breathless, all the while her mind wheedled her to run, afraid to expose her heart for fear it would be stricken dead if Mordecai despised her as much as she imagined he must.

She clutched the orchid and cut a glance in Isaac's direction in the same instant Mordecai ducked behind the screen. His scent—fresh growing things, overturned earth—filled the small space. Light streamed through the painted screen, imprinting the shadows of bats in flight across his face. It was a disturbing scene, bringing a macabre ambiance to his already angry features. He flinched when she raised her free hand to touch his sunshine bright hair, and she dropped her wrist to her side. It hurt to look upon him . . . so beautiful, so untouchable. Right in front of her, yet so far out of reach.

"What the hell are you doing here?"

She gasped, shocked by his coarseness. He'd never spoken to her with such spite, but why shouldn't he? She'd called him a classless brute . . . had said as much in her note. Or so he thought. Clenching the orchid's stem, she weighed her response carefully. "I have been seeking you for weeks."

His teeth ground. "Isaac and I went abroad the night you sent the missive. We had wounds to lick." The explanation came out with a bitter snap of his tongue.

One blink passed between them, then her full confession spilled with the force of a flooded creek. "It was a lie. Everything I wrote. My uncle threatened to harm you if I didn't do as he bade. He swore to take away your parcel of land, your cottage. After I'd done as he asked, he locked me in my chamber. When he finally let me out, I secretly sent word for you to Tatabury." Her throat lumped. "But every missive came back unanswered. I thought something horrible had happened."

A struggle crossed Mordecai's face, an attempt to hold onto his accusatory scowl. But one look in his eyes—lovelorn and lost—and she knew her sincerity had made a dent.

He exhaled loudly, as if a horse had kicked him in the chest. "I— I should have realized your bastard uncle had a hand in it."

"I hoped you would at least suspect . . ."

His face flashed red. "Had I embraced even a suspicion, I would have stormed that estate and demanded your refusal in person." He raked his fingers, smudged with soil, through his hair, mussing it. "I could kill the old sot for treating you like a caged bird." Then the anger fled away, surrendering to something gentler—something remorseful and accessible. He glanced around the screen to check on Isaac, but she knew the gesture for what it was. Like her, he struggled to keep his emotions at bay in their public setting. Turning back to her, his blue eyes brightened with hope. "We should go somewhere to talk in private. Where is your lady's maid?"

"She's home. I didn't wish her to bear the brunt of my crimes. I stole guineas from my uncle." Heat rushed her cheeks on the admission.

Mordecai shook his head. "It's not *stealing* when it rightfully belongs to you. Your parents bequeathed you an endowment."

It was true. Her uncle and aunt had taken it upon themselves to withhold her legacy lest she marry a man of their choosing. "I also borrowed one of his coaches, but I'll send that back."

Mordecai muffled a surprised laugh that faded to a concerned wrinkle in his brow. "You came all this way, alone? That's unsafe."

"I had to find you. To make you understand."

His eyes went wide with something akin to wonder and pride. "How did you gain entrance here, unescorted?"

"I met a priest on the steps outside. He walked in with me." She paused, pressing her lips together. "I asked him something, Mordecai."

"You did?" His gaze fell to her mouth, warming it—reminding her of all the furtive kisses they'd shared in her uncle's gardens, hidden behind copses of honeysuckle and ivy.

"I asked him if the license you drew up for our nuptials would still be permissible after so many weeks. He said it would." The hand holding the flower had started to tremble. Mordecai reached for it.

"You still want me?" he asked. "Despite my station . . . my lowly status. I thought you needed more than I could offer." His rough, callused hands served as a foil to the vulnerability of the query.

Dropping the orchid, Lynora cupped his jaw. "Did you not hear what I said? Those were my *uncle's* sentiments, not mine. I do not give a fig for wealth or prestige. I want only you and Isaac. That's all I need to be happy. Our family." She sobbed. "It has been hell without you."

A mix of elation and compassion passed across Mordecai's features.

"Ah, Lynora. A lady of the ton should not use such profanities." He shifted his chin to kiss her palm, sliding down to her wrist, tasting her pulse.

"Curse the ton." She curled her fingertips around the soft shell of his ear. "I am your lady, Mordecai. Not the peerage's. And you have taught me to speak my heart. Do you want *me* still?"

He wrapped his arms around her, a delicious encroachment of masculine heat and gruffness. "Yes." He kissed the tip of her nose. "Lord, yes. More than my own life." He nuzzled the coil of hair dipping from beneath her bonnet.

"Please forgive me," she whispered. "I never wanted to—"

"Forgive *me* for not fighting for you. So many weeks wasted due to my stubborn pride." He drew back momentarily, long enough to glance around the screen and wave Isaac to come to them. While awaiting his arrival, Mordecai pinned her to the wall. His lips found hers and she savored his flavor, his forgiveness. Her palms trailed his face, fingertips skimming over his whiskers. He broke the kiss, tucked the loose coil into her bonnet and rearranged the tie beneath her chin. "I'm ashamed. I've been a coward. Working late in the lab every night . . . hoping to forget you instead of seeking a way to win you back."

Tears edged her lashes and she touched the hair feathering at his collar. "I'm so glad you didn't forget."

"I couldn't. I had a constant reminder." From inside his shirt's lapel, he withdrew a cord of braided thread. Dangling on the end was the twine ring he'd made for their original nuptial plans.

She gaped. "You've been carrying it all these weeks?"

Smirking, he held the band up. "Not one step outside the cottage without the weight of it against my chest—anchoring me."

She sniffled as he slipped the ring off the cord and onto her finger.

"With this ring I will thee wed," he whispered, pressing his forehead to hers. "With my body I will thee worship, and with all my worldly goods, sparse as they may be, I will endow upon thee. According to God's holy ordinance—"

"And thereto I will give thee my troth," she finished, tears filling her eyes.

Mordecai smiled against her lips as he kissed her. They had practiced the vows so often they both knew them by heart.

"Marry me, Lynora. *Today.*" The luminance of his smile melted all reserves of ice between them, leaving only trust and forgiveness burning hot and bright.

"Yes." She dug a matching twine ring from within her reticule. "I made you one, too . . . while we were apart. In hope you wouldn't let me go." Tears ran down her face and drizzled from her jaw.

He traced the trails. "I will never let you go again. Not ever."

"And I will never leave you. You *nor* Isaac."

In that moment, Isaac had come around the corner of the screen, thrilled to see her—ecstatic to hear she was there to stay—but less than happy to depart the Egyptian exhibit for which he had gained a new appreciation. Mordecai had pacified the child by buying a toy kaleidoscope from a gift cart stationed at the door on their way out to get married. The very same toy that had lay burning in their cottage, when Mordecai set flame to Lynora's trust and left their nuptial vows in a pile of ash and soot.

Every night, upon reliving the memory, Lynora fell asleep to the agonizing knowledge that her husband had altered then abandoned her, as the rancor of his bitemarks pulsed on her neck, keeping time with the beat of her broken heart.

CHAPTER 8

In the mornings before sunrise, Lynora educated herself on her new life by wandering down to the Sanctorum of Enlightenment. Although each room and hall of the castle portrayed opulence and elegance, although each had its own charm and mystery, this one held a special thrall for her.

Located on the first floor, the Sanctorum provided an ample supply of books and scrolls, and she spent many an hour there, absorbing all she could of her new world—trying to make sense of things. There she had learned of the genesis of the Desmodai race and their barbaric lifestyle, and came to understand her husband's role in her own warped fate as a hinge in the door that separated the mortal and immortal world. She'd been told he was punished for his crime, but no punishment could countermand such a betrayal.

To give up a life of privilege and wealth for her husband had been difficult enough, but to awaken in a world where every law of nature was twisted and tangled like threads unraveled from a spool—well … it left her sanity shaken. Each time she attempted to rewind the strands of reason, she learned something new that snipped the coils loose.

Did Mordecai even care about her present state? Did he feel remorse for misleading her that fateful night? And what of Isaac? How was he faring with news of her death so soon after his brother's supposed demise? Lynora had made a promise to retrieve the child from the orphan asylum, but now the only way to make that happen would be to commit a crime so vile and violent, she couldn't even contemplate it.

The Sanctorum personified radiance and purity . . . an antithesis to the dark confusion and frustration that often plagued her. White floors stretched as lustrous as a frosted pond. Along the four white walls, plaster pilasters with three dimensional carvings of swans and garlands were set in vertical increments. Silver festoons of Florence satin draped the oversized windows. On warm evenings, the sashes were thrown open and the curtains shifted in the breeze to brush across an idol standing like a beacon in the daylight. The likeness was of Eset, also known as Isis: goddess of sun, compassion, and nature. It was the idol's presence in the room that inspired the chamber's title "Sanctorum of Enlightenment."

However, there was another statue that held special meaning to Lynora: a life-sized image of Sekhmet, a completed twin to the bust from Piccadilly's Egyptian exhibit, that kept watch over the castle grounds outside. Though the statue was often painful to look upon, as it tied Lynora's past to her present in an inescapable knot of memories, Lynora purposefully sought Sekhmet today on her morning march with the other neophites. She needed to borrow strength from the stone carving for the challenge that awaited her in a few hours.

Crisp air rushed into Lynora's lungs as she brought up the end of the line, trudging along a pebbled path behind her eighteen neophite sisters. She nudged her twine wedding ring and peered over the heads of the others to better see Heron—leading the group as the Sister Superior. Her fawn-brown braids parted as she bent her head forward, revealing a shaved spot at the base of her skull where a swatch of ivory skin bore a scar shaped like the sun.

Reaching toward the matching scar on her own nape—peeking

out at the opening in her iron neck cuff—Lynora shivered. Two weeks ago, she received this brand alongside another girl who had recently arrived at the castle. The shape was carved into their flesh so it remained rough to the touch—a tangible reminder of the vows they'd made: Never to injure a human unless their own lives were in danger; always embrace nonlethal means to appease their blood lust so they could walk in the sun.

"My neophite sisters, nurture the strength of your bodies, hearts, and minds," Heron shouted. "Just as Sekhmet did. With pride and honor, we unite to defend what's left of our humanity."

"Cleave to the light, and spurn the darkness!" All the neophites chanted in hand-fisted unison, their knuckles a procession of knots reflecting the pink blush of dawn. In the distance, the surrounding white stone walls and forest glistened with dew.

The summer had been warm, and autumn's first frost had delayed its coming. On the castle grounds, everything still thrived: carnations and lilies thickened the air with their spiced sweetness; honeysuckle dripped like lace across latticed archways and bees buzzed all around the blossoms. Even the peacocks were confused as to the season. The males dragged their trains of plumage in a dazzling array of color while they searched for snakes, seeds, and insects to eat.

Lynora stepped over a stream no more than a hand's width across. Her flat-soled boots slapped against a limestone walkway that flanked the entire circumference of the enclosed courtyard. Behind her, Castle Gwyndolaire's looming shadow chilled her shoulders beneath her shirt, and she imagined Mother Nenet's painted eyes looking down from the highest tower, watching her fledglings.

It was the mother's practice to bestow her rescued girls new names for anonymity. She drew inspiration from birds, as birds represented resilience—some flying thousands of miles to survive the most brutal seasons of their lives. Lynora was appointed "Starling" due to musical abilities that put her in league with songbirds. The other new neophite took the name "Wren", a tribute to her fierceness alongside a delicate bone structure and mournful bird-like eyes that shimmered, deep-set, within her brown skin. Wrens, though one of the smaller breeds, were known for facing cats head-on to save their nestlings.

Lynora studied Wren on their march. Though all the other sisters had their natural hair fashioned into braids for their day's work—exhibiting a rainbow of blondes, auburns, chestnuts and sables, Wren's locks hid beneath a pseudo black chignon.

Although her hair's true color was the same purplish-ebony hue as Lynora's, the natural texture—coils that sprung tight and wiry—was a far cry from the sleek style of the Sisterhood's costume wigs worn for uniformity on outings. Lynora's own locks had regrown long enough to braid, yet today, like Wren's, it was tucked up in a matching wig, as they were the only two with assignments that would take them outside the castle gates. The completed disguise included protective iron neck cuffs and bracelets that juxtaposed silver against the metallic gold maquillage hiding their complexions. For such excursions, they always wore riding breeches, long-sleeved men's shirts, and boots in lieu of the more exotic airy full trousers, slippers, and sleeveless tunics the sisters sported daily behind castle walls. Though a nod to European fashion, it still maintained their defiance as a style no proper English lady would ever be seen in.

Lynora had rolled up the sleeves to her elbows because the crisp linen felt foreign everywhere it touched after so many weeks of wearing silk. But there was another discomfort even more foreign grating at her very core: this would be her first venture out since the change, and her spirit railed against the possibilities.

The line of girls approached the lattice-enclosed sparring yard where Sekhmet kept guard. In a wave of rustling tunics and trousers, her sisters passed the stony sentinel and separated, off to mind their morning chores in different areas about the castle yard. Lynora needed to accompany Wren to the ash grove for their shared task; however, she halted in front of the spacious frame where Sekhmet stood, one half of her heart aching over the reminder of her time at the museum with Mordecai and Isaac, the other half intrigued by what she'd learned since she'd been here.

At the Piccadilly Museum, the bust of Sekhmet had only consisted of a head and neck, as fragmented as the scholar's portrayal of the role the woman played in Egyptian history. Now, Lynora knew the whole truth.

In the earliest years of Desmodai civilization, neophites were rounded up and killed—bearing the blame for their own victimization. It was the uprising of rebels, both Desmodai men and women, who found such action cruel and immoral. They smuggled stray neophites into Alexandria, a city in Egypt where a powerful warrior named Sekhmet was rumored to be harboring halflings she'd found living in desert caves.

The Desmodai rebels presented Sekhmet with a proposition. They needed her to find the castoffs a place in society where they would be tolerated, if not accepted. The leaders of each undead city and province had agreed to give the altered women permission to live if they could co-exist among humans, for therein they could help the Desmodai flourish. They were to act as mediators between the underground cities and the surface. Sekhmet accepted, even allowing herself to be changed to a neophite, so she could better understand and guide the women who were now her charges.

As the dawn brightened to strands of yellow and orange, a blue, hazy shadow lengthened across the ground in front of Sekhmet's statue, making it appear to stand taller. Reverently, Lynora trailed a fingertip along the marbled jawline where a glint reflected off the smooth surface. In places, rough spots caused by weather and age dulled the sun's glare, giving the carved features a blunted, serene countenance. A tunic—engraved to swirling perfection—surfaced the torso, and haram-style trousers ballooned then clasped at the ankles, mirroring the clothing Lynora and the other sisters donned most days.

The statue's stony palm clenched a chiseled ammut: a pronged hair pick that represented the seven-inch iron-tipped weapons each neophite wore tucked in their hair or wigs at all times.

Sekhmet assigned neophite ambassadors to go out from Egypt all over the world, to provide sanctuary for any neophites they might find. She trained each ambassador in the arts of fighting, and how to hide in plain sight via masquerade. All of Tatabury thought Gwyndolaire to be filled with libertine and immoral women. Now, illumination gave their walk new luster. These ladies Lynora had once mistaken for esoteric outsiders, were in fact great warriors.

Lynora drew confidence from the thought and knelt for a moment of meditation. So intent on her veneration, she didn't hear the footfalls scraping behind her until a hand caught her shoulder.

"Starling." Wren's voice was firm, much like her grip.

Their gazes locked. Lynora had grown accustomed to seeing the cat-like curls of black makeup streaked around every sister's eyes. They wore it every day, putting on a fresh coat each morning upon waking. It no longer struck her as garish like it once had, not now that she understood it was *apotropaic* paint. The iron and kohl mixture gave the neophites immunity to the Desmodai's flickering gaze so they couldn't be hypnotized. Coupled with the wrist and neck cuffs, it was a neophite's best form of protection against being bitten or seduced by their otherworldly enemies.

"Should've known you'd be here," Wren said with a frown.

Lynora returned her attention to the statue as she stood. "One never expects, when they step into a museum exhibition filled with lore, that one day they'll experience the mythos firsthand."

"Yes, we are but the rubble that gods and goddesses leave in their wake." Wren gestured toward the grove of ash trees. "It's time to tend the bats." Her change of subject was unsurprising. She never liked speaking of life as it was before. "We've only a couple of hours before we leave for our assignment."

Stomach flipping at the reminder, Lynora fell into step behind her, relishing the sun's warmth as they left the shade of the trellis.

Wren eyed the path beneath them, half of her painted face veiled by the castle's shadow. Lynora found it hard to believe her new friend shared her age. Wren had a turbulent aura—a hardened, cynical edge. Though her beauty could not be contested, a deep sadness rimmed her dark blue eyes beneath their iron-tinged lining and belied the light of youth on her face. She rarely teased, and aside from when her expression tightened to stone, often looked to be on the verge of tears. Her full-lipped pout contributed to the illusion.

Yet it *was* only an illusion, as she wouldn't dare give in to any such tender emotion. She embraced only anger. Justifiable anger.

They passed groups of their sisters—some tending the goat pens, others the flower and vegetable gardens, the remainder washing laundry and feeding the peacocks that scuttered back and forth, adding dashes of vivid color across the grounds. One group of sisters looked up as they passed, several of them grimacing at Lynora with disdain.

There were two means whereby a person could become a neophite halfling: a bite from an infected human—a full Desmodai or a neophite—that festered and infected the soul; or the exchange of blood between an assigned Mentor and a consenting recipient. Of the eighteen neophites residing in the castle, Lynora was the only one altered because a Desmodai man had loved her so fiercely he couldn't bear to be away from her. This had earned her admiration from some, envy and acrimony from others.

Meeting the looks cast their way, Wren paused to pick up a stick so Lynora could match her stride. "You would win more friends here, were you to show that you are serious in regaining your humanity. Here you are, one of the few who knows your attacker. One of the few with the means to lure him to you, to reclaim your humanness. Use this advantage. It would earn their respect."

Lynora's teeth clamped her bottom lip. "You *know* that I'm serious. I have to find a way back to Isaac."

"*A* way back? There is only one way." The ire in Wren's voice snapped harsher than the wet clothes being shaken out by the laundry crew in the distance.

Wren clasped Lynora's hand, the jewels on their bracelets capturing the sun in rainbow glints of light. Her gaze tracked the twine on Lynora's left ring finger—so humble compared to the gems upon their arms. Yet it meant more to Lynora than all the treasures of the castle.

"You believe your husband still lives inside that monster. That's why you wear his chains. You claim to want your humanness, yet you can't part with your love for him. This makes you weak." Her button nose fidgeted like a rabbit's.

Lynora squeezed her friend's fingers, a gut reaction. Just one glance at her ring, and she remembered how her groom's eyes had looked on their honeymoon when her shyness and hesitance drove him out into the forest to begin with. She'd seen that same gentle blue gaze again when he came to her on the night of her alteration. "What if he sleeps . . . deep within the monster? The discerning side of him. A dormant angel. How can I be responsible for clipping his wings?"

Wren's eyes narrowed. "You are not responsible. He lost his wings the night he turned to their side—to the darkness."

"I sent him to his lab on our wedding night. It's my fault he was courted and seduced."

"The Brotherhood would've broached him one way or another, and he still would've made the same choice. The gardener you love is no longer within that beast. You would do well to forget his humanness altogether. For you will never see that side of him again." Wren jerked her fingers free from Lynora's then resumed walking, scraping the path with her stick.

A silent scream shook Lynora's chest as she followed. Yes, she hated the monster that had changed her. But how could the goodness that had once lived within Mordecai's human soul simply vanish?

"It isn't as hopeless as you think, Starling," Wren interrupted her musings. "Men are easily replaced. They're all the same." Her stick trailed the grass alongside her delicate ankles.

"People are not cut of one pattern. Mordecai was unique, gifted . . . brilliant even." Lynora despised talking about him in past tense. "The first time I saw him, he was gardening at my aunt and uncle's country estate in Bath . . . barefoot." A bittersweet smile tweaked her lips. "He wanted nothing between him and his plants."

Wren whipped aside a low hanging branch where the path wove between two trees. "And here I thought you were to inspire me with some sensuous tale of romance. So, you have a proclivity for bared feet. I'm sure we can find a grape-stomper for you to marry, once you're free. And you'll get an endless supply of wine, to boot."

Frowning, Lynora blocked the branch's backswing then passed Wren to take the lead. "You want sensuous details? When he worked, his shirt hung free from his pants' waist, draping his backside like a cape, and his muscled shoulders sparkled with sweat. Each time he stroked the stems of his plants—caressed their leaves, and tilled the earth with his fingertips—I found myself daydreaming I were a flower. Wishing he would touch me with such tender reverence. That I could give him pleasure in return."

Wren groaned from behind and Lynora gleaned some small satisfaction as she envisioned her friend's expression tightening in annoyance.

"Still suspended in a world of fairytales. You're far too naïve to be here among us," Wren snarled. "Tomorrow night, we will don pretty dresses to seduce and siphon blood from noble men. A detestable ceremony we endure due to your husband's bloodthirsty kind."

Lynora cringed at the reminder. "Are you nervous?"

"It may be my first Gwyndolaire gala, but I'm well-versed at playing the whore. Remember? I sold my body as haymarket ware."

Lynora glared over her shoulder. "What you did for your sisters and your stricken father . . . you sold the only thing you could to keep them from starving. You're selfless for that."

"Mayhap. But your Mordecai is not. If he does still retain his human side, it makes his betrayal all the more detestable. For he altered you without telling you what it would entail. Despite the goodness you say he embodies, he was thinking of no one but himself. That doesn't sound like the loving gardener you idolize. Even you can't refute that."

Lynora whirled around to face her companion. She pressed her lips against a rush of nausea—triggered more by the acknowledgement of Wren's inarguable truth than the swirling surroundings.

"As I said, there's only one way back." Wren prodded Lynora's chest with her stick, digging the knife of candor deeper. "In order for you to return to the living *and* Isaac, someone will have to end your husband's immortal life."

CHAPTER 9

Mordecai longed for an end to this torment. The caustic realization seared his brain as he chased a victim through the shadows of the Miseria Chambers—the hive-like structure of underground caves used solely for practice. The human had been captured earlier by Drakkarh and brought into the under-realm for this trial run.

Reapers in training learned the art of stealth while well-hidden from mortal eyes. This minimized the chance of making any mistakes topside and exposing their kind. They couldn't have the mortals believing in monsters, after all.

Monsters. Mordecai would have laughed at the word; but laughter was too pure an emotion. With his brother out of reach and Lynora dead, the only thing that drove him was thirst—a convoluted and compulsive pull. Even faced with the knowledge that his fragile bride had burned alive due to his recklessness, he still craved blood. That insatiable need to feed proved he no longer had any shred of humanity left within.

So why did he still feel human enough to grieve?

His shoulder blades pressed against the rough arch of a tunnel, spurring some loose clods to fall from the walls. He shut his eyes and listened to the patter, fought the tears that threatened to join the rainfall of dirt. He tried to remember Lynora's beautiful serenades on the lyre in hopes to block out the whimpers of the victim who scrambled along an adjacent tunnel like a frightened rat.

Mordecai wanted to go back. To reclaim innocence lost, to open his eyes and see Isaac and Lynora picking flowers or playing hide and seek outside their cottage. To be blinded by sunlight. Blind to the havoc he had wreaked.

It was morning on topside. Yet outside of these caves, within the depths of Nocturnus, the entire populous rested in their sanctuaries. That's where Mordecai wanted to be. His sanctuary. Where he could miss his family in private; where he could torture himself with memories of Lynora's songs and sweetness in peace.

"Get on with it, nursling!" Drakkarh's voice bellowed from the other end of the tunnel, as intrusive as any slap. The dusky-eyed regent had been assigned to supervise the slaughter once Mordecai caught the victim.

Clenching his jaw, Mordecai forced himself to resume his search.

Despite the temporary reprieve from his grounding collar while in these tunnels, he'd been dreading this day for the past two weeks of training . . . dreading his introduction to the full potency of the *Wisdom*. To date, Mordecai had sampled the wanton trespasses of harlots in preparation, but the crimes this man had committed were much more sinister. This man had tortured and killed five innocent people topside, and was to be Mordecai's first true sampling of the darker sins. Mordecai's flesh prickled at the thought of allowing such evil to engulf him—even if only for an instant. Couldn't they have brought him a thief instead?

Scenting the quarry's repugnant sweat, Mordecai rounded a bend, his footing agile and sure despite the darkness. He needed no light to see in the gloom. To him, the outlines of his surroundings were clear with colors distorted to variant shades of gray. On the other side of the tunnel wall, his victim's panicked breaths grew more desperate.

In the beginning of this run, Mordecai had procrastinated, chasing the quarry without use of his inhuman strength or spirit advantage.

He did manage to capture the man twice. But despite his rotund form, the victim was desperate, feverish to survive, which contributed to unexpected fleetness. Having shoved Mordecai to the ground, he escaped both times.

Now, tiring of the grim spectacle, Mordecai opted to end the chase. Even though he knew what poison awaited him, this man's blood still called to him, an invisible hand clenched at his throat. Dusting off his shirt lapels, he gave himself up to mist form.

He drifted weightlessly through the tunnels in spite of a heavy soul. It was an odd sensation, swimming as a cloud—soundless, formless—covering fifteen feet of crawl space in one sweep. For a moment he relished the feeling . . . the closest thing to omniscience a man could achieve. Until he realized this was the closest he would ever come to imagining how Lynora felt, gliding as an angel in heaven.

A loud thud in the adjacent tunnel shattered his agonized thought. The quarry had collided with a boulder in the darkness. Mordecai filtered through miniscule holes in the wall to arrive where the man writhed on the ground a few feet away, stalled by a dead end.

How apropos.

Drifting toward his hunched victim, Mordecai materialized. His booted feet, the last to form, crunched the broken rocks just inches from the sniveling man's face.

"Oh, Lord . . . please . . ." The man shuddered on the ground— his knees raw with cuts, his pants stained red, and his plump fingers clenched like bloated caterpillars across his eyes. "How did I get here?" He sobbed and tightened his hands over his face.

The scent of his blood trembled on the tip of Mordecai's tongue. Some Reapers claimed to feel a surge of poetic justice when cornering their condemned prey, the rush of a vigilante ending the brutal reign of a criminal. Mordecai wondered what he should feel—for this man, for the broken society that spawned such deep soul sickness it drove humans to behave as beasts.

Without a word, he lifted the victim and pinned him against the wall. Mordecai's flashing eyes trailed lights across the man's face. He turned the man's chin to expose his neck, studying the bite marks left from earlier, when Drakkarh had hypnotized the quarry to bring him here.

"No! God help me, no!" Tears trickled down the victim's face and double chin, tiny tributaries which joined the pools of dirty moisture gathered within folds of neck fat. His moist flesh made him difficult to contain, like a slug that kept sliding through Mordecai's fingers. "Please . . . please . . . "

Mordecai nearly lost his hold as the man struggled to break free. "I wonder." He murmured as he dulled the flash in his eyes. "Did *your* victims plead in such a way for their lives?"

The murderer grew still, seeing only a gardener's studious stare now, calm enough to have a conversation. "What—are you a *Bow Street Runner*? Is this prison? I demand a trial!"

"You've already been tried and found guilty." Before the man could react, Mordecai clutched his coat lapels, leaned forward, and punctured Drakkarh's previous bite marks just enough to release a slight amount of numbing toxins from his fangs. He licked a droplet of blood away and trembled inwardly, his body screaming for more. But he wrestled the temptation to gorge himself. He wanted to remain aloof, to avoid an emotional connection with this murderer. The man's legs folded and his shoes slid along the pebbles.

"I have him!" Mordecai's outcry echoed through the tunnels as he wrestled the man. Within seconds, Zebulon, the lead Reaper, stood behind him. They were so close in body type and size, he could've been Mordecai's shadow. The victim had begun to plead for his life again in a hoarse, grating whine.

"Finish it." The Reaper's chilling command curled along Mordecai's shoulder and stiffened his neck hair. "He hasn't the mind of a child. If ye just sample his essence with a sip or two, ye release just the altering agents in your saliva that weaken his muscles. Ye must drink deeper than ye ever have . . . lead him into a full trance by releasin' the proper amount of toxins into 'is blood through yer fangs. Otherwise, he can still scream, lead people to witness his abduction. He must be inanimate *and* silent if yer to provide a successful spirit shroud to levitate 'is passage to Nocturnus."

Mordecai paused, panic slithering through his heart. "Can we not simply knock them out . . . wallop their heads with a brick?"

Terrified by the graphic debate taking place over him, the victim cried out—a yelping wail that echoed through the tunnels.

Zebulon snickered. "Well, that wouldn't be very civilized of us, would it?" He clenched Mordecai's shoulder from behind. "Ye very well know why we can't do that. Now get on w'it."

Mordecai's body tensed. Yes, he knew, just as they couldn't cut out a victim's tongue to silence them. Leaving behind smears of blood, or any sign of a struggle, was forbidden. And to render a human unconscious or dead during the capture tainted the blood with a stale taste, even affecting the texture. It became an undrinkable, stagnant sap. The victim had to be semi-conscious, partly awake albeit paralyzed throughout the entire process, until the moment the last of their blood was drained away to be added to the communal cocktail.

It wouldn't do Mordecai any good to debate further; he would only end up locked in a sarcophagus again if he didn't make the effort. What did it matter . . . he couldn't feel any more a murderer than he already did. He had killed his own bride.

Biting back an agonized roar, he repositioned his mouth, aching for release from this pain. His jaw widened, fangs sliding deep into the quarry's neck to pierce an artery. A river of hot blood burst across his lips. The warmth dulled his memories, numbed his regrets. Lost in rapturous gluttony, his suction tightened and the liquid gushed down his throat. Heat spread to every limb as he gulped and gulped again, the man's sobs only making him crave more.

Even in this frenzied ecstasy—Mordecai understood what he needed to do next. Wrap the man in his spirit, the same way he bound his clothes to himself when he translated, like a spider shrouding his prey in web.

But as the victim grew silent and Mordecai prepared to turn to mist, the *Wisdom* overtook. The quarry's most recent sins—vinegar dregs of murder and the burn of coarse-ground pepper, indicative of rape—rose to the surface of Mordecai's consciousness. The flavors scalded his tongue. He groaned in dreaded anticipation of the rush.

Smothering a scream, his head tilted back and the motion ripped his fangs free. Mordecai's body shuddered, his mind replaying the evil deeds of his prey: A crimson splash scattered across a window pane like tainted raindrops. He watched himself, in his quarry's clothes and body, slice a man's throat . . . a husband trying to protect his wife. The meaty taste of lust surged through him. He turned to the woman in his mind. Tears streaked her lovely face as she pled for her husband's life. Mordecai threw her to the floor with fat hands that weren't his. Repulsed by his touch, she fought him, enhancing the need to overpower her, defile her. Then, in a moment of macabre insight, Mordecai saw the sick man's twisted rationale—as this was his revenge against a father who had beat him as a child until he bled . . . against a mother who had taunted him for his worthlessness and did not care to stop the abuse.

Motive . . . Mordecai tasted the motive and nearly gagged on it.

Growling, he dropped the quarry. He heard the man's neck snap upon impact against the ground.

"Ye cretin!" Zebulon's fury rung out in the hollows.

Yet Mordecai couldn't think beyond the *Wisdom*. He clamped his palms to his throbbing temples. He crumpled against the limestone wall, bound by the demented man's blood, an unwilling participant in a rape he had never committed, in a tragic childhood he had never experienced. When the vicious crime ended with the woman's death, he wept.

"Get up, nursling!"

Mordecai caught the glint of Drakkarh's gold ring as a harsh jerk on his shoulder shook him back to the present. He hadn't even realized there were two Desmodai standing over him now.

"Do that topside," the regent seethed, "and not only will you cost us the quarry, you will damn the handful of witnesses you'll draw with your blubbering. Each one will have to die to save your anonymity."

The words sunk into Mordecai's dizzy head. He would need to learn to postpone the rush somehow—draw his prey down before the *Wisdom* hit full force.

He stood, his insides jittery as if the blood in his veins clambered to become his own again, to flush out the contagions of the quarry's essence.

Drakkarh lifted the corpse and his nose curled in disgust. The man's bladder had emptied when he took his last breath. To Mordecai, the scent of urine was a welcome distraction from the filth he'd just experienced.

Drakkarh bared his fangs. "Never feel remorse for a human."

"I saw his motivation!" Mordecai screamed, no longer able to float above the waves of disgust and regret racking his body. "Why didn't anyone warn me?" Raking back his hair, he glared at Zebulon.

The lead Reaper laughed as Drakkarh flung the corpse his way.

"Go get your work done. Leave the body. I'll care of it," Drakkarh said.

Zebulon snapped a nod, then glared at Mordecai while shaking his waist length hair as if in pity. The white tips settled around him, the color of aged bones. "Ye'll ne'er be a Reaper. Yer far too soft." With that, he kicked the dead criminal aside as he left Mordecai alone with the regent.

"You idiot." Drakkarh narrowed his dusky gaze. "That's why the populous only drinks diluted blood. The communal cocktail suppresses the grisly insight into singular, personal motive. Every Reaper must encounter it cold. It is part of the training."

Mordecai suppressed a gagging sensation and dragged his hand across his lips. "I don't want it. I don't want to *feel* what they feel . . ."

"*Perfect.* The flavor of that distasteful communion. It's there to help you break ties with empathy. That is the only way your sanity will survive this calling."

"So, I'm to stop caring? What will separate me from the beasts of the field if I lose that ability?"

"Humans are the beasts. I've witnessed their abominations over the centuries, watched one senseless war bleed into another until mutilated bodies fade into the compost of tomorrow's trees, and precious blood is wasted on the poppies and laurel. They are barbarians . . . their own worst enemy." Drakkarh clutched the corpse's shirt lapels and shook him like a rag doll. "Why do you think they call this rush of insight *Wisdom*? It's our release from the curse. We are the hierarchy. The sooner you realize this, the better. T'would help you get over your sainted Lynora's death."

Mordecai lunged at Drakkarh. The dead body toppled from the regent's hands. Standing on the quarry's lifeless arm, Mordecai crushed the regent against the wall. "Speak her name again and you will join the corpse beneath my feet."

Drakkarh sneered. With just a flash of his eyes, Mordecai's knuckles cramped until he could no longer hold the regent's lapels.

Stepping back, Mordecai worked out the kinks in his fingers. One day he, too, would master the hypnotic gaze enough to use it on others of his kindredship. He could hardly wait.

Drakkarh dusted off his vest—the same deep red hue of his burgundy hair. He gestured to the adjacent tunnel. "Your guard awaits you at the entrance with your collar. Go home. Rest. Prepare yourself. You'll practice until you can utilize that gardener's ability of persuasion that Augustus waxed so poetic about. You won't be a free citizen again until you prove yourself an able Reaper." He glared at the corpse beside their feet. "Slaying a human is no different than slaying an animal. They are here for no other purpose than to sustain our thirst. If not for their vile, sinful nature, we wouldn't have to take so many, to make a cocktail that dilutes their shame . . . just to keep us from suffering other men's depravities seared into our souls. Consider that."

Drakkarh spirited away with the corpse, leaving Mordecai to contemplate his apathetic spiel. Each and every Desmodai had once been a human. Some of the regents still seemed to remember that, yet Drakkarh had forgotten.

Mordecai gripped his aching head as the rape victim's face transposed with Lynora's in his mind. Silent tears crept down his face.

Perhaps Drakkarh was the wise one after all; perhaps being a Reaper *was* the answer to abandoning humanity; if so, Mordecai would embrace it . . . for he would do anything to forget.

CHAPTER 10

Lynora could no longer remember why she once feared bats. Now, when she wasn't sparring in the courtyard, making blood pudding in the kitchen, educating herself in the Sanctorum, or composing songs on her lyre in the music chambers, the bat grove was her favorite sanctuary.

Together, she and Wren plunged into the small thicket of ash trees where only the castle's highest turret remained visible in the distance. Overhead, the twisted branches shaded them from the sun, though several leaves had prematurely succumbed to autumn and shuffled beneath their feet in a shifting carpet. Lynora's nostrils stung with the odor of bat dung—an amalgamation of rotten eggs and ammonia. The guano's rich nutrients, when combined with goat marrow and sprinkled upon the castle grounds, kept the flora thriving well after most flowers had died along the hills outside of Gwyndolaire.

Wren ducked into the shed then reappeared carrying two miniature shovels, two buckets, and a pair of gloves for each of them. Expressionless, she handed Lynora hers. Wren had been chosen for this task three weeks before Lynora arrived, as she wasn't the least bit squeamish of the creatures—a trait uncharacteristic to that of most women. Lynora, however, was paired with Wren due to her musical ability. Drawing from her knowledge of pitch and rhythm, she developed an unprecedented means of communicating with the pipistrelle. Once she overcame her apprehension for the creatures, she found herself respecting their cleverness and fortitude. In some ways, tending them had helped soothe the absence of Isaac in her life, by giving her something small that depended on her care.

Wriggling her fingers into the stiff gloves, Lynora glanced overhead where roosting boxes, mounted twelve feet high upon each tree, housed their sleeping bats. There were twenty abodes, and four bats lived in each one.

Standing on tiptoe, the girls scraped bat dung off of the round predator guards encircling the lower quarter of each trunk at shoulder height. Along with collecting the fertilizer, the metal shields protected the bats from ground-dwelling rodents and snakes.

After Lynora deposited her bucket and gloves in the shed, she spotted Wren climbing a trunk to access a roosting box. Today, they would search for any cracks or splits in the wood, then next week, they'd fill any deficiencies with mortar to keep the bats warm in the upcoming winter. They would also slather a new coat of black paint onto each box's exterior to help retain heat from the sun. This level of upkeep had kept the roosts in place for almost a century without splintering or falling apart.

Lynora climbed one of her assigned trees, utilizing the wooden pegs where they wound in increments around each trunk—providing a ladder that trailed up and over the guard. She'd just approached the shield's metal ridge when a hand grabbed her ankle above the edge of her boot. Lynora snapped her attention to a group of six sisters encircling the trunk below.

The one holding her foot—Raven—tightened her grip, fingernails biting hard into tender flesh. She was two years younger than Lynora, wickedly beautiful with hair the reddish brown of harvest leaves and piercing eyes the color and shape of shelled almonds. She'd already threatened to break Lynora in half during three different sparring sessions. Judging by her determined expression, she intended to make good on her sadistic threats today.

Tendrils of pain uncoiled from Lynora's ankle to her shin. She tried to jerk away but it almost cost her footing. Pressing her lips together, she clenched the pegs on the other side of the trunk, hugging the rough bark to her chest.

"Come down, Starling," Raven crooned, the tiny freckles along her nose disappearing as she crinkled it tauntingly. "I came to show you something."

"Go back to scrubbing our bloomers, laundry nit," Wren gritted out from the canopy above, having reached her roosting box. "We're doing something important."

"This is between me and the princess, *Wrench*." Raven motioned with her chin, sending three of her companions to gather around Wren's trunk and keep her treed.

Gut tightening, Lynora stayed on her own perch until Raven's two remaining accomplices gripped her other boot's heel and tugged, offsetting her balance.

Lynora managed to make the descent with enough grace to land on her feet. The moment her shoes hit the leafy carpet, she plucked her ammut from her wig. The hairpiece didn't budge, held in place by pins.

"One on one, Raven." Wren started to descend the pegs on her tree. "Or I tell all the other sisters how it took the six of you to defeat the weakest fighter in the castle."

A combative fire kindled in Lynora's stomach. She wasn't weak. Wren had been training her in private, and over the last two weeks she'd made marked improvement. But arguably not enough to take on three opponents.

Her heart pounded as she and the trio faced off.

Huffing, Raven gestured to her two friends to stand back. She slashed at Lynora with her ammut's iron-tipped end, having freed it from her hair. Her feet shifted to fortify the lunge. Lynora blocked with her forearm and clipped Raven's elbow on the downswing, winning her a nasty cut that would heal within hours. Though a neophite could not heal spontaneously like a Desmodai, they did heal at a faster rate than common humans.

Blood dribbled down Raven's arm and her eyes widened in surprise. Lynora raised her stick, smirking. Raven jabbed forward and Lynora blocked again. Her opponent shifted, off-balance; but it was a trick, for in the span of a breath Raven executed a front sweep with her right leg. She caught Lynora in the left knee, sending a shot of lightning pain through her nerves.

The ground slammed into Lynora's back and shoved the air from her body, hollowing her lungs. Raven straddled her, pressing her flat on the ground. Pebbles and crispy-edged leaves ate into Lynora's back as she struggled to catch her breath.

With one hand clamped on Lynora's shoulder, Raven leaned forward and jammed the hair-stick against her jawline. "Poor little princess. Violated by the Desmodai knight who loved you too much. So confused . . . so torn."

Lynora's skin bristled as Raven's free hand moved from her shoulder to the iron cuff at her neck, scraping Lynora's collarbone as she pried the protective piece off to reveal the bitemarks underneath.

Raven sneered. "He left you such a pretty love bite; your flavor must be irresistible." She leaned close. Her mouth almost touched Lynora's—so close Lynora could taste her breath of sugared musk. Without preamble, Raven raked her rough, hot tongue across Lynora's forehead then faked a gag. "Appears to be an acquired taste. For filth."

Lynora spat at her.

Raven's thighs tightened around Lynora's ribs as she swiped spittle from her chin. "You think you're better than us. But you're wrong. All you need is a good look at yourself. Then you'll see how monstrous you truly are." From beneath her tunic, she withdrew a small silvery square. It caught a gleam of sunlight, flashing onto Lynora's face.

The three sisters at the base of Wren's tree edged closer, their expressions flickering between anticipation and something that resembled dread. Within her periphery, Lynora caught a glimpse of the reflective surface. For an instant her flesh appeared gray and began to flake away like ash. Lynora slammed her eyes shut, twisting her head back and forth. Her throat clamped tight with the struggle.

She'd read about what happened to neophites who looked directly at their reflections, knew her fate should she fail to escape: her eyes would lock upon themselves—as if an unseen force nailed her gaze to the glass. She'd be a helpless bystander to her soul's decay. Her skin would appear to crumble. The old flesh would peel off, though only in her image, like a snake shedding its scales, leaving nothing but emptiness staring back. From that point forward, she would never have a reflection again. The shock of the vision would strip away any memory of a past or sense of identity, leaving her mind forever lost to madness.

Lynora screwed her eyes shut—tighter still. Every muscle tensed as she fought a futile battle against Raven's hold.

"No!" Lynora heard Wren shout. A scuffle ensued and she could only guess Wren had broken through the neophites guarding her, only to be tackled by the remaining three. "Don't look, Starl . . ." Wren's voice muffled as if someone shoved something into her mouth.

Lynora squared her legs to push up her lower half in hopes she might alter Rose's balance, but a shooting pain twisted through her knee. She collapsed again.

"Just one peek, you sniveling debutante. And you can forget your sad, sad plight." Growling, Rose attempted to force Lynora's eyes open, pinching the skin around them. Thankfully, tears rose to the surface, helping to blur Lynora's vision as she strained to keep her head turned.

Familiar sounds stirred overhead. Thumps and chitters from

within the roosting boxes. Hearing the waking bats, Lynora grasped desperately at a plan. With Wren settled safely on the ground, it would be the perfect recourse. Dragging one of her arms free, Lynora kissed her fingers, inducing a high-pitched squeak.

A shrill chirrup answered in return. She recognized the source, even with eyes shut. It was Rime, the one-year-old albino with fur as white as frost, and wings, face, and feet the color and sheen of fuzzy, ripe peaches. He had always favored Lynora, as if he sensed their similar situation. They were both so different from those they cohabitated with, yet inescapably linked to them through their blood.

"Sun-bright!" Lynora shouted while wrestling against Raven. "I need a favor."

"What's going on up there?" One of the girls holding Wren asked with a suspicious quiver in her voice.

Raven resituated atop of Lynora, glancing overhead. Taking advantage of the distraction, Lynora shoved her off. The mirror slammed into a rock and shattered. Swiping tears from her eyes, Lynora stood. She suppressed the shooting pain in her knee and squeaked her fingers again.

Rime responded with a chittery-chirp. In a rush of rubbery wings and squeaks, all eighty bats—each with tiny chains jangling on their legs—burst out from their roosts to follow their albino leader, swirling around the girls, twisting their clothes with currents of wind.

"Call them off!" Raven shouted. Her arms flailed as the bats formed a brownish-black funnel around her.

Seated aground, Wren laughed at the other sisters who scrambled toward the thicket's entrance, only to be hemmed in when half of the bats dove across the opening. "Fair comeuppance for such bad form!"

As Raven and her companions engaged in a tug-of-war for their hair and clothes against the bat funnels, Lynora helped Wren stand. Together, they opened four wooden cages and Lynora called to Rime with her kissing song. He led fifteen of the bats into the enclosures, which Lynora promptly latched shut. Then she directed the rest back to their roosts with a final hooting whistle.

Raven hunched on the ground, arms curled over her mussed-up hair, tunic disheveled and off-center. Her accomplices panted and whimpered around her in similar poses.

Wren stepped over the broken glass, kicking the silver shards toward Raven. "A mirror. Really? Have you gone mad?"

"No. But I'd like to see *her* go there." Raven slanted a glare at Lynora.

The two stared at one another, ammuts clenched once more within the fists at their sides.

The shrubbery rustled as Heron plunged into the thicket. The long sleeves of her silk tunic fluttered like wings. Her gaze shifted from the weapons in their fists to their disheveled clothes and hair. "Mother Nenet saw the bat funnels from the tower window. What's the cause of this?"

Lynora opened her mouth to answer, but Wren silenced her with a look and raked several leaves over the broken glass with her boot's toe.

Heron studied the eight girls, frowning. "So, you've nothing to share?" No one would meet her gaze. She grabbed both Raven and Lynora's hands, forcing them to drop their ammuts. "Our war is with the Desmodai. Unless you're sparring under my supervision, you're not to use any weapons on one another. Raven, you shouldn't even be wearing your ammut today, as you're not leaving the grounds. Where is your naturlege?"

With a downtrodden expression, Raven shrugged. The naturlege sticks were made to look similar to the girls' ammuts—painted silver and carved into the same shape. But since they were made of juniper heart-wood as opposed to iron, and had healing properties, each girl marked them in some definitive way. It was how they knew which stick was safe to use in sparring.

"Fine." Heron's scowl deepened. "You'll both sit at Mother Nenet's hands at dinner this evening. I'm guessing you'll be a bit more forthcoming with her. You six . . ." She motioned to Rose and her friends. "Off to tend your tasks. This afternoon, we begin preparations for the blood gala. Go now."

Lynora propped her shoulder against a tree to watch them clear out. Raven tossed a scowl over her shoulder as she laced her ammut in her braid and slipped through the opening toward the peony gardens.

Heron lifted Lynora's ammut and handed it to her. She furrowed her brows. "Are you hurt?"

Lynora shook her head. She exhaled through her nose to ward off the spasms in her knee as she shifted her stance. Wren paused beside her to straighten the wig seated lopsided on Lynora's head then snuggled the ammut within the chignon.

Heron's face softened. "Do you need me to see to your leg? Perhaps you should retire to the infirmary hall."

Lynora noticed mirror dust glinting in the sunlight between the leaves piled on the ground. She placed her sole atop it. "Thank you, Sister Superior. But I wish to complete our outing today. The novice carriers have trained hard for this test." As if in answer, the bats fluttered in their cages. Rime gnawed on a wooden bar, eager to go.

Wren squeezed Lynora's arm in a show of support.

A smile of sympathy curled Heron's painted lips. "It won't always be so difficult here," the superior said, picking up Lynora's discarded neck cuff and handing it to her. "For some, the envy is fresh. Yours is a story we should all like to own. To be chosen as opposed to preyed upon ... would make it easier to live with, somehow. Still, the others will one day see that you stand to lose the same as each of us. That perhaps your trek is in fact even harder."

Nodding, Lynora slid the neck cuff into place over her pulsing bite marks.

THE WISDOM OF BLOOD

"Be safe on your journey, both of you." With that, Heron ducked out of the grove.

After waiting a few moments, Lynora shot Wren a glare. "I can't believe you protected Raven."

"We're akin to bats, not rats. Sisters don't snitch on sisters. Raven is young and insolent. She and her accomplices will be shown the path to loyalty and devotion once our Sisterhood learns of the malevolent attack against one of our own. Better they punish her than Mother Nenet. The lesson will be deeper ingrained coming by way of her peers."

Lynora pursed her lips, uncovering the glass shards on the ground. Since mirrors were forbidden at the castle, none of the sisters could manage their maquillage without one another's help. They even practiced sparring blindfolded so they might learn to trust their other senses besides sight, in case they ever needed to close their eyes and ward off a Desmodai assailant that might hold a reflective shield to gain an advantage.

"Where do you think she acquired such a thing?" Lynora toed some dirt across the shimmery dust.

Wren shook her head. "Probably during one of her merchandising runs to Tatabury. The sentinels can't watch us all. They must've took their eyes off her for a minute; that's all it takes for one such as her. Why do you think Mother named her Raven? Because she's a scavenger. She's clever and feeds on carrion."

"You're calling me carrion?"

Wren shrugged. "She'll peck at you until you prove you belong to the living. Fight for your life. Only then will you earn her respect."

Lynora's teeth clamped her bottom lip to refocus the burning sensation in her knee. "It's your respect I'm in need of gaining, and we both know it."

Wren rolled her eyes. "You shouldn't come today with that hurt knee." Her inflexible expression softened an almost negligible amount, like a rock weathered by heavy rains. "It's a far walk to the cemetery."

Lynora gritted her teeth. "I can endure it." Though she sensed Wren's concerns had nothing to do with distance. Wren worried for what waited at the end of the hour-and-a-half jaunt. Today, they were to carry the trained bats to the entrance of Nocturnus. Wren had already visited that gateway two weeks ago when she accompanied four sisters and one neophite sentinel to town to sell the merchandise supplied by Nocturnus. On the way to Tatabury, they took a detour through the cemetery so Wren could find her way when the time came to test the novice carriers. Mother Nenet had refused to let Lynora go on that sojourn, fearing it too soon for her to be exposed to her past.

"You're still not hardened enough to step outside these gates." Wren picked up two cages and prodded Lynora's waist with one, as if to demonstrate her softness. "These sympathies that rule you, they'll cause you to make weak choices . . . to be victimized once more."

After rolling down her sleeves so the cuffs covered her iron wristlets, Lynora secured the remaining cages and squeezed the wooden handles in her grip. "I may sympathize with the man he was, but I'm not so deluded as to believe I can ever trust him again." It was an honest statement, though she secretly wondered if she could trust *herself* to resist what awaited at the end of the hour-and-a-half jaunt.

Being in such close proximity to Mordecai's under-realm would bring startling clarity to the nightmare she'd experienced last night upon falling asleep. The perforations on her neck had been pulsating unbearably, perhaps that's why she'd found herself dreaming of her husband's underworld, adrift in a gondola along a river of blood and sins. Demons lined the dark shore, welcoming her home. At tunnel's end, Mordecai waited, glistening and lovely, open palm held out. She went to him and as they bit one another in violent fits of passion, their blood flowing into the river, the torrents swept them away. She had awoken, gasping for air.

She'd accepted that the throbbing bite-marks would never heal, that each neophite suffered such a fate, eternally tied to the Desmodai who had changed them. But for Lynora, there was another tie . . . an emotional bond, making her want him despite everything he had done. More than want—a need beyond desire. Her spirit longed to unite with his, joined as eternal mates.

He wanted it too. She could sense his thoughts, how he yearned for her. This was unique to their situation . . . a consequence of their blood exchange. No other neophite had sipped the blood of their attacker.

However, recently, the mental tie held a bitter tang of closure. Lynora had felt Mordecai grieving her death. She broached Mother Nenet with the subject, who admitted she'd led the Brotherhood to believe Lynora had died in the fire. Her husband was in mourning, thinking her gone forever. Lynora agreed it best to uphold that charade; he could never know she'd survived.

At least with Wren and Lynora venturing out in daylight, there'd be no chance encounter with Mordecai, as the Desmodai populous would be at rest.

Clenching her jaw against an unwanted pang of disappointment, Lynora followed Wren out of the bat grove, limping. She didn't dare ask her companion to slow down, but as the iron-pike barrier to outside came into view, she nearly stumbled over her own feet.

The sentinel on guard dragged the gate open, and the keening screech raked through Lynora's bones. Wren rushed through, impatient to be on the way.

"You must prove yourself fit to accompany me . . . match my steps." She tossed the dare over her shoulder. "Otherwise, be the victim Raven believes you to be and stay at the castle with your knee propped on pillows."

Lynora leapt forward in spite of a jolt in her leg that mirrored the one in her heart. She had no intention of being treated like a fragile debutant. And she would not be a victim. Not today.

Her gaze fell to her ring.

Not ever again.

CHAPTER 11

Lounging within his sanctuary chamber, Mordecai leaned his shoulders on the arm of his chaise couch. Although darkness and silence surrounded him, sleep betrayed him. He couldn't stop thinking of his victim.

After his experience with the *Wisdom* in the Miseria Chambers, his body yearned for the release of dreams. According to his longcase clock, it was early afternoon topside. When sunlight warmed the earth, all of Nocturnus slept. He, however, would not sleep today. After witnessing that woman's rape and murder, he could no longer deny Lynora had also been violated . . . misled, then killed at his hands.

He stood, lungs heavy as if he'd been inhaling mud.

All of those weeks in solitaire. All of that wondering, worrying. Where could Lynora be? How was she handling the changes? He had even faced the terror that she might have looked in a mirror. But all had been for naught. For his bride had been dead before the sarcophagus lid even slammed across his face.

The torture of it was that he still felt her heartbeat in his soul. That on his tongue, he could taste her breath—alive and strong. He would have sworn she still lived, that her thoughts were as consumed by him as his by her, but how could she have survived such a fire?

Fingers trembling, he lit a candle. The spark danced and teased him, brought to life distorted images of his bride screaming in the midst of an inferno while the walls crumbled around her. Jaw clenched tight, he held his palm over the candle, staring at the back of his hand. The flame's glow illuminated his veins through his pale flesh.

How deceptive, that he appeared to have the inner workings of a human. Desmodai did not require air to breathe since they fed off of the oxygen-rich essence of humans. Yet in the beginning years of each individual's immortal walk, their heart would still throb and their blood still pulse along its given path—spurred by compulsion rather than necessity. As though the mind and body refused to relinquish the faculties once necessary and instinctual for life. However, that instinct wouldn't last forever. One day, his body would forget the old impulses, and he hoped, along with that physical separation, his mind and heart would forget what it was like to *feel* human.

Inch by inch, Mordecai allowed his palm to fall closer until he could smell singed flesh. The nerves screamed and shot dagger-like impulses to his elbow, but he held fast. He would heal within seconds of drawing back, a benefit Lynora hadn't shared. Cursing, he yanked his palm from the candle, the flesh black and ragged like parchment curled by flame. Before he could blink, his skin smoothed, returned to the spectral white of a new moon. As perfect and flawless as his every possession in this place.

The contents of his domed chamber spun around him: his armoire filled with lavish clothes; his walls, draped with velvet panels in alternate shades of scarlet and ebony; patterned rugs rich in ornamental style; his library case, filled with the history of mankind, those unsuspecting souls who were now his prey.

History. Prey.

Mordecai sat heavily on his ottoman. One month after he had asked Lynora to elope with him and she sent a note refusing, she found him and Isaac visiting the museum on Piccadilly. Perhaps, had he not been so distracted by her presence there . . . by the fact that she came to offer him her undying devotion . . . perhaps he would've paid attention to the Egyptian exhibit. He would have viewed the display instead of leaving early, and been on guard against such creatures. The very creatures he now considered his kindred.

He had rushed his brother and Lynora from that museum, driven by the unrelenting need to make Lynora his before anyone could stop him again. The same motivation which pulled his strings on the night he altered her.

He'd only wanted to keep his promise to never leave her again . . . to be with her—forever young. He'd wanted to bring her down into this unique society of wise and regal people. Yet he didn't give her the courtesy of choosing.

He grimaced at the gold gilded mirror on his wall across the chamber. Once a neophite became a fully realized Desmodai, there was no longer a risk of madness upon seeing themselves. How many times had he worshipped his reflection since he'd been changed? The influence, the wealth, the alluring beauty of metamorphosis. A lowly gardener rising to a king.

Those things he had hoped to escape: the fall of his family, the resulting poverty. Such a deep yearning, it had made him easy to seduce.

His mother died when he was six years old. Throughout the remainder of his childhood, his father, Cornelius, tried to evade loneliness by traveling, leaving Mordecai in the care of an aunt who lived in Tatabury. Meanwhile in other corners of the world, Cornelius acquired a bizarre assortment of herbs, plants, and bugs for experiments, siphoning away Mordecai's heritage. When his father returned without a guinea to his name, he sold his estates in order to hold onto his scientific equipment and findings. Later, he tried to regain the properties through gambling, but instead lost his family's title to an ivory-turner. The dicer was so skilled Cornelius never had a chance, and neither did Mordecai's claim to earldom.

Shortly after his father vanished without explanation, a wet nurse appeared on Mordecai's doorstep with a three-month-old half-brother he had never even been told of. With nothing to go on as to Isaac's mother's identity, Mordecai slipped into the shoes of his father and never looked back. Isaac's first step was taken along the footbridge at Haven's creek, his tiny hands holding tight to the rails. His first words had been, "Go . . . go far." The lad was always happiest when exploring new places and scenes. And Mordecai had been there for each accomplishment, aglow with pride. He wouldn't have traded that time for all the money in the world. Then again . . . that's exactly what he had done.

Isaac. At just the name, Mordecai's stomach turned upon itself. He had robbed his brother of not only his care, but Lynora's as well.

If it were permitted he would reveal himself . . . but no.

Isaac could never know he lived, for it would be the cruelest of taunts to dangle that hope for a relationship which could no longer be.

The highest and most sacred law in Nocturnus protected all mortal children—an addendum to the Sanctioned Conversion Decretum. Any child under the age of seventeen was not to be taken as feed or coerced to come into the Desmodai fellowship.

The law came about upon the foundation of the Desmodai magistrates in the very beginning, when there had been talk of bringing children down so they could fill the chambers with laughter and light. The lawmakers deemed it unethical to change a human before their piquing years. So, from that point, any interaction with them was forbidden.

Were Mordecai to cross that line, even Augustus and his pretty words would fail to deliver him from the wrath of the sacred vessel— or worse.

Raking his palm down his stubbled chin, Mordecai stood and

walked over to the mirror. He glared at his image, nose to nose. Better this way. Isaac was an exceptional child. He had never been ill a day of his life. Not even with a cold. And if he ever got a cut or a bruise, it healed within minutes. Mordecai was convinced his father had found some sort of miracle inoculant during his travels, which he then gave to Isaac in his infancy before abandoning them.

Knowing this, Mordecai had to believe the boy would live a long and prosperous life. Best to break all ties now, so his brother never learned the truth. Mordecai couldn't bear to have Isaac know of his own murderous path that originated with Lynora's death.

A knock from outside jarred him from his dark musings. Shoving himself from the mirror, he pulled some trousers on under his night shirt and opened the door.

At first glance, he saw only his appointed guard a few feet away, sitting against the tunnel wall. The brood runner's head jerked in his direction, then looked down again at a book he was reading. He obviously hadn't knocked.

Mordecai scanned the surroundings. The lapping canal wound past his sanctuary chamber, twined into the distance like a liquidized street. The damp scent of the water curled through him, a strange comfort in a strange world.

A rhythmic scrape stirred the stillness where a gondola the size of a rowboat—docked next to the black cobbled walkway leading to his steps—was being pummeled by wavelets. The luminary blossoms he'd planted three months ago lined the tunnel walls in hanging pots and glossed the surroundings with a soft glow. Shifting water caught the light and glittered like a night sky.

All was peaceful and hushed while the populous of Nocturnus slept: no gondolas carrying passengers to work or leisure pursuits; no one strolling along the narrow walkways on either side of the water. Though Mordecai preferred moving in spirit form, most of the Desmodai had been undead for so long they'd lost appreciation for this unique mode of transportation. To act human was more exhilarating than any supernatural stunt they might pull.

Hearing the hum of a pulse, Mordecai leaned slightly forward. Something alive and breathing stood before him, undetectable to the eye.

"Krig," Mordecai mumbled. "Show yourself."

There was a slight movement, level with Mordecai's thighs, like a rift in the atmosphere. Then a sparkle of scales flashed from the gargoyle's head leading down to his toes until he was visible. Mordecai had only had the servant for one week, and each time he looked upon the creature, it chilled his bones to think it had once been a Desmodai man like himself.

The gargoyle ogled him with vast, inquisitive eyes. It was the one thing that set this individual apart from the other diminutives. Instead of serpentine, his eyes were kitten-like—for lack of a better description. Inquisitive, mischievous, and endearing in one sweep of long, thick lashes. For some reason, they hadn't deviated like the rest of him and seemed strangely out of place on such a hideous form.

Krig's fingers, spindly as spider's legs, clasped beneath his chin. "Master . . ." His airy voice drifted upward, like wind rustling through reeds on a lake.

Mordecai reached down and caught the gargoyle's scaly wrist to haul him into his chamber out of the guard's earshot. He latched the door behind them. "Tell me what you saw topside. Hold nothing secret."

Distracted, the gargoyle gimped toward the flickering candle. Slobber drizzled from his stretched-out lips. "Baubles . . . pretty baubles . . ." He touched the flame and yelped, falling to his backside.

Rolling his eyes, Mordecai helped him up. "Sit over there, would you? No. Don't touch it again, Krig. It's not a baub—"

Another screech.

With a sigh, Mordecai lifted the candle to the highest shelf on his library case.

Krig's gaze shot from one side of the chamber to the next. He shuffled to Mordecai's armoire, opening the doors. "Aaah . . . baubles?" From over his shoulder, he gawked at Mordecai, seeking permission.

"Fine. If I give you some glitz to play with, would you settle on the couch and concentrate?"

Krig nodded idiotically and stumbled back as Mordecai sorted through his apparel.

Mordecai tugged free a dress coat with sapphire-encrusted buttons then motioned to the couch. After the gargoyle climbed into place, Mordecai laid the coat across the creature's lap just beneath his protuberant belly.

A daft smile ruptured Krig's face. His teeth, like a cluster of miniature icicles swathed in moss, clicked together. All the while, his fingers crept across the glistening buttons and fondled each one. "Master . . . good. Master . . . kind."

"Master wants to know what you saw topside. Is the cottage truly gone? Burned to the ground as they said?"

If possible, Krig's eyes grew even wider. He kicked out both legs as if he were a frog and leaned back on his elbows. "Ashes . . . sparkle. Krig bathe in them. Krig taste." His slitted nose curled. "Krig no like."

Knees weak, Mordecai flopped down onto his ottoman once more. He felt as if he were drowning, but he had to know. "Did you find any sign of Lynora? Her body. Were there . . . any remains?"

Krig's wormy lips smacked. "Lynora . . . light?" He pointed to the candle. "Light for Master?"

Tamping down a wave of despair, Mordecai sighed. "The brightest that ever shined."

Krig's legs stilled as he straightened his back. "Light," he lifted a hand and clamped his fingers in a fist, "snuffed. Ash to ash." The glaze over his eyes shifted to piercing intelligence for an instant then dulled again.

The confirmation punctured Mordecai's soul. This eternity that stretched before him was now nothing but a dark void.

He shut his eyes against gut-wrenching spasms. "Was there anything left? Anything salvageable?"

Silence.

Mordecai's eyelids snapped open and Krig's ears drooped guiltily.

Mordecai glared at the creature's bulging belly. He had studied the gargoyles closely throughout his tenure in Nocturnus. There were three inherent traits every one of them shared.

Firstly, they had no discernable scent. It vanished during the change, making it easy for the creatures to meld into the background without a trace. Secondly, they had flaps that folded around their stomachs like a pouch, made of excess skin which had nowhere else to go after the shrinkage of the body. In these pockets, diminutives hoarded anything glittery they happened upon, like grotesque packrats. And lastly, their naiveté was nothing more than a brilliant stratagem to cover up a penchant and talent for thievery.

Mordecai had experienced such embezzlement first hand, when a different gargoyle robbed him of several bags of gold coins he'd saved to carry topside for Isaac on the night he went to retrieve Lynora. He'd once hoped he could trust Krig not to betray him in such a way, but it appeared they were all alike.

"You fat-pated lizard." Mordecai lost all patience. "You found something, didn't you? Show me."

Sloughing the coat to the floor, Krig tumbled down. In a matter of seconds he blended into the surroundings. "Krig no find . . . no find baubles. Master be kind."

Whimpers drifted all around the room as the gargoyle sought escape. Mordecai blocked the door. Other than the equipment, journals, and specimens he brought down to Nocturnus on the night of his change, that weaver's cottage was the last tie he had to his past . . . the last tie to his wife and brother's memories.

"Listen you little fungus. I don't care how pretty the object may be. It's mine by right. Open your pouch and let me have it, or I shall rip you down the seams."

The gargoyle's whimpers grew to full-fledged sobs. "Master find new baubles . . . other baubles." The sniveling swirled about the room, impossible to pin down. "Krig love his baubles. Much colors . . . pretty colors. Master be kind . . . "

Mordecai growled. He had no idea where the diminutive was. Blasted grounding collar. Since he couldn't fade himself to spirit form and flush the gargoyle out, he would have to use hypnosis.

"Look, Krig. You give me what's in your pouch and you can have two coins. Glossy, polished coins that dance. See?" Silver light glinted from Mordecai's gaze onto the velvety walls of the chamber.

The gargoyle came into view again, mesmerized by the flares beaming from Mordecai's eyes. He waddled closer. "Ooooh . . . pretty baubles. Krig make trade? Make trade with Master?"

Mordecai stretched out a palm. "Hand it over first. Then you shall receive your just reward."

With a dizzy grin, the gargoyle shoved his spindly fingers into his pouch, fished around, and drew out a loop of gold and silver keys in shapes and sizes of which Mordecai had never seen. "Oop . . . magic keys." He snickered sheepishly, shoved them back in his pouch, then retrieved a charred kaleidoscope.

"That's Isaac's," Mordecai whispered on a groan. His fingers closed around it. He thought upon his last night with Lynora—so enraged she threw the toy at his face. She had hated him at that moment. He had merited her hatred. Merited the remorse and guilt he would now bear for an eternity.

"Much colors . . ." Krig pointed to the prismatic sea glass in the kaleidoscope's wide end.

Aiming the lens toward the candle, Mordecai lifted the narrow eye piece and peered within. Somehow, even with the damage caused by the fire, the glass had retained its beauty. Flicking his wrist, he turned the cylinder to change the variegated patterns, then paused when the design melted to clarity like a painting, as if he looked through a telescope.

He could see an aged castle of bricks and stone—gray and solemn as a winter sky—set within the bowl of a lush, green valley. Then a grove of ash trees. But this was no painting, for a flutter of movement broke upon the landscape where a woman, fragile and graceful—tiny as a dancer in a music box—spun beneath a funnel of bats.

"Heaven's light." A breath caught in Mordecai's lungs. His focus tightened on the image, and he heaved a shuddering gasp upon recognizing the familiar silhouette. "*Lynora.*"

PART II:
KALEIDOSCOPE

"Gaze no more in the bitter glass
The demons, with their subtle guile,
Lift up before us when they pass,
Or only gaze a little while...."
~William Butler Yeats

CHAPTER 12

Unblinking, Mordecai watched the impossible scene unfold within the kaleidoscope. Wearing a shapeless tunic and billowy trousers, his bride perched in some branches beneath a funnel of flying bats. In the distance was a grove of ash trees, a trellis courtyard, and elaborate windings of peonies, foxgloves, day lilies and carnations—all abloom out of season.

Her black hair had been gathered in a braid. And her skin, once so pale he could see the veins in her wrists, glittered gold. A dark line of charcoal accentuated her chartreuse eyes. She moved with the grace of a butterfly, lifting one hand to her mouth, as if to guide the flapping pipistrelles into roosts along the trees.

So stunned by the sight, Mordecai nearly dropped the toy; as his fingers scrabbled to keep hold, the cylinder turned again. This time he saw an archway of roses—wild and thorn-filled—rich with blossoms of deepest crimson, just outside the walls surrounding the castle in the earlier scene. And there in the midst of a brilliant afternoon, playing her lyre with a most peaceful smile upon her face, was Lynora—again wearing the same odd clothing. A tiny girl sat at Lynora's feet, weaving a wreath of roses as Lynora serenaded her.

He turned the cylinder once more. Now his bride leaned against a brick wall in the presence of a priest. Behind the holy man, lightning pierced a gray sky and Lynora wept, her metallic makeup and black liner running streaks down her face. Mordecai groaned, aching to reach inside the glass and touch her.

What could it all mean?

"Reward now?" Krig asked, breaking Mordecai's concentration and blurring the scene to nothing but distorted color.

Mordecai drew back from the peephole, convinced he must be losing his mind.

"Krig have coins?" The gargoyle's wide gaze was ponderous as he pointed at the lights cast on the walls by Mordecai's hypnotic gaze.

"Ahh. Your coins." Mordecai blinked—muting the flashes of silver to reveal his normal eye color.

Krig scowled. "Master lie! Master tricky-trickster!"

Mordecai snatched the creature's wrist before he could fade back to camouflage. "You have your tricks. I have mine." He reached in his pocket and drew out a shiny copper. "Fair play, I'd say." He pressed the coin into the gargoyle's hand. "You would have received a bagful of these had you not tried to steal from me. Lucky I don't tie you up and feed you to the mummers."

At the mention of this, the diminutive's sobs turned to desperate pleas. "No Master . . . no mummers! Krig *shrink* from mummers . . . Krig hide."

Opening the door, Mordecai rushed the gargoyle through, almost knocking over Augustus as he came up the walkway.

"Next time I send you on an errand," Mordecai snarled after Krig as the gargoyle gimped away nuzzling his copper treasure between sniffles, "you will be required to turn out your pouch upon your report to me."

Augustus grinned and opened his mouth to speak but Mordecai jerked him inside before slamming the door shut upon his guard's watchful eye.

Mordecai coaxed Augustus toward the couch. "I am surprised to see you out at this hour. Will Florentia not miss you in her bed?"

"She is still at rehearsal." Augustus picked up Mordecai's fallen jacket and smoothed it on the cushion next to him. "Though I cannot fathom what she could have left to learn. They are to perform the Pantomime of Alexander the Great. It isn't as if anyone has lines." An unsettled cloud crossed his face, but cleared the instant he met Mordecai's gaze. "Evan told me you haven't been sleeping of late."

Mordecai frowned. "My apprentice needs to learn to keep things in confidence."

"He thought I should check on you. Imagine my surprise to see you acting so . . . enlivened." Augustus grinned again. "What has gotten into you? You're practically sweating. Not an easy feat for someone with ice in their veins."

Mordecai scooted the ottoman close and took a seat. He held out the kaleidoscope. "What do you see?"

Augustus arched an ebony brow. "A . . . child's plaything?"

"Inside. Look inside." Mordecai forced the kaleidoscope into Augustus's hand.

"Ah, yes," Augustus said, peering within. "I had forgotten how delightful these are. Such beautiful rainbows. Such intricacies." He lowered his hand. "Say, perhaps I might borrow this for Florentia's entertainment? She's been so crestfallen of late."

"You . . . you saw nothing but colors?"

"Um. Colors, yes. And shapes."

"But nothing distinctive, like a portrait, or an outline even?"

"A portrait?"

Mordecai's hands clenched his hair, tugging at the roots. "Of course, you wouldn't. I'm going mad. I was a fool to think I could ever forget."

"Forget what?"

"How I wronged her." Mordecai eased his hands free and stretched out his legs. "I have never told you of our history. What she gave up for me."

"No, you have not."

"Because I'm not proud of it. Her status, her wealth, everything . . . she disowned it all. Just so she could marry me, a simple gardener. This is why I was so determined to give it back to her. Why I took my place here without hesitation. The wealth, the prestige; it called to me."

Augustus nodded, encouraging him to continue.

"The first time I saw her, I was tending the gardens for a Baron and Baroness in Bath. Her aunt and uncle. Disgusting couple. The man was out of his trousers half the time, chasing the chamber girls and lady's maids. The woman was drunk and oblivious by noon each day. Had they or their help kept a closer eye, perhaps Lynora and I would never have met. But one afternoon, this woman-child tumbled through a path between some rose bushes—long, midnight hair wound all about her head—so elegant in her clumsiness. She asked me question upon question about floriculture and gardening techniques." Mordecai grinned, but felt his eyes stinging.

"At first I ignored her. Beguiling though she was, she was the unchaperoned niece of my employer, and he wouldn't approve. But he was a careless buffoon, and Lynora was relentless. I began to answer her questions—clipping the conversations short. Giving her just enough that she'd leave me be. Then one day . . ." The smile curled higher on his lips. "Up she walked touting a lyre. I had no idea what she planned to do; I was in the hothouse trying to revive my newest orchid hybrid that refused to bloom. I growled for her to leave, in hopes she'd scamper away in fright. Instead, she looked me in the eye and said her music could tame any beast, and nurture the most recalcitrant of plants. Then she played for me and my orchids on the spot. She returned every day until the flowers blossomed—hearty, voluptuous, and vivid." Elbows propped on his knees, he clutched his temples again. "And damned if she didn't tame the beast as well. It got so that I fell asleep each night dreaming of her eyes, her inquisitive mind, her *music*. Such sweet songs. I fell utterly in love. Even while I was awake, thoughts of her possessed me. I wanted her. Wanted her every moment of every day. I can hear her music, still. Oh, Augustus, she has . . . *had* . . . a gift with the instrument. I suspect the angels are envious at her presence, what with their discordant harps." Mordecai moaned and slumped forward. "I thought if I could forget my humanness—the experiences, the feelings—I could survive an existence without her. But I always see her when I close my eyes, and now even when they're open I'm seeing her as if she were alive."

Frowning, Augustus draped a hand on his shoulder. "Your guilt is fresh. I can assure you it won't always be so difficult. The day will come when you can distance yourself from such memories. From the regret. The day will come when the pain will be nothing more than a dull ache in the furthest corner of your soul. You have an eternity to lie this to rest."

"She gave up everything for me . . . twice in one lifetime. Even an eternity won't be enough to forget that." Mordecai gripped his thighs. "She will haunt me. Just moments ago, within that very toy, I saw her. She was dressed as a Gwyndolaire sister. She was wearing their costume, with her face and hair made-up queerly. Dancing with bats. So fragile. So graceful. So out of place. She would never have tolerated bats, you know. They terrified her."

Augustus's hand fell away and his demeanor shifted, as if shocked. "Wait, bats? Are you saying you saw her at the *castle?*"

Mordecai nodded, swiping moisture from his lashes. "A likeness of it. Though I haven't seen it since my youth. But this couldn't have been real. The gardens were exquisite. The blossoms bloomed far beyond their seasons. I even saw some wild roses outside the walls, such as I've never seen. It must be her spirit in purgatory. I sent her to her death. And now, I'm going to lose my mind as punishment." When he met his friend's gaze, he was surprised to see a smile on his face. In fact, Augustus appeared to be beaming.

"You think this a jest?" Mordecai began to stand, prepared to storm to the other side of the room, but Augustus held him down.

"What you have just described is no delusion. My brother, you've had a *vision*. It must be. Your bride is living amongst the Sisterhood." His jaw worked in thought. "That is so like Lady Nenet. Clever fox that she is. To burn down your cottage for a distraction ... then carry your bride away. They fooled us all by faking her death."

"What?" Mordecai's throat clenched. "That makes no sense. There was a small girl in one of the scenes. Are there any children living at the castle?"

"No. Lady Nenet would never allow that."

"So, it must be a dream. A wish born of my sorrow, spawned to haunt me in my dark, endless hours." Mordecai ground his fanged teeth and slumped deeper in his seat.

Augustus grinned. "Enough with the dramatics. Hear me out..." He nudged Mortdecai's shoulder. "There is a tie between Mentors and their neophites. It remains until the neophite reaches full realization. They are joined on a spiritual level, and the Mentor can focus on his mark. Wherever they may be, however many miles span between them, he can sense how his neophite is faring. The one thing the Mentor needs is an object shared between them on the night of the alteration. Where did you get this toy?"

Adrift between hope and disbelief, Mordecai stood and paced the room. "Krig." He waved his arm. "Krig found it at the remains of my cottage."

Beside him now, Augustus handed back the kaleidoscope to halt Mordecai's stride. "You and Lynora both touched it that night?"

As his fingers closed around the slick brass, Mordecai nodded.

"Often, a Mentor can mentally glean a sense about their neophite, share their feelings. Much like you've said all along: you never believed her truly dead, as you could *feel* her. But this ... this is something more. Something rare and fortuitous. Since your conductive object is *visual,* you have been gifted with visions of her. I've heard rumor of such occurrences, but never experienced it or known any other who has."

The gravity of what Augustus said started to sink in, and working like a counterbalance, began to lift away the weight on Mordecai's heart, though he wasn't quite ready to relinquish his doubt. "Am I seeing her day play out? Is this in present time?" Mordecai peered in the peephole again, facing a mélange of broken color. "And why can I see nothing now?"

Augustus's broad shoulders shrugged. "You could have been seeing yesterday, today, or even tomorrow. With practice, you will learn to manipulate the visions so you can pull them from the past, present or future at your will. But once you master one span of time, the other two will be lost to you. You must choose if it's more important to see her in the now or in the future." Augustus paused as Mordecai tried to look within the toy again. "As to why you see nothing at the moment? You must be missing your balancing element."

Mordecai drew the peephole away from his eye. "What is that? How do I get it back?"

Augustus shook his head. "'Tis individualized. Something that works as a medium for you, bearing the brunt of any negative emotions so you are receptive to altered perceptions. You will have to discover for yourself what it is. But for the moment, you can rest assured that Lynora is faring well." He smiled. "The Gwyndolaire Sisterhood will take good care of her. Lady Nenet is one of the wisest neophites on topside. And there's not a single mirror in that castle, so you needn't worry for Lynora's sanity, either."

Mordecai set the kaleidoscope on the library case. Cupping Augustus's face in his hands, he teetered between laughter and tears. "Do you know what this means, brother?"

Augustus clasped Mordecai's wrists and laughed with him. "Yes." He gave a slight squeeze with his fingers. "Lynora is safe. You can resume your life here, free of guilt."

Mordecai's joyous laugh died in his throat. "No . . . I-I'm free of nothing. I saw her with a priest. Lynora is a moral woman. What if she went to him for absolution? What if she confessed to him? She could be in grave danger if he realizes what she is . . ." Mordecai strained to speak around the lump in his windpipe. "I must go topside, immediately."

Augustus freed himself from Mordecai's hold. "Now, you're jumping the river when you should be taking a bridge. There is no way Lady Nenet would let Lynora out into the commons in her condition. She keeps a tight rein on her charges. They're only allowed in the furrows, or in town as a group. This could be something from the past you're seeing. I suggest you wait it out. Once your collar is removed, you'll have more options."

The past.

"Lynora did mention meeting a priest at the museum the day of our wedding." Mordecai shook his head. "But in the image, she had the made-up face of the Sisterhood. It has to be present, or future . . ." He clenched his jaw, remembering the stormy sky behind the priest.

One of the drawbacks of being locked underground was he never saw the weather changes. He'd been asking Krig about the sky each day—wondering if perhaps his cottage garden might spontaneously bloom again at some point, given enough moisture. According to the gargoyle, there had been a dry spell topside since Mordecai first entered Nocturnus. No heavy rains to speak of. Which meant the lightning scene must take place in the future—a future that could be as soon as tomorrow.

Arms and legs jittery, Mordecai paced the floor. "Lynora must stay away from the church. Men of God will never sympathize with her plight. I need to warn her. Better yet, bring her down where she'll be safe." The iron ring around his neck seemed to squeeze tighter. "Damn this collar!"

"It makes no difference." Pulling out a poetry tome from the bookcase, Augustus flipped through the pages. "Neophites are of our blood. They can sense our kind. Smell us even in mist form. To keep the peace, none of us have dared try to breach those castle walls. You cannot break through without putting our way of life in danger. And there are sentinels posted outside the castle every night. Regardless that they are female, they are well trained in defensive strategies and shan't hesitate to kill you."

"Once I'm capable of taking spirit form again, I can go. I just need to hide my scent somehow."

The book sloughed shut in Augustus's hands. His darkly luminous complexion paled by degrees. "The only thing that neutralizes our scent is to be surrounded by roses. You'd have to drift in wearing a rosebush. And daresay there's nothing subtle about that. May as well paint a target on your forehead."

Mordecai snatched the book from his friend to fit it back in its slot and smirked. "Wearing a rosebush, aye? How about a *thicket* of roses? I saw some, growing outside the walls."

Augustus scowled. "And what? Hide within and lure her out to you? Should you even manage the first two steps of such a plan, a far viler fate than drinking from the sacred vessel or being torched by the sun will await."

Mordecai huffed. "And what could possibly be worse than either of those?"

Augustus's voice lowered to a foreboding murmur. "To die at the hand of the woman you love."

CHAPTER 13

"Kill your husband, and you can walk in the open without hiding, unencumbered by costumes and lies." Wren's snarled words carried over to Lynora, biting harder than the cage handles that dug into the bends of her fingers. "Or you can let me do it for you. Once he is dust, one way or the other, you can live."

"I was simply making a statement … that my wig itches," Lynora said while trying to ignore the sweaty discomfort at the edges of her hairline.

"And I'm simply telling you how to make it stop, forever. Either shush your complaining, or fix the problem."

Lynora pressed her lips tight. The duo kept to the hills, winding through long grasses and woodlets to avoid the main road. Despite that they wore maquillage and wigs, just as for town visits, Mother Nenet demanded they steer clear of populated areas when training the pipistrelle. The rumors in Tatabury painted the castle's Sisterhood in an unscrupulous light—tolerable on some unspoken level, much as any house of harlots. They were not so much outcasts, as curiously immoral. But to be caught carrying cages of bats would border on paganistic mystique, which would pique interest from the church. *That* they did not need.

Pipistrelles carried nocturnal missives between Mother Nenet and the Agnate Brotherhood. Given their history, bats trusted the Desmodai where common birds would not. However, one drawback to using the pipistrelle was their size. They were one of the smallest species of bats. Even as adults, they grew no bigger than a winter wren. This made them less intimidating to commoners as they flew overhead in flocks. However, it also eliminated the practice of attaching scrolls to their legs with metal clamps as was customary for homing pigeons. Instead, the message was scripted in shorthand on a small square of parchment, coated with wax to protect the ink, then rolled and tied with a ribbon affixed by a wax seal. This ribbon linked to a miniature chain and cuff that stayed in place on the bat's right leg at all times. The system worked without interfering with the bats' nightly meals of lacewings and mosquitoes while in flight.

Today, Rime would complete his final test of distance training. Over the past month, Wren had taken the albino bat—accompanied by two sentinels and the fourteen other novice carrier bats—to stretches of one quarter mile all the way to a-mile-and-a-half from home. The cemetery was three miles. If the bats found their way back today, they would qualify as efficient carriers.

Wren squinted up at the sky. "A storm is building. We'd be wise to hurry."

Lynora looked overhead, surprised to see the clouds. It had been some time since they'd had a good rain. She matched Wren's pace. Now only a twitch of stiffness remained in her knee, not enough to slow her down.

A buzzard croaked as it cut a groove in the bleak sky and Lynora bit back a wave of panic.

"Why so quiet, Starling? Our destination?"

A gust of cool wind caught Lynora's riding breeches and plastered them to her legs. Her fingers tightened on the cages in either hand. Sometimes Wren was much too perceptive.

"I'm worried for the bats' safe return," Lynora offered a half-truth. "They're more susceptible in daylight as you well know . . . to carnivorous birds."

"To humans," Wren added, her expression unaltered.

It was an unfortunate course for the pipistrelle to train during the day, but night belonged to the Desmodai. Mother Nenet enforced stiff curfews at sunset, locking the castle gates and appointing sentinels—made up of four select neophites—to hold the Sisterhood safe within the walls, and the Desmodai without. She barely suffered the race, and wanted no chance for corruption. Thus, all of the neophite activities were limited to daylight.

The only exception was once a month when the mother herself would leave the fortress walls at night, always accompanied by Heron. Lynora had seen them, peering out her bedroom window from four stories high on the south side of the castle. They wore black cloaks and followed the road to the cemetery. Even pushing a three-wheeled cart without a lantern, Mother Nenet moved with grace and stealth, a liquescent shadow across the hills, as if she needed no light. As if her eyes were acclimated to the night.

Mother Nenet and Heron wouldn't return until they'd reached the gateway of Nocturnus and retrieved merchandise: drapes and decorating articles, bolts of raw silk, or newly carved trinkets of pomegranate wood. In exchange for vending the Desmodai goods on market days, the Sisterhood received any silk product they desired, free of charge. Every hand-made item was immaculate, but Lynora was partial to her daily wardrobe, as tunics and trousers were far more comfortable than the stylish corsets and gowns she'd grown up wearing.

Wren capped the final hill and the footbridge came into view. Seeing the familiar landscape, Lynora could smell the clover of spring days long past; she could taste the tang of cider from picnic lunches, feel the tremor of her lips as Mordecai leaned in to steal kisses while Isaac chased butterflies a few feet away.

The very last picnic they shared, Isaac had come racing to them after exploring, his blue eyes vivid with fear. He sobbed in Lynora's arms and tried to describe the hideous troll he saw living in the shadows beneath the footbridge. Mordecai investigated, but found nothing. They had attributed the incident to the child's imagination. It was understandable. The place had an eerie feel about it, being within sight of the graveyard and so quiet. Even the creek silenced its gurgles as it ran beneath the bridge's wide, dark archway.

Back then, Lynora and Mordecai didn't know that diminutive gargoyles often came topside during the day to do the bidding of their Desmodai masters, that it was rumored they had a way in and out of Nocturnus beneath the small bridge.

Isaac had in fact seen a real monster; she was relieved he'd never know that truth.

Lynora followed Wren down the slope where Haven's Creek slithered along one side of the graveyard. The sunken headstones, draped with withered ivy, appeared spectral in the dim sunlight and pre-storm fog. From this vantage point, the Cromwell Mausoleum loomed above the graves, larger than a cottage yet smaller than a chapel. Lichen coated the building's limestone walls in the way that cobwebs would coat an untouched windowpane.

It was the final resting place of Monarch Edward Cromwell—the man said to have provided shelter for Mother Nenet's predecessor when she first arrived over a century earlier. It was his castle in which they lived now. Though the details weren't recorded, that first neophite guardian had managed to strike a bargain with him for the deed. Upon his death, Edward's body had been shut inside this mausoleum and the doors sealed. Now the building stood gray and lonely, a tribute to the solitude of the afterlife.

The arched fretwork door—with lacework copper designs—was guarded by two stone women on either side, one holding a sword, and the other a dove. A third woman, jutting out from her waist above the door, held a baby in her outstretched arms. A cool gust blew the scents of mildew and limestone Lynora's direction. It tickled her nostrils as she stepped out into the patchy sunlight. She was relieved of one thing at least: that she and Wren could now brave the open and no longer hide.

Any part of the town or countryside unoccupied by upright and ethical humans was called the farrows, and could be walked by the neophites or Desmodai without breaking any Decretums or rules. The cemetery fell into this category, as the towners were superstitious to a fault and wouldn't come near the graves unless to bury someone.

Upon descending the hill, Lynora found herself almost running to keep from seeing the demolished cottage that she'd shared with Isaac for a month and a half. Were she to take a right turn and follow the winding trail fringed with dandelions, she would find herself in the midst of the rubble on the other side of Coventry Hill. The thought of Mordecai's once-upon-home, fallen to dust and sifting on the wind, revived her heartache for the child and the pain he must be feeling at his loss of family.

A waterfall's roar grew steadily closer.

"This way." Wren kept to the creek where it branched off to a deep stream and strode toward a massive wall of overgrown shrubbery and vines. The thicket spanned from east to west for a full mile and provided a barrier impenetrable to the eye between the graveyard and the entrance to Nocturnus.

Wren ducked through a camouflaged opening in the thorny shrubs and Lynora matched her steps, barely avoiding a snag in her sleeve. Several thorns caught her wig and tugged as she spiraled through a labyrinth of vines and branches so chaotic, they cut the daylight to a greenish-blue tinge. The bats flapped and scrambled atop one another in the cages. Her hands resituated their hold and she plunged through a break which opened to a clearing.

Wren stood there already, still as stone, staring at the waterfall nestled in the crook of a valley several yards below. Overhead, the clouds rumbled and stitched the sky closed. The wind chilled and whipped about the girls' faces.

Together, they descended a steep, rocky trail. Lynora bartered glances at the entrance's ghastly beauty. Water cascaded from a hilltop at least twenty feet above. A gradual descending embankment of trees and greenery enclosed the resulting pond—almost the circumference of a small lake.

At the base of the waterfall, two headless angel statues, covered with moss, stood larger than rearing horses and faced one another in the froth. Glistening with droplets, their wings curved upward over their shoulders to meet in the center. The pond was said to be five or six feet deep. The statues sat upon a scaffolding of rocks, holding them high enough to be viewed in full.

"The Waters of the Morose." Lynora pursed her lips, taking the final three steps off the trail onto the pond's margin. "I grew up hearing the pond was undrinkable. Everyone believes it cursed from the people who leapt off the waterfall to crash onto the angels' wings when life became too difficult to bear."

Wren smirked—an expression caught between respect and disdain. "No one ever made that leap. The Brotherhood planted those tales. People fear suicide is contagious."

"And fear is the strongest deterrent. I never would've guessed it was a gateway."

Wren shrugged. "I never would've guessed there was need for one."

Lynora swallowed a lump from her throat. "I read about how it works in the sanctorum."

"I have it memorized." Wren said in a mocking tone. "The Desmodai enter and exit the tunnel in mist form if they're going out on their own at night. But if it's an official courting trip for the Agnate, or goods are being brought up for us to sell, the statues swivel, face away from one another to allow a carriage passage. There's a mechanism beneath them. Separate platforms that operate on gears.

A grand tribute to the brilliant minds of the murderous race."

Frowning, Lynora tracked the blue water's surface with her eyes, unable to make out anything beneath for the reflection of the cluttered sky overhead. "I didn't read far enough to know what triggers them." Talking over the water's roar, she set the cages at her feet and held her chin up to embrace a cool spray from the falls.

"The wheels." Wren's long, painted eyelashes sparkled with tiny droplets of moisture. The golden paint on her face also bore glistening specks, giving her the semblance of a Fabergé egg embellished with crystal beads. "The Desmodai carriages are formed to fit perfectly into grooves on tracks beneath the water at either side of the gates. There's a switch in the gutters that activates the machinery."

Envisioning Post-chaise carriages drawn by robotic horses, Lynora bit back the taste of bile. This was how Mordecai had been taken from her on their honeymoon. Weeks later, on the night of her alteration, it was the absence of such a carriage combined with Mordecai's scent that signaled foul-play to Mother Nenet. She'd been scouting the hills along with two sentinels when they stumbled upon the cottage. Had they not interrupted when they did, Lynora would already be exiled to the under-realm.

Her attention flitted to the headless angel statues, stirring thoughts of her own fallen angel. Was Mordecai in there now . . . hibernating in the depths of his darkness? After all he'd done, he had no right to slumber restfully while she battled the dreams of the damned.

Wren struggled with a latch on one of the cages. "Time to release them." She cast a glance to the sky as thunder boomed overhead. "The rains will come within the hour. We need to get back."

After opening the cages, the girls stood aside and the pipistrelles swept out and upward, their chains glinting against the murky clouds. Though the other bats had no hesitation, Rime hovered above, as if torn between leaving Lynora and heading home. Fingers to her lips, Lynora whistled and squeaked to urge him onward.

Wren frowned. "You've coddled him too much lately. He'll never succeed for Mother if he begins to expect you to accompany him each time and give him permission."

Studying his movements, Lynora noticed him circling the cemetery. "No . . . he's watching something. On the other side of the thicket."

Gathering up the empty cages, they wove their way through the overgrown labyrinth. Unfamiliar voices rang out, halting the girls before they stepped into the graveyard. Lynora strained to see through the impenetrable vines surrounding them but could only make out voices.

"Do'n ye see it?" One man spoke in a panicked, whimpering tone. "Up there! White as white. A ghost bat is a *omen*. Do'n ye know that? Told ye we should'n ha'e come. A boneyard is the devil's garden."

"Shush up now." A second man's voice rattled as if he was gargling stones. "It's nothin' but a bird. Yeh. A dove or some such."

"A dove? It was flyin' with the other bats. They'n had chains on their legs. The devil's bondservants, I'd say."

"Fool. Stop your dallyin'. Old man Cummings want us look at the headstones, and that's just what we're gonna do. You take that side."

"An' what am I to be seekin'?" The whimperer's voice moved slightly closer to the thicket and Lynora sucked in a breath. Wren shook her head.

"Look for children's graves. And dates. Yeh . . . dates of their deaths. He wants to know if there's a past history of mass illness . . . like what's takin' place at the orphan house now."

Lynora gasped before Wren could cup a hand across her mouth.

"D'ye hear that? D'ye hear it, Leander?" The whimperer's footsteps shuffled away from the thicket.

"I heard somethin' alright . . . mebe it come from the mausoleum!"

"Told ye it was a omen! I'm a leavin'."

Both sets of footsteps kicked up. "What'll we tell Cummings?"

"Tell 'im he'n face his own demons."

Once the shuffles and voices faded, the girls broke through to the cemetery side.

"I must see Isaac!" Lynora tossed her empty cages at Wren's feet. Rime still hovered overhead, unsettled and undecided. She sympathized. A thousand emotions whirled within her as well, muddling her logic. But logic didn't matter. Being only a short walk to the orphan home, she refused to turn her back on Isaac again.

"Absolutely not!" Wren's painted face hardened to a rock; small cracks appeared around her dark eyes, like as an eggshell tapped with a spoon. "I would just as soon break every bone in your body and fold you inside one of these cages. I'll not let you endanger yourself or the Sisterhood."

The anxiety gripping Lynora's heart was far stronger than any physical threat her companion could make. "I can't go back without knowing that he's well."

Thunder rolled again overhead.

Wren's eyes whittled to slits. "There is a reason why we go in groups to town, Starling. Why the mother mixes mortal blood with goat's marrow and animal's blood for our pudding, why we wear scarves over our noses and mouths after the donients are hypnotized during the blood galas. It's to control our thirst, to rein in a need that could overtake and cause us to cross to full realization. Were you to be exposed to such temptation, alone—"

"I would only be tempted by fresh blood. I'm sure the children are bandaged if they have lesions. I won't be close enough to even smell it. I'll merely peer in a window."

"What would you say to Viscount Cummings if you're caught? How would you explain your presence?"

Calling Rime down, Lynora held out her palm for a perch. He landed softly like a fallen leaf, tiny claws prickling her flesh. Her thumb stroked his fur. She recalled her experience with the custodian of the home when he came to pick up Isaac so many weeks ago. He kindness made him easy to deceive. "I'll send Rime ahead as my escaped pet." She nudged the chain on his leg. "He has a leash, after all. They already believe us exotic. I only need to see Isaac once, from a distance. Then I vow to leave."

Wren caught Lynora's arm where her bracelet hid beneath her sleeve's cuff. "There are other dangers as well. What if your gaze catches in a mirror?"

"I'll be vigilant . . . avoid any shiny surfaces." Lynora spoke with more conviction than she felt.

"Not good enough. Wait until it's your time to make a trip to market, then you can check on the boy." Wren tightened her clasp at the edge of the thick bracelet—squeezing to the point of pain.

Lynora knew, if it came down to a battle of strength, Wren would win. "Isaac is my family. Would anything stop you, were it your sisters or father? Would you put it off until it was *convenient*?"

Wren released her. "Then I come, too."

Shaking her head, Lynora took off her bracelets and handed them to Wren, lessening the oddness of her style as much as possible. She kept only the cuff around her neck to hide her bitemarks. "No. You're to provide my alibi."

Wren wrinkled her nose at the jeweled wrist guards and tossed them into an empty cage with a clang. "What alibi?"

"Tell Mother Nenet that the storm confused Rime, and I set out to find him. She'll be angry, but it's plausible. She knows my fondness for the bat." Lynora waited for Wren's response. Receiving none, she turned toward the footbridge leading into town.

"*Lynora is dead*," Wren hissed behind her.

Lynora stopped short upon hearing her mortal name used in such a sentence.

"Even if he's knocking at heaven's gate . . . you do *not* let that child know your identity. You are Starling of the Gwyndolaire Sisterhood now. See that you don't forget that."

Nodding once, Lynora strode onto the bridge.

CHAPTER 14

Lynora watched Tatabury's main street resolve to quiet clarity in the distance.

A light mist had started to fall, dotting the cobbled road, the homes, and the shops with glitter. The Cummings' Asylum for Orphaned Children was a three-story townhouse in pristine condition, complete with gingerbread-colored bricks and a creamy-frosting trim. Under any other circumstance, such a charming building—set off alone on the cusp of town—stood as a beacon to the homeless and weary; but today, it reflected the dark, wind-swept murk of the sky overhead. A sinkhole of sickness.

Perhaps she was worried for naught. After all, Mordecai had spoken often of Isaac's hardiness against infections and illness. The boy even healed at an exceptional rate—she'd seen that for herself. The very peculiarities which she had fretted over upon his induction to the orphanage could possibly be his saving grace.

Yet if by some chance Isaac *were* sick, who would sit with him, holding his hand? Who would read to him, or stroke his hair until he fell asleep?

She tugged at the jeweled cuff upon her neck, tying to subdue the throbbing pulse of her bitemarks underneath. Her anger at Mordecai's thoughtlessness grew with each step.

Once she reached the asylum's pebbled walkway, she released

Rime and squeaked an instruction. She followed his flight around to the back of the house, drawn by the sounds of children's squeals and laughter. Hidden behind an English hedgerow, she peered through spiky green leaves. A blonde-headed boy led a group of five children into the yard. They ran beneath Rime as the bat flapped toward a Goat Willow tree. Scooting closer to the hedge to escape the soft drizzle, Lynora lifted her arms, providing protection for her painted face and chignon against the leaves and their pointed edges.

Isaac had grown. He looked . . . healthy. Happy even. Her spirit leapt with joy, thankful for the resilience of children. Whatever illness had hit the orphanage, it hadn't claimed him. His plump cheeks flushed with excitement and he started to scramble up the tree to capture Rime. Lynora bit her lip, debating if she should call the bat to her, but before Isaac even made it past the first branch, a woman's voice drifted out the back door.

"Any of ye stragglers be wantin' a warm meal, best get inside and dry off."

The gaggle of chattering children tumbled past the bush. They arrived on the doorstep, and took turns wiping their shoes on a rug before they stepped in. A short, portly middle-aged woman propped the door open while holding a shawl clamped around her shoulders. A red and black rosary peeked out at her neck.

Isaac was the last one in. "There's a bat in the Goat Tree, Miss Plum. A white bat! A phantom from another world . . ."

"Is it now?" Shading her forehead from the drizzle, the woman's eyes squinted in the direction of the tree. She gripped the rosary beads at her neck—as though on reflex. Her face was red and pocked like a ravaged apple, but she had a cheery countenance. "Hmm, I don' see it."

"You don't think it a sign, Miss Plum? A sign that my friends aren't coming back? Just like my brother and Lynora . . . "

Lynora's hope withered at the pinch in Isaac's voice.

The housekeeper released the rosary and pulled her shawl across ample bosoms. "Now, ye well know your friends'll be back. Those children are only with the bishop in London until they feel shiny again."

"Shiny as gold?" Isaac asked.

"S'right. Mebe it was a dove ye saw. Doves are good omens, Master Isaac. Mebe it's to bring some Providence our way, hmm? Now, get inside. After lunch, ye and the others are to help me mop this filthy house." She rubbed his back as they shuffled in.

The door closed and the soft patter of rain on the leaves became the only sound. Gratitude welled within Lynora—for their obvious kindness toward Isaac.

Seeing him so well-cared for should satisfy her. Yet she wanted more.

She wanted to be the one to hug and comfort him. To cradle him in her arms and tell him she was alive; that she loved him and would keep her promise to never leave again. Since the day Mordecai first introduced his little brother, she had thought of the child as her own. Now, he was the closest thing to a son she would ever have, unless the neophite curse was broken.

Damn Mordecai for leaving her with this impossible choice.

Her heart weighed like a stone in her chest, and she bowed her head against the ache, trying to find the strength to stand and walk away.

"Would you like to come in?" A man's voice from behind, honeyed-smooth and low, startled her. She shot up, turned on her heel, and nearly fell into the hedges.

Catching her hand, he steadied her. She worked herself free, a startled breath tangling in her throat as she looked up into the face of Father Lucien, the young priest who had assisted her at the museum on Piccadilly months earlier. What was he doing *here*, in Tatabury?

For once, she was grateful for her heavy maquillage. She couldn't have him recognizing her back. A lock of hair dipped across his forehead and stuck to his wet lashes. Realizing she stared, she averted her gaze to his shoes and felt her face flush—another aspect of walking the line between immortality and mortality. Though her blood was chilled enough to pale her skin, in moments of physical excitement or embarrassment, her heart still had the ability to pump heat into her cheeks.

"My Lady, did you hear me?"

She needed to leave—lest he ask why she was standing out here watching the children. Although she managed to meet his gaze again, fear crept from her spine to her neck and jaw, clamping down on her tongue.

His grey eyes strayed from hers to study the clouds, lit sporadically by lightning. "I'd say within the next few minutes, we'll have ourselves a righteous cleansing of the earth. The Viscount and Viscountess are out for the day, but you're welcome to come in and stay warm by the fire until the storm passes."

Before Lynora could respond, Rime swooped down and perched himself squarely on her shoulder. Wet and shivering, the bat nestled against her neck cuff. She cupped a protective palm over him.

The father's mouth gaped. "I've never seen such a sight."

Lynora didn't know if he was referring to her ornamented neck, or the bat.

"Does it belong to you?" He clarified as if reading the confusion on her face. "Is it tame?" Although his voice held no accusation, Lynora panicked. The last person she should be socializing with was a priest, no matter how understanding he'd been upon their first meeting; no matter how different he'd seemed. No man of God would condone what she'd become.

"I—I really must be going." No sooner had she said this than the skies opened on a downpour. If not for Father Lucien's quick reaction, whipping off his cloak and holding it over himself and Lynora, her wig and makeup would have been a lost cause—her identity exposed.

She had no choice but to move alongside him as he strode toward the asylum's back door. He hunched down, confined within the space beneath the cloak. His clean-shaven cheek almost touched hers. Up close like this, she noticed a leanness to him, yet a broadness through his shoulders that alluded to a prior state of heavy musculature. She held her tongue, blanketed by his musky scent of myrrh. As his body pressed to her side, Lynora was reminded of his limp. Her gaze caught on the familiar cane looped over his elbow—his shepherd's crook. She almost smiled, remembering its metallic clack at the museum.

Upon stepping in the back door, Lynora entered a stuffy kitchen. A burning sensation against her backside urged her away from a coal stove where an orange glow flickered. In the room's midst was a butcher table crowded with shiny, copper tureens of hot soup. She avoided catching her reflection in their polished surfaces. The scent of potato and onion stock filled her nose as she scanned for a safer place to look. Two sideboards held bowls half-filled with sweetmeats, breads, and sliced mutton. In the next room, the sound of whispering children joined the scrape of silverware against dishes.

Lynora found herself a corner, hidden well out of sight of the doorway. Disturbed by the silverware's clanging, Rime wriggled beneath her hand, his cold snout shoved between the neck cuff and her collarbone's indention for comfort.

"Miss Plum"—the priest bowed his head into the dining room to address the maid—"after you see to the children's meal, might we have some fresh tea brought into the game room? We have a guest." Ducking back in, he hung his dripping cloak on a peg. That lock of hair still hung over his left brow and Lynora itched to straighten it.

"Would you like something to eat?" he asked.

She shook her head, although the sugarplums looked tempting. They'd always been her favorite: minced figs, almonds, and cocoa, rolled in a coating of sugar. As a neophite, the only human delicacy she could keep down was sweets. But she didn't dare take time to eat here, or even drink for that matter. Isaac might see her. He would never recognize her in the masculine clothing and garish face paint, but the pain of being denied a chance to talk with him, of having to pretend she didn't know or care for him would be intolerable.

"I must be going. Do you have an umbrella I might use? I will see it returned to you within the week."

The priest offered that charming side-long grin, putting weight on his cane from time to time as he led her into a room adjacent from where the children ate. The game room's raised ceiling presented an airy draftiness—a comfort after enduring the stifled heat of the kitchen. The walls were hung with fern-green cotton damask, and all of the woodwork, including the fireplace and hearth, gleamed with satiny layers of white paint. A pine cabinet and a multi-drawered escritoire furnished the open space, along with a cushioned settee and two velvet wing-chairs facing one another on a patterned rug.

"I suppose a crippled priest must seem lackluster company to a young lady such as you." Her escort stood at a lit fireplace and refreshed the cup of tea he must have been nursing earlier.

Steam from the silver kettle curled over to Lynora's nostrils, tangy with a hint of citrus and cloves.

"Why else would you choose this"—he gestured to the window with his cane—"over sharing tea with me?" From behind sheer curtains, rain gushed down the panes as if someone were throwing buckets of water at the house. "Or perhaps you simply don't like tea." A soothing chuckle shook his chest.

In spite of his humorous tone, Lynora felt shame for her insensitivity, for behaving as if they were strangers—especially after how kind he'd once been. Yet she had no choice. "I mean no offense. I simply have far to go and must be on my way."

He settled his cup on a table beside a chair and propped his cane against the wall. Running a hand through his hair, he at last caught that wayward strand. "Even were I to lend you an umbrella, you would be soaked before you reached the end of the walkway. And umbrellas offer little protection against lightning. Surely within the hour the storm will dwindle." His gaze trailed the collar on her neck, then shifted to the furry lump perched atop her shoulder. "Besides, wouldn't want your little desmodus to get chilled, would you?"

Shocked by his flippant use of terminology she'd only recently learned herself, Lynora sunk into the confines of the velvet-cushioned chair opposite the one he'd chosen. Gently, she tucked Rime's sleeping form into the folds where her shirt bunched around her pant waist. "What do you know . . . of the desmodus?"

"Ah. Vampire bats." Sitting across from her, he studied the crackling fire and took a sip of tea. Lynora watched his clear, olive complexion, glazed to shadows and light by the flickering flames. "I have been studying them for some time. At first by choice. Now . . . by necessity." His square jaw twitched, carving shrewd lines into his masculine profile. "Today I had resolved my studies futile. Had just raised a prayer for guidance and strolled outside to watch the children play, when I saw this . . . statue of gold . . . hiding in the hedges." He shifted to look at her. "You may resemble an idol carved of precious metal. But I believe God sent you to me."

"*God* sent me?" Taken aback, Lynora swallowed a bitter laugh.

"Angels take many forms in biblical accounts," he added.

"I assure you, I'm nothing of the kind. I lack the wings . . . and the halo of light."

Father Lucien's mouth drew to a wide, straight-toothed smile even more inviting than one of his half-grins. Before he could reply, the thunk of children's footfalls drummed up the steps to the second floor, indicating the children had finished their meal. The ample Miss Plum muddled into the game room with a porcelain teapot in hand along with an extra silver cup.

She took one look at Lynora and nearly dropped the piping hot brew. Her double-chin bubbled beneath her neck as she gritted her teeth. She wobbled to the hearth to pour fresh tea into the silver kettle. The extra cup settled with a clink on the tray, unfilled.

Wiping the side of the silver pot with a cloth napkin, the woman mumbled, "Shameless. In a house full of children, seducin' a priest." Her tongue clucked in resounding agreement. "*Foreigners.* Rag-mannered mollies, all of ye." Then out the door she shuffled.

Lynora's host arched his brows at her.

Try as she might to hold her tongue, Lynora couldn't stop from defending the ladies of the castle. "Believe what you will, Father. Rumors abound. But we are not wanton or solicitous. We're merely entertainers. A means to an income so we might keep the castle that provides us sanctuary from a nightmare existence few others could ever conceive." She pinched her wrist, missing the protection of her bracelets, of the tall, stony walls and the iron gates. The realization of how truly foreign she was now, in this world she once belonged to, crackled through her chest like ice forming on water.

Placing his saucer at his feet, the priest leaned forward. His compassionate expression melted some of the frost gathered around her heart. "I am Father Lucien Tanden. My home parish is in London. I'm not here to judge you, nor to be your confessor. I've come to help these children, nothing more."

"Oh." Lynora stroked Rime in an effort to regain some composure. "I am Starling, of Gwyndolaire."

He surprised her by cupping a palm over the hand that protected Rime. "Be you an angel, an idol, or even a songbird, you are an answered prayer. For you hold within your grasp what I suspect might be the key to an illness isolated to the children within this home. And you have knowledge beyond any I have met, as you have tamed the desmodus."

She tamped the urge to flinch. "This is no vampire bat. He's a pipistrelle. He feeds on bugs . . . moths, lacewings. Not blood."

A tiny crinkle etched between the priest's brows. "Of course." His hold on her hand grew warmer. "The pipistrelle. I remember reading of them. No. They aren't of the desmodus genus, are they? But perhaps similar enough to give us some insight into their habitudes?"

"You say you have been studying them?" His cryptic statement in the museum resurfaced in her memory: *I'm here for something most unnatural.* Was he referring to the children's illness even then? It couldn't be. When she first sent Isaac here, there was no talk of any plague.

"I've collected many books over the years." He gestured to an avalanche of biology and zoological tomes piled in a far corner. "Only recently have my studies brought me to this home, where I find words in print are nothing to life experience. I borrowed two of the viscount's groundmen today. Sent them to the cemetery. They returned with stories of a haunted mausoleum. Of ghostly bats . . . one such as yours, white with shimmering pale wings and a chain upon its leg. I thought they had gone mad. Then you turn up with the little culprit in tow. God sent you to me. I'm sure of it. The only question is, are you willing to share your command of these creatures to help me solve this ghastly riddle?" As he released Lynora's hand, his gaze caught on the bulge at her knuckle where her twine ring resided.

"Why you?" she asked, tucking her left hand beneath Rime's furry body while keeping her right palm securely atop his folded wings. "Where is the physician? An ordinary priest is ill-prepared to solve the mysteries of the flesh. Your expertise lies within the realm of the spirit."

"Ah. But you see, this illness is both spirit and flesh, yet neither— all at once. And I," his attention flitted to the bat and back again, "am not your ordinary priest."

His words held a cautionary note, reminding Lynora of the danger she was putting herself—the entire Sisterhood—in by being here. From the window behind him, she could see the rains had slowed.

She began to gather up Rime, halting abruptly when a child's piercing cry from upstairs shattered her eardrums. Like a chain reaction, several other screams broke loose along with a rush of slamming doors.

Rime's head shot out from beneath her hand and her host's complexion drained deathly white. The next few minutes swam in chaos. Father Lucien scrambled for his cane and took the stairs two at a time, making up for his lack of grace with gritty determination. Cradling her shivering bat, Lynora followed.

Miss Plum nearly bowled them over when they reached the upper floor. Her lips writhed like a gasping fish. "It's happen' again, Father." She indicated a cross from her forehead, shoulder to shoulder, then her chest, before kissing her crucifix. "I-I was puttin' the younger snips down for their naps. The pain took one. Had to hold her to the mattress . . . and the markings . . . Oh, sainted spirits!"

Father Lucien clasped her hands to calm her. "The other children?"

"Shut up in the rooms, afeared to come out. Tis little Amelia . . . the furthest door down the hall. She's restin' now. Poor lil tot. Just getting' over a cold, and now this. Oh, Father, I don' want to send another child off to London. . ."

"First we send for the physician. We'll notify the bishop only if we must." Father Lucien limped toward the one door ajar in the dark hallway. Faint yellowish light streamed from the room. Without looking up, the housekeeper bustled around Lynora and descended the stairs, her shoes pounding a staccato rhythm.

Lynora hesitated, wondering which room was Isaac's, and then hurried to catch the priest. Father Lucien paused at the partially opened room and glanced over his shoulders as she caught up to him in the gloomy corridor.

"I hope you're as inured to strangeness as you appear to be," he murmured. "Few people can endure such a sight as this, without trading their dreams for night-terrors."

He tugged a crucifix from beneath his collar and stepped within.

CHAPTER 15

Father Lucian whispered a prayer for all the innocent souls living in the home, kissed his crucifix, then made his way across the room toward the window.

Lynora halted at the threshold, one hand clenched to the frame and the other supporting Rime. Inside, heavy jacquard drapes blocked the outdoor light. Two rows of iron-framed beds lined opposing walls, with one long table between them. This hosted a wash basin and three unlit candles melted to stubs. Within the eerie half-light, everything appeared distorted, a false reflection of reality.

Metal rings screeched on a rod as Father Lucien opened the drapes, splashing the surroundings with a watery-gray film. Flashes of lightning made the room appear to tremble. The priest laid aside his cane and knelt at a bed beside the window where a tiny form lay curled beneath the covers. He stroked the girl's reddish ringlets and spoke softly. There was no question he had bonded with these children.

Although she felt like an intruder, Lynora couldn't resist inching in a bit further. The priest's strong shoulders blocked her view so she relied upon her other senses to paint a picture. The little girl's irregular breath rattled deep in her chest. Disconnected coughs broke from her mouth. Father Lucien murmured questions that the girl would not, or could not, answer.

Lynora ventured another step before the scent hit her. A floral sweetness, tinged with decay. *The scent of a Desmodai.* "That smell . . ."

Father Lucien held a tiny wrist in his fingers and turned it in the light. "A common feature in such cases. The site gives off a perfumed aroma. This always occurs when the wounds spontaneously manifest themselves."

Spontaneous wounds? Were these children being attacked?

Lynora looked about the room, but could see no sign of any other occupants. No spirit shroud of mist to trick the eye. It was senseless to conjecture, for even with an overcast sky, a Desmodai would be committing suicide should they walk the earth during the day.

"The church believes this is a form of stigmata. These wounds will heal within an hour—as spontaneously as they appeared, leaving no scar behind." Father Lucien's voice recouped her attention. "Amelia is the sixth child to have experienced it in this asylum."

Lynora's shoulders tensed. "Is not the stigmata a spiritual phenomenon, affecting an individual on a personal level? How could it be contagious? I've never heard of such an outbreak."

Father Lucien shifted his lame leg. "Precisely why I am having trouble believing it. This is unlike any miracle I've ever seen. It leaves the victim a hollow shell. Catatonic, as it were. I refuse to accept that God is responsible for such atrocities upon innocent children. Something is amiss. Thus, I'm seeking other explanations."

"The desmodus?" Lynora asked, hugging Rime closer, unsure of the connection.

"I realize it's far-fetched. But I read an article where a vampire bat once hid within the chimney of a home. At night the beast would find its way into the children's rooms and drink from them. It would return each night to the same wounds, pulling back the scabs and drinking more. It was so small, it slipped in and out without any indication of its presence. I thought perhaps we had such a prey, possibly infected with some disease. I've searched the chimney, but surely there are other places such a creature could hide." His shook his head. "Still, there are oddities that don't conform to a bat. The fact that it occurs in daylight being one. I read they are mainly nocturnal?"

Lynora clenched her teeth, her mind still on the Desmodai scent. "Yes, unless trained otherwise. You said oddities—plural. What are the others?"

"The mist. There's mist in the room when the puncture marks first appear on the skin, according to our witness. One child has been present at several of the spells. He has claimed seeing two victims rise in the air . . . float on a cushion of mist. The little blonde boy who nearly captured your pet earlier—"

"Isaac?" The name slipped before Lynora could stop it. She bit her tongue and a sharp pain shot through her mouth.

Father Lucien turned slightly, just enough to catch her in his peripheral view. "How do you know his name?"

The pull to Gwyndolaire and safety called her, but her need to protect Isaac was stronger. "I . . . I heard the housekeeper call out to him. When I was behind the hedge looking for my bat." Rime wriggled in Lynora's hand, as though punctuating the lie. "You were saying something about children floating?"

Father Lucien turned again to the patient. "Yes. Although levitation is not unheard of in spiritual phenomena, the mist is isolated to these children's experiences, as is the catatonic state. No other stigmatics on record have incurred such a negative consequence of the miracle." The little girl moaned and Father Lucien drew out his crucifix. "She's unconscious for all intents and purposes, but I don't wish to frighten her in case she might hear us somehow. Allow me to bless her, and we'll retire downstairs to talk." With that, he began reciting the Lord's Prayer.

Lynora grew silent. Curiosity niggled in the back of her mind, fluttered like a moth trying to break into the light. Before it could materialize, the hair on her neck raised. The Desmodai perfume had faded, making way for another aroma: salted-sweet and metallic . . . a scent that teased her, curled through her entire being and made her salivate.

It was the scent of fresh mortal blood . . . yet more possessive in its calling than she could have imagined. The bitemarks beneath her metallic collar pulsed, her veins twisted beneath her flesh like snakes writhing in agony, and her heart balled up to a fist—hammering at her ribs.

Temptation sang within her: *Drink, drink.* Led by the song, she took another step closer, cradling Rime between her breasts with one hand. She licked her lips. The bouquet swelled within her lungs. Two more steps and she glanced over Father Lucien's left shoulder. On either of the girl's inner wrists, as well as in a ring around her forehead, beads of blood—crimson and glossy—mimicked the wounds of Christian faith, as if she had been crucified wearing a crown of thorns.

Entranced, Lynora scrabbled for some hint of empathy . . . some spark of humanity as she wiped drool from her mouth. Even hearing the victim's grunts and groans, even while regarding her tiny, freckled face, the beautiful droplets of scarlet glistening ripe upon the tender, pale flesh sang louder.

Drink, they said. And oh, how she wanted to. Just a taste.

One harmless taste.

Thirst became her master—a malevolent desire to quench the sand coating her throat. The priest would have to be removed first. Lynora knew how to break a man's neck. She had been taught many useful things over the past weeks.

Free hand trembling, she loomed behind him, nearer . . . nearer yet . . . inches from clutching his nape. Her fingers positioned to snap his spine. She imagined the crunch of bones, the choked strangle of his last breath. A heavy darkness soiled her soul, driven onward by the blood's song.

So close now, she felt heat radiate from his flesh to hers. Her mouth watered in anticipation.

Rime screeched out from beneath her hold, jolting her awake.

Father Lucien jerked around just as Lynora twirled on her heel and lurched toward the door. She gagged, repulsed by her instincts. That she would even consider harming the priest or that precious child brought the true ugliness of her fate to light.

She was an infection. A soulless, damnable blight on society.

She plunged through the doorway and nearly toppled into the physician coming in. The door frame scraped the side of her wig, dragging it to the floor along with her ammut. Her thirst still called to her—a distant but incessant beckoning. Afraid to stop long enough to retrieve her articles, she stumbled ahead. Children opened their doors at her clumsy passage, curiosity getting the better of them. Through tear-blurred vision, she saw Isaac staring with an expression of bewilderment.

What if it had been him bleeding in that bed? Would she have wanted to . . . ?

Sobbing, she lunged toward the stairs. Her breeches and shirt scraped Isaac as she teetered down the narrow hall. He caught a glimpse of Rime wriggling in her hand then his gaze caught on her face. His expression contorted to horror and he slammed the door.

She lumbered down the stairs, ignoring Father Lucien's calls from behind. It was a struggle to outrun his uneven footsteps, as if she trudged knee-deep in sludge.

Bursting through the back door, she toppled into the garden.

"Thank God for you, sun-bright," she whispered to Rime. After nuzzling her bat's soft fur, she released him to the gray sky, sending him homeward with a squeak of her lips.

Though the storm had passed, glimpses of lightning sparked some clouds in the distance. A cool breeze filled her, clearing her mind with the scent of damp earth and shrubbery. Her unholy thirst shrunk away and was replaced by a white-hot surge of nausea. She dropped to her knees in the mud, heaving as if to vomit—though her stomach had nothing to purge. Head dipped down, she leaned against the wet, scratchy bricks of the asylum and shut her eyelids, allowing the wind to dry her tears. Her real hair caught in the gusts, trailing free from the pins that earlier held it secure under the wig.

She sensed the priest's arrival; heard his breath laboring from his race to catch her. "You dropped . . . your things." He gulped a breath and crouched down.

She took the wig and ammut without looking up. The faux hair caught on her buttons as she cradled her disguise to her chest. "Forgive me." A strangled apology caught in her throat.

"Forgive you?" A warm, smooth finger touched her natural hair— the strands that dangled at an awkward angle across her forehead. He grazed the corner of her eye and drew back his finger wet with black and gold smudges. It occurred to Lynora that her maquillage must be nearly cried off. She gripped her thigh with her free hand, bowing her face lower.

"There's nothing to forgive," Father Lucien said tenderly. "You're no different than others who have witnessed this. When the Viscountess first saw the blood, she turned greener than dishwater and had to be carted off to bed. Your reaction is the most graceful to date. Certainly the most caring. To be so overcome with emotion at the sight of a wounded child is nothing to be ashamed of. Are you sure you don't need some tea? A bite to eat, to fortify you for your walk home?"

Mortified by his respect and kindness—so undeserved and misplaced—Lynora burrowed her fingernails into her leg. In this moment, were she alone, she would take her ammut stick and drive it into her cold, fiendish heart. The poor man had no idea. No idea what vile horrors she had earlier thought to perpetrate upon this household.

"I've tarried too long." She stood. Her hair fell across her face, managing to keep half her features from his view. She forced herself to think back on the child's odd wounds, nothing like the bitemarks a bat or a Desmodai would leave. Perhaps it truly was the stigmata. "It's not a vampire bat plaguing these children, you can rest assured. I wish I had more to offer." She started for the path that led from the orphanage.

The father stepped aside, although his attention intensified on her profile as she passed. "Again, you manage to escape the wrath of tea-time. Something stronger might be more to your liking. Coffee, perhaps? Miss Plum makes a mean pot. Should you come back this way one day, I shall have her boil some."

Lynora stalled, though refused to look at him. The thought of never seeing Isaac again gouged into her chest with such intensity she couldn't breathe. But she couldn't make false friendships that would turn deadly at a drop of blood, couldn't hide like a leech pilfering joy as she watched Isaac grow and play from behind a mask.

"I will never return." *Not until I'm free of my curse.* The unspoken caveat grew sour on the back of her tongue.

Father Lucien stood in silence for a moment, then she sensed his departure toward the house by the sound of mud squishing beneath his feet.

Her gaze fell to the twine ring on her finger as she walked in solitude toward the footbridge—to the farrows and the cemetery with its welcoming dead, far away from the living who were endangered by the ghastly nature of her half-life subsistence.

No one was there to hear or see when she cursed her husband, but the vow she made to regain her humanness required no witness to burn a deep and lasting brand in her heart.

CHAPTER 16

Mordecai held the kaleidoscope to his eye.

Though it had only been a few hours since his discovery, he'd been checking at every opportunity—worried of missing something important. Until he could master zeroing in on one specific timeframe, he would have to hold hope that Lynora hadn't yet visited any priest. He was wracking his brain to think of a way to get to her, to stop her before she made such a dangerous move, but until he'd completed his Reaper training, the collar and guard held him imprisoned beneath the ground.

At least he knew she lived. Despite that a part of him was furious with the Sisterhood for lying to the Agnate and himself, he couldn't help but be grateful for their intervention. It had been unbearable, thinking her dead.

Seeing movement in the cylinder, Mordecai perked up. Lynora came into view, standing at the charred spoils of their cottage. Sunset limned her in shimmering violet hues. She looked around, her makeup smeared and her hair unkempt, then knelt to dig a hole in the mud. He wondered *when* it might be, considering it was well past twilight on topside at present. Was this moment yesterday, today, or tomorrow?

She continued to dig. It appeared she was burying something. A seed, perhaps? Was she trying to revive proof of their past, or simply searching for any remains, as he'd had Krig do? If only Mordecai could stand beside her in that very minute, so they might grieve their loss together. It didn't matter what Augustus had said. Mordecai refused to heed the warning: that to stand anywhere close to his bride would endanger his undead life. Augustus had insisted Mordecai would no longer mean anything to Lynora, other than a way out, because until a neophite reached full realization, they could become mortal again by snuffing out the life of the one who altered them. But Mordecai knew, no matter how furious or desperate she might be, they were bound by vows and love. She could never kill him.

As the scene began to fade from the lens, Mordecai though he saw a shadow in the wreckage behind her—as though keeping watch. Was she with someone? Most probably one of her sisters, or a sentinel. Augustus had made it clear that the mother didn't allow the young neophites out on their own. Before Mordecai could decipher anything more, the image completely vanished, leaving only blocks of color. He closed his eyes and allowed the scent of soil and herbage to saturate his senses, to remind him of work yet to be done.

He had been in the Solarium since the sun set a little over three hours ago—grafting together different species of plants in a corner alcove where two long tables housed his experiments.

Centuries before, upon the conception of Nocturnus, the Agnate constructed this greenhouse beneath the ground, so plants could regulate oxygen levels for the diminutives. Being the one rectangular quarter in all the city, the Solarium Chamber accounted for an eighth of the underground domain, second only in size to the Vakara Chamber where the Desmodai thespians and symphony performed two evenings a week for all of the populous.

The complexity of the greenhouse bordered on genius. To prevent the Solarium's ground-level, thick-planed glass ceiling from being visible to the topside, the original Desmodai architects extended a wide stream off of Haven's Creek to run across the roof. During the day, the sun filtered in from the high ceiling—magnified through a depth of three feet of water. Which meant while Mordecai slept safely tucked away in his chamber, the Solarium maintained a sunny atmosphere for the plants. The soil boasted a robust richness that also nurtured their growth. Due to the underground locale, the climate remained temperate all year around: cool in the summer, warm in the winter. The plants never went dormant, for no seasons controlled their cycles. An irrigation system branched off in enclosed tracts from the canal to both water the plants and power fountains.

Mordecai's favorite characteristic of the Solarium were the hillocks—no higher than his shin—that added character to the landscape. In the short time he'd been here, Mordecai had managed to introduce a creeper vine into the gardens, and it now encompassed a fourth of the grounds. Other than the glass ceiling, it truly felt as if this was the outdoors. At night, when he worked here, the moonlight infiltrated the stream that ran overhead and lit the walls with fluid bluish-green reflections, providing a peaceful environment.

Sometimes, when a full moon graced the sky, a rainbow spanned the Solarium, painted by the humid atmosphere. The rainbow played out, beginning with a strand of deepest ebony, then tapering to variants of gray and ending in white. It was an unusual sight, and melancholy in its fragile beauty. Yet in those moments, Mordecai realized with deep regret how he missed the sun, the wind, the color . . . all the potpourri of human life. Yet he did find solace in these gardens, surrounded by things both natural and unnatural.

As if cued by that thought, Krig turned his coquettish eyes up to Mordecai. He sat at Mordecai's feet, entertaining himself with his collection of keys and jeweled buttons. As he lined the objects up along the grass, he stroked each one and cooed an odd, happy little tune.

Mordecai crouched. Several of the jewels looked suspiciously like the ruby buttons gone missing from his China crepe tailcoat. He glared at the gargoyle.

Moonlight filtered in from the glass roof, silvering Krig's scales as he responded with a gruesome, toothy smile. "Master . . . see messes?" Krig pointed at the kaleidoscope in Mordecai's hand, an obvious ruse to distract Mordecai from his crime. "Master's light . . . Lynora . . . make messes in colors."

"It is not Lynora that's made the messes. It's me." Mordecai held up the toy and sighed. "Did you gather the fireflies like I asked? We must feed the luminary flowers tonight."

Krig gestured toward two glass jars filled with dancing lights. Then he prodded the kaleidoscope in Mordecai's grasp. "Colors . . . make Master cross."

"I'm cross because I know where those ruby buttons came from, little thief. You can consider them your pay for the week." Mordecai stood. Triggered by his movements, two strands of creeper ivy slipped out from the grass and snagged Krig's treasures.

Mordecai grinned as Krig yelped and tried to wrestle the sentient plant. The creeper had taken a liking to the diminutive, and often teased him this way, yet always surrendered the plunder in the end.

Although Mordecai's amusement at the spectacle helped him tolerate Krig's thievery instead of breaking each one his long, sticky fingers, there was another detail—discovered just tonight—that held Mordecai's righteous indignation at bay. Through some form of poetic justice, the gargoyle was Mordecai's balancing element, absorbing his cluttered emotions so he could concentrate on visions within the kaleidoscope. Which meant he couldn't see Lynora in Isaac's toy, unless Krig was at his side.

Sighing, Mordecai secured the kaleidoscope within his apron's pocket and ducked into the tool shed, fishing out some shears along with a rigid ladder. He couldn't wait any longer for Evan, however out of character it was for his gardening assistant to be late on a night they were to prune the pomegranate trees.

Angling the ladder against a ten-foot trunk, Mordecai climbed five rungs. The wood felt rough beneath his bare feet. Leathery leaves raked his face and neck as he moved among the branches. A nectarous scent surrounded him. The Desmodai ate pomegranate fruits to curb their sweet tooth—a craving inherent to their diet of blood. Though very flavorful, mortal blood had little sweetness to it. Pomegranates offered this missing element, and being a plant, perpetually replenished its yield. In Greek mythology, the bloody-juiced fruit was known as the "Food of the Dead". The Desmodai often had a grand laugh over this.

Mordecai ascended two more rungs and cut away branches jutting from the canopy. He moved aside to let the clippings fall then studied his pristine palms. No matter how hard he worked now, they wouldn't get soiled. It was as if the dirt abhorred him as much as the bugs. He never thought he'd miss the feel of mud caked upon his skin, but he did.

The pomegranate trees—along with mulberry bushes, willow grasses, China Roses, and various wildflowers—thrived in the rich soil here. The mulberry leaves were stripped often, as they provided fodder for the silk worms of the Desmodai sericulture.

Upon finishing the first tree, Mordecai started on another. He peered through the canopy when the brass doors at the entrance squealed open and thudded closed. Evan strolled over and removed his cloak, hanging it on a peg hammered into the tool shed's frame before scraping mud from his boots. "Started without me, old chap?"

Mordecai shrugged. "Night is dwindling."

Evan squatted beneath the ladder to gather the clippings. The stripped leaves would provide mulch for the gardens. The branches would be wheeled out in a cart and taken to the Desmodai artisans for carving. Hinged ring-boxes and knife handles made of the creamy, yellow bark were sold in the under-realm shops or topside by the Sisterhood in Tatabury's market—along with the sericulture's silk goods.

Mordecai and his apprentice worked without pause. They had to be on the other side of the Solarium's walls before dawn's first light. Insulated with velvet cushioning—the doors remained locked throughout the day to prevent any sunbeams from entering Nocturnus and harming its inhabitants.

Once Mordecai had pruned the last tree, he brushed wood particles from his clothes, eased down the ladder, and helped Evan collect the remaining branches. With five hours left till sunrise, they opted to rest and share a pomegranate. They sat on the grass beside a sculpted fountain's basin. Water trickled behind them, pouring from a pitcher held by Selene, the moon goddess.

"So, did you contact the Agnate about making Lynora a citizen?" Evan leaned his head against the fountain's stony rim, draped his muscular arm across a knee, and balanced his half of the snack between lax fingers. His pale face reflected a blue halo of moonlight, his features so flawless he favored a god of marble himself. A god with dimples.

Mordecai gouged into his half of the fruit, seeking seeds. "Regent Ezra wasn't keen to allow it. Despite how Lady Nenet lied to the Brotherhood about her death." Mordecai flung some viscous pulp into the fountain, his jaw tightening. "He said anything that happens in her domain must be respected. Since I broke the Decretum, she doesn't answer to them. They answer to her. And Lynora was in her jurisdiction to do with as she pleased." Placing the seeds in his mouth, Mordecai savored their sweetness in hopes to tamp down the bitter taste of the words. "Bloody ridiculous how much power that woman wields."

Evan made a grunting sound, an ingenuine attempt at sympathy. "So, are you ready to release Lynora at last? To get on with your eternity and stay out of danger?"

Mordecai glared at his friend's hopeful expression. Both he and Augustus had made their concerns very clear on the matter of him meeting with Lynora. "No. I convinced Ezra she would be an asset to our world. One that he personally couldn't refuse. I told him how she composes songs the angels would envy. Holds herself with the grace of a swan as she's playing them on her lyre. She's an enchanting performer." Mordecai's hand slid into his apron pocket to nudge the kaleidoscope. He wondered if she was playing her music now, entertaining her sisters.

Evan munched on some seeds and swiped the red juice trickling from one corner of his lip. "Genius tactic. Ezra is enthralled with any kind of musical talent. And that's an instrument we've never had in our symphony." Then he shook his head. "But I don't understand how someone so brilliant can be so stupid. You're going to die for this obsession."

Mordecai swallowed his fruit and growled. "It's not an obsession. It is love. I can convince her to forgive me, to become one of us. All I need is to see her in person. Ezra said he'll submit her for the Desirable List and plead her case with Lady Nenet."

"That easily? Despite his passion for our symphony, I'm surprised by that. Lady Nenet is unlikely to allow any of it."

"She doesn't have a say if Lynora opts to choose me. Besides, the *all imperious* 'mother' gets something out of it as well. She gets to know I'm suffering."

"How's that?"

"Ezra's help is contingent upon my trial run as a Reaper topside and how successful I am." A rush of nerves filled Mordecai's stomach. His first unsupervised capture was scheduled for two nights from now, and his entire life with Lynora hinged upon his ability to survive a dizzying intake of Wisdom without going mad.

Evan elbowed him. "Buck up, Mord. I can take your mind off Lynora *and* your Reaper obligations. Let me lend you one of my ladies. Kylia has voiced a particular interest in you."

Mordecai stretched out his bare toes. "I don't want to have a tryst, nettle brain."

"How can you so easily dismiss the women of our world? They are the essence of perfection. And—I am pleased to relay—adept in the artistry of seduction; they'll do things to your body mortal women would cringe at. You should at least taste the forbidden fruit before deciding which tree you wish to be pruning for the rest of all eternity." Evan swallowed his last bite.

"Lynora's is the only fruit I wish to taste." Sprays of water speckled Mordecai's nape as he scooted closer to the fountain. He tossed aside his pomegranate's rind. Several coils of creeper vines inched forward and towed the castoff behind the fountain.

Evan watched the exhibition with a strained turn to his brow. "That plant is beyond disturbing, Mord."

Mordecai chuckled and dragged his hand down his whiskered chin. "You've nothing to fear. She's quite fond of you."

He had taken great pains to ensure this batch of vines knew other masters besides himself. In fact, each member of the Agnate Brotherhood had spent time enough here to earn the plant's trust and loyalty.

"Still." Evan's dimples vanished with his frown. "It truly unnerves me."

"This from a man who faced sea serpents and never flinched."

Hundreds of years earlier, the Brotherhood approached Evan for his hydrographic abilities after he mastered a means to map the earth's bodies of water—a means that would aid the undead race in their navigational prowess. Evan accepted and became a Desmodai maritime consultant, commandeering Nocturnus's submersible ships known as the Dasyatis. The bodies of the vessels were fashioned in the form of mammoth sting rays with large, pectoral wings and bodies of copper wrapped around silver skeletons. Each ship could hold a crew of twelve Desmodai along with a full shipment of silks, carved goods, tableware, and furniture. Their weighty ballast tanks along with the tail's manually operated propulsion system carried them far beneath human maritime affairs. Evan had told Mordecai story upon story of the creatures he'd seen living beneath the depths before he'd been suspended to dry land for entertaining undead vixens in the hull of one of the Dasyatis ships.

Licking his fingertips clean, Evan stretched out his legs and crossed his arms behind his neck. "Well, back to the subject of Kylia, I suppose there's a bright side. It will be my duty to comfort her after your heartless rejection." His lips curved on a sly grin and his dimples deepened.

Kaleidoscope in hand, Mordecai peered within. Nothing but prisms of broken color glared back. His gaze darted around the chamber in search of Krig. "Where is that little fungus?"

Evan ran a hand through his reddish-blonde hair. "I let your gargoyle out when I came in. He took his keys and scrambled away. He seemed terribly bored."

"Bored." Mordecai snorted. "Time is the least he owes me. He's always stealing from me. He's to stay at my side."

Evan's mocking laugh carried across the Solarium. "Such reliance upon your servant. Are you sure there's not more to it than him being your balancing element?"

Mordecai strummed his fingers on his thigh. "That's ridiculous."

"Not so. I say there's a bit of affection there. Perhaps you even feel sorry for the chap."

Mordecai tucked the kaleidoscope away. Krig's Desmodai identity had been Josiah Simmel, the previous gardener to Nocturnus. In fact, Mordecai had been brought down to take his place. This was why they assigned Krig to him, as he already knew the inner workings of the Solarium. Though diminutives often had no memory—or at least no *perception*—of their past life, they still clung to familiar rituals of work or natural inclinations toward the most basic routines.

Evan was right; this knowledge did have a bearing on Mordecai's sympathy for the creature. He identified with him, even understood why the little toad liked to steal. Perhaps why all of them did. Their attraction to glittering things appeared to be tied to their loss of beauty, as if the sparkles and glints of the world held some sort of magical curative for their deformities. It was the same reason Mordecai spent as much time as possible in his gardens. To make up for all he'd lost above ground.

As the creeper vines twisted and twined affectionately between Mordecai's toes, he quietly pondered Josiah's sentence.

The Desmodai gardener had broken into the Apostate Chamber and tampered with the Feed List, adding a nobleman's name who was marrying his lady topside. Krig—Josiah—couldn't accept her going on without him, even though it had been a decade since his 'death'. He'd expected her to stay a spinster and live alone, mourning him until her last breath. An ethical and innocent mortal died due to his jealousy and arrogance. The only reason he wasn't exposed to sunlight was due to his knowledge of the Solarium.

So yes, Mordecai sympathized. How easily he could have shared Krig's fate. Some would say the crime he'd committed was just as contemptible: forcing his bride to walk a road she would never have taken if given the option.

He thought upon his vision of her, standing in the ashes of their cottage. What if she'd gone there to bury her love for him? To say goodbye forever? Although he managed to sound confident to others, in truth, he knew the only way he could ever earn her forgiveness would be to reunite their family—to bring Isaac into their care.

Unfortunately, by becoming an immortal creature, Mordecai had damned any chance of that to hell.

CHAPTER 17

"Why so quiet all of a sudden?" Evan asked over the fountain's trickling song, his eyes closed.

"Pondering why you were tardy tonight." Mordecai lied. He glanced up at the glass ceiling, meditating on the moonlit water's subtle movements to soothe his conscience. "Please tell me it wasn't one of your liaisons."

"Something much more noble, in fact. It involves our dear friend Augustus and his bloodmate."

Mordecai jerked his gaze back to Evan. "Is Florentia still having problems?"

Though only the Reapers had to endure the vilest sins in singularity, even the common populous experienced a lethargy or sorts from the diluted Wisdom in the cocktail of combined blood. The disorientation lasted a week, like a severe hangover. But for some, the malady lasted from feeding to feeding. Florentia had been battling such an extreme case of soul sickness for years.

Evan's lashes opened to slits. "She went missing tonight. Augustus grabbed me on my way over and begged my help."

"Why didn't he send for me?"

Evan sat straighter and motioned toward the sealed door where the guard waited on the other side. "He didn't want your personal brood hound coming along."

"Two more days of this." Mordecai tugged at the collar. "Two more days and I'm rid of the albatross guard. So, is Florentia all right?"

"Precious little. We found her topside, on the edge of Haven's Creek. She was rolling in the mud . . . giggling like a school girl. And her eyes." Evan's sarcasm faded. "Her eyes had rolled into her head, white as mushrooms. As if she had them turned within herself, reliving a memory. She was in some sort of euphoric fog."

Mordecai tried to picture Augustus's lovely, regal bloodmate, sprawled out like a possessed child and ruining her immaculate clothes. "What was she doing there?"

Evan shrugged. "Hard to say. Augustus first saw her at the entrance to the slatturns. When she spotted him, she bolted like a rabbit on the run."

Mordecai could hardly fashion the thought of Florentia at the slatturns. That place was the equivalent to the slums on topside—rife with the most debase and degenerate of their kind. In years past, the brood-runners had tried once or twice to clear it out. But every world has a dark-side, and in a realm as dark as Nocturnus, there were shades of black so deep no light could penetrate them. Thus, the occupants were left to themselves, provided their filth didn't seep into the upstanding populous.

"We managed to get her home." Evan's lashes fell again. "She was coming back to herself when I left."

Mordecai studied Evan's boots. "That explains the mud on your heels. How close was she to the margins?"

Evan propped the back of his head on the fountain's lip. "She was actually a few feet within the thicket. It's stormy tonight. It made for quite the macabre scene—lightning crackling in the sky like some well-timed theatrical effect as we dragged her down to the gates."

Mordecai shot to his feet, nearly toppling into the fountain. "Lightning? Oh, devils no. Were there puddles? As if it had been raining all day?"

Evan stood and dusted off his brocade breeches. "Well, yes. Wait, are you thinking about the vision you had?"

"I saw lightning behind the priest. It was raining in torrents. It could've been today! I-I have to go topside. I must know she's safe!"

Evan shook his head. "Let me get this straight. You wish to be her shining knight. How's that to work? Your armor has chinks in it." He flicked one of the dangling garlic cloves on Mordecai's collar. "You'll make no distance up there with this on."

Brushing Evan's hand away, Mordecai shrugged off his work apron. "I survived an entire life topside without the ability to hide in mist."

"But then you didn't have a scent that gave you away."

"There's a small cove of wild roses around the Gwyndolaire back entrance. I can hide there. I only need to get past my guard here in Nocturnus and to coax Lynora out of the castle to me."

"Assuming that's where she is at the moment. What if the priest holds her captive? Or worse—"

Mordecai gripped his friend by the lapel. "If he has dared to disturb even a lash of her eyes, I dine on holy blood tonight."

Evan's expression iced to shock. "You wouldn't."

Mordecai didn't respond that indeed, he would. After experiencing the *Wisdom* at its highest potency, a priest's blood would go down like sweet wine in comparison. But he had no desire to provoke a debate on the state of his soul.

Despite his insatiable lust for women, Evan was a deeply religious man. Some might say that made him a hypocrite, but he was sincere in his fervor. Before he had been altered, he served as a Privateer—a pirate licensed by some seventeenth century king to attack enemy shipping. Even then, as a sea-thief, he had held the Bible sacred, ingrained in him from his childhood.

To this day, he sought a loophole to assure he still had a place in heaven should his preternatural life ever end. So desperate, he often went topside in disguise once or twice a month when the priests offered midnight confessionals to those other than their parishioners. Evan said himself that if there were there a chamber of worship in Nocturnus, he'd be sitting podium-side each time the doors opened.

Mordecai glared at the Solarium's entrance. "I'll take the passage through Haven's Creek footbridge. A tight squeeze, but I'm sure I can manage. I need you to retrieve Krig. Quickly. I must be back before dawn or I'm dead."

"You're dead the minute you leave this chamber. Have you forgotten? The Agnate has forbidden you to do anything until you're officially a Reaper. Besides, I thought you were to let Lynora decide for herself. Are you opting to change her against her will?"

The rape victim's face flashed through Mordecai's mind. He winced. "If I have to lug her down to Nocturnus on my shoulders, so be it. But I'll find a way to hide her here as a neophite . . . I'll not force her to full realization against her will. No. She'll learn by watching us that we're not demons who crave blood and murder mercilessly. She'll see that becoming one of our kindred is the safest choice—for her. And for Isaac as well. He's better off never knowing about the alter world."

Evan scowled. "Wait two more days and you can go without all this covert scheming."

Clasping Evan's shoulders, Mordecai yanked him close. "As you pointed out, Lynora may not have two days. She's not undead like us. Anything could happen to her up there. I go tonight."

Evan tugged free. "You won't fool the guard. Unless you have some twin brother who's willing to play the diversion."

Mordecai studied his apprentice from head to toe, nodding as an idea slowly took form. "I've one better. I have you . . . and a mummer with my face on it."

Mummers were Mordecai's successful attempt at merging a plant with an invertebrate species: a giant flower pod his father had found in Asia, and an octopus segment from the sea, kept packed in ice. After utilizing laboratory methods and pollination by hand, Mordecai was able to rely upon the plant to carry out its natural cycle thereafter.

He had perfected his first successful mummer here in Nocturnus weeks before he was put in solitaire. Originally, he hoped to create a hybrid that could change its color and texture just as an octopus blended with rocks, algae, or coral when avoiding predators. But nature had had its own hand of cards to deal, and what came about surprised even him.

The pods, each one the size of a cabbage, were balloon-like in appearance with alternate stripes of white and brown. Reddish colored suckers ran the length of the brown stripes. Each pod housed a unichambered core filled with an inky paste.

Whatever had possessed Mordecai to dip his hand into a pod on that day of genesis, he couldn't say. But when he drew his arm back, the inky goo conformed to him, took on his flesh's color, and dried within an hour, casting a perfect likeness of his fingers, palm, and wrist. A "glove" of sorts. Even when he pulled it off, it retained his hand's image, down to his fingernails and veins.

Had Krig not been curious, had the gargoyle not tried on the "glove", Mordecai would have never known the extent of its retentive capabilities. Once fitted upon Krig's spindly fingers, it veiled his scales while retaining Mordecai's coloring and shape. The knuckles moved in all the right places and the palm-lines and fingerprints matched Mordecai's perfectly. Yet it was fleshy and soft, like a real hand.

As required of him, Mordecai had reported the mummer discovery to the Agnate before his incarceration. When he returned to the Solarium after his month in isolation, he found that four of the ten pods were missing. Only the Agnate had access to his lab—being familiarized to his creeper vines. He tamped down the urge to question their intrusion and instead resumed his research, making a perfect cast of his face—facial hair and all—to put on Krig. Just like with the glove, it took on Mordecai's flesh tone, his mannerisms and musculature, in the same as it merged with Krig's own flesh. Even when Krig would move his features beneath, the mask compensated, retaining Mordecai's likeness with the movements, as if he were the one that smiled, or frowned, or yawned. It was as if Mordecai were looking at his own head slapped upon a diminutive's body.

There was only one drawback. Though it appeared to be a harmless mask, it was a biological and botanical entity. If the mummer stayed on for too long, it would attempt to root into its wearer's flesh for nutrients. Krig experienced this first hand, and had Mordecai not been there to peel the mask from his face, the mummer would have suffocated the gargoyle. As a result, Krig was now terrified of the pods and steered clear of them, fading away and screaming when he came within inches of one.

"Hold still," Mordecai scolded Evan after coaxing him to sit at the table so he could mold his mummer mask around the apprentice's flesh. "You're the one always saying we need more excitement in the under-realm. I would think you'd be up for this challenge."

Having already traded clothes with Mordecai, Evan slanted a second worried gaze to the thicket of trembling wildflowers where Krig's wails drifted up aimlessly. The gargoyle hadn't been happy when Evan brought him back, and unhappier still once he realized what the two men were planning.

Mordecai rolled his eyes. "I told you. The mummer won't attack unless you wear it for more than an hour. Besides, the gargoyle needs oxygen. We're pure uncompromised Desmodai. Immortal. Worst it can do to you is bring some discomfort."

Evan groaned. "Such a reassuring bedside manner," he mumbled as Mordecai patted the mask into place on his lips. "I'm only doing this so you'll give me a good reference upon my next evaluation. I'm ready to sail again."

"And I'll ensure you're sitting seaside in no time." Mordecai stood back to study the result. Evan's build was so close to his own, his hair color barely a shade darker—he made a stunning double. "How does it feel?"

"Comfortable, if a bit tight around the cranium. Always told you I had the bigger brain."

Smirking, Mordecai slapped his friend's shoulder. "I must admit, I've never seen you look more handsome."

"Perhaps," Evan said, "I'll pay a visit to Kylia while you're out. She might be more receptive to my propositions were I you."

Mordecai narrowed his eyes. "You do, and I'll deck your sanctuary walls with creeper ivy."

Evan shuddered then surrendered to a grin. Incredibly, the mask even hid his dimples.

Mordecai shook his head. So strange to see his own self smiling and winking outside the borders of a mirror. It almost felt as if he were standing face to face with his father, Cornelius. He had never realized how strong their resemblance until now. The only difference was the stubbled chin. Cornelius would never have abided whiskers.

"No talking to the guard." Mordecai strode over to wash his hands in the fountain. "Your voice would give us away. Keep your head down. Let the brood-runner escort you to Augustus's sanctuary chamber. I always visit him in the evenings, so it's in keeping with my routine. I'll sneak out of the Solarium once you leave. When you're inside the chamber and out of the guard's sight, have Augustus help you remove the mask until you don it again for my return."

"You're sure it can handle a second wearing?"

"The mummer has amazing retentive abilities. It will retain my likeness until returned to the pod. Only then will it forget and become liquid again." Mordecai dampened a clean rag in the fountain and wrung out the excess moisture. "Keep it in this cloth until I get back."

Taking the rag, Evan wriggled his chin back and forth. "Too bad you hadn't time to make a mask of me. You could trade in your wallflower tendencies and tour the streets of Nocturnus as a blinding beauty."

Mordecai shrugged into Evan's cloak. "You forget; here even the wallflowers are blindingly beautiful, and that's thanks to me." Upon that statement, he gathered a bouquet of glowing star-flowers and tucked them into a small basket before slipping boots onto his feet. "Wait at Augustus's sanctuary. Once I'm successful in reaching Lynora, I'll return to the solarium before dawn and send Krig to fetch you. Then put the mask on again and meet me back here. We'll leave together and carry the pomegranate branches to the craftsmen in the morning. Thus, it's a customary end to our workday."

Mordecai watched his own frown harden Evan's face. "You can't possibly accomplish all of this in four hours . . ."

"Why not? We're faster than typical mortals, with or without our spirit forms. I'll be back before the sun cracks the horizon." Mordecai fastened Evan's borrowed cloak into place over his grounding collar, then shuffled through some papers on his experiment table. "Here." He tied a paisley neck cloth in a ball-room knot around Evan's throat. "I've been wearing this over the collar on my walks to and from my sanctuary. It will hide the fact that you don't have one."

Evan lifted a hand to stroke his new facial hair. "Remember your promise, old chap. Do not shed any holy blood."

Mordecai shook his head. "I vow not to slay the priest *only* if he hasn't harmed Lynora. That's the extent of my word."

"Suit yourself," his friend said. "It's your undead soul that hangs in the balance."

CHAPTER 18

After leaving the orphan asylum, Lynora had taken a detour to explore the lifeless remains of Mordecai's cottage. Upon arrival, she stumbled over a collapsed archway of wild roses and honeysuckle. It once stood tall enough for her and her goom to exchange wedding vows beneath. Now, the petals clung in black crinkly snarls and the trellis splintered and frayed, rather like a putrefied skeleton of some serpentine creature. The disrepair mirrored her marriage. There was no possibility left. No chance for reconstruction. Only tainted memories, buried beneath silt.

Standing on the dregs of her and Mordecai's defeated plans, Lynora made peace with the decision she'd made—to do what must be done so she could return to Isaac and take him far away from the strange happenings at the orphanage; to free herself of the monster that threatened to take over her mind and body. Knowing she could never kill Mordecai while wearing the symbol of their past commitment, she slipped off her ring, dug a hole in the mud, and shoved the circle into the ground . . . pressed it deep with her thumb until the silt burbled up and oozed over itself, leaving not even a thread of twine showing through. She'd thought she had heard something stirring in the brush behind her, and for a moment had a sense that Mordecai was watching her every move, but when she turned around, she was alone.

Twilight was long past when she arrived at the castle. The sentinels allowed her entrance with raised eyebrows in lieu of questions, meaning Wren had been faithful to relay Lynora's false alibi. Ill-prepared to face anyone, or to hear I-told-you-so from Wren, Lynora disrobed to bathe in a stream that ran through an isolated cove in the courtyard. The wet foliage glistened around her—a crystal illusion beneath the silvery moon. Its beauty gave her clarity, and as splashes of cold water erased the black smudges dried beneath her fingernails and caked in the ridges of her palms, she rinsed away the last sediment of her past and cleansed herself of her gardener.

After shrugging back into her grimy clothes and checking on Rime, Lynora crept into the castle. The neophites were gathered at the long table in the Banquet Hall for their social hour. The Sisterhood ate one meal of blood pudding a week, as a neophite's appetite differed from that of a pure mortal's. Every other evening, they snacked on sweets and drank tea while sharing any challenges they faced in their new life. Then they would retire to the Flower and Willow Hall where Mother Nenet taught performance skills and game techniques to entertain the nobleman during their galas.

Lynora skirted past the Banquet Hall's arched doorway. Heron—holding a pastry to her lips—saw her but didn't say a word. Lynora ascended the winding stairs to her chamber on the fourth floor in solitude. She knew, judging by the superior's concerned expression, she would receive a visit from the mother tonight.

Absentmindedly, Lynora prepared for bed and climbed beneath her covers to wait.

Images of Mordecai slammed within her, loud and unsettling. Something had changed. Her husband wasn't grieving her death anymore. She could feel him yearning for their union deep within her soul; and with each passing minute, his thoughts grew louder. In answer, the bitemarks upon her neck ached anew as if freshly made. Mother Nenet had warned her she would always be tied to Mordecai through them. Unless, of course, he no longer lived . . .

Weariness and dread cinched her lungs, wrung them like rags until her breath came out in a groan. She touched her naked ring finger where the skin was smooth—worn from being rubbed by twine for so long. She finally flipped to her stomach to silence the nervous tremors and fell into a fitful sleep, startling awake when her chamber door opened with a creak.

"Starling, my daughter. Are you awake?" Mother Nenet's rose-scented perfume wafted in.

"Yes, Mother." Lynora rubbed her bleary eyes, having no idea how long she'd slept. She threw off her covers and sat on the bed's edge. So far as she had seen, Mother Nenet was a compassionate warden, and—as Wren was always swift to point out—seemed especially tolerant with Lynora. However, it was possible the mother's patience had worn thin today. Sitting up, Lynora wrapped a shawl around the shoulders of her gauzy nightdress to curb a sudden chill.

Mother Nenet glided into the shadows, taking a seat beside her. Lynora couldn't see even a hand in front of her face, but she sensed two eyes appraising her. Even after all these weeks, she still felt like a stranger to this grand woman. The mother kept to herself throughout the day. Too many tasks within the castle to employ. She started on her business before dawn while everyone else washed their bodies in the cold streams of the courtyard then dressed in preparation for constitutionals. Heron acted as their instructor throughout the day. Lynora never saw Mother Nenet until supper.

Seated beside her in the darkness, she envisioned the mother in all her stately elegance: her pastel dyed day-gowns of finest silk and lace; her hair, dark as the sheen of a nightingale's wings, drawn up in a chignon bound by a length of silvery beaded crepe; her face and eyes always painted, never nude.

"Nostalgia is dust." The mother's voice—as soothing as a wind chime—courted the air between them. "It dulls all that is familiar with a deceptive haze. You sleep unkempt tonight. Eyes naked; neck and wrists exposed. What would you do were trouble to seek us in the shadows? You've misplaced all I taught you, due to sentimentality over your past."

Lynora winced; while preparing for bed, she'd reverted to her old ways and left herself exposed. Although she had tucked her ammut beneath her pillow in case she needed a weapon, she suddenly felt naked without her jeweled armor.

"How did you know I was struggling with my memories?" She searched her night desk in the dark until she found her bracelets then pressed the cold metal into place at the base of her palms. Before she could do the same with her neck cuff, the mother picked it up in her gloved hands and held the glistening emeralds against a moonbeam. Reflective sparkles of green spangled Lynora's white gown.

"Why else would you flee today? To chase a bat in a storm . . . you're wiser than this. You're not the first to hear the old world's call. Did anyone see you?"

Lynora couldn't think how to bare her experience without stumbling over her awkward confession to the priest. "A priest from London. A stranger, mostly."

Mother Nenet's breath stilled. "Go on."

"I was angry. At the town, at the people. At everything they say of us. They're wrong; I didn't wish for him to believe it."

"His opinion mattered to you. Why, if he's a stranger?"

Lynora pinched her forearm until the skin retained bumpy imprints beneath her fingernails. "He's staying at the orphanage."

Upon another loud intake of air, the mother placed Lynora's neck cuff on the night desk, then drifted to the window. She threw open the drapes. Starlight gilded her silhouette as she looked outside. "You went to visit the child. And saw the priest by accident."

"The priest saw me, rather." Lynora ground her teeth. "I heard the children suffered a plague. I had to know for myself. At that moment,

Isaac's safety was my only concern." She patted the scars on her neck, trying to dull the ache.

Mother Nenet turned around. "Is he ill . . . your Isaac?" There was a strain to her voice, no longer lyrical but tight and jaded like rocks scraping a brick wall.

"Isaac is fine, for now."

The mother answered with a curt nod. "What is this plague?"

"The church is calling it the stigmata, but the priest has doubts." Lynora sought the words to describe the scene to the mother: how there were indications of Desmodai involvement if not for the sunlight and the appearance of crucifixion wounds in lieu of bitemarks. But she couldn't admit any of it without admitting her own vile temptations. Shame and terror closed her throat and stiffened her tongue. "I need more information."

Mother Nenet's lacy sleeves rustled against the window sill. "Viscount Cummings . . . he runs this asylum?"

"Yes." Lynora fidgeted on the mattress.

"First thing in the morning, the Viscount will receive an invitation to the gala tomorrow eve. I did not intend to invite him, but you can question him while he is under hypnosis. Perchance you can glean more intimate information this way. He is not the outsider the priest is."

Her willingness to dabble in the lives of the townsfolk took Lynora off guard. "Thank you, Mother." She kneaded her hands. "But why would you help me after my disobedience?"

"I'm helping the children, Starling. Not you."

The muscles in Lynora's fingers eased. Why had it never occurred to her that perhaps the mother loved children, missed them even? After all, she was barren like every other neophite.

Mother Nenet looked out the window once more. "Did you expose our lifestyle to the priest?" Her question was soft. Not at all harsh like Lynora would have expected.

"No. I simply informed him that we're entertainers—nothing more."

The mother nodded. "That is good. Such a learned and educated man has surely read of mummers, ancient performers who wore masks and took part in pantomimes. We're very like the mummers of old." Mother Nenet slanted her neck and the window framed her lovely profile.

"Yet we're not; we charge men a price to seduce them, take what we want while they are entranced by our neophite wiles and charms. Perhaps we could invite women to the galas as well . . . so we wouldn't have the reputation of courtesans. Isn't their blood as good as any man's?"

Keeping her back turned, the grand lady lifted her shoulders on a deep breath. "It is difficult to be separate; I understand. But we must have a valid reason for the galas. The townsfolk think we use our charms as a means to win investors who will fund our silkworm business. Thus, we invite only the wealthiest of noblemen—as they're generous when catered to, and more willing to leave with their purses lighter if their ladies aren't present to provide a conscience." The mother glanced over her shoulder and for a fleeting moment, Lynora thought she saw her irises gleam, though it must have been a trick of moonlight. "We're not just thought of as courtesans, but also artisans; everyone presumes it's how we pass time in this castle. This keeps jealous wives and sweethearts at bay. They leave us to our solitude so we might make the pretty dresses and the wooden trinkets that decorate their bodies and halls. In the minds of righteous women, we're libertine coquettes with foreign customs—tolerated like the cobwebs in the highest corners of the tidiest cottage, so far out of reach none wish to strain themselves with our abolishment. Better this than we drop from the heights and scuttle beneath their feet, either poisoning them or getting crushed ourselves."

Mother Nenet closed the drapes and Lynora strained to find her outline in the darkness. She thought she heard a rustle at the doorway behind her, only to find the mother leaning her hip against the desk.

"Would you see your sisters dead, Starling. . . or fall to madness for lack of sustenance? Were we not to appease the beast, we would each of us become his vessel of destruction. Our noblemen donients live, none the worse for their contribution—blood and money alike. We use one for anonymous charities, the other for own livelihood. They return to their wives and mistresses, remembering nothing but a sense of contentment and satiation. Our gift to them in gratitude for their gift to us."

Any response balled in Lynora's throat. It was a question of survival for everyone; what more was there to say?

"Tomorrow night we will have a blood-letting gala . . . your first." As Mother Nenet made her way to the wardrobe and opened the door to showcase Lynora's costume for the gala, her gown's hem swished along the floor. "Many men will fill the Flower and Willow Hall. Donients whose blood will feed our hunger. You must learn our way of life now. As we both know you have no place with the mortals." She paused, then raised her timbre an octave. "You must never return among children. That was very dangerous."

She said this as if she knew all that Lynora had faced of her evil nature today.

Lynora's stomach tilted. "I *will* belong among mortals again, one day."

"Oh?"

Biting her lip, Lynora fisted her hands in her nightdress, trying to assuage the hollow ache of her ring finger. "I'm going to vanquish my husband."

"Ah. Brave intentions. However, you will be battling not only your love for the man he was, but his seductive prowess as a Desmodai. You must be strong enough to conquer *yourself* before seeking him out. Otherwise, I fear such a challenge will cleave your heart in twain."

CHAPTER 19

As Mother Nenet said goodnight and slipped from the room, Lynora clamped her jaw to keep from admitting what her instincts told her: Mordecai roamed the moonlit hills at this very moment, searching. She tamped down her alarm, for even should their unearthly connection give her whereabouts away, the sentinels protected the gates. She could avoid him until she was fully prepared, so long as she stayed on the castle grounds.

Lynora strained her ears for any sounds in the adjoining bedchambers. The answering silence was a comfort—a promise of the vocation and routine that were hers for the taking now. The sisters were in the dance hall on the second floor of the castle, far out of range. Being the night before the gala, they would practice for hours: dancing, gaming, conversing. Lynora touched her knee, no sorer now than when she first awoke this morning. Perhaps, with her newfound mission to regain her humanity, she could at last win Wren's respect. She crossed the room to open the curtain once more and propped her forehead against the cold glass. Outside, a dense fog sat upon the gardens. Holes appeared and vanished where the pipistrelles flew, catching their supper. Where she once feared that nightly sojourn, now it gave her peace.

Her breath clouded the glass on a sigh, then she turned and strode back to her bed. She left her nightdress on, belting it around her waist with a satin cord. In the corner her lyre waited—the one possession her sisters had saved from the fire. If they were to practice for the blood-letting, she would carry down her instrument and join them.

Utilizing the moonlight from the window, she eased into her slippers and slid her ammut from beneath her pillow. The iron glimmered like a u-shaped dagger, both ends pointed and lethal. She wrapped her hair within it, sweeping the strands into a chignon. Though she couldn't manage her full maquillage and wig without a sister's help, she blindly brushed a thick coat of deep, golden powder over her face and neck, then stained her lips with saffron-tinted wax. Next, she sought her jeweled neck cuff, only to find it wasn't on her desk where the mother had left it.

"*Baubles?*" A hissing utterance erupted out of thin air.

Lynora gasped.

"Pretty baubles." The eerie voice sang in teasing consonants.

"Who's . . . there?" Lynora spun in the dim room until her gaze caught on a spatter of indentions swirling the covers atop her bed, much like footprints. She stared in disbelief as a shift in the air—a momentary flash that resembled scales—appeared to hold her neck cuff between long fingers. In a blink it faded into the background once more, as if her bejeweled armor hovered atop her mattress alone, glittering and afloat.

Straining her ears, Lynora heard breathing. Her eyes narrowed as she inched closer to the bed, closer to the mysterious floating neck armor. What was this strange magic?

"Master . . . need light," the eerie voice muttered.

Lynora swallowed a scream. Before she could even gather her bearings, the neck cuff bounced almost to the floor and drifted out of her bedchamber. It hovered in the hall, waiting for her to give chase. For a split second Lynora considered involving Mother Nenet, but the embellished piece bounded down the long, marble corridor and she feared she'd lose it.

The jewels embedded in her wrist and neck cuffs were her fortune. Upon each challenge a neophite mastered, she received a gemstone to fill the indentions in the armor. It was security; should they one day be human again the precious stones would be theirs to sell for currency—a means to a new start. Lynora had already earned seven garnets, four amethysts, and two faceted emeralds. After having her past stolen, she refused to lose any part of her future.

The armor bobbed as if held by an invisible hand—waiting for her to follow.

Lynora locked her door—a force of habit—then trailed the jeweled glint through the halls past the other bedchambers. Careening toward the dungeon stairs, the cuff reflected the moonlight where it shone in slivers through the opened doorways.

Once she turned the corner, Lynora's slippered feet crept down the stony stairs leading to the dungeon's blackness. Losing sight of the jewels in the darkness, she hesitated at the last step. The odor of damp limestone and rusted metal enveloped her. Though she'd been down here many times when they stored the blood pudding, she was accustomed to the wall torches being lit. The cadence of dripping water in pitch-dark disoriented her.

Just as she debated reversing up the stairs, a breath warmed her hand where she clenched the satin belted at her waist. A queer glowing flower appeared in increments, as if drawn out from a pocket.

"Master say give . . . light to his light."

The blossom lit the room with its halo of soft gold, more tender and alluring than any candle. Her invisible thief fully appeared this time—a wash of scales in iridescent green, a body with a bulbous head, pointed ears, and the eyes of a forlorn kitten. It was the ugliest creature Lynora had ever looked upon; yet there was an infectious curiosity in its long-lashed gaze, as if it wanted to be liked.

She knew in that moment what it was. A gargoyle: some wretched Desmodai leveled to slave status for a horrible crime.

"Light." The creature's clear, moss tipped teeth opened to a smile as it held out the blossom with spidery hands.

"A star-flower," Lynora whispered. This had to be the gift Mordecai had meant to give her on their honeymoon night—the hybrid sundew that had changed their lives forever.

Cautiously, she took the last two steps into the dungeon and reached for the luminous bloom. As she grasped the stem, the thief's smile pulled even higher, so that the corners of its lips appeared to touch its ears.

Fondling the petals in her hand, Lynora held a breath in her chest. "Mordecai . . . is it you?" She could hardly bear to think it, much less say it aloud. She'd heard he was punished in some vile way, but *this*? Is this why she'd sensed him tonight?

A repressed surge of pity gathered at the base of her tongue— burning and sour like stomach acid.

The diminutive raised his brow. "Krig." He pointed to his scaley chest. "Krig . . . servant. Master send Krig." His voice rustled. "For light . . . and baubles."

Lynora blinked back relieved tears. She cursed herself for caring. In truth, it would be so much easier to take Mordecai's life were he locked in such a form.

She pointed to the neck cuff in the gargoyle's grasp. "Give that back to me. It's not yours."

The gargoyle's mouth twisted to a sad frown. "Krig want baubles." He took several clumsy steps backward. "Krig need baubles. Make Krig pretty . . . like Master." His stick-like fingers raked down the tufts of hair on his scalp, as if he were grooming himself.

Nervous shocks speared throughout Lynora's body. "Where is your *master*? Is he here?"

Even as she asked, she knew there was no way Mordecai, with his scent, could've made it past the sentinels and into the castle. She would smell him herself were he in this dungeon. For further assurance, she waved the flower and painted the walls with light for assurance. Boxes of blood pudding sat in one corner. In another were piles of scalped hair—flayed off of Nocturnus's Feed List victims once the corpses had been drained for the populous—and donated to the sisters so they could be dyed black and woven into wigs.

Rusted chains hung from the ceiling in intervals where human-sized, empty cages lined the walls, their double-gates askew like the skeletal wings of macabre birds. Lynora had never seen these filled; rumors abounded as to what they may be there to house: a stray Desmodai awaiting their death sentence, or a neophite gone mad from seeing their reflection. At the very least, they served as a reminder that rules and decretums were to be obeyed or containment would be practiced.

"Master say . . . light follow baubles," the gargoyle's hissing voice burst through Lynora's macabre musings.

She turned back to see Krig's toes disappear through a three-foot hole in the wall. Wood gaped and splintered at the opening where someone had pried the slats free. A tapestry—with flowers, animals, and human figurines twining in a fanciful dream sequence—covered that wall. Now, though the left half still hung in place, the right folded down to reveal a tunnel's entrance behind the busted wooden slats. Lynora had noticed the arabesque in the past, thinking it too beautiful for hanging in such a gruesome dungeon. Now she understood its purpose.

How long had this secret tunnel been hidden? Did Mother Nenet know, or was it nailed shut before her predecessor's arrival over a century earlier? Surely if she knew, there would be sentinels appointed to guard it. It must lead outside the castle wall. Where else would the gargoyle have come from? Diminutives hadn't the ability to mist through cracks and holes as their higher kinsmen did, and the courtyard walls were too high for one of such stature and awkwardness to climb.

Gulping against a dry throat, Lynora knelt down to face the tunnel—intent on catching the creature before he escaped the castle's sanctuary. Fine hairs draped the jagged wood at the opening, dangling in gossamer strings as if yanked from the gargoyle's head. Taking a deep breath, Lynora tucked the back of her gown's hem into her belt to form makeshift trousers, then ducked low and plunged into the hole. She held the blossom's stem between her teeth to light the way as she maneuvered on all fours. The plant had an acrid taste that tingled on her tongue.

Something scuttled in front of her hand—a spider desperate to escape the castle. The neophites emitted some sort of repellent through their blood. One of the few advantages they shared with the Desmodai. It kept their castle pest free. Grit and pebbles raked between her fingers and jabbed at her knees as she crawled ahead.

She strained to see anything beyond the flower's glow. The one power Lynora envied of the Desmodai was their ability to see in the dark. Krig's coos moved closer, as if to navigate her direction. The tunnel was a straight-shot with the exception of an interstice in the middle where it widened to an aperture on the right. Avoiding the opening, the gargoyle continued to veer left. Lynora paused where he bypassed, distracted momentarily by a shut door that caused that hallway to end abruptly. Her nose caught the scent of roses swelling out from the keyhole. She held the flower up for light, wriggling the latch. Finding it locked, she pressed an ear against the wooden frame but heard nothing within. Roses were forbidden in the castle; Mother Nenet was the only one who ever sported the scent, being as her favorite perfume was rosewater. Yet this aroma was stronger by far than any small spattering of floral tinged water.

Krig's cooing began to fade in the opposite passage. Lynora tore herself away from the mysterious chamber, knowing Mordecai must be waiting outside the castle walls. She secured the ammut tighter on her head and scrambled blindly into the depths, determined to retrieve the neck cuff before the gargoyle escaped the tunnel and forced her to take chase outside where night ruled alongside the wicked Desmodai.

Mordecai waited in the midst of a rose thicket. Jewels of raindrops and starlight crowned the plants. While waiting, he had occupied himself with the intricate vines and thorns serving as walls around him. Just as the vision had revealed, these roses were an undiscovered genus. A moss-like fur coated the leaves and stems and exuded a spiced aroma separate from the scent of the petals themselves. Their combined fragrance was far more concentrated than any he had ever smelled, even when wet from all the rain. One single bud plucked free had the potency of an entire rose garden.

The blooms were true to their color through the kaleidoscope's lens— a crimson as deep as the velvet flow from a punctured artery. He drew off the hood of Evan's cloak and arranged it across his grounding collar for a closer look. Owls hooted and the echoes of bats drifted on the night air. A gentle wind shuddered the leaves and swirled mist around him like a foreboding omen, a reminder of the night he'd done the same to Lynora in spirit form. At that thought, he began to worry. Too much time had passed, and he wondered if Krig had failed to lure his bride here. What if the little clod had been captured?

Dawn was an hour away by now. Best case scenario, if Lynora followed the goblin and encountered Mordecai, she'd scream at him. Worst case, she'd attack him.

He had two advantages: their marital commitment to one another, and being stronger than her physically. He would carry her to Nocturnus before the sun's first light—whatever it took.

His attention drifted from the rose petals to the twine ring on his left hand.

This would've been such a fitting place to celebrate his bride's triumph over the fire: a rose grove, so like the one where they'd shared their first kiss in her uncle's gardens. Just thinking of her voice in that monumental moment and he was lost to the memory—a wave of nostalgia so all-encompassing it swallowed any other sound until he was there with her again.

"You say it's the perfect rosebud?" she had asked. Her beauty shone bright that night . . . even with twilight closing in overhead, he'd felt the warmth of the sun in her smile.

"The most perfect specimen I've ever seen," he'd answered back while holding the rose in question behind him—its thorny stem wrapped within a linen handkerchief.

"Stop teasing, Mordecai. I wish to see it."

He arched a brow. "Hmmm. I'm not sure your unspoiled eyes can brave such a grand sight." Grinning, he tucked the blossom into the front waist of his trousers, the linen hanky a slick barrier between his bare abdomen and the thorns. "You want to see it so much? Pluck it free, my swan."

Her gaze trailed his naked chest and paused at his trousers' waist. A flush crept into her cheeks and neck, noticeable even in the purpling dimness. Licking her lips, she took a step back toward the brick wall looming behind her. "It's a hopeless farce." Her voice trembled, as if stirred by the same cool breeze shaking the leaves on all other sides of them. She crossed her arms over her chest as she forced her attention back to his face. "Dare I even try, you'll push me away, like you always do."

"Not this time, my lady. For weeks on end, you've followed me about these grounds . . . tantalizing me and my flowers with your siren songs." He glanced at the lyre she had propped against the bricks. "Speaking to me as you would a beau, a lover. I'm finished running from you. A man can hold honor for only so long."

Her eyes widened as he rushed her until her back was flush to the wall. He meant to see it through. To scare her off. She'd been far too trusting of him, and he feared—should she not learn the lesson— some other man would spoil her when she'd finished her games with Mordecai and moved on. His hands planked either side of her head to pin her long hair to the bricks, the silky waves a direct contrast to the roughness beneath.

His lips hovered above hers and he murmured a final warning. "We both know the blood in your veins is far too blue to mix with the likes of a gardener. So, either play out your hand, or go back to your uncle's splendid mansion and be the debutante you were bred to be. I am no one's toy."

Even now he remembered his struggle for self-control as her soft, cool fingertips slipped beneath his pant waist to drag the rose free and toss the handkerchief to the wind.

She lifted the petals in triumph to the darkening sky. An expression of wonder crossed her face. "I seek more than a plaything, *Gardener*. And my blood burns every bit as red as your own." She punctured her fingertip on the rose's thorny stem, and held the weeping wound inches from his eyes.

He tightened one hand in her hair and used the other to capture her wrist. Plunging her finger into his mouth, he sucked the blood away. A whimper shivered in her throat and she dropped the rose. Her eyes fluttered half-closed . . . her knees gave. He caught her around the ribs, lifted her against the wall, and pressed their mouths together—a moment so powerful, he swore he felt the bricks behind them crumble, only to realize when he opened his eyes and found hers looking back, that the wall *between* them—erected by upper-class strictures and prejudices—had collapsed.

To think a mere thorn prick had crumbled those societal boundaries and enabled their love story to begin; how ironic, that another instance involving blood threatened to end it all. They had much practice smoothing over the biases between two different sects of society, but this . . . this was two completely different worlds.

A rustle of grass from behind forced his attention back to the present. He faced the thicket's opening, unable to react before a rush of white gauzy fabric lunged for him. A leg bent around his and forced his knees to give. His shoulder blades slammed into the muddied ground and wet grass licked the bared skin at his nape just above the cloak's collar.

By the time he realized what had taken place, a light weight pressed on his abdomen, a set of thighs straddled him, and his hands were pinned above his head.

His bride's chartreuse irises glared at his chin, her thick lashes slanted to prevent their gazes from fully meeting. It appeared Krig caught her washed clean of the Sisterhood's apotropaic eye-paint, so she took care to guard against his hypnotic powers by looking away. He felt a sense of pride at her cunning.

"Lynora."

"Lynora is dead. You will address me as Starling." In one swift move, she released one of his palms and loosed the metallic hairpiece from her head. Her hair fell to her shoulders as she jabbed the dual points at his sternum, puckering his vest. He bit back a hiss at the iron's burning sensation through his clothes. He caught her fingers with his free hand in an attempt to restrain the u-shaped weapon.

"What's the plan then, *Starling*?" he asked through clenched teeth, consumed by myriad feelings. She appeared to hate him, yes. But more importantly, she was here, *breathing and whole,* touching him.

"The plan is to gut you from stem to stern," she answered on a snarl, "and resurrect Lynora's life."

CHAPTER 20

Triggered by the metal tips at his chest, Mordecai's instinct overtook. His spine tingled in an attempt to translate to mist. In the same as the collar held him grounded, the miracle overcame him: Lynora was alive. His bride was here, and she would never kill him. He allowed himself a moment of awe and wonder, relaxing under her straddled position, liking the feel of her legs wrapped around him.

She seemed to sense his thoughts—in an obvious struggle to hold her gaze averted.

"Master's light . . . slippery." Krig's voice came from behind and Mordecai spotted the creature looking over Lynora's shoulder, grinning absurdly.

"Got past you, did she?" Mordecai asked, unable to suppress a grin of his own.

Lynora slanted a scowl at the gargoyle. Taking advantage of the distraction, Mordecai snagged her elbows and twisted, affording distance between his chest and her weapon. He held her there, still seated atop him.

"Stop grinning like a fool," she seethed. "After all you've done, you're unworthy of any shred of happiness."

"After thinking you dead all this time? Thinking I killed you? How could I be anything but happy to see you living and breathing—resurrected from my dreams?"

Lynora wrestled against his hold, huffing when she couldn't escape. "And you, from my nightmares. You, who stole everything from me. And you're still doing it."

"Master's light . . . follow baubles." As always, Krig interjected at the worst possible moment. From his peripheral, Mordecai caught sight of the jeweled neck cuff he had seen in the kaleidoscope. The one he had specified the gargoyle take.

"Krig found tunnel . . . open door." The diminutive jingled something in his pouch. "Magic keys."

"A tunnel. Well done, resourceful little thief. You have well pleased me."

Panting from the physical exertion of keeping Mordecai contained, Lynora ground her teeth. "If you two are quite finished stroking one another's egos . . . we can finish this."

Mordecai smiled again, despite himself. His bride wasn't afraid of him anymore. Steeped in admiration, he realized how much the Sisterhood had helped her. How much they had shaped her. He had to admit, he found her new courage quite alluring. "Finish what, my love?"

He watched her neck muscles tighten in the moonlight. "My walk as a neophite. With your death, I'll reclaim all I lost."

Mordecai almost laughed. She could never hurt him. Even with her made-up face flecked with tunnel dust, even with her hair disheveled and her gown unkempt, she was still the essence of purity and kindness. "Ah. So . . . how should we do this, little swan? Let me cast the dice. Do I lay here immobile, or should you wish to chase me around for a bit? Which would make a livelier bedtime story for your neophite sisters?"

Krig snickered but clamped his mouth shut when Lynora glared in his direction. "Your next, sticky fingers." Her attention returned to Mordecai, still not meeting his gaze. "This is no game, and it isn't your gambit to make. I hold all the cards." With that, she jerked her elbows free and the iron points found him once more, working holes through the fabric above his sternum. The metal hissed with steam as it touched his flesh. Mordecai winced, surprised by her strength and determination.

Did she truly intend to . . . ?

Her knees tightened around either side of his waist with pressure enough to snap a human man in half. She dug the ammut further into his chest, nearly breaking skin. He clutched her thighs, struggling to topple her off. He would have to be careful—defend himself without harming her.

Krig whimpered from the grove's entrance, then tilted the stolen neck cuff so the jewels caught a slash of moonlight. The glint struck Lynora's face. She closed her eyes for an instant. It was all Mordecai needed to lock her in hand-to-hand combat. He flipped her over and scrabbled to clutch her wrists, but the bracelets she wore burned his skin. She broke free, retaining her hold on his waist with her powerful leg muscles. Though he sat atop her now, his ankles became tangled in his cloak, rendering him defenseless to loosen her grip.

Growling, she slipped a leg around him and reversed their positions. They rolled from one side of the thicket to the other. Krig jumped out of the way and hissed as they sloughed through mud and soggy grass.

Hairs raised along Mordecai's neck as it hit him full force this was not the delicate and docile girl he remembered. This was a neophite bent on revenge. He rolled her over and pounded the back of her hand against the ground until she dropped the iron stick. He shoved it out of her reach and stripped off his cloak to free his legs and arms, covering the weapon and Krig simultaneously with the heavy fabric as he tossed it aside. The gargoyle seemed content to hide, mumbling to himself beneath the drape.

Mordecai held Lynora down. A soft breeze turned in his hair as his gaze lit on her tangled locks, splayed like midnight shadows all around her head. His attention slid to the bitemarks on her neck. "All this fuss over a little necklace?"

Lynora shifted her focus to the grounding collar on his own neck, now bared without his covering. Winded from their tussle, she tried to catch her breath enough to speak. "That cuff . . . will one day be my livelihood. Those jewels . . . will help me survive without needing to rely on any man." She sucked in a breath. "It's an honor to earn it. Much the opposite of your necklace, yes?"

Mordecai winced. Not only had she become adept at wielding weapons, but also words. He stretched his body to cover hers. Propped on his elbows, her curves and clefts cradled his lower torso. Her aroma, her proximity, threatened to waken the beast he was trying to keep at bay. "I'm wearing an adornment," he lied about his collar, his lips almost touching hers as he spoke. "The cloves are an aphrodisiac. Can you feel their power?" He joined their fingers, banking her hands to the ground on either side of her head.

"No. But I smell their stench. And you speak with the forked tongue of a cornered snake." She tried to jerk free. Her face contorted to a scowl. "I understand it takes extreme meditation for you to translate. That is a mixture of brass and iron on your neck . . . it inhibits your concentration. It is a *leash* for a rabid dog. I hear tell that even the door frames in the under-realm are lined with the metal mixture, so none of you can filter through as mist and impose upon one another's privacy." She still wouldn't look him in the eye. "It appears perfection can indeed have flaws."

Mordecai ground his teeth. He didn't like the way she said that. As if he were an amusing plaything with a broken winder. He tightened his hold on her. "A Desmodai has no flaws. Only vulnerabilities put upon us by your blasted sun goddess."

Her panting breath swirled with his, a chilling wisp of condensation between them. "Yes. Eset was brilliant. Most especially with the Bisu water." In the time it took him to blink, Lynora had wound a leg around his and twisted her lithe body so deftly he found himself beneath her again, his clothes absorbing the grass's moisture without the cloak's barrier. "So tricky," she sneered, "how it only affects you if it's drank or injected into your body . . . to touch it to your flesh merely leaves you wet. Misleading enough that a quarter of your populous became stupefied before you realized what was causing the gargoyle mutation."

Krig's embarrassed moans erupted from beneath Evan's cloak in the background. Neither Mordecai nor Lynora acknowledged them.

"Been pouring over the history scrolls, have you?" Mordecai asked her. "Aren't you a good little pupil? But you should be apprised . . . I wear this collar to appease your warden, the Grand Mother. It is my punishment for altering you."

"A punishment disproportionate to the crime, if you ask me. I know your laws. You could have been changed to a diminutive, or bared to the sun. Would have been better that you had." Lynora tried to stand, but he clutched her waist and reversed their positions again. Pinning her down, he relished the press of her breasts against him as she struggled for the upper hand.

"Better," he said, lowering his head close, "because it would have allayed a murder you can't bring yourself to commit. You made an sacred oath to me, and I to you. Those promises forever bind us; we are to protect one another. Not *kill*."

"I promised myself to you in life, not in death. There is nothing *sacred* left of you to hold me to any vows." Her lovely lips seared him with the remark. She growled and shoved her hands upward, causing his fingers to slide to her bracelet. He hissed and jerked back. She clutched the iron collar at his neck, squeezing so his skin folded to pinch against it. A spark of animosity ignited her expression. With her metallic makeup reflecting the moon's bluish slivers where they streamed through the vined canopy, she looked like a fallen angel.

Determined to set them both on common ground—the angel and

the devil—he rolled then stood, lifting her to her feet with him.

"Lynora, please. Let us be civil, let us talk and find our way."

"Civil? You've made us mortal enemies!" Huffing, she pushed free with her left hand, causing him to note the absence of his ring upon her finger.

The sight jolted through him, cutting like a slice of lightning. "Your ring is gone. Was that why you were at our cottage? Was that tonight?"

As if shaken by his insight, Lynora's gaze finally snapped to his. "How did you know I was at our cottage? Were you spying on me?"

Mordecai ignored the question, nearly choking on the bile that filled his throat. "You've condemned me to die. Without even giving me a chance to explain. Damnit, Lynora. You are worse than the Agnate."

She stood in silence, seemingly unable to look away now that their eyes had made contact.

"Master play . . . coin on walls?" Krig tugged on Mordecai's breeches, clenching Lynora's neck cuff in his other hand. He hopped from one foot to the next, obviously excited.

Mordecai saw it then: two lights dancing across Lynora's cheeks and forehead. *He* was the source of her sudden intense focus, her softened resistance. When her eyes had met his, his hypnotic instinct had taken over—all on its own. It empowered him, yet terrified him. Another piece of his humanity must have crumbled away to make room for the adaptation. He shoved aside his dismay, for this gave him an advantage. They could hash everything out in Nocturnus, safely underground. Now that he had her wrapped within his spell, he wasn't about to release her. He would smuggle her in—make her understand.

"You did well, Krig. You will have pick of my wardrobe. As many buttons as you like," Mordecai answered without releasing Lynora from his glittering stare. "Check our path," he told his servant. "Be sure it's clear. We need to get back before sunrise." He dismissed the diminutive with a sharp nod. The leafy surroundings rustled as the gargoyle slipped through the fringes.

Intent on Lynora, Mordecai thrummed his fingertips on his thigh. "You are going with me."

Lynora edged away from the opening, moving deeper into the thicket. Spindles of moonlight streamed through the leaves to paint her with light and shadow. Despite that she couldn't escape his gaze, a fragile stubbornness crimped her brow.

His hands clenched to fists. "You swore to be with me forever. I can't live an eternity without you. You are the only thing left that connects me to—"

"To what?" she asked, her voice no more than a whisper. "Isaac? The responsibilities of a mortal world? The things you were so anxious to leave behind." She squinted, as if trying to coax her lashes to close. She growled when she failed. "You chose to walk in darkness. Threw everything away."

"And you? You threw things away, too. I made you that ring."

As though stunned by his disconnected comment, Lynora curled her left fingers. "I buried it in the place our dreams died." Her chin tilted upward.

"That is why you visited the priest. To absolve our marriage." Mordecai's flashing glare traversed her every feature to gauge her reaction.

Her haughty expression diminished. "How could you know of him?"

It wasn't an outright admission, but it was a definite acknowledgement of the holy man. An animalistic rage vibrated through his bones. "Did he annul our marriage? Is that why you buried your ring?"

Miniscule lines furrowed Lynora's forehead. "How can you know of him when you cannot move in mist form? And . . . it was daylight during my visit."

"Did you absolve our vows? Answer me, Lynora!"

"What does it matter?" she hissed. "A marriage that has never been consummated is null and void already."

"Fair enough. Then we will rectify that right now." He advanced toward her. "Take off your bracelets."

Lynora groaned, but his flashing eyes coaxed her until she dropped the metal clasps to the ground. She backed up against the wall of thorns, getting caught by her hair. Lifting her arms behind her head to wrestle the snags, she couldn't get free. Ignoring her panicked yelp, Mordecai closed in until only an inch of space stood between them. He leaned down, his lips a hair's breadth from hers.

The tremor of her lips stirred the sliver of space between them, echoing through the nerves in his mouth—an earthquake of sensation. In that moment, he wanted her so much his reasoning started to fade. She swallowed, dragging his attention to the muscle spasm in her neck. Seeing her scars, he faced the urge to taste her again. One bite was all it would take. If he reopened those wounds, she would be rapt with hunger and desire—would do anything he asked.

His fangs nudged his inner lip. He stepped close enough that her breasts grazed his ribcage. Her nipples beaded against him, an erotic response that belied her efforts to escape him. His fingers traced her collarbone, smoothed the pleats at the neckline of her silky gown. He groaned to finally be touching her. She felt like heaven. It had been so long since he had basked in the company of heaven.

The change in her was immediate and unmistakable: the scintillating purr of surrender, her muscles relaxing. His mouth watered. His lips found hers for an electric moment and she reached for him, responding with fervor.

He cupped the back of her head and nudged her mouth open with his tongue. It shocked him, the heat of their unity. He thought with her being a neophite now, their kisses would be cold. But warmth uncoiled in a rush of sweet comfort like heated brandy. He moaned as their tongues danced and played, drawing out the flame so it pulsed through his blood—a sensation achingly foreign to his undead state. Her hands tightened in his hair and she matched his urgent need with her own. But then her tongue grazed his fangs and she went rigid in his arms.

Mordecai tried to slow down, to lead her gently. His palms stroked her arms, her neck, her lower back—relishing any small contact with her. His lips followed her jaw line and stopped at her scars. She tensed more, which only exacerbated the urge to bite, to titillate. Faded though the puncture-marks were, they cried out to him and he touched the tips of his fangs to them, indenting the skin an indiscernible amount.

"Please Mordecai. Have you not violated me enough for one lifetime?" The hoarse plea reverberated to a lion's roar in his head.

He slammed his eyelids shut and slipped back to the Miseria chambers—faced with the pale and lifeless reminder of a crime he never committed. Of a woman he never forced himself upon, yet experienced the debasement as if he had.

When he opened his eyes and looked down at Lynora, the flashing lights of his irises had vanished. Fear and distrust reflected on his bride's face, and ripped his black heart in half.

Cursing, he released her and stumbled backward, trying to subdue the beast that had awakened. No wonder she wished him dead. Dropping to his knees, he watched her as she managed to free her hair from the thorns—a songbird escaping a hunter's snare.

"Forgive me." Tears blurred her image. "The Wisdom has tainted me. I no longer even know what I'm capable of. How can I expect you to trust an abomination?"

She regarded him with caution as she crouched and slipped her bracelets back into place, her face a glistening smudge of frightened confusion.

Mordecai felt a tug on his shirt sleeve. He glanced over his shoulder to find Krig had returned.

The gargoyle frowned and pointed through the thicket's opening where a glow dusted the horizon in the east—barely discernable through the fog. His ears drooped. "Master . . . die? Ash to ash."

Lynora gasped but Mordecai barely noticed her reaction. He inhaled the richness of the roses swimming on the breeze around him and stared at the impending sunrise—the slightest flicker between deep purple and burnt orange.

How long had it been since he'd seen the dawn?

"Mordecai . . ."

Lynora's voice drifted somewhere behind the dredges of his consciousness. He had no response. The horizon's seam brightened another degree. So beautiful.

This was where a gardener belonged. With the air and the wind and the rustling of leaves—with the world an ornament put on display by the hands of the sun, a vivid adornment of color and life.

On the vista, the slim light burned his eyes, but he forced them to stay open.

He was so weary. Weary of being to blame. Weary of hating himself. Weary of his selfishness. He remembered the vision he'd had of Lynora in this very rose grove, playing her lyre for a tiny girl with hair the color of night. Lynora would never have a child as long as he lived. For any daughter to be in her future, for Isaac to be there as well, he would need to give up his present. *Today.*

"Go get my brother; become Lynora again, and never look back." He stood, shakily, starting toward the entrance to the thicket.

Krig whimpered and clutched Mordecai's pants leg, trying to keep him from reaching the opening.

"Mordecai?" Lynora called out, the sound of a harp's song to his aching ears.

But his ears weren't aching. They were burning. A slight sizzle had begun along their tips. *Good.*

"Mordecai!" Lynora caught his other hand but he refused to stop.

He dragged her and Krig along behind him, plunging through the entrance and out of the shade. In the same instant he felt a glorious blistering heat along his face, a strange squeaking sound broke from Lynora's lips. A sudden flutter of a hundred tiny wings encompassed the clearing. A black sheath of bats eclipsed the dawn and engulfed him. He crumpled to the wet grass, cloaked within their high-pitched cries . . . blanketed by their dark, musky warmth.

CHAPTER 21

"Take this panel and secure it to that column."

Morning light beamed through the multiple windows of the Flower and Willow Hall where the blood gala would take place this evening.

Trying not to think of Mordecai, Lynora clasped the twelve-yard length of silvery silk offered by Wren. Balanced on a ladder, she tied the fabric to a pillar in the far corner. Wren took the panel's excess and, using her own ladder, wrapped it around alternate columns so the fabric scalloped along the cathedral ceiling like an ocean's waves; sunshine highlighted the silk to a shimmering fray.

The sisters had started to decorate the dance hall a few hours after dawn. When Lynora had returned from the tunnel, she drifted up the dungeon steps before anyone woke, exhausted and quiet as a phantom. She changed her clothes, washed off the mud and found Wren to apply her maquillage—complete with apotropaic eye-paint. She returned the favor, and the two girls joined the others in the hall.

To keep up appearances was Lynora's only concern at the moment. Her sisters couldn't discover what was hidden within the dungeon's secret tunnel—that a Desmodai waited in the furthest throes next to a trapdoor which led outside the castle gates; that he was wrapped in a wreath of roses and slept beneath a cloak. No one could know how she had betrayed the mother's charity and kindness—all of their kindnesses—by bringing what they despised most right within the fortress walls.

No one could know she had betrayed herself, proving too weak to watch him die and win back her life.

Plumping a cucumber-green velvet pillow, Lynora placed it in the circular pattern of cushions centered on the hall's glossy marble floor, impressed by their progress thus far. At each of the four arched entrances, Rose and another sister had arranged carnations and lilies in long stemmed vases attached to the door frames. Sconces—hung like copper vines along the walls—held lavender scented candles. When lit later, they would gild the ornate wallpaper with golden light and evoke a relaxing scent to aid in hypnotizing their guests.

Now all that remained was the food preparation. Lynora followed the sisters to the kitchen where the scent of roasting pheasant wafted from the doorway. The banquet's menu for their guests consisted of poultry, asparagus, peas, buttered celery, and candied walnuts for dessert.

Lynora went to work coating the walnuts in a simmering maple syrup and cinnamon mixture. Wren laid out the glazed nuts to dry.

Lynora tried to keep up a rhythm despite the effects of a sleepless night. After wrapping Mordecai and his sheath of pipistrelles within the cloak, she and Krig guided him the entire way from the rose thicket to the tunnel's entrance, racing as quickly as the weight of the bats allowed. Upon using Krig's key—which she still wondered how he possessed—the gargoyle helped her lift open the trapdoor of iron. They dived into the tunnel just as the sun burst out in its full glory. The bats rushed back through the opening before Lynora sealed it behind them. Had they been one minute later getting underground, no bats or cloak could have saved him. Her husband would be a pile of ash.

And to think, that was exactly what *he* had wanted.

He'd seemed to be in some sort of trance . . . for when the tunnel door slammed shut, he came back to himself. Before Lynora knew what was happening, he drew her into his arms and caressed her—everywhere. Between kisses, he said, "Thank you for forgiving me. You saved my life. I owe you everything."

It shocked her, how terrified she had been at the thought of losing him to the sun. Especially after she'd planned to kill him herself. The fact was, she had seen the gardener today, watched him entranced by the dawn—heartsick for the sun. He didn't worship the darkness as she'd feared; he was enslaved by it. So even though a monster ruled his body, the man still lived within his soul. She'd seen other indisputable glimpses of him . . . when he pulled back from his intent to ravish her, despite his body's reluctance to comply . . . when he had been willing to offer himself upon the altar of sacrifice, just so she and Isaac could be together again.

And to think, for a moment, she'd thought he might somehow be the monster responsible for what was happening to the children . . . due to his inexplicable knowledge that she'd met with the priest.

Lynora stirred the walnuts faster. But after Mordecai had attempted to free her from his curse by walking into the sun? A monster would never cave to such chivalry. And she could never kill him now.

"Starling! You're slinging syrup everywhere!"

Lynora shifted her focus to Wren, finding gooey droplets clumped in her upswept hair and faded apron.

"Oh, Wren. I am sorry."

"Where is your mind today?" Wren swiped the drizzling syrup from her temple.

"Is there something bothering you?" Sister Heron looked up from shelling peas and focused on Lynora. "If so, speak it now. Tonight, your donient shall portray what type of woman he desires onto you, whether it be sweet and helpless, or fiery and aggressive. To play that role, your inner-self cannot be struggling. This taints the canvas."

On the other side of Heron, Rose stopped cutting celery. Knife in hand, she leaned against the wall. "How can little Starling portray any kind of woman, when she is not yet one herself?"

Heron tried to wave her away, but Rose stayed in place, puckering her fingertip with the knife's point. "One whose petals have never been opened by a man, never savored the flavor of sensuality, cannot stoke the fire to light her eyes and mesmerize her victim. Our princess wears her innocence like a millstone around her pretty neck. Is this not true, Starling?"

Lynora shifted from foot to foot. Every sister in the room had stopped their preparation to wait for her answer; even Heron turned back to Lynora.

Rose drilled the knife deeper in her finger. "Perchance we should give our princess some mortal blood, straight and undiluted. Let her experience the Wisdom. That would cure her insufferable walk as the Virgin Mary. Then she might finally be of some use to us."

Lynora pinched the bracelet at her wrist, remembering how Mordecai had said the Wisdom had tainted him. She hadn't had time yet to ask him what he meant by that.

"Enough, Rose." Heron stood and set aside her bowl of peas. "Starling, show me your eyes. Prove her wrong. Summon the light within. Without it, you cannot hypnotize a donient. You will have to stay in your room during the ceremony tonight."

Lynora groaned inwardly. If she couldn't attend the gala, she wouldn't be able to speak to Viscount Cummings about the children in the orphanage, about the illness. But how could she summon the fire of the neophite while on display, when she'd never even learned to master it in private practice? She thought upon how it felt to be touched by Mordecai in the rose thicket, then again this morning in the tunnel as he thanked her . . . how a part of her had wanted to surrender, to learn all he could teach her. Now, standing here without that intimate insight, she felt every bit the child.

From her peripheral, Lynora noticed Wren sidling closer to Rose. She wasn't sure what her friend intended, but knew it couldn't be prudent.

"Starling?" Sister Heron touched Lynora's arm. "Show me the fire in your gaze."

Before Lynora could respond, Wren shoved Rose against the wall, causing the knife to puncture her fingertip. A red blob oozed from beneath the blade. Snarling, Rose lunged at Wren and they dropped to the floor, strangling one another.

Just like that, everyone forgot Lynora. Heron and a sentinel wrestled Wren and Rose apart then escorted them to the Infirmary Hall. Both sisters were warned that if they fought again before the gala, they would be locked in the dungeon's cages until Mother Nenet could counsel them.

Lynora had plans to visit Mordecai later that afternoon during meditation when everyone retired to their rooms for two hours. She hoped Wren and Rose would keep their distance from one another until then. To have such a captive audience in the dungeon when she crept into the tunnel could prove deadly for her husband, not to mention herself.

Without a star-flower to light the way, Lynora had to lean on her fighting-blind training to sense her way through the darkness. She crawled along the tunnel in her tunic and billowy trousers, her already tender knees being pummeled by the terrain. The muslin pouch at her waist nudged her arms, heavy with a pomegranate and a deck of cards she'd brought to occupy Mordecai's time until he could leave.

She made a wrong turn and, forgetting to rely on her other senses, slammed her head into the wall. Dirt clods pattered around her as she stifled a cry. Resituating her ammut in her hair, she massaged her throbbing forehead. A duo of silvery light danced on the walls of the tunnel, then settled on the path beneath her hands.

"Are you protected?" Mordecai's low, husky baritone carried across the darkness.

A pang of appreciation bolstered Lynora; the fact that he didn't want a repeat of earlier, to accidentally pull her into his gaze, validated her growing trust in him. "Yes, my eyes are painted."

"Good. Follow the lights. Otherwise, you'll bust that pretty head again."

Lynora tightened the pouch on her waist and complied. When she came within feet of him, he maneuvered his muscular frame on a turn and led her past the adjacent tunnel. Here Lynora paused and noticed the door of the strange room remained firmly shut, just as it had been when she crept back to the dungeon after dawn. She had mentioned her curiosities about the locked chamber earlier, upon leaving her husband down here alone. She wondered if he'd seen or heard any movement in her absence.

"Mordecai—"

"Shhhh…" They continued for another long stretch until they reached the tunnel's end—well out of reach of anyone in the castle— where the iron door waited and the passage opened wide and tall enough for them both to stand.

"I have heard no sounds from the room," he answered her unspoken question. He shut down the flash of his eyes. She could feel him in the darkness, patting dust off his clothes. From his vest, he drew out another glowing flower. He burrowed the blossom's stem into a crevice in the wall for a makeshift torch. An amber haze filled the small recess. "And I also have seen no movement. I watched it most of the morning after I woke. Even tried to open it—discreetly of course. There will be no breaking in without a key."

Lynora inhaled sharply and his eyes rounded.

"Krig," they both said the name simultaneously.

"Do you think he has one that would fit?" she asked.

"He well might. He has an entire ring of them. Perhaps at the least, there's a skeleton key we could try. But he's not here at the moment. I sent him back to Nocturnus. He must inform my friends to carry on with the masquerade, else I meet my death."

This thought made Lynora's stomach kink. "Do you trust him to get by your guard?"

"Yes. He was a brilliant Desmodai before his punishment, and even with a lesser brain, seems to be quite resourceful."

"But will the plant mask your friend is wearing work for so long? I didn't spare your life today, only for you to lose it when you return."

Mordecai's flesh glimmered like moonlight in mist, too dim for her to read his features. Yet she knew her concern had touched him when he leaned over and kissed her temple. "You are an angel." His mouth moved to her ear. "How I love your tender heart." The scent of roses from his wreath titillated Lynora's nose, reminding her of the roses she'd smelled in the cryptic room.

She gazed back into the long passage from whence she'd come. Without her husband's flashing lights, the void stared at her like a mouth agape—dark and hungry. "I want to see inside that chamber, Mordecai. It holds answers to questions I have not even thought to ask. I sense it."

His hand cradled her elbow. "Krig will be back at dusk to help me open the trapdoor. I'll have him try his keys before we leave for Nocturnus. I'll send news through him, if we find anything."

"Perhaps I am impatient." She took off her pouch and offered it to Mordecai. "There may be record of it somewhere, written in the time of Mother Nenet's predecessor. It could be I simply haven't found it yet. It is said the Monarch Cromwell kept journals. Perchance they would mention the room."

"It has always struck me odd," Mordecai's fingers slid over hers as he took the pouch—an obvious effort to sustain contact as long as she'd allow, "how there's no name for your grand benefactress's forerunner. I would think that other woman would have a tribute somewhere, for all she did to establish this castle as a harborage for halflings. And odder still that Lady Nenet was alive long enough to know her, yet she's retained her youth. Granted, neophites live longer than mortals, but they age eventually."

Lynora leaned against the cold wall. "She drinks a special tea made of the Mushroom of Immortality. It grants her longevity. The Egyptians believed the fungus to be a gift from Osiris ... so I suppose it would be unknown to you."

Mordecai grunted and opened the pouch. He pointed to the cards. "What are these for?"

"To keep you entertained until you can leave tonight. And I brought you some sustenance."

Mordecai drew out the sliced pomegranate. "Thank you." He sucked out several seeds, tipping the dripping fruit her direction. "I wouldn't trust Lady Nenet, were I you." From what Lynora could make out in the dimness, he appeared to scowl. "There are secrets in this castle. Secrets someone doesn't want your sisters or you to know about."

The foreboding thought hitched Lynora's breath. This place was her home. She trusted the mother and her sisters. Without her faith in them, she had nothing. "You have no right to make assumptions about a woman you have never met."

"I might not have met Lady Nenet," he mumbled between chews, "but I have seen her. She doesn't look trustworthy."

Lynora studied the shimmer of his lower lip. "You saw her? How?"

Swallowing, he swiped juice from his stubbled chin. "The same way I saw your priest."

"You never fully explained that to me."

Upon taking another bite, he raised an eyebrow. "First, I want to know why you met with the holy man."

Lynora studied her husband—so large and sturdy he nearly filled the small room. It occurred how easily he could overpower her should he wish it. She'd opted not to wear her bracelets as a show of trust. Now she wondered if that had been a fool's folly.

Claustrophobia scuttled up her spine then slinked along her stomach with the fluttery sensation of a centipede. She pressed her shoulder blades into the wall for support. "I went to the orphanage to check on Isaac. Father Lucien was there, investigating an illness afflicting the children."

"Isaac?" Mordecai cast the pomegranate aside. It hit the wall and knocked some dirt loose in a cadence of patters. "Why did you not tell me?"

"Because he's well. Short of being in emotional turmoil over us and the sickness of his friends."

"Of course, he is well. The one thing I can thank my father for." Mordecai raked a hand through his hair as if relieved. "Tell me of this plague."

She reached into the pouch for the deck of cards. "It is of a spiritual nature, or so it seems." She dropped the bag to the floor and flipped the cards' edges between her hands. "Though I had considered that a Desmodai might be responsible."

"Why?"

"There was a familiar scent in the room of one of the affected children. The scent of your kindredship …and the priest said such a scent is common in the stigmata. But it was daylight." She paused as the unwanted memory of another scent tickled her senses. "Have you ever smelled a child's blood, Mordecai? Sweet … so sweet. It calls to your heart." Eyes closed, she battled the inner demon which had revived her appetite again, just at the thought.

Mordecai's fingers laced through hers, grounding her. "Lynora?"

"I wanted to drink, Mordecai. I would have done anything for it." She felt her face congeal with terror and shame, as if she wore a shrinking mask over her makeup.

Mordecai drew her closer. "Sweet sanctum." He cupped her face. "Come to Nocturnus with me. The temptations are too strong here on topside. Down there ... you'll be safe from the mortals. You will never have to face them."

She drew back. "How can you ask me to leave Isaac, yet again?"

Her groom's lush mouth turned on a remorseful slant. A warm, tugging sensation spread through her at the vision. It never ceased to leave her breathless, how someone with such masculine polish could at the same stroke be so beautiful. She couldn't let him know the effect he had on her ... this power to topple her resolve with just an expression—that he didn't even need to use his Desmodai prowess to render her breathless.

In silent regard, he studied her. "So ... what are we to do?"

"We?"

With a deep sigh, Mordecai backed up to the other wall and slid to sit beside his cloak, piled on the ground like a pillow. "He is my brother. I've wronged him beyond anything forgivable. But I still want to try."

Lynora rubbed her knuckle along the back of the slick cards, touched by his sincerity. "Viscount Cummings will be at the gala this eve. I plan to question him while he's entranced. Perchance he might offer some understanding of this plague."

"Oh hell. I forgot about the blasted gala. You are attending?"

"It's expected. Besides, I have to, for Isaac."

"It isn't safe for you."

"Some would say it's safer than what I'm doing now."

Mordecai's expression turned fragile, almost wounded. He looked up at her and gestured to the ammut in her hair. "You wear a weapon of iron in your hair, even after all we experienced at dawn, to defend against my kind. Yet when you're surrounded by randy men—who could prove dangerous in their own ways—you wear sticks made of wood with healing properties."

Lynora shrugged. "We use our naturleges in the blood-letting ritual; drain the veins in the donients' wrists to keep from infecting them with our saliva. The juniper wood restores any puncture marks within an hour, leaving no scabs or scars."

Mordecai looked thoughtful. "And those sticks are carved in a U-shape, like your ammuts. They're painted silver, as well, to appear metal, so that a Desmodai can't differentiate between them, unless by touch. Pray tell, how is yours marked? How could I know the difference?"

Lynora wouldn't answer. It felt as if she would be betraying herself and her sisters by saying too much about their rituals. "As the rumor goes, since the ammuts are iron, they're weighted, heavier to your kind. And they would blister your fingers should you try to touch. There's no other means."

He sighed. "So, we are back to not trusting one another again, aye?"

"Were you testing me? How can I fully trust you yet?" Her attention caught on the small snippets of his metal collar where it showed through the rose wreath around his neck, a reminder of what his gargoyle had stolen from her earlier. Her palm opened. "You still have my neck cuff, after all. I'll need it tonight to cover my scars."

His fingers cinched around something folded in his cloak. "First you grant me one question." Before she could answer, he captured her wrist and dragged her down level with him, face to face. The swiftness of his action knocked the cards from her hand so they scattered on the ground. Pebbles rolled under her knees and palms where she balanced herself to straddle his thighs.

"I want to know," his other hand caught and lifted her chin, "how you charm the men."

As he held her there, his lapel gaped open under the rose wreath to reveal his smooth, sculpted chest. The luminous white of his complexion mesmerized her. She remembered how his flesh used to twitch beneath her touch. She wondered if it still would, were she to brave touching him.

She started to stand. His eyes pleaded and his fingers locked on her shoulders. "Damnit, Lynora, I will do everything I can to respect your independence. Just please, grant me this, as your husband."

Lynora's teeth ground together. "There are different ways to be enchanting hostesses. Some of us converse with them. Others play card games." She glanced at the deck strewn on the ground beside them. "And then," she swallowed, "then there are those who perform."

Mordecai rose to his feet, drawing her up with him. "*Perform?*"

She wouldn't meet his gaze. "Dance. Dance for the men's pleasure."

"Ah." He pushed her back to the wall. His hands came to rest on either side of her head against the loose dirt and rock. "And which *tactic* are you assigned, my swan?"

She squeezed her hands to fists at her waist. "I-I am dreadful at rummy or whist … and I shy from speaking to strangers but excel in music … so I am on the performing end."

His answering snarl made Lynora's blood skitter through her veins like mice through a maze.

"It is only dancing," she mumbled.

"Ha! I've seen you practice your dancing. Such erotic grace; no man can resist a beautiful woman put on display like a wanton butterfly."

"Tell me how you know that! *How have you seen me?* Has Krig been spying for you all this time?"

Mordecai's head snapped up, his face stiff as stone. "I won't tolerate you seducing other men. You are a lady, a virgin, and a wife."

"And you are a hypocrite. Your kind uses seduction, too. The only difference is that I will not be guilty of killing the innocent victim."

"Innocent? Hardly. We feed off the dregs of humanity."

"They are human, nonetheless. Something I would give almost

anything to be again." Hand outstretched, Lynora gestured for her neck cuff. "We had a bargain. I upheld my end."

Glaring at her, Mordecai kicked his cloak's folds open to reveal her ornamented neck armor. Before she could crouch to retrieve it, he caught her elbow. "Choose something else. Anything but dancing."

She sighed. "I do not get to choose. It's the only talent I possess. It is my place to help the sisters … to earn my keep. I must feed." Grunting, she tried to yank free.

Mordecai turned her loose then, a fierce grimace on his face. "Vow to me they'll not touch you. Let them watch to their heart's content. But no touching."

"I will do my best."

He shook his head and pulled her close, his body cold and unyielding as metal. "Not good enough. I want your word as a lady. As my wife. And I have ways of watching you. Remember this."

Tears edged her lashes like crystals of ice. She refused to let them fall. "I can merely try. I am … quite inadequate at being a neophite."

He curled his fingers around her nape, tracing her tattoo. "You appear to have adapted quite well."

His fingertip's soft movement stirred a friction within her lower extremities. "I—I can't conjure a hypnotic fire in my gaze to hold a man entranced and under my power. The flame will not kindle in my soul. No matter what I try."

Mordecai's eyes narrowed and he caressed her cheek with the back of his fingers, his touch tender and intense at once. Keeping her in his sites, he bent to gather the fallen cards. "Well then I think it's high time you learn to play whist, my love."

CHAPTER 22

Lynora picked up her neck cuff and tucked it in her pouch. "You wish to teach me to play cards? *Now?*"

"How long until you will be missed?"

"One half of the hour."

"Not as much time as I'd like. But it will have to do." Mordecai's back faced her as he spread his cloak across the dirt.

She struggled to understand his reasoning. "Even should I learn the game, I will still have to dance. That's my assignment for this gala. There is no means to change that today."

Her groom sat upon the cloak and smoothed the wrinkles. After removing the wreath of roses from his neck and setting it aside—having no need to hide his scent this far inside the tunnel—he gestured to the empty space on the cloak beside him. "Sit." He watched her hesitation from the corner of his eye as he shuffled the cards. "Come Lynora. At least attempt to trust me."

"The last time I did, I awoke in a castle full of outcast women who feast on blood and play with bats." She hadn't meant to say it aloud. It simply slipped out. But she knew she'd hit a nerve.

His card shuffling slowed and his broad shoulders slumped. "I can't undo what I've done … not without—"

"Stop." Lynora gathered her trousers around her legs and sat across from him, crossing her ankles. "I am partly to blame, for all of this."

Frowning, he gazed at her. "How did you come to that?"

"You left the cottage on our honeymoon ... to ease my juvenile fears. A game of forbearance played to assuage my blasted inexperience."

"I've always loved your purity, Lynora. Do not belittle it. And it doesn't matter that I went on an errand for you. Even had I not, they would have found me, regardless. And I would have made the same ill-fated choice. Because I am an arrogant fool."

Lynora reached for his hand. "Enough name-calling. All is not lost. I have been thinking on this. Studying it. There is another way back for us."

His eyes locked on hers. "Another way?"

"I read of it in the Sanctorum. It is a bit more complicated. Whereas, a neophite can simply kill their Mentor to be free, a full Desmodai must kill their Mentor, burn his heart, and drink the ashes in Satsuma water. Were you to do this, you and I would *both* be human again. We could return to our life as it was meant to be. Isaac, living with us, sunlight always surrounding us. The means to have your child, returned." Her voice shook despite her efforts to hold strong. "Find your Mentor. Kill him."

Mordecai's jaw muscles bunched. He seemed shocked and disturbed by her suggestion.

"You didn't know of this?" she asked.

"No. I've made few friends. And those I have rarely speak of such things." He glanced down. "It's impossible anyway. Anyone courted by the Mentory is approached by at least six Desmodai and hypnotized during the exchange of saliva and blood, so they cannot know their Mentor's identity."

Even in the dim amber light, Lynora could see an uneasy strain across his brow, as if he mulled something over; something he wasn't quite willing to share. It appeared he had yet to learn to trust her again, either.

She played with the hem of her tunic. "Are you happy ... in Nocturnus?"

He snapped the corner of a card between his finger and thumb. "In some ways. All my life, I have sought such company. People who are wise, discerning. Who serve a grander purpose in life than simply to attend balls and indulge in inane pleasantries such as smoking cheroots or playing billiards. Now, I've found a place of higher order and thought. A near perfect society, it would seem. But I am nothing short of miserable without you and Isaac there."

The honest strain of regret in his voice stoked Lynora's compassion. "They are barbarians, Mordecai. For all their talents, for all their great discernment ... they are still as flawed as the mortals you sought to escape. There are other means whereby they could survive, if they chose to—like the Sisterhood."

"If only. Things would be so much simpler if we could find a way to integrate animal blood into our diet, to stretch it so that less would be required to satisfy us. But the Agnate has tried. No one can tolerate the mixture. It affects us like influenza. It has to be flushed from the system with pure human blood, or the Desmodai will dehydrate and die. It is not by choice. We would prefer to have a diluted mix such as yours. Were we to ever find to a way to block the sins from the flavor like you do, it would be so much easier to bear. None of us wish to be monsters."

"Perhaps you are not *all* monsters." She glanced at his feet. "I assume you still garden barefoot?"

Without looking up from shuffling the cards, he nodded.

Lynora reached out to still his hands. "There then. A monster wouldn't do that."

Wincing, he shirked her touch. "But my toes are no longer tanned. For the sun abhors me."

Noting the defeated set of his jaw, Lynora wondered again if that was the cause of his trance earlier. If his longing to see daylight had overtaken all reason. "You must miss many things."

"What I miss most, are nights by the fireplace, listening to you play your lyre while Isaac and I engage in card games. I miss letting the boy trump me, time and again … simply so I might earn an appreciative smile from your pretty mouth, and sweet rewards beneath the sheets when we retire to bed. And, I miss holding you in my arms as we sleep."

Lynora quivered, her nerves alight with fantasy. "But we never had such moments. I never even spent one night with you and Isaac."

"You did in my dreams, Lynora. You still do." Growing silent, Mordecai dealt out thirteen cards first to her then to himself before stacking the remainder in the middle, flipping the top card face-up. "What of you … were the changes in your body … difficult?" His gaze shifted up, a pained light behind it.

"Excruciating." Lynora would not pull punches here. He needed to know what he'd put her through. "I thought I was dying. Then when I realized I wasn't, I longed for death. I hated you for—" She stopped herself short upon seeing his frown.

"I made short-sighted choices, for which I'm sorry. You'll never know *how* sorry." He didn't look up again.

She watched his long fingers, the deftness of his movements as he resituated the cards. There was a slight tremor to his hands now. She remembered how those hands had touched her in the rose thicket, stroking her over her clothes. He had felt nothing short of human in that moment, just like now. But with him so close to her here, with his rose wreath cast aside, he smelled of wilted flowers and moonlight. The essence of a Desmodai—lush and seductive. The opposite of what he once was, yet somehow still beguiling to her. She wondered … was it the man that called to her, or the beast?

"Did you hear me, Lynora?"

She shook herself out of her reverie, unaware he'd been talking. "Sorry. No."

"Listen this time." His husky command strummed a chord deep within her. "The game's rules are important to your success." He pointed to the stack of cards in the middle. "This is the stock. And this is called a trick…" He laid down a three of clubs from the cards which he'd fanned like a peacock's tail in his hand. Lynora studied his card, unsure what to do.

"Do you have one of the same suite?" he asked. "If not, you may play another suite, but forfeit the win of this trick to me."

She struggled to splay out her cards so she could see each one, using her thumb against her palm to hold them in place like Mordecai did. She smiled upon accomplishing the feat, though her cards appeared more like a ruffled hen's tail-feathers than a peacock's. She drew out a seven of clubs to lay it atop his.

Mordecai grinned. "Splendid. Your seven is a better play than my three. So you win this trick." He nudged the two cards toward her, his hand grazing her thigh. She tried not to notice her body's instant reaction, a tensing and throbbing in sordid and sundry places.

Mordecai appeared unaffected by the contact and proceeded to remove his vest. She watched his shirt lapels fold to reveal his chest once more, fighting the urge to reach out and trace the cut of his muscles. His physique was somehow even more masculine and alluring now, in that there were no rough edges. Everything had been filed to perfection.

"Now, Lynora, take the card off the top of the stock and add it to your hand, and I'll draw one from the deck. That is how whist is played. First, we compete to win good cards from the stack to add to our hand; then, when the stock is empty, we try to win the majority of the tricks." Mordecai tilted his head, studying her as if to gauge her reaction to his next words. "And as added incentive for you, upon each trick you win, I'll remove an article of my clothing."

Lynora's breath caught. She clutched her tunic's neckline.

"I do not expect you to reciprocate in kind," he assured her. "You will understand my stratagem soon enough."

And so the game proceeded. Lynora pleased herself, catching on much faster than she would have imagined. Within a matter of minutes she had won five tricks and Mordecai was down to only his trousers. By this point, watching his abdomen ripple as he tossed his last stocking behind him, she began to feel a spread of warmth throughout her body, all the way up to, however strangely, her irises.

"Your move," he prompted.

She couldn't look away from his half-naked torso long enough to take the top card from the deck.

Tilting her chin up with a fingertip, Mordecai centered her attention on his face. In a slow and carnal sweep, his tongue eased out to lick his lips. Lynora's heart skipped at the sight. She remembered how his mouth and tongue had felt on her breast on the night of her alteration, the way they seared her flesh despite the chill—an erotic dance with frostbite.

Shocks of tumbling pleasure rushed between her thighs, and she felt as if the entire room were afire—glowing red and hot around her.

"Ah, very nice." Mordecai's words slapped her awake. Her eyes stung as she refocused on their surroundings, surprised to find everything truly was cast in tinges of red. That was the warmth she'd felt in her irises. The heat of a neophite's lit gaze.

Mordecai leaned closer, and as if reading her thoughts, said, "Yes, isn't it splendid? With just one lesson, you've ignited your power."

Coming back to herself, she smoothed the fabric along her trembling legs. He wasn't teaching her whist so she could alter her performance for tonight. It was all a ruse to help her conjure the fire so she could protect herself. Gratitude swirled within her chest.

Mordecai's lips lifted on one side. "Perhaps we'll try one last lesson. Just to perfect the talent." He leaned forward, his chilled finger running from her jaw to her neck. "In just a blink, you can protect yourself from man and monster alike. All you need do to bid the flames, my swan, is trade your pristine feathers for the coat of a vixen."

Watching her as he did it, he drew his fingertip across a card's edge, slicing the surface flesh. Blood oozed out.

Her heartbeat peaked to near implosion.

His hand lifted to balance the crimson bead, causing her to salivate, an echo of thirst so strong she had to fight the compulsion to leap to her feet and attack him.

"Now, anytime you think on something you crave, something you desire to the point of a burning, white hot ache within your very core—your gaze will ignite."

Trembling, Lynora crossed her ankles tighter, feeling the very ache he spoke of along her pelvis.

As if hearing her thoughts, his eyes dropped to the place between her legs. "For me, my most fierce desire is what awaits beneath that fabric. I would give up my very immortality to touch you there."

Her face grew hot.

He eased closer, careful not to lose the shiny, bulbous swell upon his fingertip. "You see, this ache cannot be the draw of sustenance alone. It must be intertwined with passion, bittersweet and hot. Like the mating of a man and woman. As you have never experienced such intimacy," both of their gazes locked on his hand, "you shall have to think upon the closest experience you've had."

His breath mesmerized her with the scent of sweet pomegranate as he knelt on one knee. His finger nudged her mouth. Just as she had done that night of altercation, she gripped his wrist to hold him there. She forgot about the gala. She forgot about the neophite gaze or the mysterious room further down the tunnel. A wicked decadence swirled through her, an indomitable need that crushed any other thought to dust.

Mordecai's cool blood drizzled onto her bottom lip. Anticipating the flavor, she sighed. Her lashes fluttered closed. Weaving his free fingers through her chignon, Mordecai tilted her head back. Her tongue tipped out to taste his flow, starving for it.

As she drank, she peered up at him. In a beautiful display of lust, his nostrils flared. When her eyes shifted to the opposite wall, a red glow pierced the dim surroundings like torches.

"You've mastered it, Lynora," Mordecai encouraged.

She smiled and coaxed his finger deeper into her mouth. Her tongue curled around his digit to draw out more blood.

With Desmodai grace, Mordecai guided her to lie on the cloak without even mussing her tunic. He fell upon her. The hard planes of his half-naked body settled against her. His fingers wove through her hair, holding her neck still so he could kiss her forehead, her brows, her temples and cheeks. "Lord, how I've missed the feel of you."

Lynora released his finger from her mouth. An anguished pang shook her. It mattered little that he had crippled his Desmodai power over her by showing her the flame, for he had strengthened his prowess as a man—as her husband. And, having glimpsed the gardener still within him, she no longer had the will to fight. "I've missed you, too."

Nuzzling her ear, Mordecai maneuvered his free arm to circle her waist. His palm sculpted her lower back, tracing the intricate contours there.

She clasped his neck and coaxed his mouth to hers for a deep kiss. Her lips opened to him and his tongue nudged inside. The union brought warmth, and Lynora drank of it, starving. Her hands lifted to his nape and tangled in his hair.

Their breaths clashed as she regarded him intently, running her hands along the thick billows and crests of his back. His chilled flesh quivered beneath her touch.

He moved his lips down her chin, feeding on her sighs of pleasure. He trailed his tongue along her neck. She felt him stiffen for a moment as he bypassed her scars, as if it took all of his strength not to taste her. Then he lifted the hem of her tunic and eased away the lacy chemise beneath to expose one breast. She whimpered as her nipple speared upward in response to his chilled breath.

He took her into his mouth, sending needles of sensation through to her sternum as he sampled her with patient gluttony. His palm glided down her belly to the tie at her trousers' waist. She trembled and his mouth stole her gasps of breath.

"Mordecai…" Her voice broke his control and his fangs made an impromptu appearance. She felt them indent her breast as he eased her from his mouth and withdrew his hand from under her tunic, cursing.

Propped up on his elbows, he regarded her intently. "We are rocking an ocean, and I can't contain the waves."

"I am not so fragile as you think." Anesthetized with unfulfilled passion, Lynora attempted to lure him close again, to ease the ache within her core.

He remained immoveable. "You are breakable, where I am not." He tugged her tunic back in place. Remember last night, being trapped in the thorns? How I almost …" The guilt in his eyes nearly broke her heart. "I'm not myself, Lynora."

"You said that then." Lynora's fingers trailed his bare shoulders. The shimmer from his skin reflected back on her fingertips and followed them, as if she trailed her hand through a moonlit lake. "You said the Wisdom tainted you. What did you mean?"

In tender silence, he raked a strand of hair from her face, his expression pained.

Then something occurred to her. "Twice, you have given me of your blood—and I drink of you willingly."

Mordecai averted his eyes. "Yes."

His fangs glimmered, stirring in Lynora an unexpected desire to feel them penetrate her pulsating scars. She forced her voice to hold steady. "You could have tricked me. It would have been easy enough. You could have hidden mortal blood in a vial; placed it on your finger.

Made me think it was yours and brought me to full realization. Why haven't you?"

In lieu of a response, he yanked his hand from hers and rolled her so they were both on their sides. He curved a palm over her hips along her silky trousers. An expression of pure torment clouded his face, as if some memory sliced through him. It made Lynora hurt just to watch.

"Mordecai…"

"In our past, we had practice smoothing over the biases between two different sects of society. But this … this is two completely different worlds. I cannot unleash my passion on you, unless you are strong, like me. Or unless I become like you again. Ultimately, one of us will have to sacrifice their world in order to be with the other. I can't reclaim my humanness, and you can only if—"

"No." Lynora pressed her hand to his mouth, her despondence caught in her throat like a wad of thorns. "That is no longer an option. Speak of it no more."

Silent, he sat up, straightened her clothes, put his shirt on, and drew her sideways onto his lap. The rose leaves rattled as the discarded wreath lodged beside her folded legs. She felt his desire for her beneath her buttocks, sending tendrils of fire through her veins. She wished she could know him now … merge the man and monster to fill the void his absence had left within her for so long.

He swept aside her tangled chignon and kissed her nape. A wave of chill bumps rose on her flesh in the wake of his lips.

"Everything has changed," he murmured. "Last night, I planned to beg you to give me a second chance. I hoped to take you on a tour of Nocturnus, to show you the beauty that a life there could afford us as bloodmates. But now I know … you are better off without that world. Without the Wisdom." His strong palm traced the curve of her neck. "Without me."

Lynora was shocked at the terror his words evoked. "No. You can't be saying goodbye. I-I need help with Isaac."

Nodding, Mordecai drew her into another kiss. "And you shall have it."

His tongue tasted of fruit and Lynora responded with hungry enthusiasm until he pushed her off of him.

"Enough." Breathless and scowling, he resituated his trousers. "When I'm alone with you like this, I can't seem to keep myself from touching you."

Lynora's cheeks warmed. "I must go anyway. The guests arrive at sunset." She situated her pouch at her waist, laced their fingers, and persuaded him to stand.

Growing somber, Mordecai glanced at their joined hands then up again. "Will you be playing your lyre tonight?"

"Yes."

A smothered groan shook his chest. "Do you still play just for pleasure?"

Lynora hesitated. The question was more intimate than if he had asked if she still dreamed of him. For he knew, as well as she, that every song her fingers birthed were compositions of her love for him. "I-I have been learning a movement from 'Water Music'. It is said Handel wrote the collection to regain favor with his majesty."

Mordecai wrapped a tendril of her hair around his thumb. "I wish I could have heard this piece."

She caught the hand which held her hair and pulled his palm to her mouth to kiss it. "Perhaps you will one day, if I have the opportunity to accompany an orchestra. It is meant to be a tribute to the sea … and the sea has many voices, not just one lone song." Balanced on her toes, she reached up to peck his cheek. "Do not give up just yet," she whispered against his cool cheek, though in his eyes she didn't see even a glimmer of hope.

A momentary hush weighted the air between them, as neither wished to voice their dread at parting.

"If you learn anything from Viscount Cummings, about the children?" Mordecai broke the silence.

"I'll send my bat to bring you a message. I shall decorate the parchment with glittery buttons, thus Krig won't miss it."

Once her husband had nodded his agreement, Lynora took two steps backward.

"Wait." Mordecai caught her ribcage and lifted her gently, holding her in midair. His head tipped up to regard her with a hungry intensity which sent all the need he had forced her to suppress sluicing into her depths—a fluid smolder so heavy it gathered in her belly then settled between her thighs.

"Remember everything I taught you tonight." The rasp in his voice vibrated through her as he set her down again. "Ignite your power, and neither man nor monster can steal what belongs to you—not ever again."

CHAPTER 23

"Master . . . thief? Thief like Krig."

Mordecai watched the gargoyle's scales reflect swatches of moonlight. "I'm borrowing. Understand? *Borrowing.*" Mordecai talked low to preserve their hiding place behind a thicket of blackthorn shrubs. On the other side of the brush, a boisterous crowd of men in costume took the main road to the Gwyndolaire Castle. Horse hooves and carriage wheels stirred clouds which carried the stench of dust and animal dander. Snorts and whinnies blended with men's laughter.

"Master tricky-trickster." Krig smiled his ghoulish smile.

Mordecai suppressed an answering growl. His little companion was taking this much too lightly. "Shush your bone-box and help me peel off the man's costume. Oh, and find his invitation. No one gets into the gala without one."

Mordecai worked swiftly in the darkness, grateful for his Desmodai vision, even more grateful for his hypnotic ability. He was fortunate to have spotted a man so close to his proportions walking in solitude along a moonlit path through the woods. And he had a full face mask, no less. Most of the other attendees wore domino masks that merely rounded the eyes and the space between them, like a raccoon's disguise. That would never have sufficed. His pale flesh and dark lips would have given him away.

Loud innuendos and chortles cracked the cool air on the other side of the thicket—eager men anticipant of their night of presumed pleasures. Mordecai sneered. They had no idea what they were in for. "I did you a favor, old man." He patted his victim's cheek and removed a three-corner hat of black velvet trimmed with red plumes.

Mordecai placed it on his head. "So, what do you think, Krig? Haven't seen a Tricorne in years. They went out with the eighteenth century."

Krig wrinkled his slitted nose.

"What?" Mordecai thrummed his fingers along the brim. "Does it not suit me?"

"Master need mask." Krig peeled the Venetian disguise from the stranger's face, the stiff, silver fabric molded in the handsome likeness of Adonis. "Master . . . Greek god." He snickered.

"Ah. Well said." Mordecai fit the mask on and resituated the hat. "Now to find my Aphrodite, hmm?" His voice muffled beneath the cover; he wished he could get caught up in Krig's infectious enthusiasm. But things had taken a very disturbing turn since he'd last seen his bride. "I'll get the cloak. You check his pocket for the invite."

The stranger wore a domino cape, a voluminous, red silk cover that would trail all the way to Mordecai's ankles when fastened around his neck. It would hide his clothes, the rose wreath, and the grounding collar in one fell swoop. Mordecai worked at the fastenings around the man's neck while Krig fished a gold gilded envelope from his breast pocket.

They both paused when the stranger sighed. Muscles tensed, Mordecai waited for his slow, even breaths to resume, then slipped the cape away. He traded Evan's cloak for it, intending to come back later and exchange them again before the man awoke.

By all accounts, his victim was asleep. Interesting how the training for a Reaper had assisted Mordecai in such a benign venture. Instead of seducing the man to give him his blood, Mordecai enticed him to hand over his clothes without even a word passed between them. And as a reward for his cooperation, Mordecai convinced the fellow to take a little doze. He would not wake until morning, and would have no memory of the night's events.

Mordecai hadn't intended to come to the gala, despite his qualms over Lynora's erotic performance. But when he and Krig had went to unlock the door in the tunnel's mystery room, they'd found it already ajar. Assuring no one was within, they searched the room. And what Mordecai found made his undead blood boil.

He drew out the silver, pearl-beaded scarf and held it up in the moonlight. He knew it was Nenet's. He had seen her wear it in one of his visions through the kaleidoscope. Combined with his other discoveries, he deduced that not only was the grand lady of the castle a liar . . . for all he knew, she might also be dangerous. He wasn't taking any chances. Lynora needed to know the truth tonight.

"All right, Krig." Upon tucking the scarf in his trousers' waist, Mordecai fastened the domino cape at his neck, turned up the high collar, and stuck the invitation in his vest pocket before working silky, black gloves onto his hands. This would help him avoid any interactions with iron.

He handed the diminutive a sterling. "You've been a great help. Now I want you to go to Nocturnus and tell Augustus and Evan that something important has come up. Tell them I'll return before dawn."

Krig's wormy lips twisted. His globular, thick-lashed eyes shot to the dark horizon.

Mordecai patted the creature's scalp. The scales and tufted hair snagged his gloves with tiny popping sounds. "I will not get stranded again. You have my word. Tonight, I'm a slave to the clock. All right?"

A soulful frown dragged the gargoyle's chin. "Blood smell. Master . . . go mad?"

"Yes. To be present for the draining ritual would make me lose control."

The gargoyle nodded, ears down.

"And I can't have anyone bleeding me, either. They would realize in an instant that I'm Desmodai. I'll have Lynora help me out through the tunnel's trapdoor before dinner is served. The ritual begins after all the guests have full bellies."

Krig's face brightened and he dropped the sterling into his pouch then blended into the surroundings. For an instant, Mordecai considered the Desmodai lifestyle that Josiah had once lived, the inanity and servitude which now imprisoned him as Krig. A wave of pity and compassion overcame him. Despite his best efforts, he was becoming fond of the little toad.

Mordecai awaited the rustle of grass which indicated the gargoyle's escape into the hills. Then he glanced through the shrubs toward the road.

In the distance, cradled by the valley, Gwyndolaire cut through the moonlight and mist like a fortress of frost. Fitting abode for Lady Nenet, who Mordecai now considered an ice queen. He parted some leaves for a view of the road and debated joining the other men.

A line of horses cantered by. He recognized some of the men's voices. He would have to avoid them in particular. Surely there was some lone attendee going slowly enough that would warrant a companion.

He saw his mark bringing up the end of the procession—a man with a cane, dismounted and leading his horse. Mordecai paused long enough for the fellow to get four feet's lead. Then he crept from the shrubs and caught up, stroking the horse's glossy neck with his gloved hand as he arrived.

The horse startled and Mordecai eased back. He'd overstepped—had hoped the rose wreath would allow him to pet the horse, but at least he could be in closer proximity to the beast without stirring her into stampede mode.

From behind a domino mask—black, with silver-embroidered ivy around the eye slits—the man settled his mare then gave Mordecai a once over

"Beautiful mare." Mordecai said by way of an apology.

The man nodded a thank you, but said nothing in return. A hint of myrrh emanated from his flesh and Mordecai tried to place his identity. The cane was unusual, and would be unforgettable to anyone who had seen it. This was no one Mordecai had ever met in Tatabury. Exactly what Mordecai had needed, a stranger.

His companion limped onward. With marked reluctance, he leaned on his walking stick as seldom as possible, an obvious effort to hide his need for it. Despite his powdered wig and top hat, his lean body gave his age away; he couldn't be more than upper-twenties. His shoulders stood broad and straight with the poise of youth. He had once been more muscular, apparent by his confident carriage. Mordecai supposed the man had reason to be confident, considering all the other guests appeared to be in their late thirties or older.

"Don't find many dappled grays with white points." Mordecai attempted conversation, using the horse again as a starter. He needed it to look as if he and this man were acquaintances when they arrived at the gate, to better allude the Gwyndolaire Sentinels. "Looks to be a mix of a hackney pony and a saddlebred. Where did you find her?"

A swarm of gnats encircled the stranger's neck. He swatted them away and adjusted the collar on his shin-length, black satin cape. "I procured her in London, five years ago."

Mordecai moved aside as the gray mare whinnied and nudged her owner. "Do you visit there often? London?" The gnats took a dive across Mordecai then darted off as if startled away, though he hadn't raised a hand to them. He cursed inwardly, hoping his companion hadn't noticed.

Leveling a sidelong glance at Mordecai, the stranger fondled his horse's muzzle. "I live there." He spoke with hesitance, as if turning something over in his mind. "Close to Piccadilly."

"Truly? I understand the King's Theatre is the most fashionable place to be seen."

The man leaned on his cane for a few steps. His mouth lifted to a one-sided smile. "The opera is exquisite. As is the Egyptian Hall. I try to attend a showing there at least once a month when I'm home. But the Dewstone Theatre . . . nothing could compare to that. I used to go once a week, before it burned to the ground."

A saddened tone punctuated the statement, but Mordecai's thoughts had reverted to the day he, Isaac, and Lynora were at the Egyptian Hall. His wedding day. The memory reminded him of Lynora's buried ring, and revived a deep sadness.

Taking several steps in silence, he squelched the emotion. No time for remorse. He needed to concentrate on befriending the stranger. "So, you came all the way from London to acquaint the ladies of Gwyndolaire, aye?"

Beneath his mask, the man burnished to crimson and made a strange sound like a strangled cough. "I'm here . . . on business. Not for carnal pursuits."

Mordecai did a double take at this reaction. Something about this man seemed almost . . . celestial. Why would someone who oozed goodness from his pores be seeking company with prostitutes? He didn't seem like every other lecherous scoundrel Mordecai had seen thus far. Here to frolic with what they assumed a castle full of harlots but too ashamed to show their identities, thus the costumes.

Perhaps this fellow hoped to lose the shackles of goodness. Could be he'd come to glean some worldliness. Mordecai bit back the urge to laugh. If so, this young philanderer would get his comeuppance, just as they all would.

"I must wonder how you managed an invite," Mordecai blurted. "The Gwyndolaire are quite selective in their clientry. I've ne'er heard of anyone outside our locale attending these galas."

The stranger fished in his pocket for a gold-embossed envelope identical to the invitation Mordecai now had in hand. Before he could respond vocally, a colony of pygmy bats swooped across the road, emitting high-pitched, chirping songs. Both men ducked out of the way.

The resulting swish of air rushed through Mordecai's cape and swirled the hem, prompting him to remember how the winged creatures had saved his life this morning. "The bats are in rare form tonight. Do you suppose they're searching for love?" His Tricorne hung cockeyed over his mask and he resituated the brim.

"September ended their mating season," the stranger answered, straight-faced. "The females give birth in June or July."

"Ah. So you study the pipistrelle. Is that why you're here?"

His companion's jaw tightened on a spasm beneath the shadow of his half-mask; his gaze focused ahead on the looming wrought iron gates of Gwyndolaire woven with ivy and fragrant honeysuckle. Two sentinels, clad in tunics, trousers, and thick makeup, waited just within. With their delicate figures draped in mist, they looked more like little girls playing make-believe than the hardened killers Mordecai knew them to be. But if they perceived even one whiff of his scent, their true nature would emerge. His fingertip traced the wreath of roses beneath his cape.

"My greatest pleasure in life is to learn," the man said, taking up Mordecai's earlier line of conversation. "Of late, my preferred subject is bats. Most especially the desmodus."

Mordecai stalled upon the word. The mare almost collided with his backside. Her owner circumvented the impact by a harsh downward tug on the reins. The horse snorted an objection.

Catching the commotion from the gate, the sentinels tightened their expressions. They gestured to an alcove lined with torches where all the guests had been directed to leave their mounts and carriages. The stranger led his mare over to the others, arranging her reins to drag the ground. She flicked her tail and nuzzled the grass.

"Sorry to startle you." The man directed the hushed apology to Mordecai as he returned, his gaze serious within the eye slits. "I suppose to study vampirism seems a gruesome pursuit. The creatures are parasites. Furry leeches."

Mordecai clenched his teeth. "Just because we don't understand their habitudes, that gives us no right to assume them repugnant monsters, does it? There is grace to be found in their determination to survive."

"Survival at the expense of other lives is not grace. It is murder. I realize they are slaves to instinct, but they carry disease that often kills their prey. Thus, they are dangerous vermin."

Ignoring the throb in his temple, Mordecai continued alongside the man, one hand tightened to a fist. "Not all of their victims die. Only those rife with sickness or weakened already. Only those that offer nothing of substance to their surroundings. It is not a crime to rid the world of its deficiencies."

The stranger hooked his cane over an elbow and limped several paces without its aid. "I am speaking of soulless animals. Why do you take offense as if I denigrate your closest acquaintances?"

Mordecai found himself begrudgingly grateful that their arrival at the gates superseded any need to respond. He and his unwitting companion sized one another up from beneath their masks while the sentinels inspected their invitations. Mordecai shut down his breath, fearing the women might sense the chill upon each exhalation. He moved his ribcage in a pantomime gesture, trying to appear natural.

None too soon, the guards waved them through into the gardens. Lanterns—encased in globular, multi-colored parchment shades—shimmered like rainbows among the plants and lit the path to the castle's arched doorway.

Mordecai heard the gates latch behind them in the distance, fighting a sense of dread. Taking one last taste of the outside air, fragrant with flowers and alive with the gurgles of miniature streams and waterfalls, he stepped across the threshold behind the crippled man into a candlelit hall where everyone waited to be led upstairs to the gala room. Sheep for the slaughter; or perhaps more like sheep for the shearing. They would be left unharmed, after all.

He clenched his teeth beneath his mask, hoping all would go smoothly. If he was caught, he would throw himself on an ammut before any connection to Lynora could surface.

It would be his atonement: a quiet death, to restore her life.

Their guide called it the Flower and Willow Hall.

The dome-ceiling room belied the gothic appearance of the castle's exterior. The comforting scent of lavender numbed the senses. A soft amber glow decked the walls where candles flickered in sconces of copper-wired ivy—the brassy metallic tone matching the makeup that hid each girl's true identity. The marble floor had been sorted into four sections by dried greenery that was bundled and tied with colorful silks. Shadow and light danced in fluid reflections along the polished tiles, as if water glazed them.

In each of the sections three to four neophites stood, directing their donients to sit on pillows. Noticing the deck of cards in one neophite's hand, Mordecai assumed that these were the separate levels of entertainment. He searched for the dancers, his gaze distracted by the rich palate of silk party gowns—each a different color, each a different design. The only consistency was their golden faces and black hair, or rather, wigs. Each woman wore the same style—braids clacking with beads that matched the embroidery and lace of their individual costume.

His gaze stalled on one neophite in the furthest corner beside the south door, standing alone and looking lost. A lyre's empty case gaped open against the wall behind her. *Lynora.*

She was so beguiling; mysterious yet lovely in a gown of dusted peach embroidered with hues of green thread and lace which shimmered like jeweled frogs hidden in the folds of the fabric. A wide emerald green sash draped the empire waist—tied in the back—complimenting the jewels on her neck cuff. The lower half of the gown hugged her closer than was proper, showcasing her curves.

His body responded to the vision with a resurgence of hardening discomfort. How splendid that womanly shape had felt against him earlier in the tunnel. When she'd been about to leave, he was going to allow it; to surrender to goodbye. But she'd reached up to kiss him one last time, and he could resist no longer. He'd pinioned her to the wall and wrapped her legs around him so his fingers could find their way past the waist of her trousers, touching that intimate part of her he'd never breeched.

A growl smoldered in his chest at the memory of how her eyes, at first widened in shock, surrendered to heaviness as she became drunk with passion. In that moment, the walls had finally broken down between them. He felt it in the way the moans shook the back of her throat—such unladylike sounds, yet more feminine than anything he had ever experienced. He felt it in her trembling body as he held her in his arms to absorb the aftershock. Tasted it in the rapturous tears running down her cheeks.

To have shared the experience with his virginal bride was more exhilarating than the first time he flew above ground as a spirit. He had brought her to ecstasy, and now owned a small part of her that no other man would ever have. His gloved fingertip touched the mask over his nose and lips, remembering the scent of her arousal, the flavor of her appeasement. It had taken all of his will-power not to give in and claim her fully at that moment.

But he wanted to make love to her with premeditated leisure and tenderness, without dreading the appearance of his blasted fangs. He wanted to swathe her in romance and poetry, so she would know it for what it was in his heart: his eternal devotion and loyalty through the summation of their beings. Monogamy and fidelity. That is what he wanted to offer. An eternity of it. Anything less would be unworthy of her. Somehow, he would find a way.

Returning to the present, Mordecai cursed under his breath. He'd lost sight of her. His attention tracked the crowded Flower and Willow Hall. In a distant corner, two other sisters wore similar styles as Lynora, albeit differing colors, and danced seductively for the men seated before them on pillows. His stomach sunk. Every other neophite donned traditional dresses, the skirts wide with crinolines and petticoats. The body-clinging fashion set Lynora's group apart as dancers. He had driven her to this . . . battling her shyness so she could pilfer blood from a roomful of strange men.

His guilty conscience was eclipsed by her reappearance as he saw her stepping out the side door into a dark hall. No one else noticed, so he made his way behind her at a distance.

Devoid of torches, the corridor lacked the warmth of the Willow Hall. Up ahead, Lynora spoke to someone in hushed tones. It sounded like a man responding. Following them up a flight of stairs, Mordecai heard a rhythmic thump with each step they made.

The hem of Lynora's gown vanished through a doorway. Mordecai paused for a moment then eased open the door enough to sidle within the room, latching the lock behind him without a sound.

While Lynora whispered to her companion and struggled to light a candle, Mordecai ducked behind a velvet screen in the corner. He caught the scent of myrrh on the air and realized her guest was the man of earlier—his crippled, bat-slandering acquaintance. It occurred to Mordecai he had never even asked the man's name. He had been too annoyed by his one-sided view of the world.

The room illuminated. Next to the candle's halo, Lynora's metallic-gilded face and painted eyes glimmered like an exotic arabesque come to life. Mordecai's gaze intensified on her companion. His fangs nudged his lips as he wondered what sort of sins might flavor a crippled man's blood.

CHAPTER 24

Lynora struggled to calm her heartbeat. The scars at her neck pounded. What if she was sensing Mordecai's departure? He should have left before now. Perhaps he had found something in the underground room that held him up. Still, at least he would soon be safe.

That's more than she could say for herself.

The excuse she gave to the other two dancers bought little time. How long could it take to find a 'misplaced' lyre, after all? Were someone to explore the corridor, they would find her instrument right where she left it, wrapped in a velvet cloth and propped beneath a table. She could only hope they would be too busy entertaining their donients to notice her absence.

If she were discovered here in the Luminary Hall entertaining a priest . . . what would her punishment be? Worse, what would *his* be?

A full body shiver shook her to her toes.

"Are you all right, Lady Starling?" Father Lucien removed his domino mask.

Lynora sighed, grateful to see his face. When he first motioned to her from the corridor outside the Willow Hall, she hesitated. Only when she glimpsed the distinctive cane on his elbow did she recognize him and leave the gala so they might talk.

Without the mask, he looked like himself again, short of the powdered wig. His strong forehead and tender, angelic features opened up and eased her discomfort.

"We do not have much time." Noting how he favored his lame leg, she directed him to a cushioned chair. "Tell me why a man of the cloth would enter a den of harlots."

The moment she said this, Lynora thought she heard a hiss from the far corner of the room where a velvet screen cast shadows on the wall.

She waited but heard nothing else, other than the whisk of satin as the father wrapped his cape around his torso to sit.

His gray eyes reflected the candlelight. "Well, a certain lady once told me that the town's conceptions of this palace were misguided. Or was I misguided to believe her?"

Turning her back, Lynora meandered toward the two arched, stained-glass windows against the east wall. Her slippers scraped the pebbled tiles where jade, white, and lavender designs glistened like mosaics in the firelight. She stopped at a table centered between the windows to plunge her hand into a bowl filled with multi-colored marbles. The slick, glassy feel of the orbs between her fingers cleared her thoughts.

She considered a response. She should tell him she lied. That they were in fact prostitutes. What better way to make him leave and never return? What better way to protect him?

But her pride could not bear the words.

"You have no answer, then?" The father's voice held no blame, only concern.

Lynora spun around to study him. Her braided wig clacked with the movement. "You have yet to answer me. Why are you here?" The mist must have lifted outside, for bright moonlight diffused the stained glass from behind her, dotting the father's olive skin and the opposing wall with variegated colors and shapes. In any other circumstance, she would have been awestruck by the splendor of the vision. It was as if a hundred luminaries, lit with prismatic flames, cast patterned groupings about the room.

Father Lucien lifted off his top hat and wig. The signature wayfaring lock of hair dropped over his forehead. His fingers raked it back and rubbed his scalp. "This wig is infected with parasites, I'm sure of it. I must wonder how many are latched onto me at present." He smoothed down his hair. "Least I shan't lack for company."

His half-smile appeared and filled Lynora with a new surge of worry. He was too good to be here. Too kind to get caught up in these happenings. She could not have him being drained of blood tonight.

"You aren't one for small-talk, are you?" The father held her gaze.

Her mouth clamped tighter.

"Ah." He untied the cape, allowing it to fall from his broad shoulders and conform to the chair's back. "I see I'm to get nothing out of you until I account for my presence."

She raised an eyebrow.

He propped his elbows on his knees and clasped his hands. "Truth is . . ." Long lashes fanned his cheeks as he studied his feet. "I've been praying for some means to come to you. I have something important to discuss." His attention toured the room, followed the colorful lights on the wall. "But it is nigh impossible to break through a fortress such as this." His focus returned to her and she wondered if he was referring to the castle, or the walls she had erected around herself.

"When the invitation to the gala was delivered to the Viscount this morning," he continued, "it was as if God's very Hand placed it in mine. I saw the Gwyndolaire seal pressed upon the envelope. Heard Viscount Cummings discuss the event with the deliverer. When we were alone, I reprimanded him for partaking in what was rumored to be a night of carnal pleasures. I scolded him so fiercely that he turned over his invitation to me in ransom for his guilty soul. He never suspected I planned to use it myself. To find you."

Another sound—like a smothered snarl—came from somewhere

in the room. Lynora supposed she imagined it, so shocked to hear Father Lucien admit to such deceit. She moved to stand before him. "Is it not considered sacrilege for a priest to trick one of his flock?"

The half-smile returned. "Ah. But he is not of my flock. I told you, my parish is in London. And besides this, I did it for his own good. His wife was quite perturbed upon the delivery of the invitation. I intervened to save the marriage—the church's most sacred institution."

Lynora clasped her hands together. Her gown's full sleeves fanned across her abdomen and draped down to her shins. She remembered her own husband, his promise to be watching her tonight through some mystical means. Every moment spent alone with the priest was putting the man's life in danger from all sides. Mordecai's protective predilection was not to be trifled with. Should he perceive the priest a threat, he would kill him. Holy or not.

"Forgive me for my brashness, Father, but could you please get to the point? We are both in grave danger being alone in such a way."

"From whom? Who is holding you here, *Lynora*?" He stood upon saying her name and caught her hands between his.

She gasped. "What did you call me?'

"Lynora Dureance. I was right to suspect that there was some fantastical story behind you're being amongst these—women. I pray to God you are not like them. That you only faked your death."

His final words clung to her ears, sucking at her courage like leeches. There was no underplaying the accusation behind them. "How do you know my name?"

The priest released her hands to pluck a small brass cylinder from his pocket. Candlelight reflected off the shiny, polished metal. "Isaac asked me to give you this." He pressed the chilled brass into her palm. "It is a kaleidoscope, though a very rudimentary one. It needs a stone within the holding to present the colors within. I gave it to Isaac a while back. He sent it with me tonight. Said you would understand the significance of such a toy."

Moisture drained from her mouth. Isaac knew she was alive? But how?

As if hearing her unspoken question, the priest answered on his way over to the bowl of marbles. "Yesterday. You were there to see about him. I didn't realize it of course. Though it struck me odd when you said his name."

The marbles clapped against one another, animated by Father Lucien's fingers as he dug through the bowl. He drew out one orb—a swirl of half red and half white. "You almost had me convinced that you overheard Miss Plum call out to him. But while we were standing outside, when you had cried much of your makeup off, I thought I recognized you. Then Isaac confirmed it. Sometime after you left, the maid went upstairs to tuck the children in and found him gone. Since it was twilight, I went seeking him, worried for his safety. I barely made it over the footbridge before he came running my direction from the other side. Apparently, he'd snuck out and followed you to the burned remains of his cottage home. I took him back to the orphanage where he verified my doubts. He had recognized you, just as I had."

Closing his fingers over the marble, the father took the brass cylinder from Lynora, his soft, warm hands grazing her skin. "You are so cold. Is that why you tremble? Perhaps you should sit."

Lynora shook her head. She needed her footing, if nothing else. Questions swarmed her mind and the room rocked around her. Isaac had followed her last night without her even realizing? And why hadn't Mordecai mentioned his brother's presence? Had his all-seeing eye missed that detail?

"It's not too late for you, Lynora. I do not know what has brought you to this place from the day I saw you at the Egyptian Hall. But I suspect this is the first time you've ever partaken in such a . . . gala." The father flipped the cylinder—hollow on one end with a lens on the other—and nestled the marble into the open side, fastening it with a hinged clamp. He leveled the lens with Lynora's eye and coaxed her to look within.

Scarlet fireworks met her gaze.

"You can turn away," his whisper cloaked her face in the scent of myrrh. "Reclaim your innocence before all is lost." On a twist of his fingers, the marble shifted from red to spotless white, altering the starburst of color.

Lynora's heart ached. If he only knew how much she had lost already . . . the inconceivable murder she would've had to commit to reclaim it. "You gave Isaac this kaleidoscope?" She pulled back and struggled to steady her voice, desperate to take control of the conversation.

"When I first came to the asylum weeks ago, he wasn't speaking. They said the entire time he had been there, he hadn't said a word. I tried to reach him—tease with him, read to him—in hopes to see a smile or melt the frost in his eyes. But he wouldn't respond. He just sat and ate and slept."

Tears ran lines through Lynora's maquillage, but she could not stop them. It hurt too much to think of Isaac imprisoned inside himself in such a way.

"Then one afternoon," the father's gaze followed the droplets where they clung to Lynora's jaw before dripping to the floor, "I took this out to look at it," he touched the cylinder, "and it was as if a window opened in the boy's soul. I told him I bought it in London, showed him how it worked. Then he started to jabber like a bird freed from the confines of a cage. I could hardly keep up with his stories. He has quite the imagination. He intends to be a great explorer one day. To travel the world."

Against an excruciating bought of nostalgia, Lynora tightened her hand on the toy.

The priest tapped the glossy brass with his fingertip. "Isaac wanted me to ask you if you are queen of this castle. He wanted to know if that's why you haven't returned for him."

A tearing pain sliced her heart. She doubled over and fell to her knees. The father cradled her elbows to steady her descent, kneeling with her.

"Please," Lynora cried, "please tell him for me . . . how much I love him and miss him. Please tell him . . ." Meeting the father's gaze, she choked on the profound discernment in his eyes. "Tell him I never intended to leave him. I—I had no choice."

Father Lucien's expression softened. He lifted a finger to her cheek and wiped away some makeup. "Your tears are like ice water. And you are so pale under all this glitter and glint. It's as if you're drained of blood and nourishment." Concern furrowed his brow and he braced her shoulders. "You should tell Isaac yourself. Come with me tonight. Leave this place and your unholy benefactress. I know what it's like to lose someone you love dearly. Do not put him through that again." A pained line etched across the priest's forehead—the residue of a tortured memory. "I don't care what you've done; nothing is so unforgivable that you should have to die to the ones you love. The ones who love you. And he does, Lynora. The little lad needs you. You are his family. Come back to him."

"It's impossible," Lynora whispered.

"No. Bishop Lauden is coming to Tatabury tonight to pick up another afflicted child from the asylum. Tomorrow, I am going to insist he take me with him to London. I want to visit the orphanage's other sick children that have been under his care there." He paused, his jaw twitching. "Why don't you and Isaac go with me? He would love the trip. It is only a few hours in the carriage. You can make a new life for yourselves in the city. And I will be available as a friend, to guide you. I know your husband is dead. That you feel alone and abandoned. But I shall help you find work, a means to live, so that you can take Isaac away from the orphan house. There is too much sickness there. Though he seems untouched by it, I dread that he must bear witness to it any longer."

Lynora freed her chin and covered her face with her palms, trying to ignore the throbbing ache in her scars. Thoughts of being around Isaac, around the scent of any child's sweet enticing blood, tormented her, pierced through her gut like a red hot poker. "I would do nothing but put him in harm's way. Let him be a child. Let him live happy. Free from the atrocities on this side of the world. I will not expose him to it."

Father Lucien tugged at her wrists, opening her face to him. "To what? The Lord gives us each an inner voice, and yours is telling you that you don't belong here. You need only listen."

Jerking from the priest's grasp, Lynora leapt to her feet. "No. The Lord no longer counsels me. He abhors my kind. You can't possibly understand. You are a sainted man of God." Lynora tried to look away, but the father caught her ruffled sleeve.

Lynora heard another hiss somewhere in the room, or perhaps the pop of a candle?

With his elbow banked on the chair, the priest pushed himself to stand, recouping her attention. "I've only been a priest for eight years. Before that, I was a *Bow Street Runner*. I served under Sir John Fielding as a detective. Our troop raided gaming houses, quashed riots, hunted elusive criminals. I have seen my share of sin."

Lynora balked. She would never have suspected he'd had such a past. He seemed so docile, so celestial.

"Due to my father's success in the troupe, I was hired as one of the youngest detectives," he continued. "Started when I turned sixteen. I suppose, to thrive on bedlam at such a tender age, theories and postulations tend to take over my imagination at times. But I don't believe I'm imagining what is taking place in this castle tonight. That there are creatures walking among us."

Lynora's pulse slammed in her temples, making her dizzy. "Whatever do you mean?"

"I sense evil in this place. An evil I'm intimately familiar with." His gaze swept the floor. "The last case I had as a runner revolved around the Dewstone Theatre on Piccadilly." As he spoke, he started to tap his cane on the floor in a nervous gesture. "Set designers and thespians alike had reported sightings of a dark devil in the rafters."

Lynora chewed her lip, trying to contain her panic.

"That case was personal to me," he continued, "as my sister was an actress there. I feared for her safety, though chose to keep my investigation quiet. I now realize I should have told her everything." Anguish swept over his face, quickly replaced by determined lines. "Some said the devil would appear in the midst of a white haze, that his eyes glittered like gold coins in the darkness, proof in their minds that he was from hell. With its locale next to a dinner-club, the building was often overrun with roaches. But upon the appearance of this . . . apparition . . . the infestations ceased to be. One bystander from the street reported watching a wave of bugs pour from an open window once—as if someone cast out a bucketful of black water. This led me to study Egyptian lore, as I remembered reading something similar as a youth . . . something in their mythology."

He hung the metallic cane over his elbow as if to stop his nervous fidgets. "There was an ancient Egyptian civilization that rose up from Necropolis, the city of the dead—spawned by the bite of bats. They were given directions on the walls of their tombs—hieroglyphics that pointed them back to the world of the living. But to stay, they had to slaughter humans, and drink the blood of their victims. It was said that the earth itself, nature itself, rejected the race, disdained them. The sun would torch their skin to fry," he fused her gaze, eyes alight with a feverish spark, "and insects were repelled by their very presence."

Lynora almost gagged, feeling as if someone had poured sand down her throat. "Why would you put any bearing in such macabre fairytales?" she stammered, trying to buy time.

A sidelong grin turned his lips, no longer charming for its cynicism. "Because men record similar stories all over the world. From the orient, to Greece, to the European imperials."

Lynora attempted to conjure her hypnotic gaze but his line of sight flitted to the stained-glass windows behind her. The colors danced across his face, distracting and perplexing.

"How can something rooted in beliefs that are shared by each and every race be discarded as mere fairytales?" When he stopped gazing at the windows and focused on her again, he squelched her inner fire with his next observation. "You were able to face the sun at the orphanage the other day. So, I deigned you and the Gwyndolaire ladies pure. But I saw something tonight . . . a swarm of gnats avoiding one of your guests on the walk here . . . which has made me question my judgment."

Lynora's breath hitched, not even curious as to whom the priest spoke of. For it was her life that hung in the balance now. Father Lucien seemed to know everything. Why didn't he simply kill her? What was he waiting for . . . validation?

"In Jewish demonology," he watched her, "there is a prostitute demon that glides through the night, searching for the innocent— children, and babes—thirsty for their pure blood. She is called Lilith. In lessor known lore, she disguises herself as a governess, a nanny. The children call her Nanetta. Does that name ring familiar to you?"

Lynora slapped away tears. "You think Mother Nenet is responsible for this heinous crime upon the children? That this gala has something to do with that? No. I have been beneath her guidance for months . . . I would have seen signs. Are you to accuse me next?"

The obstinate crease between Father Lucien's brows softened. "I would like to think you are removed from all of this. Your concern for Isaac seemed genuine. In fact, you remind me of my sister the last time I saw her. Your age, the color of your hair. Your virtuous nature. I believe that's what drew me to you at the museum upon our first meeting." He shifted his bad leg, stroking his cane's handle. "It had been eight years since I'd lost her, that day I saw you on the steps of the Egyptian Hall. I'd chosen to visit there to try to make peace with it all. An attempt to understand what went wrong the night I set out to capture the theatre's demon. The night I set out to prove he was indeed a malevolent being." The priest's eyelashes folded closed. "The night I killed my sister."

CHAPTER 25

Upon Father Lucien's confession, Lynora clenched the kaleidoscope until its hinges bit into her palm, torn between sympathy for his pain and fear for herself. "I cannot imagine you being responsible for anyone's death."

He shook his head. "I had the brilliant idea to climb into the rafters and wait for the apparition. He was rumored to arrive after sunset, so I settled in my hiding place a half-hour before. He appeared right on cue, across from me on the other side of the oil-lamp chandelier. When I realized he was watching my sister below, I feared for her life. I leapt toward him . . . thought to use the candle fixture to spirit me across. A foolish move. The chain was rusted through and the brackets yanked from the cathedral ceiling with a deafening squeal. I fell alongside them, and my leg was pinned beneath the apparatus. I laid there, helpless, as oil ran from the lamps and flames lapped up the paths. The painted wooden sets, the lavish fabrics and stage curtains, everything combusted in a matter of seconds." His jaw twitched. "I lost consciousness to the sound of my sister's cries, unable to even see her for all the fire."

Lynora stared at the candle's flickering flame, letting it paint a glare upon the back of her eyelids to blot out the compassion she felt for a man who might very well be her enemy.

"I came to believe in God that night, Lynora. As when I awoke, I found myself lying outside the inferno that was once the theatre, and had no explanation as to how I got there—as to why I was the only survivor. I suffered a few minor burns and scrapes . . . and the crushed left leg. But my sister . . . she was so badly burned they found nothing but ash." His voice cracked. "I went into the priesthood—penance for my part in her death. Though I have never been able to get past the guilt. So, when the chance came to help these children, I asked for the opportunity to serve."

Lynora wanted to comfort him, but had to hold her features devoid of emotion, still unsure of where she stood. "You came so God could prove that goodness still resides within you, the goodness I see each time I look in your eyes. He will not disappoint."

Staring at her, peaceful resolution smoothed his features. "Perhaps not. For I believe I was sent to save you as much as those children."

His hand heated her wrist where he still held her sleeve tight.

"Would that it were so simple, Father. There is no salvation for me now. No other side. No hope. And for your safety, you must leave and never return." Hearing music begin downstairs, Lynora started for the door. "They will be serving the food now. I know a way you can slip out while everyone's distracted."

Grip tightening on her sleeve, Father Lucien turned her to face him. He took the kaleidoscope from her hand and tossed it to the chair. "I will not leave without you."

"What?"

"If you can yet be saved from this unholy lot, it is my duty to escort you out. As I told you once," he finally freed her sleeve and smoothed the wrinkles in the silk, "I am not your confessor. But I am here to help. First, I must know if you are in league with the women of this castle. Could you hold this?" He held out his cane.

Puzzled by the strange request, Lynora took it—musing over how lightweight it felt despite its metallic appearance.

"Do you find it unwieldy . . . bulky?" he asked, closely observing how she handled the walking stick.

Lynora narrowed her eyes. "No . . . should I?"

"Hmm." His fingers disappeared within his vest pocket, seeking something.

Lynora had just tightened her grip on the cane, ready to defend herself, when in her peripheral, two round lights appeared alongside the colored reflections on the wall opposite her. The scars at her neck surged to a screaming throb. Discernment rushed along her spine, as brisk and startling as a glacial mountain stream.

It couldn't be. Mordecai would never have made it in past the gates.

But then, this *was* a masked ball. And she had given him the means whereby to veil his scent.

In one quick shift, the flashing lights panned to the priest's chest and then his neck, lighting his carotid artery. Before Lynora could turn and seek the source, Father Lucien drew out his hand and held up something shimmery.

A mirror.

Taken by surprise, Lynora's eyes locked upon her reflection. The cane slipped from her hand and rolled away, but even its clank on the floor failed to break the mirror's spell. She whimpered, unable to free her gaze, seeing her flesh molded and decomposed, flaking off, piece by piece. She tried to shut her eyelids against the ghastly vision, attempted to rub her face to assure it wasn't real, but her body betrayed her—frozen against all efforts to move.

A snarl drifted over the screen in the corner like a deadly fog. "Drop the mirror."

Jolted, Father Lucien lost the trinket to the floor and Lynora's trance shattered with the glass. Her insides felt scored—scraped and raw. Her legs weighed heavy as she turned in front of the priest to face the tall form which skulked from the shadows. Mordecai's powerful frame appeared even more intimidating in a red domino cape and Venetian mask. He tugged at his gloves and crossed the room in four strides.

"You . . . ?" Father Lucien's acknowledgement of Mordecai caught Lynora off guard. She glanced at the priest over her shoulder, still hazy and tottery from the mirror's effects. It was all the distraction Mordecai needed.

In one silken move, he swept Lynora into the chair. The cushions hugged her while the kaleidoscope jabbed her in the hip. Mordecai caught Father Lucien, fingers clenched around the priest's jugular. He dragged him to the wall, lifting him so his feet dangled.

"You needn't concern yourself over Lynora's abandonment, *Father*." Mordecai's angry voice resonated over the priest's guttural struggle for breath. "I am her husband, merely *partly* dead, mind. And I'm not going anywhere. Most sacred institution and all that rot."

Lynora eased her shaky limbs from the chair as Father Lucien wrestled for his life. With his good leg, the priest managed a sharp kick, tagging Mordecai in the gut, an adroit move obviously perfected in his runner days.

It took Mordecai by surprise, but he countered and maintained the upper hand. His hold tightened around the priest's neck. Father Lucien gripped Mordecai's wrist in a vain attempt to escape.

When the priest's complexion shaded to deep purple, Lynora came to herself enough to leap onto her husband's back. "Mordecai, no!" She secured an arm-lock around his expansive shoulders until her feet swayed free of the ground. She grunted, straining to hold on as she worked free the naturlege from her wig with her free hand. "Let him go." Her lips skimmed Mordecai's nape. "He is a priest."

"A squall of sin rattles behind that collar, Lynora. I suspect there is lust for you hiding in his blood. What say I have a taste and see?"

Lynora tightened the arm crooked around Mordecai's neck. She nudged the wooden points in place until they puckered his throat, knowing they would be ineffective against him. "Put your fangs away, Mordecai."

"Your healing stick can't hurt me. And this man suspects what you are; he was holding a mirror to you."

"It was a test. No doubt he's heard that an infected soul shows no reflection. He doesn't realize what my mind would go through to reach that state. He would never have done it otherwise. He's my friend. And he's been nothing but kind to your brother."

Mordecai snarled. Muscles tense, he guided the father to the floor in an unconscious heap. Then he wrenched his arm around to help Lynora down from his shoulders.

Tucking her pin in her hair, she crouched and found the priest still breathing. "You are fortunate." She glared up at Mordecai. "Had you succeeded in killing him, you would be no better than the Reapers that terrorize our backstreets."

He appeared taken aback by the statement. "They are only serving our society."

"I realize they are the sole means to the survival of Nocturnus. But I can never condone what they do. How can you? What they take so heartlessly. It is rape. It is rape of a spirit and murder of a soul, regardless if the victim is a degenerate or not."

He shook his head and eased into the chair. Though she couldn't read his face for the mask, his eyes held pain enough to betoken a roomful of grieving people.

She hated to have been so blunt. But a Reaper had changed Wren, and among her sisters, at least three others had been mistaken for someone on the feed list but somehow managed to escape. There was obviously a flaw in the Desmodai precepts.

Still, she hadn't meant to put Mordecai in such a category. He was far from a Reaper. He was merely a citizen in Nocturnus. Merely trying to survive.

Father Lucien started to stir. Looking into his tender, gray eyes, Lynora did the only thing she could think of. She thought upon her and Mordecai's interlude in the tunnel when he had brought her rapture with a touch of his hand. Then she pinned her fiery gaze on the priest, forbidding him to remember anything of this night, coaxing him to sleep. His head bobbed forward and his eyes snapped shut. Being her first attempt, she was pleased how well the hypnosis had worked.

"We must get you both to the tunnel." She waited for Mordecai's response. He still appeared wounded by her earlier statement. "Come, Mordecai. Help me. The music has ended. Dinner is over, the blood-letting is underway. We have little time before the others realize I'm gone and come up."

In a silent fugue, Mordecai stood and hefted the priest over his shoulders. Lynora snatched Father Lucien's cloak and covered him. Then she lifted his cane. After pressing her ear to the door, she released the lock.

The door flung open against her, thrusting Lynora back. Heron and Raven stood at the threshold with pinched mouths. Lynora's mind raced as Mother Nenet appeared behind them, the velvet that once covered Lynora's hidden lyre crushed to her chest.

"It is as I said." Raven spoke first.

"Starling, explain yourself." The Mother's painted lips tightened.

Arm braced across Mordecai's chest, Lynora eased back into the room with him, searching for an explanation. "I—I . . ." She gulped then gestured to the priest with his cane, "I thought he was Viscount Cummings. I fear the walk up the stairs was too much for him. He fainted. I asked this man to help me carry him down." She and Mordecai exchanged glances. Candle light glinted off his silver mask.

"Foolish girl! No one is to separate from the others on this night. I told you I would help with the Viscount." The Mother's bird-like eyes narrowed at the priest where his face peeked out from the cloak. "I do not recognize this man. He's not the elderly Cummings. How did he get past the—"

"What is that?" Raven stepped over the threshold and pointed to Mordecai's neck. His cape, drawn open by the body balanced across his shoulders, exposed the rose wreath and grounding collar for all to see.

Lynora caught the flash of Mordecia's eyes at the same time Raven did.

"A *Desmodai*!"

"Capture him!" Mother Nenet's command echoed in the room like thunder.

Lynora lunged forward with the cane but Raven's kick to the lungs doubled her over. She dropped the walking stick as her breath caved in on itself. From her peripheral she could see Mordecai step toward her. "No! Run, Mordecai!"

Her husband flung Father Lucien into the chair and sprinted for the windows, losing his Tricorne hat. The fallen cane rolled beneath his feet and he slipped into the crushed glass, winning cuts which would heal in moments. Heron and Raven tackled him before he could regain footing.

Raven held her ammut to his throat while Heron cinched his arms behind him, pressed iron handcuffs in place over his gloves, and forced him to kneel.

"Please Mother," Heron's voice quavered, "have mercy. Allow Starling to leave the room."

"Ha! She should bear witness." Raven pressed the iron points harder against his jugular, her eyes aglow with fury. "Tonight will be her salvation. The rest of us must go on in misery until the day we die."

Still struggling to breathe, Lynora clutched the mother's sleeve. "Please," she fought back a sob, "I beg of you. Send us both away. I will live with him in Nocturnus." She spoke the words like a warrior, though her courage floundered at the thought.

The mother jerked away to stand over Mordecai. "He has broken too many Decretums to be released. But for you, Starling, as you are a daughter to me, I will grant him one last request. Do you have one,

Desmodai? And stop flashing your eyes. Such spellbinding has no power over me." Splaying her gloved hands, she reached up and dragged her own ammut from her chignon. Raven opened his shirt to expose his chest for Mother Nenet's deadly blow.

Lynora felt the pierce to her heart as if it where her own flesh waiting to be gutted. "No! He has goodness within . . . I-I have seen it." Her gaze met her husband's for an instant and gratitude transmitted through his blue eyes, though a pained hopelessness soured the sweetness of the connection.

"The Brotherhood never looks beyond the veneer of their sinful victims when they make their feed list." Raven glared at Mordecai. "They kill anyone they deem evil, never once peeling away the layers to see if goodness lies beneath. So why should we offer them such mercy?"

Lynora tried to rush at Raven, only to have her feet swept from beneath her by the mother's swift reaction. Her knees hit the floor and a shattering throb shot into her thighs.

"Enough." Mordecai growled. "Stop hurting her. I shall submit. All I ask is that you remove the scarf tucked in my waist band. I believe it is yours." He directed this to Mother Nenet.

The mother shifted her stance. "Raven, assist him."

As Raven drew out the beaded panel from his waist, Lynora shoved herself to sit up. Why did Mordecai have the mother's favorite scarf?

A muffled hiss came from beneath her husband's mask as he looked at Mother Nenet. "I know of the secret you hide, *my lady.*"

"Do you now?" She smiled, a wretched, hate-filled smile. "Desmodai, you have a strange way of convincing me to let you live." Her tone iced with ire. "Remove that mask from his face. I want to look upon him as he dies."

"No!" Lynora tried once more to throw herself in front of him, but Heron caught her and held her down.

"Close your eyes, Starling," she whispered, a cool rush against

Lynora's ear. "It will be over soon. And you shall be whole again . . ."

Whole? She'd never be whole again.

Sobbing, Lynora clenched her eyes, hatred for the mother and Raven burbling up within, joined by hatred for herself . . . for her inability to rise and take on the entire Sisterhood and the Agnate. This was wrong. All of this killing was so wrong.

Memories of her and Mordecai walking the hills with Isaac's hands held between them rose up from a sacred place in the past, surfacing like a double-edged sword to slash her most tender hopes. She'd been a fool to think they could ever find some way back to happiness in this warped reality.

Tears wet her hands, slimy from where they smeared her made-up face. Her throat felt like a rock, hardened to hold back her sobs. The silence seemed to go on forever, broken only by the rustle of the mask slipping away. Then a sharp yelp forced Lynora's eyes open.

CHAPTER 26

Mordecai's mask dangled from Mother Nenet's gloved fingers, her scarf pooled on the floor at his knees. His face was bared for all to see. But there was no gash in the flawless skin of his chest.

Raven held the iron prongs at his neck steady, confused by the mother's reaction.

"Cornelius?" Mother Nenet backed up to the door, staring agape at Mordecai.

Mordecai squinted in disbelief. "You knew my father?" He tried to break free but the cuffs prevailed. "Do you know where he is?"

Mother Nenet appeared to be in a trance. "The resemblance. I never . . . expected . . ."

Heron and Raven both watched the mother in bewildered silence, waiting for her instruction.

Seizing her opportunity, Lynora shoved Heron away and leapt for Raven, catching her wrist and pinning her ammut to the floor despite the ache in her knees with each movement.

Mordecai fought to free his arms but Heron had regained footing and clamped his head in her crooked arm, lifting it so his chin tilted upward. Veins bulged in his neck.

Raven outmaneuvered Lynora and caught her neck in a vise as well. Lynora struggled to catch her breath, twisting her lower body to try to break the hold.

"Release him." Upon the mother's command, everyone stilled. "This man's blood will not be spilled at my hands." Mother Nenet kept her face turned away, unable to hide the tremor in her voice.

Man. Lynora turned the word over in her mind. The mother had called Mordecai a man. Not a monster.

Heron drew back and got to her feet.

Raven reluctantly freed Lynora, spitting in her face.

Wiping the spittle away, Lynora sucked air through her strained windpipe. She pointed to the chair. "The other man . . . he is the priest I told you of." She stared at Mother Nenet. "He came . . . to apprise me of Isaac's welfare."

Mother Nenet's shoulders tensed.

"Please," Lynora pleaded, her hand cradling her throat. "Let him leave as well. I hypnotized him. He will remember nothing."

With her back turned, the mother waved her approval. Heron helped Raven to her feet and forced the younger sister from the room, leaving Lynora, Mordecai, and Mother Nenet alone.

Lynora crawled to her husband, swept aside the mother's fallen scarf, and caught him in her arms, drawing him close. She inhaled the scent of roses at his neck, tasted his lips with a swift kiss.

"His handcuffs . . . I need the key . . ." She turned an imploring glance to Mother Nenet.

"There is a latch which will release him," the mother answered, her back still turned. "With their weakness to iron, there has never been a need for a lock."

The moment the cuffs clicked open, Mordecai caught Lynora against him in an intense embrace. "My guardian angel," he whispered. "My wife."

So relieved to have him alive, Lynora nuzzled the crevice of his neck beneath his chin, felt his stubble at her forehead as he uttered the words over and again. *My wife.* His fingers tangled in her hair—a tender, possessive gesture.

From outside the doorway, Mother Nenet pivoted on her heel. "I received the missive from your Regent Ezra. I understand he's considering giving Lynora a place on the Desirable list and a tour of Nocturnus, contingent upon certain . . . factors."

Lynora noted the mother's avoidance of details, and wondered what she'd meant by *factors*.

Stroking Lynora's hair, Mordecai nodded. "The Agnate has granted her permission to visit Nocturnus during the Liminal Ridotto celebration—a preliminary to citizenship should she decide to stay. If things go as planned, I'll send the carriage in four nights."

Mother Nenet glanced at Lynora. "It is your choice, Starling. It is your eternity. What do you wish?"

Lynora stiffened. One side of her wanted to stay. But another, darker side—the part of her that still loved Mordecai—wanted to visit his underworld. To disprove her nightmares and witness how he lived now. "I wish to see it. But beyond that . . . I can't say."

The mother's eyes narrowed. "This is highly unorthodox. Such a thing has never been done. Once a neophite is in Nocturnus, they are led to realization and remain there forever."

"Well, her situation is highly unorthodox so it bids some leniency." Mordecai ran his fingertips along Lynora's neck where Raven had left marks. "She is my wife. Surely you can find it in your . . . *heart* . . . to give her some rope." An unspoken exchange flickered from the mother's eyes to Mordecai's as she appraised the scarf he had picked up. He tossed it to her.

She caught it, fondled the beaded fabric with reverence. "I only hope you do not hang her with it." Her jaw clenched beneath her maquillage. "I could tell the Agnate of your presence tonight. Ezra would surely withdraw his generous offer. And you would face the sun by dawn."

"I had my reasons for coming," Mordecai retorted. "Just as you do for your choices. Now secrets bind us. Such decay is better left entombed, lest it infect the innocent around it."

Mesmerized by their strange exchange, Lynora wanted to scream out for answers. But she was exhausted. Emotionally spent. And her thoughts were too heavy and tangled to pick apart.

"Your carriage will stop outside the gates." The mother sighed. "And Starling will come to you. If any of your kind stray onto my grounds, I will have my sentinels kill them. And you will die as well, regardless of your parentage."

Mordecai's head snapped in agreement. Lynora frowned again at their cryptic negotiations.

"I am sure you have already been missed." The mother focused on Mordecai's grounding collar. "You should leave immediately. I do not want brood runners sniffing at my castle walls. As for you, Starling. . ."

Lynora shivered under the mother's scrutiny. Mordecai's strong arms tightened around her, assurance he wouldn't leave her to fight alone.

"In my heart, I believe you belong here—in the world of goodness and light. But for the preservation of this castle and our lifestyle, you must decide where your loyalties lie, once and for all. In four nights, you shall make your choice. And it will be final."

With that, she was gone.

Mordecai drew Lynora up as he stood. His dazzling smile lit the room. "You have permission."

Lynora's palm grazed his stubble. So ecstatic to have him alive—beast or man—she even found herself admiring his fangs.

"Do you know what this means?" He caught her hand and pressed it to his lips. "No sneaking out. You can bide the entire night with me. We'll finally have a honeymoon."

Lynora couldn't bring herself to share his enthusiasm. In a mere twenty-four hours she had gone from wanting to kill her husband, to saving his life twice. And now to be a visitor in Nocturnus. "How did you do that? How did you convince her? And her scarf . . . where did you get it?"

"Lynora." He stroked her face, trying to center her attention on him. "There will be time enough for such questions later. I must leave before your benefactress changes her mind and opts to kill me and any chance we have to be together."

Nodding, Lynora helped him situate the priest on his shoulders again. "You will take care of him? He is my friend, and Isaac's as well."

Mordecai rolled his eyes. "I will secure your priest on his horse and lead them to the footbridge at Haven's Creek. It's up to the mare to find her way back to the asylum after that."

"That's all I can ask of you." Lynora handed him the cane.

His forehead crinkled upon grasping it in his gloved hand. He struggled to hold it off the floor. "This is so cumbersome . . . how does he use it to aid in his walking?"

Lynora took it back, lifting it high as if it were a feather. "Of course . . . it must be hollowed out wood, inlaid and lined with pure iron. He was testing me with it."

Scowling, Mordecai rearranged the priest's body on his shoulder for better balance. "Well, isn't he the devious little holy man?"

Lynora smiled. "Not so little."

Mordecai glared at her.

Her cheeks warmed. "In *courage*, Mordecai. He's very resourceful, and adept at protecting himself as well. Such a man would be a wonderful guardian for a child." She bit her lip, wondering why she hadn't considered it before. "Isaac has wanted to return to London since that day at the museum. I would like to see him away from the sickness. And we must face that you nor I will ever be able to offer what he needs now." Her voice broke on the final sentence, forced to swallow the ugly truth herself.

Mordecai's features turned to stone. "No. I'm not willing to give my brother over to a life of hypocritical saints and duplicitous sanctimony."

Hearing the hurt behind his response, Lynora opted it was too soon. Mordecai needed time to consider the rightness of her idea once he was nestled in his home underground. His undead life had been threatened twice over the past twenty-four hours, and he still had to make it back into Nocturnus without being noticed; he couldn't make such a monumental decision until he finally felt safe.

Having tucked the cane in the back of the priest's cloak to keep it from touching Mordecai, she led her masked husband and his holy burden downstairs. The guests' mortal blood had already been drained and was shut within vessels to veil the scent. The crowd of men slept in the Flower and Willow hall—deflated puddles of masks and costumes. Lynora winced as she passed them. She was glad to have missed the ritual, at least this time.

The donients would wake on their own in an hour or so, unconscious of any trauma to their bodies due to their hypnotic induced euphoria. The Gwyndolaire sentinels would serve the prepared dessert to replenish their bodies, then the men would be sent home, where they would reminisce their night of erotic pleasure, each filling in voids of memory with his own sordid imaginings.

Relief swept over Lynora upon realizing her sisters were already upstairs in their rooms. In the morning, she would withstand glares and chides enough for a lifetime. But at this moment, she needed solitude to absorb it all: Mother Nenet's reaction to Mordecai and their new covert alliance, her own change of heart toward her husband, her upcoming stay in Nocturnus, Isaac's knowledge of her existence, and the plague at the orphan house. Too much to make sense of on a weary mind.

Once within the entry hall, Lynora opened the doors. Mordecai resituated the priest on his shoulders, lifted his mask, and moved in for a kiss. His tongue's gentle possession of hers stoked anticipation for the love-making yet to come. "Four nights," he murmured in her ear. He then turned to step between the sentinels and into the darkness beyond.

Lynora shut the double doors and leaned against them. *Four nights.* Such a short time until she sailed on the river of blood and sins.

PART III: LULLABY

"A simple child, that lightly draws its breath,
And feels its life in every limb,
What should it know of death?"

~William Wordsworth

CHAPTER 27

Mordecai drifted through the halls of the orphanage. He had already checked downstairs, found nothing out of the ordinary. Now his mist blended with dust motes, drifted by windows where moonbeams infiltrated the seams of heavy drapes. Sylphlike, he eased from room to room, suffused in a smoky haze between the cracks of doors, hovering over the sleeping children in search of the familiar blonde hair.

In the back of his mind, Lynora's words taunted him. *"Have you ever smelled a child's blood, Mordecai? It sings to your heart."* He kept his distance from the drowsing orphans, just out of reach of their scent. The thought that he might endanger these innocent children tormented him, made him cautious.

Earlier tonight, he had endured the Reaper's Oath Ceremony, finally earning freedom to go topside alone without his collar. At the moment, he was to be hunting victims for feed. But he had taken a slight detour from his assignment. He held himself accountable to Lynora and Isaac above all else. Never again would he place his or Nocturnus' needs over theirs. Had he been so conscientious in the beginning, none of them would be in this predicament.

He would not let them down this time.

Upon entering the last room, he found three beds within, only one being occupied. Mordecai took form silently next to it. Reverently, he slumped into an armchair to watch his brother. Moonbeams gilded the boy's glistening blonde hair and long lashes. On his plump face, a smile turned his mouth to a half-moon in his sleep, and he looked just as he had when he was a babe—like a cherub.

The sight warmed Mordecai's icy blood. The boy had grown . . . changed so much in the short time since he had last seen him. The ache to touch him, to stroke his hair like he had every night of Isaac's seven years, nigh undid him.

Back in his mortal past, Mordecai spent a lot of time with Isaac when he was a toddler. But as Isaac got older, to feed and clothe his growing brother, Mordecai had started to garden from dawn until dusk, and only took Isaac with him occasionally. By the time he returned home at night, Isaac's governess—whomever she was for the week—often had the child already tucked abed. So while Isaac slept, Mordecai would sit and watch him sleep for a half hour or so. Then, he would go into the cellar to conduct his experiments in solitude.

He had missed out on much of the boy's youth—had planned on making that up after he and Lynora married and had a babe of their own. Planned on working less in the cellar and spending more time with his family.

That was all lost now. Never would he watch his own child sleep. Never would Isaac have the chance to teach a little nephew to capture tadpoles, or a niece to blow the tufts from a dandelion. And never would Mordecai watch as Lynora donned the vestments of motherhood, the budding ornamentation of their love that he knew would have become her to perfection.

He had pondered his vision of Lynora in the rose grove with the small girl over the past two days. And the more he thought upon it, the more he saw a resemblance between them. Had he been seeing a future that could never be? A taunting echo of his heart's deepest longing? Unquenchable remorse bruised his soul—a contusion so black and raw, he could not move for cringing beneath the tenderness of it.

Finally, forcing himself to stand, Mordecai prepared to translate again. He hadn't seen anything out of place here. Had found no clues that could shed light on the cryptic illness. No signs of other Desmodai. Now he felt a pull to leave. He couldn't bear to be so close to his brother and not hug him—talk to him.

Leaning over Isaac, he allowed himself one last indulgence. He tipped his palm across the tuft of hair that stood straight up from the child's forehead. The notorious cowlick. Mordecai grinned at the feathery rush when the strands reached toward him as if magnetized.

"Goodbye, Isaac. I hope one day you can forgive me." The words were nothing more than air, but he needed to spend them. He would never have the chance again.

Much as he'd tried to ignore it, Lynora's suggestion about allowing the priest to raise Isaac made more sense each time he thought on it. After experiencing the Wisdom, seeing firsthand the abuse some children endured, Mordecai could not deny that Lynora was right. His brother deserved a stable future—somewhere other than Tatabury. Mordecai would have to look past his petty jealousy, let the child go with Father Lucien, despite the fact that the priest had obvious feelings for a married woman—no matter how much Lynora denied it. She was simply blinded by his pristine collar of white.

But that had no bearing. Lucien also cared for Isaac. That was all that mattered.

As Mordecai drew back his hand, Isaac's eyes popped open and a muffled yelp cut the silence of the room. Panicked, Mordecai started to mist, but Isaac leapt from under the covers and threw himself around his legs, breaking his concentration and sealing him to his corporeal form.

"You're alive!" The cherubic face burrowed into Mordecai's thigh.

Mordecai nearly crumbled, grateful they were the only ones in the room. The warmth of the boy's breath, the wetness of his tears—such a soothing salve for his soul. Bent over, Mordecai held him, arms absorbing the sweetness of the embrace. He smelled sunshine and dirt, and just a hint of boyish sweat . . . the essence of his past.

"It's not a dream." Isaac's head turned from side to side against Mordecai's leg. "It's not a dream. You're back!"

"Shh." Mordecai eased into the chair again, perching Isaac on his lap. "You musn't wake the house." He wiped the boy's wet face.

Beneath his glistening lashes, Isaac's sleep-filled irises were the lavender-blue of hibiscus flowers. "Lynora said you died. But I knew you'd come back. I knew you would. Miss Plum—she said it was a dove in the tree. A good omen, she said. She was right." Tiny indentions stamped the plumpness of his cheeks.

Mordecai tweaked them with a finger. How he'd missed those dimples.

"You smell funny, Mord." Little fingers traced Mordecai's lapels. "And where'd you get these dandy clothes?" Isaac scoured his drowsy face with his palms then tried to refocus. He planked his hands on Mordecai's shoulders for balance.

Mordecai slanted his face out of the moonlight. "I – I bought them."

"So, we're earls again?" Isaac's instant smile turned sour. "Wait. Where have you been?"

"Somewhere far away." Mordecai clenched his jaw. "A place only grownups live."

"The pillory?"

Mordecai laughed quietly and tickled Isaac's ear. "Such an imagination. Though, I suppose, some might consider it a jail of sorts." Lynora did. But he hoped to change that.

"What bad thing did you do . . . to go there? Did you steal?"

Mordecai gulped at the knot in his throat. "No. I . . . I made a rash decision. And there were consequences. We must all pay the consequences of our choices, yes?"

Isaac's forehead crinkled. "Lynora is in the castle now. The one with the foreigners. Is that where you were?"

Mordecai shook his head. "No, but I have been to visit her. She's doing fine. She sends her love. Thinks about you every day."

Tears seeped along the edges of Isaac's lower lashes. "Then why did she break her promise? Why did she leave? She came to talk to Lucien, but didn't visit me. She left. Why?"

Mordecai shut his eyes against the guilt. "She was feeling shy. Yes. Afraid you would laugh at her new clothes. Her made-up face." He opened his lids to gauge Isaac's response.

The boy swiped his lashes. "Is that all? Girls are so bumble-headed. I wouldn't have made jollies. It was queer, though. Made her . . . made her look like someone else. You know, like when people wear costumes."

Mordecai feigned a grin. "That's it. It was a costume."

Isaac tilted his head, sizing up the explanation. "So . . . that's why she wore the paint on her face?" His warm weight rocked Mordecai's knees as he resituated his legs. "Should've seen her, Mord. She looked like a bloody statue, she did."

Raising a finger, Mordecai touched his brother's mouth. "Isaac. Do not use such language. Where did you learn to talk like that?"

"Oh, you'd be surprised what I've learned here. I try to be good. I do. But sometimes . . . well, sometimes I just slip. Miss Plum says it's the bad fluent of others." Isaac's features melted to such a penitent wince, Mordecai nearly laughed out loud.

"Influence, Isaac. So, who scolds you when you slip?" He had to be sure his brother was being treated properly.

"Miss Plum. She sends me to Lucien . . . I mean, Father Lucien."

"And what is your fitting punishment?" Mordecai asked, half-teasing, half-fishing.

"Hello Marys. And . . . and kissing the beadery."

Stifling a grin, Mordecai corrected, "'Hail Marys and kissing the rosary?"

Fingers clamped on Mordecai's shoulders, Isaac leaned forward, his countenance somber. "Tis what I just said."

"So . . . this Lucien ever beat you with a whip? Trop you on the noggin a time or two?" Mordecai shuffled his palm across Isaac's unruly hair.

Isaac laughed. "Nah. He's my friend, a priest. He even gave me a kaleidoscope. I sent it to Lynora."

Mordecai smoothed Isaac's bedgown sleeves, cupping his elbows. "Ah, yes. I believe I remember seeing it."

"Not so nice as the one you gave me. That one burned in the fire, I venture. It had the finest sights within."

The boy had no idea. Mordecai curled his mouth to a tawdry grin, remembering this morning when he saw Lynora's naked body in full view through the lens. He was getting better at zoning in on the present with his visions . . . and he had also improved with controlling the impromptu appearance of his fangs as well as perfecting the potency of his hypnotic gaze. At times he feared was getting entirely too adept at being a Desmodai.

"So, I should get my things, then." Isaac broke loose and slid off Mordecai's knee to pad across the room, his bedgown's hem swishing at his shins.

Hunched in the chair, Mordecai couldn't move for the sudden weight in his chest.

His brother knelt beside a stubby trunk. "Won't take me long. The viscount gives us all uniforms." He wrinkled his nose as he opened the lid. "Don't much want to keep the knickers and lace tackies. But I have a lawn shirt and breeches. And boots. Suited for travelling." He dug through the clothes, his back turned. "How far is it to the castle? And where are we to go from there? Father Lucien says London is fine this time of year. In fact, he's coming back from a trip there tomorrow." Still scrounging in the trunk, Isaac yawned. "I should leave Lucien a note I think, to say goodbye."

Groaning inwardly, Mordecai knew what he had to do. Hated himself all the more for it. "Isaac, I need you to look at me now."

"Just a till. My boots are under my bed." The boy crept like a caterpillar, his nose nearly grazing the floor. He yelped suddenly, holding up his finger. A bead of red balanced on the tip. "A splinter, Mord. Can you get it out for me?"

Mordecai sat plastered to his seat. Mortification stiffened every limb. Lynora's warning butted against his thoughts again and his entire body quaked. He had to leave ... had to escape before he became a raving demon and killed his brother.

But just as he stood to translate to spirit form, he paused. He couldn't smell Isaac's blood at all. He braved stepping closer, still scenting nothing, even standing over him. He leaned down, managed to free the splinter ... and nothing.

Isaac's wound healed instantly once the splinter was gone. Satisfied, the child started to dig under the bed again.

Mordecai watched in silent retrospect, baffled by the queer experience. He couldn't possibly be immune to children's blood; it must be only Isaac's—perhaps tied somehow to his physical oddities. Whatever his father had done to boost Isaac's healing and immunities was nothing short of a radical. Mordecai would consider it more later. But for now, he needed to grill Isaac for information, and there was only way to do it without traumatizing him.

With a sigh, Mordecai ignited his silver gaze to settle on the child's nape. "Isaac. Turn around. Look at me." He utilized a tone that had always made Isaac snap to attention in the past.

Sitting up, the child tipped his chin.

Mordecai locked him into his flashing gaze. Seconds later, when Isaac collapsed to the floor in a trance, Mordecai placed him gently atop his bed. "I'm going to ask you some questions, Isaac. Do you understand?"

The boy's glazed eyes blinked in acknowledgement.

Mordecai's heart withered like a parched fruit on a vine. He hated resorting to this, but knew no other way. "You have seen the stigmata?"

Isaac nodded.

Mordecai settled his hands on either side of the mattress. "Were there any smells or voices . . . anything you can remember?"

Isaac's long-lashes fluttered as if he sought the answer in his mind. "The mist. It smells like you. And it sneezes."

"Sneezes?"

Isaac nodded, then started to struggle beneath Mordecai's arms. "Make it go away. It has glowing eyes." He shivered. "Glowing eyes that burn my brain . . ."

With a swift sweep of his hand, Mordecai shut his brother's eyelids. "Sleep now, and bear no heavy dreams."

Isaac went still. Within a matter of seconds, he snored softly.

"I'm so sorry." Mordecai pulled the covers to his brother's plump chin and kissed his forehead. "Live your life and be happy with the priest. Forget I came tonight. Forget the horrors of the stigmata. But don't ever forget that Lynora and I love you." Cursing, he slapped at his tears as he reluctantly eased away.

He refolded the clothes in the trunk to leave the room as it had been.

One last time, he glanced at his drowsing brother, then dispersed to mist, siphoning out onto the backstreets to keep his appointment with death.

Upon registering his quarry count at the Feeding Faction, Mordecai dropped off his final victim and hurried to catch the next gondola, too exhausted to incorporate the mist again. For once, he wanted to take the slower route like a mortal.

If he knew Augustus and Florentia at all, they would have some sort of celebration planned at his sanctuary chamber. A gathering of friends to congratulate him for finally being a free man. Or monster. Whatever the case, Mordecai had to disassociate himself from all the sins he'd experienced tonight and from the anguish of saying goodbye to Isaac, or he would be miserable company.

He had made five captures. Despite the cloud upon his soul, he did savor this slight victory. His prowess as a Reaper was now proved. Now Ezra could not go back on his vow to let Lynora come for a visit. Mordecai had set the record for the most quarries brought in by a single captor in one evening and refuted Drakkarh's doubt in him.

Stepping into the small boat, Mordecai gave the gondolier gargoyle a handful of coppers. "To my home, Horroc."

Mordecai settled at the stern and leaned against the cushioned seat. Dark water lapped at the hull, a soothing rhythm.

"Have one stop first . . ." The gargoyle's hoarse, hissing voice shattered the moment. "Delivery in slatturns." His spiny fingers gestured to some boxes nestled in the gondola's bow.

For half a second, Mordecai considered getting off and walking. But he was too weary from hunting—emotionally drained after his visit with his brother. "Just make it prompt."

Horroc nodded and the boat shoved off the margin to skim the canal's surface, guided by a long pole.

The gondola rocked beneath Mordecai and his eyelids surrendered to an aching heaviness. Half-dozing, he thought upon Lynora. It was selfish of him to want her here. He knew this. But every hour she spent topside cost a portion of her life. Like an hourglass exhausting every last grain of sand, she would one day run out of time. And he would be left in the world alone. He couldn't have her pass into death without him.

He considered her suggestion that he could become human again by killing his Mentor. He'd hated lying to her about not knowing his Mentor's identity. Still, in his heart, he knew she would never want him to kill a friend. And Augustus was a true friend, though if Lynora's suspicions were true, Augustus had withheld crucial truths. In which case, Mordecai would confront his Mentor before this night was over.

Mordecai's eyes snapped open on a jolt as Horroc docked the gondola outside the slatturns, turning the boat's bow too sharp with his pole. Mordecai focused on the luminous flowers embedded in the tunnel walls to settle his stomach.

"Heh. Sorry . . . rough stop." Horroc's gruesome lips lifted to one side.

Mordecai appraised the drop-off to his left where the canal was restrained by a stone lip two feet above the water's surface. From there, the craggy barricade fell on a swift decline and opened to a cavern in the uttermost depths of Nocturnus. Even at this distance, the stench of dampness and limestone suffused all other smells. Sounds, eerie even to the undead, drifted up from the cave. Hisses, cries, and laughter—too harsh and guttural to be mistaken for mirth—intermingled with singing, loud and discordant to the ear.

At the cave's entrance, the glow from within—a sanguinary hue made by stained parchment lanterns strung along the wall—presented an ambiance of threatening gloom. Combined with the dripstones that hung from the cave's ceiling like fangs, the opening resembled the mouth of a leviathan viper in strike position.

The only way to access the slatturns from the docking post was to take a steep-descending stairway. A copper gate and a gothic wrought-iron fence encrusted with moss guarded the stair's entrance. Two torches flamed on either side to light the steps.

Three other gargoyles appeared at the margin. Horroc tossed over the bow line which they secured on a rusted picket protruding from the pebbled ground. With Horroc's aid, they dragged the boxes from the boat. One of the wooden lids slid off. Before the gargoyles could reposition it, Mordecai noticed glass vials—each filled with a dark liquid—cushioned on a bed of straw. Preoccupied with his own thoughts, he closed his eyes, crossed his arms behind his neck, and settled deeper into the seat.

From behind, the pebbled walkway scraped beneath the gargoyles' feet and the copper gate creaked. "Be back . . . Master Reaper." Horroc threw the promise over his shoulder and they descended the stairs.

"*Master* Reaper. Is that so?"

Mordecai's head jerked up. He frowned as the face of Zebulon glared down at him. All he needed. A confrontation with the previous top Reaper; the man he had just defeated with his impressive quarry intake. Mordecai wondered why the scorpion had crawled out from under his rock in the slums. "Zebulon."

"The name," the Reaper's thick eyebrows slanted down, "is Zeb, lad. Least to my friends. Only my enemies call me Zebulon." The frosted tips of his full beard and moustache glistened in the torch light.

"What the hell do you want, *Zebulon*? Come to request a recount? I assure you, the numbers are correct."

Picking up the gondola pole, Zebulon leaned his muscular frame against it and turned his fingers through the white streaks that tipped his waist-length braid. He stifled a cough. "Don't care anythin' about numbers, lad. The proof is in the Reaper's ability to disown the guilt and motivations of another. It's hard, aye? Who do ye pity, after all? The victim, or the offender, who is a victim in his own right, so often. Ye've sucked back five today, so I would say at the moment," he grinned, revealing his gold-plated incisor, "yer feelin' a bit torn up by the paradox of the Wisdom." Yellow eyes glistening, he winked.

The reminder burned like acid in Mordecai's veins.

"Ah, I can see ye overestimated yer abilities. The test of a true Reaper is to know when enough is enough. Why do ye think I stop at four, arrogant bastard?" Zebulon sniffled. "Like I said b'fore, ye aren't cut for this. Why don't ye go back to being a mortal and stop stealin' my shadow?"

Mordecai tilted his head. "Go back?"

Zebulon laughed then bent over to control a hacking cough.

Silent, Mordecai mused about the Reaper's condition. Desmodai were immune to illness. Come to think of it, Zebulon's skin wasn't nearly so pale as an undead's should be. He actually had color to his cheeks, appeared almost . . . feverish.

"Yeh, go back. Kill the one that claimed ye. Drink his heart. It will even give yer little bride her humanness again."

Mordecai stared at the Reaper. So, it wasn't a rumor. Lynora had been right. The muscles in his jaw compressed like a vise.

"Aw. Let old Zeb help." The Reaper's lips—a soft pink as opposed to their typical deep red—tweaked on a smile. "Ye want the secret of forgettin'? Have a swig of this."

Before Mordecai could pull back, Zebulon had positioned an open vial beneath his nose. A heavenly aroma drifted up to snag him— salted-sweet and metallic. Every hair on his neck, arms, and legs stiffened to wire. His mouth watered, and his tongue nudged his lips where the tips of his fangs made indentions.

His gut screamed foul-play, but he couldn't listen. And he couldn't see, anything but the sweet, dark promise swirling within the vial. He had never smelled anything like it. It . . . sang to him. Luring him like a siren's call. His muscles corded in his arms, daring him to reach out and grab it.

"C'mon now, lad. See how it entices ye? This can counteract the Wisdom, guaranteed. Ye'll ferget it all. Be as a child again."

Dizziness spun Mordecai's head; his lungs flattened as he tried to hold his breath, tried to regain control.

"One taste, lad. One taste and ye'll know paradise."

Lost to his desire, Mordecai plucked the vile from Zebulon's hand. His tongue ran the rim, seeking even a droplet to sample, but there was none on the outside of the glass. Just as he started to tilt his head and toss the liquid into his gaping mouth, he heard a voice over the sounds of the slums.

A voice he hadn't heard in almost seven years.

So shocked, he lost his grip on the open vial and it plunged into the canal.

"Clumsy bastard!" Zebulon sneezed.

The vial's spell over Mordecai was broken.

Frantic, Zebulon plunged into the water. The gondola rocked. Oblivious to the water's spray coating his body and clothes, Mordecai clenched the side for balance and looked toward the slums in the direction of the familiar voice. At the entrance of the slatturns, beneath a long, jagged dripstone, he could make out two people: one, a man with his back turned; the other, Florentia.

Why was she at the slums again? Who was she arguing with? It sounded strangely like—

Before Mordecai could finish his thought, the man turned to reveal a profile so familiar, Mordecai jolted in disbelief. The spastic movement toppled the gondola and dumped him into the water. His flailing arms tangled with Zebulon's, dragging the Reaper with him into the dark, chilled depths.

CHAPTER 28

Augustus grinned as he opened the door from inside Mordecai's sanctuary chamber. "Whatever happened to you? You look as if you've been wrestling a water serpent."

"Where is Florentia?" Mordecai swiped at the wet hair pasted to his forehead. A quick scan of the room revealed only Evan and Krig. They sat on the couch, the gargoyle showing Evan his latest glittering finds.

Krig looked up with ponderous eyes. "Master . . . wet?"

"Yes, Master's bloody wet. Where is she, Augustus?" He faced his Mentor's consummate European features. "I assumed she'd be waiting here at my chamber with you. To congratulate me?"

Evan stood then brushed past Augustus, seizing the conversation. "Good eve to you, too, old chap." He straightened his vest lapels. "The nerve . . . ignoring me. It isn't as if I wore your ugly mug for two solid nights to keep the brood hounds off your back. Had you been one day later, I'd have had to attend the damnable Reaper's ceremony as you. It would've been my head being removed in lieu of your collar."

Mordecai nodded a hello. "And I've already offered my eternal, undead gratitude. What more can I do?"

"Destroy that treacherous face leech. How's that for starters?"

At Evan's reminder, Mordecai walked over to the desk. Hidden deep in the top drawer's recesses, his mask stared back at him from within the folds of a damp cloth.

Evan touched his face and shuddered and Krig whimpered something about mummers while clumsily gathering his treasures.

"I must keep it preserved," Mordecai answered Evan, "in the chance we should need it again." He rewrapped it within the cotton cloth he'd earlier moistened with rain water. The thought had crossed his mind that perhaps the man he saw in the slatterns had somehow stolen this mask, that his face was an illusion. Now that theory was negated.

If only he could have had a second glance, but when he had resurfaced from the water, Florentia and her companion were already gone.

Moisture drizzled into Mordecai's eyes. He slapped it away. "For sanctum's sake, could one of you get me something to dry off with?"

"Aye, I'll do you one better." Evan opened Mordecai's armoire and drew out a neck scarf. "Perhaps some nice, clean trappings can soothe your ill-humor." He held up a lacy, high collar shirt the color of raspberry cordial along with a pair of black, form-fitting breeches. "They say you only feel as good as you look. And you, my fellow, look like a drowned bat."

Upon laying the clothes across the couch's rolled arm, Evan brought the scarf over to mop Mordecai's brow. He took measure of Mordecai from his mud-caked, squishy boots to his slimy trousers and lopsided square-cut coat. Stopping at Mordecai's up-turned collar, Evan scraped away a film of moss with his fingernail. "Officially a Reaper for barely a day, and this is how you treat your uniform. Shameful, Mordecai. Truly shameful." He clucked his tongue.

Augustus chuckled.

Mordecai jerked the scarf from Evan and wiped his face and neck. "You want a real laugh?" He peeled his wet clothes away and replaced them with the dry ones. "I just saw Florentia at the entrance to the slatturns. How funny is that?"

Neither of his companions cracked a smile. Mordecai felt a sick ache in his gut when Augustus plopped onto the couch in a daze, nearly crushing Krig's arm.

Krig screeched and gathered up the last of his stash. "Naughty fiend . . ." he whimpered. His scales became transparent. "Naughty big-bones. Fat fiend."

"There, there, Krig." Mordecai called him over.

The gargoyle tottered to Mordecai, his scales reappearing. He latched onto Mordecai's lacy cuff and sobbed. "Krig rumpled. Krig flat and rumpled."

"Hmm." Mordecai held out the gargoyle's wrist to appraise his 'wounds'. "Evan, I believe Krig's injuries merit compensation. I've a bag of sea-glass at the Solarium. Would you mind taking him? Let him pick out a handful." He glanced down at the trembling creature. "Any color you wish, Krig."

Evan dropped a beaver hat atop his reddish-gold hair. "Why is it always me that gets booted over the fence?"

Frowning, Mordecai motioned to Augustus with his chin. Their friend had buried his face in his hands, fingers clenched through his hair as if to hold his emotions intact.

"Ah." Evan took the gargoyle's elbow. "Off we go then, little deviling."

"Master kind." Krig's airy voice drifted over his shoulder as they left. "Master goo—"

The door latched shut.

As he dressed in silence, Mordecai turned things over in his mind. He couldn't tell Augustus who he thought Florentia was arguing with at the slums. Not yet.

"You must confront her, Augustus." Mordecai's fingers strummed his thigh. No matter how he tried to steady it, his voice sounded hollow and cynical within the confines of the chamber. "Perhaps you can get through to her this time."

"How?" Augustus's hands fell from his face. The pain in his gaze cut gashes in the air between them. "She is a thespian, Mordecai. Tis what she does. She utilizes her expertise and conducts her life as on a stage. When I asked her to come here for a celebration tonight, she said there was a rehearsal for the theatre piece she's to perform at the Liminal Ridotto tomorrow eve. I gave her the benefit of the doubt." Tears raced down his cheeks. "Such a fool. She wraps her lies in clean linens and I willingly accept them as truth. I suppose I should be grateful. Whatever she has found, it has made her happy again."

"But it's a temporal happiness . . . you said yourself. She's gone at any hour, and when she returns—or worse, you find her elsewhere— she is another person altogether."

Augustus nodded. "In the mindset of a child, it would seem. An innocent, blissful child."

Mordecai blanched at the statement. Had not Zebulon used those very words tonight? *You'll be as a child* . . . And the shipment of vials the gargoyles delivered; they were identical to the one Zebulon had offered him—he hadn't realized it then, but he did now. Isaac said something about a sneeze. Hadn't Zebulon sneezed tonight, before Mordecai was distracted by Florentia? And what about Lynora's description of children's blood? Whatever was in that vial had indeed sang to him.

What the hell was going on? There was a connection. Zebulon and Florentia both were part of the puzzle, as was the orphan house. He worried Lady Nenet might be involved upon his finding in that room in the tunnel, and he suspected the man Florentia had been arguing with held the key to solving it all. Which terrified him above all else, considering who he suspected the man to be.

Mordecai piled his wet clothes in the corner. "There's something you should know, Augustus. I believe there is a substance being peddled in the slums to counteract the effect of sin. I fear Florentia has stumbled upon it."

Augustus raised his brows. "An intoxicant? No. For centuries they have tried to sell such things. It's nothing more than wine and opium. And it never works. Our composition is different than a human . . . immune to opiates or alcohol."

"I believe they may have stumbled onto something effective this time." He couldn't yet tell Augustus any more than this. He wanted to be sure.

Crossing his ankles, Augustus became thoughtful. "It does make sense. Florentia is happy for a blink, then, it's as if the delirium wears off and she falls into the muck again, even lower than before." His face tightened. "If this is true, then already she is a slave to that elusive euphoria . . . afraid to live outside it."

"We have to find out who's supplying it."

"Yes." Augustus leaned back on the couch so the arm supported his neck. "What is to become of my beloved?" He positioned a hand over his eyes. "Rethink it, Mordecai. For Lynora's sake, reconsider bringing her here. She is a gentle soul like Florentia. Should she come to realization, she might suffer the soul sickness just the same. Then we will have them both to worry over."

Glancing in his mirror, Mordecai frowned. He didn't want to admit he'd already come to the same conclusion, that his friend might be right. And now, with this new wrinkle, it complicated everything. Yet still, a part of him couldn't let go of hope. "How do I simply let her go, aye? When given the same situation, you could not forfeit a life with your love any more than I. You charmed and altered Florentia without a second thought years ago." Mordecai's gaze leveled on the reflection to watch his friend's reaction.

"You know that's not entirely true, Mordecai. Perhaps I charmed her into bed, but only when she was dying did I make her one of us. She was pinned beneath a chandelier. The entire building was about to collapse in flames around her."

Something about Augustus's description rang familiar, intruding upon Mordecai's inner musings. He didn't know why he hadn't made the connection before. Perhaps because eavesdropping from behind a screen inside a castle filled with vindictive neophites was not exactly the ideal scenario for functional thought. But now, he could pinpoint the similarities: Father Lucien's hair, the same glistening blue-black depth as Florentia's; his full lips almost identical in shape to her own; their eyes, though different hues, both trending to the same ponderous depths. The only difference was the name, Lucien. Florentia had always called her brother Luke in her recollections. "How long ago did you say you brought Florentia here?"

"Eight years."

Mordecai turned around to face his friend who still lay sprawled upon the couch. "You've never told me the details."

"Florentia prefers I don't speak of it. It hurts her too much to remember that night. To think on her past. So haven't told anyone; out of respect for her wishes."

"What say I give it a guess? That way, you haven't to utter even a word."

A doubtful look upon his face, Augustus shrugged.

"Every night for months, you misted into the Dewstone Theater on Piccadilly and sat in the rafters. You risked exposing yourself and Nocturnus all to watch a stunning, voluptuous ingénue you were obsessed with. Then one evening at sundown a young man sat in your place, hiding within the beams, waiting for you. In his efforts to capture you, he caught fire to the theater and nearly lost his and his sister's lives. Does that strike a chord?"

Augustus looked positively trapped. Mordecai half expected him to fade to mist, to make himself translucent enough to see the couch's design through him. "How could you know this? Did Florentia tell you during one of her spells?"

"No. I heard it from Lucien's own mouth."

Augustus swung his legs around and sat up, perched at the edge of the couch. "Luke is *here*, in Tatabury? Last I heard—"

"He had become a priest?"

Augustus shook his head. "No, I understood he went abroad."

"Well, perhaps only long enough to be ordained. Though I think he's a might too young still, to be good at his job. He appears to lack conviction in the celibacy department."

"Satan's knees, *he* is the priest from your visions of Lynora?"

Mordecai leaned against his library case, grinding his teeth. "That and the same. You pulled him out, didn't you? You saved him from that fire, even though he came to that theater with the intent to expose you . . . to kill you, possibly."

"Oh, this is ghastly." Augustus's words muffled as he raked a palm down his clean-shaved face, opting Mordecai's rhetorical questioning required no response. "To have him in such close proximity . . . this will only make it worse."

"Why? I thought it might help Florentia if she could see him again, even from afar."

"No. No. It is the loss of her human life, the guilt she lives with for abandoning her family . . . for having to make them believe she's dead. It is this that has driven her to soul sickness, not the taste of the sins. I fear it would be the same for Lynora. Were she to become one of us, she would grieve for your brother, always."

"So what then?" Sitting heavily on his ottoman, Mordecai scowled. "I'm to leave her in the care of a deluder and a traitor?"

"What are you going on about?"

"Lady Nenet, for all her saintly attributes. For all her 'thou shalt not condone a Desmodai's wicked lifestyle'. What a hypocrite."

A worried expression stiffened Augustus's features. "What have you learned of Lady Nenet?"

Mordecai snarled. He had learned plenty. In the underground room, he found sure indication of its occupant—Lady Nenet's beaded scarf. And there were all her secrets laid bare for him: a baby cradle, empty and unused; rose swags hanging from the bed posts to veil her scent; and the thick white cream—doctored with the same potent roses he had worn around his neck—that she slathered on her flesh every day in the guise of makeup. Not to mention the porcelain vessels full of blood. Those he had tasted. There was no hint of animal essence. Yet the flavor was impotent, the sins weak compared to what he experienced at each feeding with the cocktail.

Now he understood the brilliant logic behind the blood gala. No doubt it had been passed on for generations by other neophite guardians, started by their predecessor, Sekhmet. She learned to hand-pick her guests on the level of their sins, never allowing anyone to attend the parties if they harbored more than lust, lies, envy, or sloth in their hearts. Murderers . . . whores . . . rapists . . . child-beaters . . . these were filtered out.

That is why Lady Nenet's guest list was so biased. And when the donients were gone, the mother pilfered blood for her reserves before treating the remainder with animal essence for the neophites. This provided her a supply of pure human essence—sans the vilest sins. Thus, she didn't suffer like the rest of her kind. And he despised her for it.

"Mordecai. I asked you a question."

Augustus's musical voice grated Mordecai's already raw nerves. Thighs tensed, he studied his Mentor. Considering what Lynora had told him, what Zebulon had confirmed, his best friend was quite adept at keeping secrets himself. Mordecai couldn't help but wonder if Augustus might already know of the skeleton behind Lady Nenet's painted facade. "How old is Lady Nenet?"

Augustus rubbed his nape. "Her age?"

"She must be of ripe years to have inherited the castle over a century before I was born."

Augustus squirmed on the couch. "You think she's the neophite who made the deal with Monarch Cromwell? That's ludicrous."

"Is it? She knew the woman, in the least. And would have to be well into her eighties by now to have forged that relationship." Mordecai's scowl deepened as he waited.

His friend's mouth opened as if to respond, then clamped shut. Standing, Augustus strode to the library case and plucked out a dusty tome on herbal remedies. As he thumbed the pages absently, the stench of mildewed parchment reached Mordecai's nose.

"Ah, here it is. . ." Augustus pointed at a page where a drawing of a mushroom with a heart-shaped cap filled the corner. "She drinks a special tea, made of this."

Mordecai bit back his anger. "When my mother died, my father was desperate to find some means to live forever. The reishi mushroom was the first miracle on his list to try. He brought some back with him from his travels once. It did help retain a youthful countenance. Just as the fungus itself does not rot, the outer appearance of longevity can be passed on. But it doesn't *stop death*. Father tested it on mayflies and though their one-day lifespan extended to a week—they still died after those seven days. No. There's another explanation for Nenet's everlasting well of life. And I venture you are aware of it."

The pages flipped faster between Augustus's fingers.

"You will not find another alibi in the tome's leaves, Augustus. There is only one answer, and it explains why she wears gloves when she forges her iron weapons. Why she sleeps in a tunnel beneath the castle. Lady Nenet is one of us. She is Desmodai. And you've known all along. Why did you keep this from me?" He tried to stifle the bitterness in his voice, but failed.

Shutting the book with a thud, Augustus wedged his fists on the library case's surface. "To protect Nenet. We are all sworn, every Mentor and Regent in Nocturnus, to hold her secret from the Sisterhood and the common populous. I was afraid you would tell Lynora."

Mordecai moaned. There it was, straight from Augustus's own mouth. "I thought, of everyone, I could trust you. But your tongue is as black and twisted as the tunnels in this labyrinth."

Cringing, Augustus lifted the book back into place. "Please. You must understand, I am sworn. You've seen what becomes of betrayers in this place. You've seen the Agnate's form of justice. I-I cannot live like Krig. I would rather be cast into the sunlight."

A sharp twinge of empathy pecked at Mordecai's conscience, softened his anger. It wasn't so long ago he was facing such a fate . . . and Augustus stood up for him. "I need to know. Is Lynora in danger? Is Nenet bent on some sort of wicked revenge?"

Leaned against the wall, Augustus shook his head. "Not at all. I will tell you the Lady's story. But you cannot let it fall upon Lynora's ears, or anyone in the common populous of Nocturnus. Vow to me, on Lynora's life."

Mordecai hesitated. "All right, I vow I won't tell her, unless it becomes apparent that she's in danger otherwise."

Heaving a sigh, Augustus glanced at the books. "Fair enough. I'm sure you have heard that Nenet's predecessor was one of three neophite ambassadors sent over from Cairo two centuries ago. Sekhmet had arranged their safe passage along the Silk Road; when they arrived, they were to be presented as performers—a gift to the great Monarch Edward Cromwell—all in the name of subterfuge. What have you heard of the monarch?"

"I've seen his mausoleum, in the graveyard. The history books claim he was a recluse. Very private in his personal life."

"Ah. With good reason. Nenet had no predecessor. *She* came with the two other two neophite guardians centuries ago, and the trio became Monarch Edward's prized entertainers. He gave them the finest halls in his castle and in short time was allowing them to bring home 'disadvantaged' women they found on their sojourns to town. He had no way to know what these guests truly were. That they were neophites, just like his treasured dancers. Monarch Cromwell was a lonely man, you see, having no children. His wife had been barren, and died at a young age. All the years thereafter, he sat within the castle, alone . . . grieving. When these ladies came to him, they gave him hope. He allowed them their galas, never questioning their queerness. The girls all supposed he was just so happy to have a family again that he turned a blind eye to everything else." Augustus tugged at a thread on his jacket. "In time, the other two ambassadors moved on to other parts of England where they were needed. But the aging monarch had fallen ill, so Nenet stayed to care for him."

Holding his voice calm, Mordecai fought a bout of impatience. "None of that explains how she came to full realization, or why she lies."

"She is not the enemy you perceive her to be. Everything she does for those women topside is a selfless sacrifice. Each day, she chances being scorched by the sun to keep the Sisterhood from living in darkness."

Refusing to let her play the martyr, Mordecai stood and headed toward his pile of wet clothes on the floor to sort them. "It is as much for herself as anyone." He waved his dripping shirt. "She has found a way to bypass the tainted blood of degenerates. If only the entire Desmodai race could follow her lead."

Augustus frowned and wiped the stray droplets of water that found their way from Mordecai's clothes to his forehead. "It would take too many donients to feed us all . . . not to mention a mass hypnotism each and every time we require sustenance. Or would you prefer we live like vampire bats, hiding in holes and crevices, siphoning blood while their victims sleep? This is why we choose the higher road and take only the wicked, despite the grievous blow it deals our souls."

"The higher road. Not to hear Lynora speak of it. She hates Reapers. Which in essence means she hates me. And yet she worships Nenet, the true deceiver. Does it not inflame you? That woman is one of us, yet she bears none of the consequences. She lives topside amongst the colors of life, she feeds without suffering."

"She has suffered more than the rest of us in her lifetime. Allow me to finish the story. On his deathbed, the Monarch Cromwell confronted Nenet about her lifestyle. He had been watching, closer than she realized, and he knew there was something different about her and the others. When she told him the truth, he begged her to change him. He was terrified to die. Her compassion damned her. It was that one bite—the one which brought life to the monarch—that caused her to experience the Wisdom and brought her immortality as a Desmodai. The very thing that she, as a neophite, had always scorned and detested. And that man—the monarch—is our own Regent Ezra."

Numb with shock, Mordecai hung his soggy shirt and trousers over a chair back. The confession wound around his mind like molasses, blurring his thoughts.

Augustus continued. "Together, they faked his death; before the audience of the town, the monarch's body was sealed in the mausoleum he had prepared at the graveyard. You would not know, having never seen within, but there's a scarab ornamentation inside, similar to the ring he wears. A symbol of the covenant they made to one another. Nenet retreated to live in the castle bequeathed to her. In fear of hurting the mortals, she became a prisoner of her own making. On the night of his interim, the monarch misted out from his crypt, to honor the promise he had made to Nenet. He went into Nocturnus, changed his name from Edward, and became part of the Agnate; they let him in without hesitation upon hearing his story. For years thereafter, he supplied Nenet with the blood she needed to survive, until she accumulated enough neophite refugees to begin the galas again. He now serves as Nenet's contact in the underworld; keeps her apprised of all the goings on in Nocturnus. But she desires to be human, more than anything. She even once befriended a mortal man—though she kept his identity hidden from Ezra. The mortal was a radical visionary who thought he could make a tonic to cure her. But they had a falling out. He disappeared before the task was accomplished. So, you see, she is human, in her way. Ruled by empathy and grief. This is why she tries to protect the Sisterhood. She wants each of them to have hope for a normal future. The sort of future that she will never have herself."

Mordecai tensed. "But I understand there already is a cure. A way back, even for a Desmodai. She could kill the one who altered her, and drink their heart."

Trepidation shadowed the angles and planes of Augustus's face as he slanted his hip against the library case. "Where did you hear such a thing?"

Mordecai's patience snapped. He clenched Augustus by the lapels and lifted him off the floor. His eyes flashed lights across his Mentor's flesh. "No more lies . . . no more secrets! I want to know if it is possible for me to change back with your death, and I want to know now."

CHAPTER 29

A nervous tick plucked at Augustus's temples. He shielded his forehead from the silver glares of Mordecai's gaze. "Yes. It is possible upon my death for you to be human again, should you complete the gruesome ritual and eat my remains."

Mordecai's arms weakened, heavy with the duplicity of the one he had trusted so blindly. He settled Augustus on the floor in front of him, holding back the urge to smash him against the wall. "You should have told me from the start."

Augustus refused to look up. "It is complicated, Mordecai. I am sworn to protect the Mentory, above all else. For a Desmodai to return to humanity, he must murder the one that altered him, then cut out his heart, burn it to ash, and drink the powders in Bisu water. But it is a two-edged sword. The Desmodai must know beyond a doubt who his Mentor is. If he is mistaken, he shan't become human again and the tainted water will leave him a diminutive. So . . . now that you know, will you kill me, my brother?"

Propped against his desk, Mordecai shuddered. No matter how he wanted to dislike his Mentor at the moment, he would always respect and care for him. Augustus had proved his loyalty far too many times for him to cut him down so savagely.

Augustus frowned. "Now you understand why under normal circumstances, only the Agnate and Mentorship know who changes who. Why a pack of us attend the courting session. Why we put our neophites in a trance for the blood and saliva exchange. But you," he shook his head, "I couldn't do it. You were so perceptive, so interested and curious about the whole process. Of all the men I have Mentored over the centuries, none have been hungrier for the change. More fit for this life. It was as if I were leading a prodigal child into the arms of his family. I was just . . . so taken aback, perhaps a bit in awe. I wanted us to share the moment, something that would bind us forever."

Mordecai let himself slide to the floor. "So that is why you told me to never speak of my metamorphosis. You didn't wish for me to expose that you bypassed a law."

Augustus sat down beside him, his gaze turned on the door. "Yes, I went against the vows. Seems I'm making a habit of that, where you're concerned. I hypnotized you long enough to convince the other Mentors I was following formalities. But when you and I went into the depths of the thicket, I roused you again. And you remember the rest."

Mordecai didn't know who he was more annoyed with. Augustus, or himself. After all, this was the same situation he had put Lynora in. An escape made possible only by the death of a loved one. "So."

Augustus met his gaze. "So . . . "

Mordecai sighed. "Tell me something, Augustus. Were we to kill the Desmodai who changed you and you drank his heart, what would become of me and Lynora upon your cure?"

Augustus laced his hands in his lap. "It would be as if I had never been changed. You would be human again. Both you and Lynora. As would Florentia, and anyone else I have Mentored. It is a ripple effect."

Mordecai leaned the back of his head against the library case. "But you have no idea."

"None. And none would tell me, were I to ask. It goes all the way to the beginning, Mordecai. To our origins. No one knows who were the first Desmodai, so no one can end the race."

Nonplussed, they sat in silence.

"I have a proposition." Augustus finally broke the hush. "I will nominate you as a Mentor. Through your productive outing as a Reaper, you have proven you have the seductive abilities necessary for the courting. And you have honed your hypnotic prowess enough to use it even on a fellow Desmodai. You nigh had me in your spell earlier with the eye flashes. When did this come about?"

Mordecai shrugged. "I suppose with my practice in the Miseria chambers. I simply had to get angry enough to evoke it. But do you think I could be a Mentor?"

"Yes. You shall be sworn in and join the Brotherhood, and take a blood oath to follow our creed of silence. Honestly, it is the best way to keep you quiet at this point."

The burn of Mordecai's hurt and confusion began to dull. "And if they accept me, it means that I can be the one—"

"To bring Lynora to realization."

"If she so chooses." Mordecai felt a small vindication in this. Even after the Agnate had approved Lynora for the Desirable list, they reiterated that Mordecai would not be the one to change her. But going this route, they would have no choice but to let him. "What will the Agnate say?" He snorted. "What will Regent Ezra say? He hates me."

"He doesn't hate you; he's simply . . . stymied by you. You have that effect on the best of us."

"What of Regent Drakkarh?" Mordecai pressed, disregarding his companion's goodhearted ribbing. "Dare say his aversion to me is more deeply seeded than a mere clash of personality. He despises my compassion for the humans."

"Drakkarh." Augustus frowned. "He is a beast. Being one of the eldest Desmodai we have here, he's from the old-world way of thinking."

"The old world?"

"Before we had laws that bound us, many Desmodai thought we should deal with humans as we would animals. Confine them in cages . . . breed them like cattle so they would serve one purpose only: to provide our sustenance. Blood is regenerative when taken in small enough quantities; the human body replenishes its supply, so long as it's given time between skimmings. Some even suggested hypnotizing our prey from birth . . . to control their every thought, their every action. It was theorized as the only way we would no longer be damned to bear the guilt of their intolerable crimes. If they couldn't think . . . they couldn't sin. They would all be as children."

"How barbaric."

"Yes. The perfect modifier for Drakkarh. Barbaric. He has no respect for anyone but those of his ilk. Dislikes neophites and humans the same."

"So why did the Brotherhood approach someone that despicable for citizenship?"

Augustus shrugged. "Drakkarh has the gift of telepathy . . . something he perfected long before he was converted. It has its usefulness in our dealings with other Desmodai societies. But it is that very gift which prevented him from ever serving as a Mentor. His tie to the neophite's thoughts were stronger than your typical Mentor's. The Agnate feared he might be tempted to take advantage of that power with his dislike for the Sisterhood. So you see, he has little say on what goes on in the Mentory. You let me take care of Drakkarh. By tomorrow night, you will be absolved of your Reaper duties, and well on your way to Mentorship. Lynora need never know you serviced our feed list. Tis the least I can do." An apology colored the statement.

Relief flooded Mordecai. If he never had to withstand the taste of rape or murder again, he might be able to forget the memories one day, to displace the guilt. Grateful, he turned to Augustus and clasped his arm. "You are the truest friend I have here. Thank you for confessing all to me. Just so you'll know . . . you were the one I was to choose as a Mentor for Lynora, if I had a say."

A warm grin spread over Augustus's chin. "And I would have been honored to bring her over. But now, it will be unnecessary."

They exchanged smiles.

"I am curious, though," Augustus said. "Would you have truly been willing to walk out of this world? Forsake the camaraderie of others like you? Forget the power and immortality and live as a lowly human again, knowing all you know now?"

Before Mordecai could respond, the door slammed open and Florentia's silhouette broke the soft glow of luminary flowers from outside.

An orchid Greek gown with tapered hem skimmed her curves. A slip of pink taffeta peeked out from the front, embellished with glistening red rosettes. Long red gloves gilded her elegant arms to just above her elbows. She appeared to be dressed for a theatrical rehearsal all the way up to the flower-shaped ruby gems in her black, waist-length curls; but Mordecai knew better, as did Augustus.

Her slippered feet, light as a ballerina's, danced beneath her to carry her inside. She fluttered, arms lifted, reminiscent of a moth—not lighting on anything, unable to settle. When she saw them sitting on the floor, she squealed.

"What are we doing?" She plopped down; her skirts and petticoats bubbled out around her. She crawled toward Mordecai and Augustus, apathetic to the rustle of her gown's fine fabrics scraping the floor. Her hair's fallen, glossy curls dragged across her hands. Cleavage, plush and white, peeked out from the red velvet trim at her décolleté. "Are you boys playing? Can girls play, too?" A high-pitched giggle thrummed her throat, a startling and disturbing timbre when born of such a sensuous and womanly body.

Mordecai and Augustus sat mute, stunned to silence.

"A party is it? Where are all the friends?" Sitting up on her knees, she clapped her gloved palms. "A party must have friends. Did you know, I like tea parties? And I invite friends." She held her forefinger over her mouth as though to shush someone. "Though not everyone can see them." Leaning forward, she planted her hands on the floor between the men. "Only very special people can see my friends." Thick, dark lashes cast shadows on her cheeks. A crooked smile parted her lush lips. "You two are special. Can you see my friend? He is right behind us. His name is Luke."

Mordecai and Augustus exchanged concerned glances.

Giggling again, Florentia rolled over so her nape rested in Augustus's lap and her naked calves draped over Mordecai's thighs. He caught a wisp of her breath as she settled, scented faintly like the mixture in Zebulon's vial. He cast another knowing glance to Augustus then respectfully tugged her skirts to hide her delicate ankles.

She reached up and traced Augustus's trembling lower lip.

Her husband caressed her hair, his profile folded to distress. "Florentia, my beloved. Not again." His voice broke. "Where have you been off to?"

"Poor Augie," she teased. "Wants to keep me in shackles. Do not worry. I am still your pink poppet." Her gaze shifted to Mordecai. "I am Augie's darling." She held up the sparkling ring on her left hand. "And I adore him most of all my toys. Of all others . . ." Her fingers caught Augustus's hair and tugged him down. She smacked kisses all across his forehead and nose, as she would a pet, then pushed him away and whirled off the men's laps. Crawling, she crossed the floor to the couch and drew herself up to fall backwards onto the cushions.

"Luke, I'm hiding!" she screeched out to her invisible playmate. "You'll never find me now!" She pounded her hands and giggled rapturously. Her long legs flailed in the air. She wore no pantalets or bloomers—her nakedness laid bare for them both to see.

Mordecai turned from the sight the same instant Augustus jumped up to cover her indecency. "What devilry is this, Florentia! You mean to say you've wandered all about the slatturns in such disarray?" His flesh turned a deep shade of green as he held down her skirts. His other hand stifled her mouth in an effort to contain her giddy laughter. "This is not amusing! Not in the least!"

From his armoire, Mordecai plucked a pair of breeches and tossed them to Augustus who tried to force his wife's feet into the leg holes.

"Stop tickling . . ." Florentia laughed and fidgeted. "You're tickling!"

It took Augustus laying astride her and Mordecai's help to coax her cooperation. Then, just as her husband secured the breeches around her waist, Florentia stiffened in a paroxysm and her eyes rolled back into her head. A low gurgle shook her chest.

Augustus clutched the curls at her temples. "Florentia . . . Florentia!" His thumbs stoked her face. "Come back to me!"

Her lavender irises dropped into view again. A smile crept over her lips, made all the more menacing by the naiveté behind it.

Upon a raspy intake of air, she started to sing. "Lady-bird, Lady-bird, fly away home. Your house is on fire, your children will burn. Lady-bird, Lady-bird, so far have we flown. To snuff out our fires, more children must burn . . ." Her fangs emerged and she giggled rapturously, her little girl voice echoing to an eerie cackle throughout the small chamber.

A chill stitched Mordecai's spine. It was all he needed to hear. Someone was peddling children's blood in the slatturns; he had no doubt now.

He watched as a cloud, deadly and dark, crossed Augustus's face and golden light pulsed in his eyes like lightning. "We will find who is responsible for this poison. I want the bastard's heart sliced on a platter." Then Augustus knelt beside the couch, face buried at Florentia's ear, their black hair blending to coiled ribbons along the upholstery.

Mordecai covered her with a blanket as she settled to a drowsing snore. He should tell Augustus the truth. That he suspected he knew what this poison was . . .

But he couldn't.

For then he would have to admit to himself that the "bastard" responsible for harming the children topside was none other than his very own father: the long-lost Cornelius Dureance.

CHAPTER 30

Lynora leaned against the frozen pane of her bedchamber window. The prior night had carried frost on its wings, and coated the trees and gardens in white. Though cold and wilted, they shimmered beneath morning's pink haze like patches of iridescent lace.

This taste of winter would be her last image topside before leaving tonight for Nocturnus. Mordecai had told her of the Solarium he maintained, how the flowers didn't die in the under-realm. But what good were gardens that could never be seen in the light of day? Their artistry would be wasted in the moonlight.

Her heavy breath stirred dust along the window sill. The particles prompted a sneeze and she wondered: were she to become fully-realized, a daughter of the underworld, would she lose the little tickles at the back of her throat when a cough blossomed? The tingles in her toes when her feet fell asleep? Would she lose the warm spread in her chest, when something of deep beauty or emotion pricked her heart and stalled her breath? She'd read that Desmodai didn't require oxygen. She assumed this meant their hearts no longer drummed, their blood sat still in their veins, no longer pulsing. When she and Mordecai were alone in the tunnel, things were too intense and impassioned for her to validate or disprove this theory.

Mordecai appeared to still have some human qualities. But were they residual? Temporary dregs of a past that would soon be washed away, like remnants of precious wine purged from a bottle with a flush of clear, unforgiving water.

Would that be her fate? An empty, washed-out vessel . . . a ghost of her former self?

She turned to face the reminder of her upcoming tour in Nocturnus: the packed valise next to her bed and the cottony-sheer mull gown and cashmere shawl Mordecai sent two days ago, via Krig. Her husband had sent a note as well, to apprise her of the Liminal Ridotto and all that the gala would entail. She would be shown three of the largest and most spectacular chambers in all of Nocturnus. The Utopia Chamber, the Solarium, and the Vakara. He described in some detail what each chamber was used for. Only one stirred her to panic: the feeding chamber. But he assured her in the note that it would not be used for anything other than dancing tonight.

After they attended the party, they were to go back to Mordecai's sanctuary, alone. Lynora strolled to her bed. The dress draped her mattress—a splash of crimson against white sheets. A wry smile turned her lips. Hard as she tried to be annoyed at the color choice, it was just so . . . Mordecai. Nothing subtle about her gardener.

She turned the shawl's fringed edges between her fingers. The colors swirled in a paisley of reds, golds, and blacks. She stroked the gown's empire waist and billowy, elbow-length sleeves. Her fingertip traced the embroidered vines and leaves of shimmering crimson thread where they started at the ribbon-braided waistline and followed the center seam to the scalloped hem all the way around to the long train. An uncharacteristic giddiness tumbled through her at the thought of wearing this. The low-cut neckline, the cylindrical form. It had been so long since she had worn something strictly to please and entice Mordecai. The last time had in fact been their honeymoon night.

A surge of heat swept through her cheeks and neck, realizing this was the very reason Mordecai had sent it. For the past few nights, she had fallen asleep remembering how he touched her in the tunnel. How he pleasured her with his hands, encouraged her with sweet words and kisses until all her barriers came down and she cried out his name. He held her so gently as she floated back to herself, whispered love on stolen breaths between them.

Tonight, if she so chose, she would experience all of him. She wanted this intimacy—could not deny it. But if she gave him this part of her, would he hold true to his promise? That he wouldn't expect her to be his bloodmate; that they would only make love. She needed time to decide if the union of their bodies was enough to convince her to live in the under-realm.

Lynora wrapped a knitted shawl over her bed gown and crept into the hall. Barefoot, she strolled the long corridor where sunrise filtered from beneath each closed door. Her waking sisters rustled within their chambers. Lynora paused at Wren's room and debated if she should knock.

She was grateful to Mother Nenet for swearing the sentinels and Heron and Raven to silence about Mordecai's intrusion at the bloodletting gala. Why the mother was so compliant after Lynora's blatant disregard of all the rules, she could not say. Perhaps it all came back to her favoritism of Lynora. Or perhaps it was this secret Mordecai held over the lady's head—the one Lynora had yet to learn. Whatever the reason, she was indebted. The past few days had elapsed without any event. Lynora took up her tasks as though nothing ever happened. None of the sisters realized that a Desmodai had stepped foot onto their hallowed grounds. None but those Mother silenced, and, as of yesterday, Wren, because Lynora had chosen to tell her.

Wren was her best friend. She had a right to know where Lynora was going tonight. But Wren had been furious with the news. Lynora hoped today she might be feeling more gracious. She had no intention of leaving things on bad terms between them, in case she never returned.

A tap on the door brought Wren shuffling to the other side to crack it open. Upon seeing Lynora, she scowled and turned away, leaving the entrance ajar. Lynora inched within and shut the door behind her.

Wren's room was like all the other bedchambers. Sparsely furnished with a rosewood desk, chair, bed, and a trunk. The walls boasted the same creamy swirl as Lynora's. But this morning, the lit fireplace glazed the paint with rosy warmth—a merriness which clashed with the gloom weighing down Wren's features. Her silk drapes had yet to be drawn open. The sheer fabric clung to the windowpane's condensation, as if someone had splashed milk across the glass.

Lynora pinched the skin of her wrist, unsure where to begin. "I-I thought perhaps you might need some help with your maquillage." She winced. Wren would see through such a half-witted excuse.

Wren glared from beneath thick, black lashes. "Nice to see you haven't turned your back on all of your responsibilities. I should consider myself privileged to merit any of your time on such a momentous day. We can do yours first, if you like."

The bite of Wren's sarcasm was a step up from the shackles of silence she wore yesterday. "I am not to don my maquillage today," Lynora said. "To intermix safely with those of Nocturnus, I'm to look like them."

"So, am I correct in assuming you won't be accompanying us to market in Tatabury today?"

Lynora shook her head. "Mother Nenet says I should spend my time here, in meditation and sleep, to balance my inner thoughts so I'll be prepared for tonight."

Huffing her disgust, Wren secured coils of ebony hair off her face with her ammut and opened a desk drawer to retrieve a tray. It held four small wooden compacts: two carved with rosebuds, one with a soaring bat, and the last with a butterfly perched on a petal.

Unlatching the first one's rosebud lid, Wren revealed a loose, gold-flecked powder, made of copper coins melted down then ground to dust. As they sat facing one another on the pillows beside the fireplace, Wren glanced at Lynora's loose waves of hair. "To be prepared for tonight, you need your ammut. Where is it?"

Lynora opened the second rose-carved compact, scooped up clear vegetable wax with her fingers, and rubbed it between her palms in front of the fire to melt it. "The iron sticks are forbidden in the under-realm. As are the neck cuffs and bracelets. Now stop frowning, or this won't apply properly."

The aroma of pine-nut oil and cloves filled the room as her fingertips caressed her friend's flawless, chestnut-toned skin. She traced the familiar curve of her cheeks, the arch of her lips, and the sweep of her jaw, smoothing the wax along the delicate turn of her neck and collarbones. She couldn't help but think upon Wren's dark-skinned beauty, and how the bitterness within her soul would one day consume it like a canker. Why had this young woman endured so much pain and degradation in her life, only to come to this?

After applying the wax, Lynora tapped Wren's face with a fingertip to ensure it was tacky enough for the base-coat to adhere. "Ready," she said, wiping the residue from her hands on a soft cloth.

They sat in silence while Wren took a bowl and diluted a handful of the glittery powder with water. She stirred it to a thick paste and offered Lynora a flat, wide brush. Using quick strokes, Lynora applied the base. Afterward, she patted Wren's face and neck dry with a sponge, then dusted her with a final layer of glistening powder.

When Lynora sat back to admire her friend's bright, metallic mask, she caught sight of the pale wall behind her—how it clashed in contrast. She was reminded of Father Lucien's visit. How he had tried to convince her she could be cleansed of her sins and start anew—that her soul could be white as fresh-fallen snow.

The priest would be a good guardian for Isaac. In the note

Mordecai had sent, he granted her permission to let Isaac go away with Father Lucien. Though—at the time of his letter— Mordecai had yet to find anything that night help them solve the riddle of the plague, he had found something else, just as important. He had found his conscience. And when he closed his note with thoughts of Isaac, how he planned to spirit through the asylum one last time to whisper a goodbye that Isaac would never hear, Lynora sensed the anguish slicing Mordecai's heart on each sweep of ink. She envied those weeping cuts, for if she made the choice to stay in Nocturnus after tonight, she would never have the benefit of such closure.

Tears stung behind her eyelids as she opened the bat compact. She used a miniscule brush to define Wren's deep brown eyes with apotropaic paint, sweeping the paste of iron and kohl in long, winged shapes along her lower and upper lids.

On the note of closure, she worried how Wren would react if Lynora chose to leave. Her friend had already lost so much. And so needlessly. Had Wren not meandered into that dark alley, had she not found a fellow prostitute slumped and convulsing against a brick wall, she would not be here now. She made the mistake of trying to help, unaware that the woman's attacker—a Desmodai Reaper—had only just sedated his victim before being sidetracked by a sound. He'd wandered off to explore, leaving the prostitute hidden within some shadows. Her soft whimpers had captured Wren's attention, who didn't hesitate to assist. At that time, Wren, like any other common mortal, had no idea the sorts of creatures that occupied the darker side of Tatabury.

The Reaper returned before Wren could drag the woman to safety. Her telling of the tale was terrifying. She always described his face awash in moonlight and the glint of gold—like a piece of jewelry—as he tilted her chin up to bite her, then the words he said before his fangs punctured her neck, "You shall do my bidding now. *By blood or by guile.*"

For some reason, he didn't finish her. After the exchange of blood and saliva, he disappeared with his other victim in an impenetrable mist, leaving Wren a neophite.

How many times had Lynora heard Wren say that she wished he had killed her? How many times had she said she longed for an escape from this half-life?

Lynora hated that monster for what he had taken. She hated all of the Reapers. How would she ever be happy in a world that depended solely upon their prowess for survival?

Could she shut her eyes to the system? Live in feigned ignorance to the way they fed and hunted?

"Starling."

Shaken from her musings, Lynora finished her final curls of paint along Wren's temples.

"How do I look?" Wren asked.

"Perfect."

Wren took the compact from Lynora's palm and laid it on the tray. Lynora had the sudden urge to tell Wren everything she meant to her. How much she cared for her and had valued her guidance and friendship over the past months. "Wren . . ."

Wren's hand caught her wrist. "Don't dare tell me goodbye. I won't hear it. You will not stay. You're not like them. They're murderous leeches. Your goodness will repel their corruption like rain off a bat's wings. Tomorrow morning, you will wake in your bed across the hall, and together we'll train our carriers, and argue with Raven, and stand always in the light. Together."

Nailed by Wren's deep, soulful eyes, Lynora hadn't the heart to argue. She squeezed her hand. "Your lips. I almost forgot." Upon opening the butterfly compact, she found it empty. Not even a scrap of the saffron-tinted wax remained.

"Ah—yes. I meant to ask if I might borrow some today." Wren grinned sheepishly, a rare sight indeed.

Lynora smiled back. "Come then. Let's finish in my room."

Upon entering the hall, they spotted Raven exiting Lynora's bedchamber. The sister's naked face startled when she saw them and she turned for the stairway.

Wren shoved Lynora aside and caught up to their nemesis. Clutching her elbow, she twirled her around. "What were you doing in there, snake?"

A toxic smirk crossed Raven's face. She broke free from Wren and straightened the belt knotted at her stomach that held her morning robe closed. "Nothing. I merely wanted to speak to our princess." Her attention swept to Lynora. "Good morning, Starling. How do you fare today?"

Jaw clenched, Wren jerked Raven toward Lynora's room and thrust her inside. Lynora followed, shutting the door behind them.

"See that nothing is missing." Wren motioned to Lynora with her chin as she held her naturlege to Raven's neck and pinned her against the wall.

Raven started to laugh. "Please. As if she has anything I would covet."

Lynora scanned the room. Her lyre and the new gown were still in place. Opening the trunk that harbored her jeweled neck cuff, bracelets and wigs, she found everything accounted for. The valise next to her bed still held the articles she had packed. Then something caught her attention on the desk. She strolled over and touched her ammut and naturlege. She searched for the mark that differentiated them: three tiny indentions in the bend of the naturlege that only she would know of. She found the marks, but the sticks were in a different position than when she first left her room. "You moved these. Why?"

Raven laughed again.

"Answer her," Wren growled, jutting her healing stick deeper into Raven's flesh.

Snarling, Raven kneed Wren in the stomach, doubling her over.

Wren's naturlege clacked to the floor and Raven kicked it across the room. Like a flash, Wren leapt to her feet and clamped Raven's neck in her hands. In retaliation, Raven grappled for Wren's neck. Red light swirled between them as their eyes lit up. They both gasped for breath.

"Stop it! Both of you!" Lynora broke them apart, winning a scratch from someone's fingernail in the process. She rubbed her arm where a welt started to form. "Haven't we enough to worry about from the outside world without bickering amongst ourselves?"

The sisters both leaned against the wall, gulping air. They scowled at one another as the fire in their eyes cooled. Raven smoothed her robe again, tapping the lapels with her fingertips as if to ensure everything was in place underneath.

"Now Raven, what were you doing with my ammut? Answer me, or I'll find Mother Nenet and we can solve it together, the three of us."

Raven's grimace deepened. "I picked it up to look at it. I was curious why you had not packed it in your bag."

"Iron weapons are forbidden in Nocturnus." Wren frowned at Lynora to reiterate her disapproval of the law.

Raven clutched the front of her robe and smirked at Lynora. "Ah. I see you told *Wretch* that you are leaving. I'm curious, did you tell her of your discrepancies at the gala, as well?"

Lynora glanced down. "I did."

"Interesting. So why is it Mother forbade me to say a word, yet you can spout it to everyone?"

"Not everyone." Lynora studied Wren's face. "Only my dearest friend. It's my secret to tell."

Straightening her shoulder seams, Raven opened the door to leave. "Yes. We all have secrets, don't we, little princess?" From the doorway, she glanced back. "Though mine is more of a wish than a secret. I wish for you, Starling, the one thing the rest of us can ever have. *Peace.*"

Lynora's eyebrows raised.

"Oh, don't look so shocked. I'm not pure evil." Her teeth shimmered white when she smirked. "Besides, it is more to get you from under my feet than anything. I would be just as pleased were you to decide to live in the under-realm with your beautiful Desmodai mate." She paused, her back facing them. "Oh. But if you are still undecided," her voice carried over her shoulder, "I would find some way to take my ammut. For a bargaining chip." Her hand caressed the door frame. "I have a feeling that once the dark prince has his princess, he won't be so keen to release her back to her world of light. Even should she beg to leave."

CHAPTER 31

Mordecai could not allow Lynora to stay in Nocturnus tonight, unless he uncovered the truth today.

He and Augustus stooped through the entrance into the cavernous slatturns. Since all the other good citizens of Nocturnus slept—including Florentia—they had chosen to sacrifice their resting hours in search of the elixir's peddler. This left the way clear to enter the slums without raising questions. And Mordecai was determined to solve this mystery before Lynora's arrival, despite how being here made his skin crawl.

The air felt clammy and stale and a fine mist hovered just above the skin, an atmospheric amalgamation of dust and moisture. It surprised him that anyone would live here, undead or no. The abodes were scaffolds made of rotting tree limbs roped together to form skeletal frames, then covered with rags that did little to hide the ungodly goings on within.

On the corner of each pebbled street stood a prostitute. Hard to believe a Desmodai woman would sell herself after experiencing the bitter taste of such sins. But there were many, their alabaster skin flawless and translucent beneath the reddish lights. Whatever these women were after, it was worth more to them than any amount of dignity.

They wore nothing but their nakedness, revealing shapely legs and perfect breasts. Some of them draped live water serpents—as long as five feet—around their bodies to perform a seductive mime ritual with the reptiles. Mordecai stopped to watch this with interest, since bidding and hypnotizing animals was not one of his strong suits. He was in awe of those Desmodai that had the ability, prostitute or no.

But when the dancing proved too erotic, he and Augustus pulled themselves away from the spectacle and moved on. These temptresses were not like the hay ware of topside. They were queenly, polished as the breed demanded, and very alluring indeed to some Desmodai seeking company but having no mate to go home to.

As Mordecai and his Mentor walked on, they found other reprobates slumped on the streets, men and women alike, their clothes wrinkled and soiled, groaning or giggling, several even singing with that same childish quality of Florentia's strange spell the night before. The words of the song mimicked hers, and were even more disturbing echoing off of stony walls.

Vials littered the surroundings, identical to those on the shipment now in Zebulon's possession. Mordecai considered culling one that wasn't fully empty for evaluation, but remembering the overpowering temptation of the scent, decided the only safe way to identify its ingredients was to find Florentia's supplier—his father. And to find him, they needed to find Zebulon.

"We're running out of time. I think we should split up, double our efforts." Mordecai passed the suggestion across to Augustus after they had looked within every abode—bearing witness to more abominations than either ever wanted to—and questioned every coherent body in the east and west sides of the cavern. It was already late afternoon topside. Mordecai wanted to find Zebulon before he was scheduled to board the carriage that would retrieve Lynora.

He had heard the gold-toothed Reaper ran a gaming hell on the north side of the slatturns, where diminutives were pitted one against another to fight to the death for the entertainment of the Desmodai.

If Mordecai could find him, he could uncover his involvement then track down Cornelius—granted the man in question *was* his father, he was still having a hard time accepting such a possibility—and interrogate him on his own. Augustus was so hell-bent on revenge at this point, it was hard to predict what he might do if he found Florentia's peddler first.

Mordecai wiped his hands on his breeches. Although no dirt was on them, they still felt filthy. "You take the south end, and I the north. Then we rendezvous back here in time for us to prepare for tonight's event."

Augustus caught Mordecai's elbow. "Perhaps you should go home now. You have already wasted your sleep to help me. I shan't be responsible for you missing the carriage ride topside. Lynora mightn't come if you aren't there to coax her."

"Perhaps it would be better if she didn't. If I'm not there to greet her, she'll stay put, and be safer for it." Earlier, he had wanted to look in the kaleidoscope to check on her today, but Krig hadn't returned home since he left last night. "This should only take a few minutes," Mordecai managed, more to assure himself than his Mentor. "There's not much to the north end."

With that, Mordecai patted Augustus's shoulder and ducked through a cave-like opening in the craggy wall. Excited chatter met his ears as he plunged out on the other side. A few yards ahead of him, standing above a large pit, a ring of shouting Desmodai came into view. Red lanterns hung from poles to illuminate the scene. Several of the men held up their fists. Wrinkled slips of parchment, stamped with gold ink, stuck out from their curled fingers. In the under-realm, such papers were the equivalent to bank notes.

"Twenty pounds to ten that the little one is crushed within the first round!" a rough voice challenged.

"Ha! I wager an entire year's income against you. The little one is spry. Look at those gangles. He's the winner, to be sure."

"No blood thirst in him. He's scairt. Look at 'im. Pasted to the wall like a fly. I'm wagering on the big one."

As each man cast his notes into a hat, Mordecai swallowed the bile in his throat. He had never witnessed a gargoyle fight. To know there were Desmodai so cruel they would counter these fallen brothers and sisters, the most faint-hearted and subservient creatures of the realm, against one another for nothing but laughs and ill-gotten gain, made him nauseous. He had heard rumors that tight copper bracelets were clamped on the gargoyle's wrists and ankles, so that when they blended to their surroundings, they would still be partially visible to their opponent and the crowd.

Wasn't it enough punishment for whatever crimes they had committed, that they lived as slaves for all eternity?

He couldn't bring himself to look down in the pit as he passed by.

"That one's fading!" Someone laughed. "Cob-headed gargoyle! Don't ye know we can still see ye?"

"Brimstones. Why are we stuck with these imbecilic, cowardly toads for entertainment? Can't someone find something with a little blood lust in it?"

"I got your blood lust, Kaige. Got it right here!"

A wave of formidable laughter broke out. Mordecai strode ahead, intent on a man a few feet away holding a wager-filled hat.

"You're gonna have to beat that one to light the flame in him, Hemp!" One of the observers yelled down at the game master in the pit as Mordecai passed behind the crowd. "Teach him that if won't be a-fightin', he'll be a-dyin'."

At the crack of a whip, Mordecai saw a dust cloud rise and a tiny screech burst out. He considered trying to stop the cruelty, but the thought of Lynora's arrival infringed. He didn't have time to argue the lack of moral rectitude in such a sport. He had to find Zebulon.

Rounding the circle of miscreants, he spotted the one with the hat walking toward someone who stood alone next to a colony of dripstones. Mordecai recognized the loner as Zebulon. The man handed off the hat and strode away so Zebulon could tally bank notes. It appeared he was to make a keen profit off this.

Mordecai dug in his pocket for some guineas. "The man who's supplying the doses. I want his name and whereabouts." He tossed the coins at Zebulon's feet.

Setting the hat aside, Zebulon glanced up and sniffled. His eyes watered, as if something irritated them. "Well, well. Ye liked what I had to offer, aye lad?" He smirked, his gold tooth glinting. "Come to seek another chance at paradise? Still eaten up by the sins, I see."

The writhing image of the rape victim incinerated Mordecai's soul, and his gut clenched from the burn. He had managed to go all day without thinking of her, until now. "Give me the name, Zebulon." He gestured to the coins.

Zebulon shook his head and kicked the guineas away. "Sorry. Ye had yer chance. The elixir's all gone. We been runnin' low. But that'll change soon enough."

Mordecai couldn't help but notice the dark circles under the Reaper's eyes, the puffiness of his splotchy, reddish skin. He looked twenty years older than when Mordecai last saw him. "I know what the intoxicant is. I know you're involved somehow. I want the peddler's name, you *scab*." Mordecai ignited his silver gaze, fused it to Zebulon's irises to prevent his rival from taking mist form, hoping it would work. In the past, Zebulon had been strong enough to fight it.

Mordecai ignored the jeers and chants behind him as the spectators yelled for their chosen gargoyles. The aura from the lanterns defined wrinkles on the Reaper's face that had not been there the night before. And strangest of all, beads of sweat glistened at his hairline.

Zebulon tried to twist free, but couldn't escape Mordecai's infectious gaze.

"You look terrible, Zebulon," Mordecai said. "You could use some sleep. Give me the peddler's name and location, and I might let you go, for now."

Zebulon's white-tipped beard reflected the strange light. "Ye can keep me from translatin', but ye can't force me to talk."

"Oh, rightly so?" Mordecai clutched the Reaper's arms and lifted him so his head hit the jagged point of a dripstone. Zeb's hair parted from the tip's pressure. "Let's see if I can't siphon the truth out of you. First, we'll drill a hole in your skull."

Zebulon struggled to escape. Mordecai was shocked to find him so lacking in strength. Only a week ago, this man had been every bit as powerful as him.

Zebulon forced a laugh that ended in a spell of hacking coughs. "Do it," he offered after gaining control. "It's not as if ye can kill me."

"By jingo, you're right. Still, I doubt anyone here likes you enough to pull you off should I impale you and leave you hanging. You might not die, but I suspect it would be an excruciating way to spend eternity, yes? In fact, why not make the game interesting? How about I invite some of your patrons over there onto the scene? We could place wagers as to how long you can last without begging for one of us to kill you and end the misery. What say?"

This caught his captive's attention. "I'll tell ye what I know, if ye let me down . . ."

Keeping the Reaper entranced, Mordecai lowered him.

Zebulon grinned. "Drakkarh said one day ye'd come lookin' for yer past. I suspect the man ye seek is Cornelius. Yer his spittin' image."

Mordecai wrestled the deep despair that threatened to choke him upon confirmation of his worst nightmare. "Where in the hell is he?"

"Ah, now that's to be a bit more difficult to pin down, seein' as I consider this entire realm hell. A lot of ground to cover, it is."

Mordecai tightened his grip on Zebulon's arm. "I know that children's blood is being peddled in the under-realm." He felt no vindication from the panic in Zebulon's eyes, to have yet another macabre fear validated. "And I suspect," he intensified his hypnotic glare in an effort to steady his voice, "that you know more about it than you're letting on. Now, you are going to tell me where my father is. Then, you are both going with me to the Brotherhood, where you will confess everything—who else is working with you, how you have managed to go topside in the sun . . . and how many citizens you have infected with this addiction."

"Hmm. Ye might want to rethink yer threats. I have it on good authority that ye went topside yerself before ye were free of the collar. I have a witness—a credible witness with clout on the Agnate, mind—that says ye went to see yer bride wearin' a Venetian mask and a red domino cape. I'd venture that would put a crimp in yer plans to bring her here, were word to get out to Ezra. Not to mention the trouble yer friends Evan and Augustus would bid for helpin' ye. Tell ye what; ye keep my secret, and I'll keep yers."

Taken aback, Mordecai lost his grip on the Reaper. Suddenly, the crowd behind them went wild. An instinctive glance over his shoulder cost his hypnotic hold on Zebulon.

"Hmm." The Reaper leaned close to Mordecai's ear and nodded toward the pit. "Ye might want to watch this part." His breath smelled acrid and pungent—the stench of sickness. "I believe ye have a personal stake in the outcome of the fight, *Master*." With that, Zebulon dissipated to mist.

Mordecai's mind raced, trying to understand how Zebulon could know such details of the night he went to the Blood Gala. The only ones who saw him in the costume besides Lynora were the two sisters, two sentinels, and Lady Nenet.

He retrieved his guineas, noticing the upturned hat on the ground. Zebulon had been in such a hurry, he forgot his stash of banknotes. Mordecai picked it up.

Before he could think what to do next, the crack of the whip snapped again in the pit. This time, along with the dust, a small hiccup erupted followed by a whimpering voice: "Krig . . . no fight. No bleed. Krig hide . . . "Then a harrowing plea: "*Krig . . . no . . . die.*"

Cradling the hat, Mordecai shoved his way into the line of spectators, sickened by the heady wilted-flower stench of the crowd. In the pit below, a large gargoyle, twice the width of Krig with rolls of fat and frothy drool drizzling from its lips, hobbled toward the far side of the pit where a shadow cowered.

Mordecai shuddered. He knew the victim's identity without even seeing his servant's full outline. Krig had tried to fade, but the open wounds exposed him, along with the copper bracelets cuffed to his limbs. Intermittent scales were made visible by splotches of black, oily blood, like floating puzzle pieces.

Though Krig's face was invisible, Mordecai could catch the glint of tears streaming down the little gargoyle's cheeks. He was shocked to realize how much that pained him. Why was Krig in the slatturns to begin with? How had he been captured by Zebulon?

Hemp, the game master, yelled at Krig. "Get over there and fight, you maggot!" He lifted the leather strip, arm stretched to deliver a vicious blow.

"Enough!" Mordecai yelled.

Hemp paused and looked up.

"That diminutive is in my charge!" Mordecai's fingers tightened on the upturned hat in his hand. "Turn him loose. He is not yours to exploit!"

The game master laughed. "Is that so? Well, what do you men think?" He directed his question to the gamblers surrounding Mordecai. "Should we forfeit the fight? Turn the little one loose and concede the winnings to his challenger?"

The fat gargoyle hunkered in the pit's center. He clapped, a wide, stupid grin on his face.

Mordecai's personal space shrank as the onlookers crowded

around him, eyes shimmering in warning—too many attackers at once. He was captured by their gazes . . . held from vanishing.

"I've a year's worth of income sunk into this fight, nursling." One Desmodai, whose irises sparked like bronze flames, snarled at Mordecai. "I have no intention of losing it for a soft dandy like you."

The men closed around him.

Mordecai hesitated; he knew of a way he might save the gargoyle. But if anything went wrong, he wouldn't be topside to bring Lynora down. The carriage would arrive without him in it, and he would forfeit her trust once more, along with any chance of ever bringing her here again. If he left now, turned his back on the sadistic game, he could still make it in time.

Krig cried out woefully from below, and Mordecai's decision was made. With all the gusto he could manage, he launched the hat into the air. The stamped papers came fluttering down to the dirt. Just as he hoped, the men released their hypnotic gazes. Driven by greed, they forgot Mordecai in a mad scramble—each determined to find a bank note more lucrative than the one they had arrived with. Even in a city so far removed from human civilization, wealth was still the god that most knees bent to.

Suffusing himself in mist, Mordecai surged into the pit and wound Krig within his spirit shroud. Hemp tried to intervene with his whip but Mordecai moved too swiftly. Upon reaching the cavern's entrance, he filtered through in a sylphlike haze—still cradling Krig—and left the slatturns, never once looking back.

CHAPTER 32

"Master . . . good."

"Hush now." Mordecai stitched a four-inch gash on the gargoyle's forehead then dabbed away blood with a soft cloth. "Hold still."

"Master . . . kind. And brave." Krig winced.

Pausing mid-stitch, Mordecai waited so the gargoyle could get his bearings. Then he finished and knotted the end.

"All right, I think that should do it." After setting aside the thread and needle on his library shelf next to the bracelets he had cut from the diminutive's limbs, Mordecai gave Krig another drink of pomegranate wine. The creature clutched the goblet with his good hand and choked down the liquid.

Mordecai pried the cup away. "Easy now, little thief." On the sleeping couch, he settled some cushions around the gargoyle to prop him up in places so the blood wouldn't gather around the wounds and throb. He situated Krig's busted hand on the highest cushion, careful not to move the splint he had tied beneath his puffy fingers. Mordecai hoped the bones weren't broken. He bristled at the abuse the helpless creature had endured. He would see to it that Zebulon got what was coming to him; for the children, for Krig, for Florentia . . . the man would pay for his malevolence.

Revenge shelved at the back of his mind, Mordecai covered Krig with a blanket. The gargoyle's eyes followed his every move, one of them swollen to almost twice its size, and the other bloodshot where his opponent's fingernails had made contact. Mordecai patted Krig's tufted head until his long lashes drifted downward. Upon a small hiccup, his breath steadied to a dozing rhythm.

Mordecai sat back on his ottoman. He wasn't much of a healer. In fact, since Isaac had never had cuts to bandage, he knew little about treating or wrapping wounds. But he'd done his best. This would have to suffice until he could get over to the Solarium and gather some yarrow leaves for poultices.

At least he'd made Krig as comfortable as possible. Now, he needed to clean himself and change. The carriage had already left for Lynora, but he hoped against all odds that he could catch up in spirit form before it reached the castle.

He was tempted to look in the kaleidoscope for her whereabouts, but with his nerves so frayed from his discovery about the children— and questions of his father thundering in his temples—he didn't think even Krig could balance such an internal storm.

He'd decided now, after all he'd discovered, he had to go on as if everything was normal. He could not approach the Agnate with what he knew until he had some plausible explanation how a Desmodai could get to these children in broad daylight without burning alive. Otherwise, Zebulon would counter with his blackmailing scheme. Most likely, any chance of Lynora ever coming to Nocturnus had already been shot. But he couldn't have Evan and Augustus in trouble for his machinations on topside.

Mordecai wondered again who Zebulon's secret spy might be within the castle. He didn't believe it would be Mother Nenet, not with what he had on her. She would never be so foolish.

Mordecai sighed, wishing he had made more of an effort with Regent Ezra in the past. He would have had a prayer to make headway with the Brotherhood if Ezra was in his corner. Now, it was a stale mate. At least until he could find his father and shake the truth from him.

Resigned to the impasse, he strode over to his armoire and sifted through his clothes. He chose a double-breasted long coat the same amber hue as a field of ripe wheat. The lapels were trimmed with a horizontal braid. A row of step-cut topaz buttons lined the front, and a wide, flat collar accentuated the coat's cut-away style. Then he took out a silk square vest and fitted, twill breeches in a soft rust to complete the ensemble.

He had just secured the vest over a frilled linen shirt and fastened his breeches when someone knocked at the door. Upon assuring Krig hadn't been disturbed, he crossed the chamber and released the lock.

"Augustus told me." Florentia stepped inside on Mordecai's invitation. The aromatic perfume of ginger lilies filled the room upon her presence. Augustus followed behind and closed the door. Mordecai considered mentioning his rush for time, but there was an odd cast to his Mentor's face—a tightness; so he held his tongue.

"Oh. Poor sorry fellow." Florentia knelt at the couch in a flourishing sweep of cranberry, teal, and royal-blue skirts edged with black lace. "How could anyone be so heartless? Little thing wouldn't even say boo to a ghost." A dark, velvet glove stroked Krig's good hand. "Augustus," her lavender gaze shifted to her bloodmate, "go back and fetch our cordial. The alcohol might be wasted on us, but will soothe him."

"That won't be necessary." Mordecai shifted a glance to his friend, surprised to see Florentia in such a lucid state. "I've already fuddled him up with wine. He should sleep most of the night." From his peripheral, the mirror caught his attention. He had covered it with a velvet cloth so Lynora wouldn't inadvertently look within it. "In fact, perhaps you might take the little fellow back to your chambers after the theatrical performance later. If Lynora comes, we'll need privacy, so I can tell her everything."

Rising to her feet, Florentia clucked her tongue. "He never intended to endanger the innocents, Mordecai. He told me this." She pressed a palm across her black lace bodice.

"He?" Mordecai offered her a chair.

Gathering her skirts and petticoats, she sat down. Makeup glittered upon her face and feathers and sapphires embellished her upswept hair. She resembled an elegant peacock in her theatrical costume.

"You are referring to Krig?" Mordecai prompted.

Florentia and Augustus exchanged a cryptic stare. "No," she said. "I am referring to your father."

Mordecai felt his chin drop. He stared at Augustus. "You know—?"

Augustus shrugged. "Florentia told me his identity when I returned from the slatturns today." He appraised his wife, weariness etched in every feature. "Your father is alive and living here in Nocturnus. He is one of us. Apparently, he's been here for almost seven years, hidden in the slatturns. Florentia met him over a month ago, when she started to," Augustus paused, searching for the right word, "*occupy* the lower caverns. But he forbade her to tell anyone of his presence. Most especially you."

Mordecai's heartbeat tumbled. So it was true. All these years he thought the old man had abandoned him, or even died. Now to find that his father was a Desmodai, and the lowest form of one.

Why wasn't Augustus angry? Why was everyone so damned calm? "You know of my father? Yet you haven't sought to rip his throat from his neck?"

Florentia gasped. "Why would he do such a thing?"

Mordecai leaned against his library shelf, his legs weak. "Not to be insensitive to your condition, Florentia. But is he not the one who's been supplying you with your happy poison?"

"Happy . . . poison." A shameful frown dragged her chin.

"You need to tell him, Florentia." Augustus turned his broad back. "Tonight is the night of confessions, after all." A bitter note clipped the statement.

Trembling, Florentia looked at the floor. "You tell him."

The tension between the two was palpable.

"Well enough." Augustus rounded the library shelf. "It appears my wife is a far better actress than I ever gave her credit for."

Florentia's glistening black lashes fanned her cheeks. She inhaled a quivering breath.

Augustus's animosity toward her quaked Mordecai's foundations. He had always looked to their joining as the romantic ideal. He couldn't imagine what had brought about such a change.

Augustus thumbed the shiny, dented bracelets on the shelf. "Over a month ago, a few days after your release from solitaire, Florentia was assigned a commission by Regent Ezra. Unbeknownst to me . . . her bloodmate."

One of the broken copper loops bent between Augustus's fingers. "The Agnate had caught wind of a substance being peddled in the slums. They chose to keep this knowledge from the populous; wanted to investigate on their own first." He slammed the bracelet down with a clang. "They decided to put someone on the inside. Someone who could pretend to be in such emotional turmoil, she was beyond the threshold of decency; a thespian so convincing, the suppliers would take her into their confidence. They chose Florentia. What they didn't take into account," his voice grew husky, "was her inner battle with the sadness. She wasn't merely acting. She has always fought guilt with the feedings—"

"It is not only the sins!" Florentia interrupted, her face fraught with agony. "I can still see their faces. Luke. Mum and Dad. All these years they grieve for me. Thinking I died an excruciating death."

"We all live with regret, Florentia." Augustus raked his hand over his face. "But you let your feelings rule your actions. You make ill-wrought decisions. Can't it be enough that we dragged Luke from the fire that night? That he still lives. Can't that be enough to nullify your guilt?"

Florentia glared at Augustus's back. "You have had centuries to forget your loved ones! It's been less than ten years for me. The pain is still fresh."

"Which exacerbates your weakness." Augustus rammed his knee against the library case, rattling the bracelets. "Had the Agnate come to me, had they asked me, I would have told them. You were a liability to the cause. But you failed to inform them of your frailty, or me of your assignment." He glanced at Mordecai. "She was lured into the intoxicant's spell before making any connections other than your father."

Mordecai fisted his hands. He wanted to tell them that the intoxicant was children's blood, but they couldn't handle such a revelation yet; their relationship appeared precarious enough already. Besides, it would kill Florentia to know what she had been drinking. She already looked to be on the verge of breaking down. He would wait.

Florentia groaned. "I have forsaken the substance now . . ." She struggled not to cry as fangs jutted between her lips. "*Though it is so sweet, and so pure.*" Trembling, she swiped away a line of drool from her mouth. Her gaze locked on Augustus. "I was only obliging the Agnate's request. They said to involve you would endanger you."

Augustus raked the bracelets to the floor in a blatant refusal to face his wife. His hands clenched the library shelf's ledge. "So you endangered yourself to protect me. Have you any idea how that makes me feel? Not as a Desmodai, but as a man . . . as a husband? I am a failure."

"No. I failed. I never thought beyond the glory of the performance. They built me up so. I was too proud to say it was not in my ability." Receiving no response from Augustus, she turned to Mordecai. "Augustus told me of my wretched behavior here last night."

She looked so fragile; Mordecai's heart ached for her. He knelt beside her, taking her hand. "You weren't so bad. Just filled with bravura."

She tried to smile. "Such kind falsities." Her glove squeezed his hand. "You should know. Your father is not the evil man you perceive him to be. He has been helping me . . . standing between me and the vials, each chance he gets."

Mordecai looked up at Augustus. "But I thought he was the peddler."

Augustus strolled to the couch and clasped his hands behind him, silently regarding Krig. "No. He helps supply the substance. He's being held against his will—his captors are exploiting his scientific genius for their own foul purposes."

Doubt spun Mordecai's head. "Is that so? He looked perfectly free to me. Wasn't even wearing a grounding collar. I propose he chose this walk—chose to desert me and his three-month-old son. He lost all of our wealth; this was the only way he could think to gain it back for himself."

Krig whimpered in his sleep and Augustus reached down to resituate the gargoyle's hurt hand. "There are other means of binding a captive, Mordecai. Your father has chains upon his heart."

Florentia patted Mordecai's cheek. The velvety softness of her glove snagged on his whiskers. "They have been threatening your brother."

Mordecai remembered how terrified his tiny brother had been last night—mumbling of flashing lights. And here he thought the boy was referring to his hypnotic gaze. He'd been wrong. As though ignited by the thought, his eyes glinted, the light dancing across Florentia's forehead. "Who is threatening Isaac? Zebulon? I'll kill him."

"I've no doubt he's involved." Florentia placed her trembling hands in her lap. "But there's no proof. And we have no other details, of who else is holding your father or what this strange substance is. Cornelius would never open up to me. He fears to endanger anyone else. I am sorry. I should have told you sooner, but my vows to the Agnate would not allow it."

"Damn the Agnate and all their contemptible vows of silence!" Mordecai shouted as he shot to his feet.

Krig smacked his lips, but didn't stir or waken. A huffing sound escaped Augustus's mouth, then all that could be heard was the ticking of Mordecai's longcase clock.

"I must go," Mordecai broke the pause.

Florentia nodded. "I, too. My troupe has one last rehearsal before our performance tonight. If my husband will accompany me."

Augustus tensed his shoulders.

"Please, dearest one," she pled. "My body, my soul, my heart . . . these were never unfaithful to you. Only my thoughts, only my tongue—silent and obstinate. I am a devilry dare. I made an error in judgment. I realize now. I need you, more than any intoxicant." She stood and held a palm out to her husband.

Mordecai looped an arm around her waist. "Come, Augustus. It's not as if Florentia is the only one harboring secrets in this place."

Acceptance softened Augustus's scowl. He crossed to his wife and pressed a kiss to her gloved palm. Taking her hand, he drew her body to his. "No more secrets between us."

"No more." Florentia molded his hand to fit her cheek.

He moved his fingers to trace her chin. They looked only at each other, touching fingertips to cheeks, noses, and mouths, darkness meeting paleness, intent and intimate.

Mordecai felt like a spy, a bug on the wall. He wanted to shrink away, to give them their moment and simultaneously find his way to Lynora. But one thing still plagued him. "Florentia, before we part, tell me: you said my father never intended to endanger the innocents. Who did he mean?" This could be the proof he needed, if Cornelius had mentioned anything about children.

Florentia cast a glance to Krig. "I assume little Isaac . . . and the gargoyle. Cornelius never meant for Krig to bear the brunt of his choices."

"I don't understand."

Florentia's skirts rustled as she drifted over to stand by Krig. She smoothed the blanket beneath his chin. "When your father learned of your presence in Nocturnus . . . he grieved sorely. He did not wish this fate for you. Then I told him of your bride, your great love, and that she lived among the Sisterhood. Cornelius believed you would find a way topside. So he sent for Krig, knowing he was your servant. He gave your diminutive a special key. A key to open a way to Lynora once you made it to the castle." Florentia stepped back into Augustus's arms. "Krig was trying to return the key to your father at the slatturns earlier, when he was captured by Zebulon. The Reaper tossed him into the fighting pit out of spite, to punish your father. To spite you."

Mordecai's jaw clenched. So, not only was Isaac in danger, but his father as well. Now he *had* to keep this quiet, lest his father take the fall for someone else's crime. Despite that dark thought, a surge of gladness warmed Mordecai's body. An odd sensation for one with frozen blood. To think that his father, after all these years, still watched over him. Wanted the best for him. So much so that he assured Mordecai would have the key to the Gwyndolaire tunnel.

But how had his father come into the possession of such a key? How had Cornelius come to know of the tunnel?

Mordecai cursed beneath his breath as a possibility came to him— blinding and bright. Augustus had mentioned that Lady Nenet once befriended a mortal man, keeping his identity hidden from Ezra. *A radical visionary*, Augustus had said. One who made a tonic to try to cure her.

Who better to cure a blood-drinker's illness, than an eccentric bat-loving physician?

CHAPTER 33

When Lynora first saw the Desmodai carriage arrive outside the castle walls twenty minutes after sunset, she hesitated. Structurally, it was like any other post-chaise, aside from the custom-made coachman's box. Most chaises had postillions—boys who guided the horses by riding them—but this had a coachman, dressed in a black cape and top hat, sitting on a hinged seat affixed to the back. Ebony horses with scarlet plumed bridles pulled an enclosed cab large enough to seat four passengers. Horses that blew steam from their nostrils, and motors that whirred in their bellies. Yet somehow, their eyes were alight with both sentience and industry.

Mother Nenet had seen Lynora off at the castle door, but would go no further. The coachman waited by the chaise. He loomed over Lynora, with a size befitting a Desmodai. But she knew the moment he took her palm and helped her up, although she couldn't see his face for the shadows, it was not Mordecai. He informed her Mordecai was tardy, and it was her choice whether or not to board. She'd taken the leap. She could think of only one thing that would distract her husband from something so monumental as her entrance into his world.

And that was Isaac. He had visited the boy last night. She had to know what he'd learned.

Yet, upon arrival at the night-realm's gate, she stopped the coachman with a knock on the cab's ceiling just as the wheels engaged the tracks beneath the pond. In spite of her attempt at courage, she couldn't bear to go one inch further without Mordecai. He had promised to be with her every step.

Unsure of how long to wait before turning back, she wriggled against the cushion, arranged the soft, crimson mull of her gown like a fan at her feet. Removing her gloves, she situated her valise next to her. The essence of leather from the carriage interior mingled with the faint fishy scent of the pond outside.

The coachman squirmed on his outer seat and rocked the carriage. He had not yet spoken another word to her, and she hoped the silence would bide. She knew nothing of making small-talk with his kind.

On the other side of the window—spotted with spray from the falls—she could see the angels hiding the gateway . . . their dark shapes foreboding and mysterious. Her nightmares of blood-filled rivers rose to the surface. The crimson waves hammered at the fragile veneer of trust she'd constructed, like a storm pummeling a ship's stern.

Why had she ever agreed to come? What could she gain by this journey into the under-realm? Every part of her begged to run, to escape before her chance passed by. The last time she'd felt this unnerved was when Mordecai seduced her into taking his infectious bite. What might he infect her with now, once he had her in the pocket of his gloomy world?

No. She stiffened her spine. Raven's well-placed words had caused this disquiet in her soul, and she refused to let her nemesis ruin the progress she and Mordecai had made. He would end his own life for her, she knew that now.

In truth, Lynora no longer needed to be wary of her husband; she needed to beware of herself in his presence. She once thought his dark sensuality incited her to do things outside of her character. But now she realized it was her new nature to step over past restraints. No longer the naïve maiden, she found herself desiring different things, surviving by different rules. If anything, Mordecai had simply allowed her to see this awakened side more clearly, through the lens of his unconditional acceptance.

The wind picked up, and gales rattled the carriage door. Mechanical whinnies echoed across the water. Lynora's stomach rocked with the water's current lapping against the axle and wheels. Shivering, she wrapped her cashmere shawl tighter around her shoulders. She rarely got chilled anymore, due to the tepidness of her blood; only when worry stripped away the warmth of confidence from her soul.

She was just about to insist the coachman take her back to the castle when she heard voices outside. Pressed against the window pane, she listened as someone directed the coachman to take a walk along the margin and give them privacy. The wind made it difficult to decipher the timbre of the man's voice. But she knew of only one man it would be.

Inching over to the middle of the seat, she expected to hear a knock, or for the latch to give. Instead, mist seeped through the crevices. She fought against an annoyed frown—angry with him for his tardiness, frustrated with him for his showmanship, yet intrigued by his power and the promise of comfort and passion his touch would bring.

The mist gave way to a black cloak. She strained to see his face in the darkness, his silhouette just out of reach of the splay of moonlight on the seat opposite her. "You are late. I almost didn't come. I hope there's a good reason. Isaac?"

In lieu of a response, he scooted into the moonlight and removed his hood.

Lynora gasped and reached for the door. The Desmodai's rough hand caught her elbow and clenched, hard, his grip hot to the point of feverish. An odd sensation, for a cold-blooded undead being.

"Ah, where might ye be gettin' to, pretty polly?" The stranger coughed, his chest rattling. "I understand yer here on official business. Mayhap to join our distinguished brood." His voice sounded slurred, drunk.

But Desmodai were immune to alcohol, weren't they?

"Yer husband's been a bit . . . detained," he taunted. "So I wanted to see that we had this time together, to get better acquainted."

Lynora covered her nose with her free hand to dull the alcohol stench which overpowered his Desmodai scent. Mordecai had written to her about his handful of close friends. One was a sea-faring garden apprentice that charmed women with his dimples. The other, a Roman Adonis who used pretty words. And then the female, a thespian of unsurpassable beauty. This man did not fit into any of those molds.

"*Let go of me.*" Her command shook the window pane.

He released her elbow, but propped his leg in front of the door to prevent her escape.

Lynora ignited her red gaze as a shield.

"I've a message for yer husband. Will ye deliver it when he gets here? I'm sure he'll listen. I know I would . . . so long as ye were naked while talkin'." He flashed a grin, revealing a golden glint in his mouth. A bitter taste coated Lynora's throat.

He ducked from the moonlight's reach again, elbow propped on the door. "Yer husband cost me a profit today. Chased away some of my best patrons. And if I see him getting plump in the pocket over the next few weeks, his sterling'll be mine. *By blood or by guile.* Understand?"

Lynora stiffened. *That phrase . . .*

Levering back into the moonlight, he lowered his voice. "Ye see, Mordecai has a bad habit of creepin' into favor with himself. Of late, his head is the size of an air balloon. But I've got the means to pierce the bluster from it, be sure." He snorted. Wiping his nose with a hanky, he eased forward enough for Lynora to see his bloodshot eyes. "He thinks, as he's a fellow Reaper, he can share my throne. Ye tell him, the slatturns belong to me and me alone. He is not welcome there."

Lynora's heart fell to her feet. She couldn't have heard him right. Mordecai . . . a *Reaper*? Could that be why he acted so wounded that night in the Luminary Hall? The ugly possibility curled within her like flame, intensifying the heat in her glowing irises.

No matter how much she loved the gardener within him, this she could not forgive. If Mordecai had lowered himself to this . . . they could never have a future. Each time he returned from a hunt he would reek of death, and she would taste murder on his lips.

Tears surfaced in her eyes. Tears of anger and fear, but most of all disappointment. In herself and Mordecai both, for thinking this could ever work.

Then a chill of realization crept over her. This creature had admitted he himself was a Reaper. The hair along her neck stiffened as self-preservation overtook. Moving in indiscernible increments, she dropped her hand into the opening of her bag, eyes soldered to the stranger's.

"D'ye hear me, lovely?" he purred. "Ye tell yer cocksure husband to stay off my turf. I have power beyond anythin' yer lad possesses. I hold mortal offspring in the palm of my hand. And I can face the sun like a god. D'ye hear me? Like a blasted god." His fingers clasped her knee and squeezed. "Be my messenger, and I'll let ye off with jest one little bite, hmm?" His fangs grew long and saliva drizzled toward the points.

Her eyes fired to torches. "Be your own messenger, Desmodai spawn. And I'll let *ye* off with just one little cut." Her hand whipped out of her bag, wielding her ammut. Gaze locked on the silver weapon, the stranger released her with a yelp as she lunged forward, an awkward move in the small space of the cab.

She jammed a thigh between his legs to pin his manhood beneath her knee cap. The vicious tactic shattered his concentration, rendered him incapable of fading to mist. He whimpered as the ammut's two points wedged against his shirt until the fabric dimpled above his sternum. Lynora's shawl slipped off and her mass of dark hair fell in her face.

Her chin quivered with an almost smile; she would have to thank Wren for convincing her to bring her weapon after all. She swept aside her hair with a flick of her neck.

The man's lips pulled back in a snarl. "Ease up . . . would ye?"

She shoved her knee deeper into his groin. In the moonlight, she saw it again. The twinkle in his mouth. That familiar phrase turned through her mind: *By blood or by guile.* And clarity roared through her.

This was Wren's Reaper. It must have been a gold tooth that glinted in the moonlight on the night of her alteration, not a gleam of jewelry such as Wren had thought.

Condemnation shuddered through Lynora's blood, pounding her temples. What a sweet turn of fate. She could cure her friend. Wren would finally be whole again.

Yet Lynora had never killed anyone. She only hoped she had the courage.

With a stroke of her free hand, she opened the stranger's shirt, exposed his chest.

"Please . . ." he begged.

She thought upon how Wren must have begged for her life to this very man. "Tonight, you pay a debt," she hissed. "And I assure you, it will be by *blood.*"

The Reaper's eyes turned up pleadingly. Something within her overtook, something dark and sinister and uncaring. Her veins jittered in her arms, this turn of power an intoxicating thrill. She pinched her knee against his manhood, felt his most tender part roll beneath her. His every muscle tensed.

Following an invisible path, she positioned the ammut inches away from the opening at the bast of his sternum and held it steady. It surprised her, how docile and weak he seemed. Almost human. And his flesh, red, splotchy, and hot.

Then she noted the sweat beading at his brow.

This jolted her back to reality. Weren't all Desmodai cold and pale like her husband? Weren't they stronger than this? Did they sweat?

If she was wrong, if this wasn't Wren's attacker, could she live with such guilt?

Her jaw tightened. Yes, on the one chance she could save her friend from eternal misery. For no matter his identity, he wasn't worthy of life. He had admitted to being a Reaper.

No sooner had she thought this than the scars on her neck started to throb. The carriage door swung open, and there Mordecai stood, flawless and glistening from the waterfall's spray, his blue eyes wide with shock. "Lynora, stop!"

Before he could hook her arm and tug her off, she managed to lift her arm and lunge. Her ammut gouged the Reaper's chest. The skin healed up again in an instant. Mordecai forced Lynora off her victim and the Reaper evaporated to mist, cursing. She broke out of Mordecai's hold and slashed at the clouded haze again with her weapon—a pantomimed vengeance in token of all her neophite sisters. She watched the cloud break then swirl back together. And in a graceful, serene rush, it eased out the door behind Mordecai to be carried away by a gust.

"Lynora?" Mordecai climbed into the carriage and sat opposite her, so broad-shouldered he nearly touched both sides of the cab. The wind slapped the door shut behind him. "Why did you bring your weapon? You know it's forbidden."

Puzzled by her ammut's failure to work, Lynora glared at her husband's bewildered face. "You cost Wren her freedom! To protect *him* . . . a murderer!" In a blind fury, she dropped the iron prong on the carriage floor and attacked him with her fists, sobbing.

"Monsters—murderers and rapists! All of you!"

"Rapists?" Mordecai's fangs appeared as he caught her wrists. "Did Zebulon touch you?"

She jerked her hands from his hold. "No . . . he destroyed an innocent. He didn't rape her in body, but in spirit and soul. She wasn't on your feed list. She had goodness in her heart . . . she didn't deserve this life. I could have saved her tonight. I just needed one more chance—one more chance to deliver the fatal blow. But you let him go . . . you let him go. Because you're a bastard Reaper like him!" Against the unyielding wall of his chest, she resumed the beatings, pounded until her fists ached and her knuckles—gouged by the jagged jewel buttons on his coat—split and bled.

Throughout the attack, Mordecai sat, still as stone; he allowed her to batter him, never once making any move toward self-defense. When she stopped and glimpsed his face in the moonlight, she came back to herself, realizing the tears which streamed his cheeks and neck matched her own. Numbness descended through her limbs.

She crumpled to the floor between his legs. His arms—with a tenderness befitting a child, not a blood-thirsty murderer—gathered her into his lap.

"What have I brought you into?" he murmured. "What have I done to you and Isaac?"

He drew her against him, flattened her ear to his chest. His palm cupped her nape. He caressed her hair with one hand and lifted her knuckles to his mouth with the other to kiss her wounds. She kept waiting for him to lick the blood away, but instead, he soothed her with the cold press of his lips.

"I didn't choose to be a Reaper," he murmured against her flesh. "It was part of my punishment for altering you. I despised it, Lynora. You've no idea how the experience still haunts me . . ."

The anguish in his voice forced Lynora to draw back and look at him.

Resituating in his seat, Mordecai rubbed a hand down his stubble. "You know of the Wisdom. For those here who drink the blood in cocktail form, the sins are like a shadow of a thought, a blur of a memory that is not truly yours. The details are so jumbled, they negate one another. But for a Reaper drinking the blood of a singular victim, it becomes akin to eating from the tree of life in the garden of Eden. For to taste the sin undiluted, your eyes are opened not only to the transgressions of the man, but you are related to the depravity by association, even exposed to the motivation behind the acts. It's as if you become the offender . . . watch yourself commit the crime. It is difficult to disassociate from the guilt once you've related to the motive."

Lynora's hand curved around his temple. He rested his face against her fingers. "What crime did you witness, Mordecai?"

His eyes grew misty and he cursed beneath his breath. "Too many. But only one is with me every day. I saw a woman raped and murdered. I have not been able to displace the image. I don't think I ever will. It eats at my soul."

Lynora studied his eyes, the dancing blue hooded by torturous shadows, born of the guilt of another man's crimes. She'd never realized the Reapers bore such a burden to ease the rest of the kindredship's feedings. It cast everything in a new light.

Unable to soothe such a wound, Lynora hugged him tight, her cheek to his chest. She nestled closer, surprised to hear a heartbeat beneath his layers of clothing.

"Your heart beats," she whispered in wonder.

"For you." He kissed her fingers. "Our love carries a melody that can't be silenced."

Shaken, she leaned back again, starting to realize how much of his humanness he still retained.

Sweeping aside her curtain of dark hair, he banked their foreheads together. "I suspect, were I ever to lose you, the beat would stop. I would live on for eternity, without a heart to guide me."

Her throat constricted. "I'm so confused, Mordecai. About everything. I almost killed that man. I would have, had my aim not failed. And I wanted to kill him. I want it still, even now. I no longer know what is right or wrong."

"But I do." A tremor cracked his voice. "Go back to the castle; I want you safe. I've made so many discoveries today. One is about the children. I can't tell you the details for fear of endangering you; but I will send a message when I can."

Lynora stiffened. Could she have been right all along—that the Desmodai had something to do with the orphanage's plague? "Are you going to the Agnate?"

Mordecai looked down. "If only. Regent Ezra abhors me. He'll not listen to a word unless I have proof. I intend on finding out everything I can during the Ridotto tonight; everyone in Nocturnus will be there, which leaves the city ripe for exploration. But the Agnate is still keeping tabs on me, so I must make a mandatory appearance to pay homage to each of them, so no brood runners will be sent out to investigate my absence. After that, I'll find a means to leave early. I must seek out my father. He has all the answers."

Lynora's jaw dropped. "Your *father*?"

"Cornelius is here. He is one of us." He glanced out the window as the robotic horses whinnied. "You were right; my world is no more perfect than yours." His legs fidgeted beneath her as he prepared to open the door.

"What are you doing?" She caught his coat sleeve.

"Calling the driver back. To send you home."

"No." She met his eyes, still reeling with shock from his news. "We investigate this together. You need me. You are emotionally overwrought with both Isaac and your father involved."

"Precisely my point. I don't want you in danger as well."

"But Isaac is my family, too. And I came prepared for danger." She nodded toward the ammut on the carriage floor. "We must make an appearance together at the ball; otherwise, people might get suspicious. We can feign a moment that leads to a kiss, and be overcome with passion; that will be our excuse to leave."

Mordecai's expression shifted. In his eyes something new glimmered: respect tinged with a hint of desire. "There will be little acting to it, my swan. I'm always overcome with passion when I'm near you."

Lynora's cheeks warmed.

"I vow to you," Mordecai squeezed her hand, "I'll find Zebulon again, not only for the information we need, but to make him pay for his sin against your friend. Our Decretums forbid taking someone who's not on the feed list. The Brotherhood will see him die, and your friend returned to her humanness. But I cannot let *you* kill him."

He cradled her up-turned palm in his. "Your lovely hands were not made for killing. They were crafted for work—skilled and honorable." His chilled lips nibbled her palm, titillating her senses. "And for music, rich and mystical." His tongue tip traced the fold of flesh between her thumb and forefinger, rousing a sensation between her thighs that matched the wetness of her hand. "And for caresses— soft and sensual." He suckled her pinky, drew it deep into his mouth and wrapped his tongue around her to kindle flames within her womb. "Never, never for murder. Not when you have a monster at your disposal, bound to your bidding."

She winced, her free hand tracing his whiskers. "You are no monster. You are my gardener, chained to a world of darkness."

"And you are my only light."

His words, so beautiful and poignant, touched her deeply. She leaned in to kiss him. He coaxed her mouth open, nudged her tongue to join his, the union a fire between them. She drank of his flavor—a brandied fusion of wine and flowers. Her fingers gripped the hair at his nape and she whimpered as he clutched her body to his.

He broke the kiss, eyes lit to silvery flares. "What are you doing, unleashing this demon within me?"

"Practice." Lynora grinned. "For our grand deception at the ball."

"Ah." His fingertips traced her face. In the dim glow, longing suspended like frangible webs across his features—a sweep of opulent blonde lashes, an urgent invitation of piercing blue irises, the feral turn of primrose lips. "How I want to become your husband in truth."

She ran her hand along his thigh, relished the tremor which followed her movements and rippled his muscles beneath his skin tight breeches. Her own body echoed his reaction, quivering in secret places. She thought upon the rapture his touch could bring, and ached to do the same for him. "I want that, too."

He looped her arms around his neck. "After this is all behind us, once Isaac is safe and my father's name cleared, I shall romance you. With dancing, and sweet words, and sights more sumptuous than your mind's eye could ever conceive. I'll indulge your senses in the art of making love, and show you how every part of you is made to be my match, regardless our other differences."

He levered her off the seat, somehow managing not to bump her head or cramp her feet while he cradled her. Once he had her settled on the other side, he smoothed the skirt over her legs.

Draping her shawl over her shoulders, he watched with rapt attention as she wriggled her fingers into velvet gloves, smoothing them up to her elbows. "You look exquisite tonight. Your hair is like a blanket of midnight and stars." He took her gloved palms and kissed them.

She laced their fingers, gifting him with a soft smile. "Call the coachman, my husband." She took a ragged breath. "I am ready to see your world."

CHAPTER 34

Lynora could scarcely contain her relief when she found the river of blood and sins to be nothing more than a series of canals—dark and glittery—that wound through the underworld as a means for transportation. Seated in back of a gondola with Mordecai, the scent of the water and the slight breeze rushing through her hair calmed her.

The bow stirred whispers of waves to swirl around them—likened to a razor slicing through a panel of shimmering, sapphire satin. It would not be difficult to fall in love with the beauty and tranquility of such a place, if one could forget the corpses and bones beneath, forming the foundation.

Engrossed in her surroundings, she responded to Mordecai's attempts at conversation with grunts and one syllable answers until he grinned and gave up, resolving instead to point out each passing tunnel and abode.

Lynora had always pictured something like a beehive, when in fact it was more like a dragon's labyrinth from a fairytale, beautiful and mysterious, walls alive with lights reflected by the wavelets and Mordecai's glowing flowers. Pride surged within her, to see her husband's brilliant talents finally being appreciated and put to use.

The dismal grace and durability of the stony world mesmerized her. Passersby stood out from the monochrome scheme, splotches of color in their luxurious and fashionable evening attire—all of them headed to the ball. It surprised Lynora that anyone would walk when they could fly. She told Mordecai so, and he chuckled, a pulsing, masculine purr which radiated throughout her body and warmed her every limb.

As Lynora and her groom skimmed through the water, one of the many couples turned and looked their way. They nodded in greeting, their eyes like sun mirrored off of puddles. Lynora glanced to the bag at her feet, wishing that Mordecai had not insisted on carrying her ammut. He'd had Lynora wrap it within a handkerchief and tuck it in his coat pocket, for he suspected it would be too heavy for him to carry otherwise. All these precautions because he feared someone might find it in her valise and send her topside, or worse, take her before the Agnate. They had too much to accomplish tonight, and he wanted no extra complications. She supposed he was right. But she couldn't help wanting the comfort of the weapon within reach.

The journey along the water proved every bit as romantic as Mordecai promised. Beneath each bridge, he had the gargoyle gondolier stop. Then her husband would cup her chin and kiss her with a deep, binding tenderness. He claimed it a Desmodai tradition to secure their eternal love. Once the diminutive caught on, it would warn them of impending bridges with a grumble and an irritated roll of the eyes. At one point, Lynora and Mordecai could no longer kiss for laughing so hard at the gondolier's obvious annoyance.

When things finally settled, Lynora asked about Krig's absence. Her heart ached for his heinous treatment in the under-realm slums. So absorbed in the conversation, neither of them noticed they had reached their destination until with a practiced sweep of the guiding pole, the gargoyle docked them at the end of a long line of gondolas.

Helping Lynora step up to the margin, Mordecai caught her lower back against him as the boat bobbed. From behind, his fingers sculpted her ribs then edged along the underside of her breasts before settling beneath her arms. She stroked her palms over his sleeves when he lifted her, admiring the thick muscles apparent even through the padding of her gloves.

As soon he stood next to her, he turned to pay the gondolier. "Wait here and watch my wife's valise, Illish. We'll be attending the Vakara next." He winked at Lynora. They were to present the illusion of wanting to stay for the duration of the Liminal festivities, including the play afterward. Thus, when they left early, making eyes at one another, everyone would assume they simply couldn't hold off their honeymoon celebration a moment longer.

Mordecai climbed out and took her elbow. "Come, my swan. The Utopia Chamber awaits."

They strolled behind several other couples. Ahead, the cobbled walkway followed a curve into another tunnel. Behind, their gargoyle settled into the boat's seat, there to bide time with all the other gondoliers.

Trying to hold her anxieties at bay, Lynora searched for something to talk about. She remembered Krig's inherent need to be busy, how he seemed antsy for escape that night in the rose thicket, and wondered if it was a characteristic common to the diminutives. "Mordecai?"

"Hmm?"

"Do they not get bored waiting for their patrons to return?"

"Who's that?"

"The diminutives. They seem like such restless souls."

Securing Lynora's gloved palm around his inner elbow, Mordecai smiled. "They stay occupied," he said. "There are serpents in the waters, with rainbow-colored scales that glisten like jewels. They can grow as long as ten feet. The gargoyles make a game of hitting them with the poles to knock them out. Whoever bags the biggest one before it wakes up and swallows them, wins." He squeezed her hand. "Oh, that reminds me. Be sure not to sit upon the seat when we return. Allow me to check beneath it first. All right?"

Lynora shivered and Mordecai's laughter echoed through the tunnel they'd just entered.

"You are jesting." Lynora studied his profile. "Least, I hope you are . . ."

"I think you should sit in my lap, just to be safe."

Lynora had no response, for they had followed the bend to a looming, dome-shaped alcove recessed deep within the wall. Covered in rich, burgundy bricks and sealed with sparkling, gold mortar, the building had no windows so she might look within, only an arched, copper-hinged doorway. Soft white light came from inside, filtering between the silhouettes that crowded the threshold and awaited entry.

Lynora stalled. "I-I can't go in." She vividly remembered this chamber from Mordecai's note. This was where they met to feed once a month. It was also used for galas such as tonight, being considered one of the loveliest dwellings in all of Nocturnus. Utopia, after all, meant heavenly. But she could not imagine anything heavenly about a room filled with human prey set to writhe upon tables, or the frenzy of Desmodai overtaking them with fangs snapping and eyes flashing.

Mordecai drew her aside to let others pass. He pressed her against the tunnel's wall, out of the light, framing her temples with his palms as he leaned in. Despite the darkness around them, Lynora could see the blueness of his eyes. She wanted to crawl within the color's softness and wrap it around her. To forget everything that stood between them, if just for this moment.

"There is no turning back now," he whispered. "I don't know what you have read in your enlightenment room, or what you're envisioning in that pretty head of yours." He played with a tendril of her hair. "We do not feed in some sadistic ritual. The Feeding Faction, where the bodies are dropped and tallied, have workers called Hashers. They take care of all the preparations. They drain the blood and combine it into a cocktail. The empty corpses are then turned over to the gargoyle populous for feed. The Desmodai sit at long, banqueting tables and drink the cocktail from goblets, as if it were wine—quite civilized. The only ones who ever look upon the victims are the Reapers and the Hashers. Our commoners never have to see that side of survival."

Lynora's chin set. Her husband, in all his genius and perception, still didn't understand her aversion. "Does the fact that the victims' families never have to see the 'empty corpses', as you so callously coin them . . . does that dismiss their deaths from the hearts of their loved ones? Can it obliterate their terrified cries from your ringing head? I know that they are kept awake to the very end. What those poor people must feel when they are brought into this darkness . . . to experience their own veins being yanked from their bodies as if they were ragdolls being taken apart at the seams—" Lynora paused, aware that she and Mordecai were being scrutinized by a tall, distinguished Desmodai with white hair the length of his waist. Two braids at his temples caught on his shoulders as he offered a half-nod and stepped toward them.

Pushing off the wall, Mordecai straightened his stature and cleared his throat. "Good evening, Your Regent."

Lynora and her husband exchanged a sidelong glance. She winced. This man was a Regent from the Agnate. What had she done, going off at the mouth in such a way? She clasped her fingernails to her wrist, but the velvet gloves prevented a good punishing grip.

"Lord Dureance." The stranger snapped her husband's name with an inflection of annoyance. Lynora looked back and forth between them, gleaning perception from the strained salutations. This must be Ezra. The patriarch with whom Mordecai didn't get along.

She'd read a little about Ezra in the Sanctorum of Enlightenment. His history was far from traceable, other than his promotion to the Agnate Brotherhood. Who the patriarch was before—how he came to be here—she had no idea. There seemed to be no record of it.

"Regent Ezra, allow me to introduce my bride," Mordecai

captured her hand and offered it to the patriarch, "Lady Dureance."

Lynora smiled. She'd never been introduced as his wife with such formality, and she liked it more than she'd expected. In that moment, she regretted burying her ring so hastily.

The regent smiled back and took her gloved hand and lifted it to his lips. "What a pleasure to meet you at long last. And how is your benefactress, the lovely Lady Nenet? Is she well?"

Lynora caught the glimpse of sincere concern on the man's face. "Yes. Strong and wise as ever."

This seemed to please him. "Did you bring your lyre with you? Your husband tells me you've been practicing Handel's 'Water Music'. King George requested that very composition on his barge as he sailed the River Thames, so I thought it fitting our symphony would play it tonight. Perchance you could join them." His eyes gleamed with a soulful lilt as he released her palm.

Lynora recognized the fire in an instant. Such devotion to music and song made him seem almost . . . human. She smiled within herself. They had something in common . . . something to build on. "Do you play, Your Regent?"

"Ah." A smile graced his elegant chin. "Once, my child. Long ago. I played an Italian Baroque pipe organ. But I failed to bring it with me when I came here." He waved his hand in resignation, causing the scarab-shaped opal on his ring to sparkle in the mix of light and shadow around them. "It had over six hundred pipes and more than two thousand parts. Tis hard to explain the majesty of such an apparatus to one who has never seen it."

"But I *have* seen such an instrument." Lynora allowed a shiver of excitement to gild her voice. "In the Gwyndolaire castle, we have a room called the Euphony Hall. It houses the most exquisite harps, bass lutes, pianofortes . . . and an organ, such as you speak of. As tall as a cathedral ceiling, with gleaming pipes that encompass an entire wall. And the angels carved within the facade oversee every note that is played—good or bad. Guardians of inspiration and harmony. We would do well to envision such an audience in the playing of our individual compositions of life, do you not agree?" She studied the regent's face, found him to be every bit as lost in the description as she. They grinned at one another, the sort of acknowledgement shared by artists of the same calling.

"Mordecai," Ezra patted her gloved hand. "You failed to capture how very charming and discerning your young bride is. Had I known this, we might have put our differences aside long ago. What a waste to have deprived our realm of such luminance all these months."

Lynora felt her cheeks flush. She freed her hand to clutch the luxurious shawl at her neck.

"I agree." Mordecai wrapped an arm around her waist and hugged her close. "So . . . I can see how such a large instrument would present some rather—unique—challenges in the transportation from topside."

Lynora cast a glance to her husband, grateful he'd eased the conversation away from her.

A far-away look glazed the regent's eyes. "Yes, the organ. Challenging. And now . . . so many years gone by." Sadness drifted across his features.

Lynora was surprised by a genuine rush of sympathy for this man whom she earlier assumed would be a blood-thirsty beast. Yet there was more to him. Much more. In fact, she empathized, for she would be heartbroken to never play her lyre again. "The Greek, back in the fourth century, had an instrument called the hydraulis. It would be ideal down here. An organ that operates by converting the energy of water," she indicated the canal behind them, "into air pressure to drive the pipes. I once saw a book in the Sanctorum of Enlightenment on early instruments. I could research it for you, send some plans your way. You could build it down here, piece by piece."

Ezra and Mordecai stared at her in silence, mouths agape.

Her cheeks grew hot again. "Oh, do I speak too freely? Too

assuming, perhaps. Forgive me. I forget my place at times."

Ezra's wide smile returned to his dark lips. "Your place, dear child, is here. Among us. Such a mind, such an intuitive nature. What an asset you would be." The regent slapped Mordecai's shoulder. "I can see why the two of you are a match. Genius knows its own kind, yes?"

Lynora almost laughed at the stunned expression on Mordecai's face.

Ezra straightened his long, slate blue jacket and cleared his throat. "I would appreciate your help in the matter of the—hydraulis—Lady Dureance. And in the meantime, there is culture aplenty to whet our appetites tonight. For one, our grand symphonic talent, which you shall hear shortly. And then the splendor of the Vakara Chamber and their theatrical presentation. Shall you be attending the play later?"

"I believe so," Lynora answered, avoiding her husband's gaze lest she somehow slip up and spoil their ruse.

Ezra gestured them to follow to the door. "You would join them inside, perhaps? Warm up your instrument?" He was back on the subject of the lyre.

"She packed lightly." Mordecai provided the answer as he snagged her hand and kissed it before curling her arm through his. A contented expression softened the hard turn to his brows which had first appeared upon the regent's arrival. He fit her fingers around his bent elbow. "She is only here for the night, unless she should change her mind and opt for an extended stay."

"One never knows what changes a night may bring." Ezra offered the quip over his shoulder without turning. "One never knows."

CHAPTER 35

As they stepped inside, Mordecai tried to read his bride's reaction. Her eyes were wide, her dark lashes unmoving, her entire demeanor stiff like a dreaming, waxen doll. Could she see past her revulsion, her prejudice toward their lifestyle, to be comfortable enough to enact their plan?

He, for one, had never seen the Utopia—three times the size of Gwyndolaire's Flower and Willow Hall—look so opulent and inviting. Twelve chandeliers of brass and frosted crystal dripped from the gold papered high-domed ceiling. White light from over a thousand tapered candles cast a brilliant ambiance.

In true baroque fashion, mosaics stretched along the rounded walls, framed by plaster motifs. Depictions of mythological scenes— Greek, Japanese, and Egyptian alike—came alive in oranges, blues, blacks, so many colors the eye refused to blink until it drank them all in. But aside from some crimson splashes in several attendees' clothes and the pomegranates upon each table, there was not a hint of red anywhere in the room's decor in respect for the blood that stained the souls of its occupants.

The scent of Desmodai thickened the air. In the midst of the room, couples mingled around the great crystal fountain which resembled an intricate ice sculpture. Clear water cascaded down into the basin, where three ladies carved of glass knelt to capture it upon their heads as if being christened. One held a sword, the other a dove, and the third a baby. Mordecai worried that Lynora would see the resemblance in the glass ladies, that she would recognize them as the same statues which guarded the monarch's mausoleum on topside and ask questions. Questions he couldn't answer without giving away the fact that Regent Ezra was one and the same as the monarch, and Lady Nenet had helped him cross over. Augustus would be in grave trouble were anyone to learn he'd shared their secret with Mordecai.

Thankfully, Ezra kept Lynora occupied by describing each and every mosaic mural on the wall for her benefit. Together, the three strolled toward the banqueting tables—draped in gold cloths and cream table runners—which lined the walls to allow space on the main floor for dancing. Several Regents from the Agnate nodded a welcome as they passed. Upon reaching a small group of Desmodai women decked in lush velvets and ruffles who turned to stare at Lynora, Mordecai tensed. A mix of longing and bitterness crossed their consummate faces.

His arm tightened around his bride as he quickened his pace, relieved Lynora was too engrossed in her surroundings to notice. He had expected this reaction from some. Lynora was a neophite. The only one here. The only one that most of the populous had ever seen. Every other neophite had been brought to realization by their Mentor in carriages, the forest, or within the privacy of sanctuary chambers before being presented to the public.

Lynora was the personification of the lost purity of their past to these Desmodai women. Their mirror in the flesh, splintering into jagged shards of nostalgia.

The hair on Mordecai's neck prickled as he heard the rustle of skirts and sensed the women at their heels. They had no intention of hurting Lynora. But the questions they would ask, the accusations they would make as to her hesitance to join the race, might be enough to turn her against Nocturnus forever.

His mind raced for the best way to defuse the situation. But in less than a heartbeat, Regent Ezra halted and turned.

Mordecai guided Lynora's attention in the opposite direction, toward a scene of Perseus holding up Medusa's decapitated head. From over his shoulder, he watched Ezra's gray eyes glimmer icy white at their stalkers. Before Lynora could seek Ezra's input on the mural, the regent was already in step with them again and the Desmodai women were skulking to the other side of the room.

Through something so simple as a love for music, Lynora had made a powerful ally. Mordecai was proud of her, and had a newfound respect for Regent Ezra, as well.

On the furthest side of the room, the symphony warmed up their instruments with lively and bouncy notes. Songs for dancing. Upon excusing Lynora and himself from Ezra's abiding attention, Mordecai moved her toward an empty table hidden some ways behind the fountain where jeweled bowls brimmed with quartered pomegranates.

He seated her, offered a fruit slice, and sat down to scan the crowd. Their plan had to be enacted in front of the perfect audience and at just the right moment.

Florentia and Augustus stood on the other side of the fountain, their backs turned. Evan and a duo of Desmodai vixens spoke with them.

"Behind me." Mordecai directed Lynora's gaze. "Those are my friends I told you of. There at the fountain. The dark man and the blonde one with his arms around the two women. When either come this way. . ."

Lynora nodded, still fondling the fruit. He noticed she hadn't tasted it. He touched her hand. "You don't have to eat it. I understand."

Her forehead puckered. "Understand what?"

He gestured to a mural on the wall behind her.

She rotated in her seat. Her shawl fell from her shoulders and pooled between her hips and the cushion. The gauzy crimson of her gown skimmed her enticing curves and the train fanned around the chair's carved legs. "Hades and Persephone?" she asked.

Faced with the depiction of the Underworld's lord dragging Persephone into the flames by her hair, Mordecai could only see the rape victim from his Wisdom-induced vision in the Miseria Chambers. "The charming, resplendent goddess and the dark lord who wanted her for his own selfish purposes."

His hands absently traced Lynora's ammut inside his jacket. The best thing he could do for her, as a man and as her husband, would be to give her life back. He'd been reconsidering it ever since he'd realized the true depths of ugliness his kinship were capable of. Ever since he'd learned of the children's involvement. He had to get Lynora and Isaac away from it all. And nothing short of his death would truly free them.

Lynora's gaze settled on his hand's movement within his jacket lapel. She caught his wrist and frowned. "What you're thinking . . . it is an ill-wrought comparison. Hades did not woo her, nor court her. He dragged her there against her will."

"Nevertheless, he brought her down. And there she was in the arms of that arrogant, insatiate prince, surrounded by darkness despite the flames. Fire that chilled the blood instead of warming it. A world of death masquerading as life. The similarities . . . you see them, as well. It's why you won't eat the fruit. Persephone lost her freedom at the consumption of one tiny seed."

Lynora removed her gloves and dug out a seed from the pomegranate, blood-red and gleaming like a jewel. Opening one of his fists, she nestled the tiny delicacy on the cusp of his palm. Her small hand slid beneath his, so soft—her touch almost a whisper. "I am not Persephone. Nor are you Hades. You are an honorable gardener, whose only flaw is loving me too much."

His jaw clenched; before he managed even a syllable of rebuttal, she lifted his palm to her mouth. In one languishing pulse of her lips, she sucked the seed and its juice from his hand. Then her tongue followed the same path, a slow and sultry swath to lick away the residue. The sensation shot all the way through his arm and awoke every erogenous zone in his body. He felt weak, at her mercy. The voices and music around them dimmed to a buzz. He caught her hands in his. "What are you doing? Are they watching?" He cast a glance over his shoulder at his friends.

Lynora cupped his chin and centered his focus on her. "No. This is no act. I wanted to show you that you have won back my trust. All of it. And to remind you that you didn't commit those crimes you tasted in the blood of that depraved man. Those memories which haunt you aren't yours You didn't earn them. Stop living as if you did."

The candles domed her in a halo of light—an angel in a world of demons. How he wanted to hold her naked in his arms, this woman of rain and innocence, who still saw him as a simple gardener despite his tarnish. To feel her heart against his, her breasts flush against his chest, with no barriers between them but flesh and bones. To be nothing more and nothing less than husband and wife. But would he ever feel worthy?

Fondling her discarded gloves, his gaze toured the room again.

The Desmodai, with their innate grace and agility, carried dancing to a new level, sweeping along the floor in hypnotic waves of scintillating gowns and plush suits.

Before he even glanced back her way, Lynora had drawn him into an embrace, arms secured around his neck, head snuggled beneath his chin. She took a deep breath and the tiny gust stirred the hair at his shoulder. "I accept you," she mumbled beneath his chin.

He scooted closer, afraid he misheard her due to the song which just began.

Her arms tightened around his nape. "You are not guilty. You are a *witness*. Forgive yourself, as I've forgiven you. I accept you as you are . . . tonight, here. I accept the Desmodai in you, even the Reaper . . . and the noble man who yet lives within your soul. Know that he is there still. Embrace him. For he lives. Why else would I love you despite all that has happened?" She kissed his neck, a soft pull, yet so powerful it siphoned away his doubt and regret.

His eyes watered. The pain dulled. The horrible memory began to fade, as if a cloud passed over to obscure the details. For the first time since the Miseria chambers, Mordecai felt removed from the rape. Far, far above it. So high, he could no longer see the faces or the act. Could this be what the attacker had needed to hear all those years ago? Could this be what he had craved to feel as a fractured child . . . what had driven him to act out so viciously as a man? Of course.

Every child needs acceptance and trust—unconditional love. Those same heartfelt words Lynora had just whispered so sweetly: *I accept you.* It was if, by treating that little boy's wounds, Lynora had healed his own.

Blinking back his tears, Mordecai nuzzled her temple. "On my life, Lynora. I believe you have cured me. The Wisdom . . . I no longer taste those sins as my own."

She looked up at him and, fingers woven within her hair, he kissed her. The faint, sugary sting of the pomegranate still lingered on her tongue. Mordecai groaned when she broke their contact.

"Your friends . . . they've seen us," she whispered.

Mordecai heard Augustus speaking to Florentia as they approached from behind.

He stretched Lynora to arm's length, his back to them. "Let us leave," he said loud enough to assure they would overhear. "I want you all to myself."

Lynora locked his gaze, a bewitching concentration that made him burn to take her back to his home and bed her, sans any of this pretense. If only time were on their side this once. . .

Obediently, she took her cue. "But I thought we were to attend the theater next—"

Mordecai touched a finger to her lips. "Either we go to my sanctuary chamber now, or I take you on this table."

CHAPTER 36

Lynora cut a sidelong glance to her husband. He caught her gaze and winked. Their plan had worked. Upon hearing Mordecai's sensual ultimatum, Augustus and his lady, Florentia, had turned around without so much as a by-your-leave and retired into the sea of dancers, both of them wearing smiles on their immaculate faces.

Now, going the opposite direction, Mordecai guided Lynora between the limited space of rustling gowns and billowing coattails, his full, dark lips a determined line across his stubbled chin. As they zigzagged through the crowd, the murals and sumptuous raiment of the attendees floated by in a swash of watercolor, in and out of focus. She and Mordecai passed the crystal fountain and her attention riveted to the statues—the three women carved of glass. The water trickled into the basin in a tranquil melody and beckoned her ears beneath the instruments.

She stopped. "I have seen these topside. These very statues."

Mordecai buttoned his long coat and tried to draw her back toward the door. "Lynora, our time is limited."

Captivated, Lynora stepped closer to the fountain and bent, allowing the back spray to speckle her cheeks and nose with droplets. "At Monarch Cromwell's mausoleum . . . in the graveyard."

Mordecai stepped up beside her. "Perhaps you should ask Lady Nenet of the mausoleum once you get back." He snagged her elbow to draw her away.

Planting her feet, Lynora frowned at him. "I think it is time you tell me this secret you have over her."

Mordecai groaned and appraised the tower of cascading water. "I can't. I made a promise. She must be the one to reveal it. Ask her of my father, Cornelius. Ask her how he came to hold the key to the castle's hidden tunnel. That should loosen her tongue. Now, come."

Lynora's chin stiffened. She admired the glass statues once more. Mordecai was right. They had too much at stake to dally, and too little time. But she assured herself she would learn the truth by tonight's end, one way or another.

She turned to follow him.

"Has your gardener told you the legend of the three Eves?"

As Lynora looked to the source of the unfamiliar voice, Mordecai grumbled something about "never getting away now."

Facing them was a handsome Desmodai, his dimples boyish and teasing.

Two females, their flesh a luminous blue like shadows on the edges of a cloud, clung to the stranger's brocade coat sleeves.

"If not, I'd be glad to enlighten you." Grinning still, the man glanced at Mordecai who glared back. "C'mon old chap. Aren't you to introduce me to your lovely bride? I am assuming—by the glint in your eye and the lilt in your step—that this is the famed Lynora?" He held out an upturned palm and Lynora reciprocated.

Mordecai scowled at the two females then inclined his head toward the male. "Lynora, this is Evan, my gardening apprentice."

Evan lifted a finger. "Tut-tut. He means to say, the under-realm's most valued Maritime Consultant."

Mordecai rolled his eyes. "And this is Kylia, the leading Belladonna at the Vakura's opera house. And Ivy has a gift with the costumes."

The Desmodai damsels' heavily lined eyes toured Lynora with muted interest. They twitched their noses and inclined forward a bit, as if she repulsed yet intrigued them.

Lynora held up her chin. Despite the brave front, her pulse quickened and caught the attention of Evan's companions. Bright pink tongues moistened their lips as they gazed at the vein she felt throbbing on the base of her neck. She fought the urge to dive into Mordecai's lapels for her ammut.

Mordecai edged her behind him.

One of the ladies opened her mouth to speak but Evan interrupted, taking both Desmodai vixens by the hand. "Say, whichever of you ladies wishes to be my partner for the Séduire? I'm actually considering taking part in this one." This caught their attention and they argued over who it would be until Evan contrived a contest to solve the dilemma. "How's this . . . whichever of you returns with a live moth in hand shall win my company for the evening." A sly smirk turned his lips. "And I do mean for the *whole* of the evening." He patted the curve of their hips.

The women cooed at him then glared at one another. Lynora suspected, that just as at the castle, all of Nocturnus was pest free. They would have to go topside and search outside the gates to find such a treasure.

It appeared they deemed a night with Evan worthy of such a quest, for without a word they drifted away through the crowd in a sparkle of jewels and lace, headed for the door.

Evan's dimples deepened.

"You might wipe off that grin." Mordecai said. "If they should both return with a moth, you'll be obligated to dance the Séduire with two . . . the *whole* of your eternity."

"Aah. They'll never be able to capture a live bug. Besides, the dance is about to begin. They shan't make it back in time." Evan's grin widened and he winked at Lynora.

She wasn't quite sure what to make of him, so she concentrated on the statues again.

Evan settled his hands on the fountain's ledge next to hers. "The three Eves represent the gifts and losses of our race. This one," he gestured to the one holding a sword, "signifies our strengthened physical prowess. And the one with the bird represents those of us who can command the animals."

"And the one with the babe," Lynora took up, "represents the loss to give birth." She couldn't hide the sadness in her voice.

Mordecai stepped up and suspended a palm across the small of her back, traced her form through the gauzy fabric of her gown. His touch, meant to comfort, only exacerbated her grief. She had dreamed so long of carrying his child within her.

As if sensing turbulence between the couple, Evan shifted the direction of the tale. "Most of us look to the trio as protection."

"But we have such statues topside," Lynora pondered aloud. "They stand over the monarch's mausoleum. I thought they were human symbols, there to protect him in his death."

Evan laughed. "If so, they have been lapse in their vigil."

Lynora gazed up at him. "What do you mean?"

Evan opened his mouth to answer but Mordecai cleared his throat, an apparent signal to silence.

Catching her husband's elbow, Lynora squeezed it. "Mordecai . . . let him answer."

"Uh, I believe your husband wants to answer." Evan nodded to Mordecai, as if he had done him a favor.

Mordecai curled his lip. "Evan, have I told you of the new hybrid I've been working on? It's a fruit with seven times the tartness of a persimmon. Leave's a man's tongue so drawn up and withered he can't speak for a month. Next time you're at the Solarium, remind me to give you a bushel, hmm?"

Grinning, Evan held his fingertips under the trickling water.

"Mordecai . . ." Lynora wasn't ready to let this go.

He shrugged. "I didn't take the time to write it in the note I sent with Krig because I didn't want you worrying and making a trip to the cemetery on your own. But the night I led your priest to the footbridge, I saw candlelight inside the Cromwell mausoleum. And there was a carriage outside, with a flag heralding the colors of the church. I sent the priest's mare toward it and hid behind some brush. A man came from within the mausoleum and helped your unconscious friend into the carriage. He was dressed as a bishop."

Lynora bit her lip. "That makes no sense."

"Well," Mordecai intoned. "When he was wooing you on the night of the gala, the little holy man did mention a Bishop Lauden coming to visit the orphanage."

Lynora rolled her eyes. "There was no wooing. But yes, he did mention that. Still, it's illogical. Why would the bishop violate the halls of death in such a way?"

"The halls of death?" Evan leaned his elbow on the fountain's edge. "Sounds like a wonderful place to vacation," he crooned, mesmerized by the water drizzling from his fingertips. "Has a musical ring to it."

"Yes, well. I believe that's our cue." Mordecai laced his fingers through Lynora's. "We must be going; good to see you."

"Wait." Evan straightened his stance and dried his hand on a handkerchief. "Where did Augustus and Florentia get off to? Did you happen to notice if she was upset?"

Lynora caught the cryptic glance between her husband and his apprentice.

Evan regarded his boots before continuing. "Florentia had a bit of trouble before they arrived tonight . . . had to be sure her hair was perfect. She feared the look was . . . *childish.*" One of his eyebrows cocked. "You know how the ingénue likes to make a first impression."

Mordecai appeared distressed by the news. "Is there anything we can do to help her?"

Lynora's eyes narrowed. "Help her?" She looked from her husband to Evan, both of them wearing sheepish frowns. "Whyever would she need help with her hair from two men who know little more about a woman's grooming habits than they do an ape's?"

A snicker burst from Evan's mouth. "You never told me our Lynora was a quipster."

Mordecai frowned. "She is not 'our' Lynora. She is *my* Lynora."

In that moment the music stopped, as if the jaunty and buoyant tune broke on a chord. Lynora turned to observe the abrupt change. Mordecai's hand, heavy and suggestive on her abdomen, coaxed her to lean against the fountain as the crowd around them split up, most of the group making their way to the tables. The four couples who remained on the dance floor embraced, intent upon the eyes of their partner.

"It's been a pleasure." Evan took Lynora's hand and kissed it before strolling toward the tables.

"What is all this?" She whispered into her husband's ear when he bent his head toward her.

"The dance of lovers. It's called the Danse Séduire. Séduire is a French term, meaning 'to seduce'. It's practiced by those who wish to join as bloodmates. Until tonight, they've been betrothed, so to speak."

"I thought to become bloodmates, the male must lead the female through the Wisdom with a sip of the cocktail, or vice-versa."

Mordecai stroked her gloved hand. "Ideally. But there are those who wish to commit, that met and fell in love after they were already changed. So, this is their vow of fidelity to one another. They perform it for all of Nocturnus—much like a wedding ceremony. The movements are symbolic of the alteration ritual; the only difference is, they have no need to share a sip of human blood at the end. We should leave before it gets started; it's the ultimate insult to walk out once it's in progress—"

At that moment, someone in the symphony struck two bells. Riding the room's acoustics, the resonance blended to only one chime.

Half the candles overhead extinguished. It struck Lynora that in this realm even fire had a will which the Desmodai could bend.

The surroundings dimmed to a sepia glow. Colors muted, murmurs hushed. While Mordecai tried to lead Lynora toward the door, two Desmodai—male and female—stepped out of the circle of the symphony, instruments aside. Hand in hand, they raised their voices in a cappella, a liquid merging of song. The sultry melody stopped Lynora her tracks. Her breath hitched for fear of disturbing the sacred duet.

So entranced by the voices, she failed to realize that the instruments had resumed. Whether the brass, or the winds, or the percussion, she couldn't differentiate, as the composition blended seamlessly with the singers to a gentle ebb and flow—a reverent and sensual flux of emotion.

"Lynora, we must go . . ." Mordecai readjusted his hold around her arm. But she froze in place, captivated by the suggestive dance that began around her. The couples thrust against one another, limbs intertwined, bodies writhing. The females straddled on their partners' waists, legs wrapped around the males' lower backs. The men held their hips and the women arched backward so their long hair swirled across the floor behind them. Despite the lascivious tone, there was a grace to it, a romantic balance which honed it to the intimacy of a practiced ballet.

In a crescendo as powerful as thunder, the brass cried out, the winds swept up and down, and the percussion grew to a climax, depicting a crash of waves against a storm-tossed ship. As though mimicking the crests of an ocean, the males dissipated to mist and lifted their partners all the way to the domed ceiling. Lynora craned her neck, barely aware of Mordecai's strong frame behind her, supporting her awkward stance. Hair raised along her neck as the electric sensation of lightning pulsed overhead—stirred by the thick mist.

The women appeared to levitate in the fog, their dresses a helix of ruffles, lace, and glittering ribbons. Blood blossomed on the female dancers' necks, as if spontaneously manifested.

"The . . . wounds," Lynora murmured as the dark flow drizzled from the puncture marks in the women's flesh.

Mordecai embraced her from behind, his fingers clasped over her abdomen. "Their partners bite them when in mist form. It makes it appear to be an illusion. It is all part of the ceremony."

In a burst of bright white, the candles relit, and the dancers drifted to the ground like prismatic ashes carried on a breeze. The males reappeared upon decent, their mouths glossed with the blood of their partners, their wrists held to the lips of their mates who drank their essence in turn. Applause overtook the room at the performance's end.

Lynora whirled to face Mordecai in the midst of the embracing couples. Nothing around her registered. She could only see her husband's face. "The plague . . . at the children's asylum." She felt as if she yelled the words, but Mordecai had to lean closer to hear her.

"What did you say?"

"I have experienced this scene . . . in the asylum . . . the stigmata!"

Chaos rocked around them as the symphony took up another lively frolicking tune, welcoming all attendees who wished to dance back onto the floor. Mordecai drew her close, his attentive gaze her only lifeline to stability. "Lower your voice, Lynora."

"It *is* a Desmodai causing the sickness in the children. The levitation . . . the scent . . . the mist. I can't understand how one of yours can survive in the daylight. But I know his identity." Her thoughts blurred in her mind, too fast and furious to catch the man's name. "The Reaper with the gold tooth. The one in the carriage tonight. He said something about being a god in the sun." Her fingers clutched her neck. "He said he held the mortals' offspring in his hand."

Mordecai growled. "Zebulon. I knew he was involved . . . but I didn't realize he was responsible for going topside." He started to walk away but Lynora grasped his coat.

"And I know what the substance is," she said. "It is a child's pure blood. That's what is being peddled in your slums!"

Mordecai nodded and caught her hand in his. "We should leave . . . *now*."

"Yes. I must find Father Lucien."

This suggestion turned Mordecai's face to a mask of terror. "That holy man cannot learn what you are. What any of us are . . . he already suspects foul play."

"I'll use discretion, mesmerize him if I must. He must take me to London, where they're hoarding the children."

"You're not going to bloody London without—"

"What do you think has become of the little ones?" Lynora interrupted, her worry spiraling to a blinding frenzy. "Are we too late? Has that beast turned them?"

"No." Mordecai raked a hand through his hair. "No. In fact, he must be using some other means to make the wounds appear as the stigmata. He can't touch the children's flesh with his fangs. Their blood would no longer be pure after contact with his saliva. It would no longer hold its appeal. Zebulon has to be keeping them alive . . . siphoning off of them somehow."

"Father Lucien said the wounds spontaneously disappear an hour later. A healing stick." The answer burst out from Lynora's mouth, leaving a sour taste on her tongue. "How would Zebulon have access to a naturlege?"

"*Lady Nenet*," Mordecai answered, holding his voice low so the dancers milling about wouldn't overhear.

"It can't be her. She was so eager to help. She even asked about your brother." Lynora sobbed at the thought of the child. "Isaac!"

Mordecai grasped her arms. "We have time. So long as my father does their bidding, my brother is safe."

Before she could respond, Evan pushed his way through the crowd congregated around the dancers. He shoved Mordecai and Lynora closer to the wall, out of earshot of the others.

The dimples that earlier dominated his cheeks disappeared beneath his stiffened expression.

"A messenger came to Regent Ezra during the Séduire. The brood runners have captured your father. He had vials of something in his possession. He is at the Apostate Chamber. The Agnate is putting him on trial as soon as they're all gathered. There's been talk he'll be locked within the Solarium . . . that he'll face the sun at dawn."

PART IV: MUMMERY

"Remember then our only shape is death …
When mask and face are nailed apart at last."
~Phillip Larkin

CHAPTER 37

Lynora's only thought was Isaac and his welfare. "Go to your father . . . help him for your brother's sake."

Mordecai shook his head. "The Agnate won't let me into the hearing. In this place, it matters naught that I'm Cornelius' son. I have no jurisdiction."

"It appears your wife has taken care of that." Evan pressed a jeweled ring into Mordecai's palm. "Ezra left this for you. Seems he sees you in a new light."

Mordecai locked gazes with Lynora. Her neck warmed beneath a rush of hope.

"The regent said he will inform the brood runners to let you into the chamber," Evan continued. "You're to show them the ring if they give you any trouble."

Mordecai studied the ring's scarab stone. "I don't like it." His focus turned to Lynora. "You, facing this alone, up there."

"I am not alone. I have my sisters."

"But there's Lady Nenet." Mordecai shook his head. "Remember the cradle in that room beneath the tunnel? That room belongs to her. The cradle ties her to children. She must be involved in this. And I have reason to believe that Zebulon has a spy stationed in that castle. One of the girls is feeding him information, if not the mother herself. At this point, I'm not sure you should return at all."

Though shocked by the unexpected details, Lynora refused to cower. "I am Isaac's only hope."

Mordecai's long, flaxen lashes fanned his cheeks as he looked down, unable to argue her point.

She touched his sleeve. "Please, don't worry for me. I know Mother Nenet. She loves children as much as I do. No matter what her secret, she would never harm a child."

Mordecai clenched his jaw. "She is Desmodai. *That* is her secret. She belongs down here with us."

The room's occupants turned in hazy lines around Lynora as she struggled with her husband's hushed announcement. Evan's eyes widened.

Mordecai noticed his apprentice's reaction and shook a finger in his face. "Damnit, big ears. You are to tell no one."

"Aye. Silent as the dead." Evan made a pinching gesture across his lips. The crowd grew louder behind them as another song began. "Mordecai, you should go."

Mordecai stared discerningly at Lynora; it was obvious he sensed her inner turmoil at the accusations against her matron, but he could never know how deeply this revelation had gouged the core of her entire being.

He drew her into his embrace. Flush against his chest, she immersed herself in his scent. Confusion muddled her thoughts over Mother Nenet's unmasked identity. So many signs she had failed to see: the rosewater perfume, her disappearance throughout the day, the faint metallic glimmer of her eyes, her ability to glide across a pitch-dark room without stubbing a toe or knocking something over; her sojourns off the castle grounds at night to manage trades with Nocturnus.

The one woman she had trusted with her life. The one place she had felt at home. She had actually come to think that perhaps she belonged at Gwyndolaire. Now nothing made sense anymore.

She felt Mordecai's hand move covertly between them, patting his coat pocket. Remembering her ammut, she surreptitiously drew out the cool chill of the satin handkerchief and slid it inside her dress between her cleavage. His fingertips captured hers at her chest, pressing the handkerchief between them. "Be careful. I love you," he whispered.

He kissed the tears from her face before handing her off to Evan. "See that she gets back safely. There are six hours left of nightfall. Please . . . ride with her all the way to the castle. Go within the gates. Help her question Lady Nenet. You are the only one I trust to be her ally. Carry her out in your spirit mist if anything goes wrong." Mordecai proffered the scarab ring. "Wear this. I'll find my own way into the Apostate Chamber."

Evan took the ring and twirled it between his fingers. "But . . . what can I do?"

Mordecai scowled impatiently. "You can help her abduct the priest, if need be. You've attended midnight confessions. You know the interior of the church better than any of us. And you've always said you would give your right arm to get inside that castle and see all of those alluring neophites first hand."

"Abduction of a priest . . ." Evan studied his fingernails. "I am not convinced this is worth my soul. And I never said I'd give my life to meet the neophites. Only a limb."

Lynora curled Evan's fingers closed around Ezra's ring. "The Sentinels will not harm you if you wear Regent Ezra's signet. You can wear a cloak. All we know in the Sisterhood is the rules and symbols of your realm. We know nothing of the regents' physical appearances. Even if they unmask you, they'll still think you're Ezra."

Evan shrugged. "That gets me in the gate. But what of an audience with the Grand Lady? Ezra is the only Desmodai she has ever had contact with. She will know his face."

Lynora patted his wrist. "We have leverage. She obviously wants to keep her true identity a secret."

"Yes. Her true identity. There's even more of a comfort." Evan inched the ring on his finger. "I want a holiday after this, Mordecai. A long, paid holiday. Better yet, I want you to use this newfound clout you have with Regent Ezra to get me reinstated as a maritime consultant within a week."

"You have my word." Mordecai's attention returned to Lynora, hands clutched to her shoulders. "Make no move for London without me." After brushing his lips over hers, he strode several feet away then stopped to glance over his shoulder. Despite his physical perfection, there was an anxious wrinkle drawn across his forehead: a worry line.

Lynora had never seen him look more human.

Pressing a kiss to his fingertip, he held it up then vanished in a cloud of mist.

The carriage flew across the dark terrain. Lynora and Evan had little time for pleasantries, too busy practicing their act for the Sentinels at the gate. Though their rehearsal proved incidental. Upon one look at the scarab ring, the Sentinels escorted Evan—hooded cloak and all— into the castle. With the lateness of the hour, the other sisters had already settled in their chambers for the night and silence wreathed the grand rooms. The Sentinels left Evan and Lynora to await Mother Nenet in the Colloquium Hall, located in the center of the third floor.

This one room in the castle reminded Lynora of the chambers in Nocturnus, due to its octagonal shape. Mossy colored silk panels comprised the ceiling, coming together in the center so they resembled an inverted dome. Lilac wallpaper covered the spaces between a succession of picture windows. Opened velvet curtains, the same mossy hue as the ceiling, admitted a continuous view of the curved hallway where the remaining rooms on the floor formed a rectangular frame around the Colloquium.

The eight walls of the chamber, along with the ceiling's draped fabric, gave the impression of being enclosed in an enormous tent. In the past, Lynora found this a cozy sensation, but tonight she felt trapped. The sconces mounted on the walls between each window flickered an eerie aura which only exacerbated her unease.

"She'll kill me. The instant I drop the hood." Evan's deep voice carried an undertow of anxiety. He plopped onto a Grecian sofa and strung out his legs, crossed at the ankles.

"No. We have a bargaining chip." Lynora paced. Her hand grazed the curved back of a parlor chair. How could she conspire against a woman who had been nothing but unselfish and giving to her? She felt like a traitor.

A knot fisted in her stomach. She didn't want to be on this side of the bargaining table. Honestly, she didn't care that the mother was a Desmodai. What she did for these women was an even bigger sacrifice due to that truth. But . . . why hide it? And what of the cradle? If the mother was responsible in any way for those poor children's fates— that Lynora could never forgive.

A sense of urgency flooded through her as she thought of Isaac. They needed to get him, but she had decided to confront Mother Nenet first, glean any information she might have. Isaac was still safe for the time being. But she wasn't sure what would become of the boy should Cornelius die at dawn. The peddlers would no longer have their scapegoat. No matter what happened, they must rescue Isaac before sunrise. This gave them only five hours. And there was still the issue of the abducted children.

"Is it true, Starling?"

Lynora whirled around. "Wren . . . "

Sitting up, Evan burrowed deeper within his hood. He inched his sleeve just enough to expose the Regent's glistening ring.

Wren clutched the door frame, complexion bared of makeup and lovely in its dark, umber despondency. A light robe covered her bed gown and her hair fell in fuzzy ebony coils down her shoulders and back—still damp from a bath. "Your scars, they're unopened." Her voice held a tremor.

"What are you going on about?" Lynora touched her bitemarks, felt the coolness of her skin.

"Raven saw the carriage arrive, she said there would be only one reason for you to be sent back, that they discovered your ammut and now you'll be forbidden to ever return. I assumed you attacked Mordecai for biting you again in an attempt to force you to stay."

Startled, Lynora took a step back and almost toppled a pottery vase behind her knees. A sweet perfume filled the air as she steadied some long-stemmed lilies with her hand. "How would Raven even know I took my weapon? You're the only one who saw."

"After you left earlier, she came to me . . . said that she wished you hadn't been such a coward, that if you were any kind of a warrior you would have taken it. I told her you did. She was thrilled. In fact, she actually began to laugh hysterically. It was very disconcerting to see her so filled with glee. She's typically such a crosspatch. So, I wrestled her to the ground and forced the truth from her." Wren drew a U-shaped silver stick from her décolleté. "It seems, this morning when we caught her in your room, she had made a switch. She got an unmarked naturlege, from our spares that we keep for the gala. She switched it with your iron one. So the ammut you carried down is in fact made of juniper, nothing more than a healing stick. She had your real weapon under her robe when she left your room. This is it."

Lynora reached out and took the iron weapon, trembling.

"I turned her over to Mother," Wren continued. "Raven is spending the night in the dungeon's cages, if you wish a word with her."

Lynora ground her teeth. What was it Mordecai had said about a spy in the castle? Could it have been *Raven* all along?

Wren's dainty nose wrinkled. "I must admit, her idea was

ingenious. But bad form, nonetheless. For her to replace the ammut with the naturlege endangered your life, should it have been threatened. Also, she ensured you wouldn't have been able to use it to reclaim your life, had you so decided. And—should anyone catch you with it—you would be escorted here and banished, which you have been."

Eyes hot and watery, Lynora yanked the ammut—no, naturlege—from her cleavage and thought upon Zebulon's escape, how the prongs had no effect; if she'd been wielding her real weapon, things would've gone differently, and Wren might be cured right now.

She dropped the false weapon on the roundtable in the center of the room and put her iron ammut in its place, forming a chignon in her hair.

"I-I wasn't banished," she mumbled, not having the heart to tell her friend that Raven had cost Wren her freedom, not her own.

"What then?" Wren turned her full attention to Evan, as if finally taking time to notice him. "From the window, we saw you being escorted in by . . . that." Her soulful brown eyes flitted toward Evan then back to Lynora. "Why else would *it* be littering the castle if something hadn't gone wrong?"

"Excuse me. I'm not some pebble that fell from her shoe," Evan said from beneath the hood. "I have a name."

Lynora cleared her throat.

Evan wriggled on the sofa. "Or rather, a title. You will refer to me as Your Regent, little bird. Show me due respect."

"I don't respect swine. And my name is not bird. It's Wren." Her fingers tightened on the door frame.

"Ah . . . no. I believe I've one that suits you better. Bristle-bird."

"Bristle?" Wren slammed the wood beneath her palm. "Such fine manners for a patriarch, wouldn't you say, Starling? It appears the murderous breed is every bit as genteel as they are merciful."

Evan stood and calmly smoothed the fabric where it clung to his broad chest. "You mean, lure a town-full of upright and moral men under the pretense of pleasure then drain them of blood while they writhe in a paralyzing trance, merciful? Merciful like you and your sisters."

Eyes lit to red flame, Wren snarled. "It is because of you and your kind that we have to dredge such swill to survive." Her sheer robe swished at her ankles as she stepped across the threshold. She scooped the discarded naturlege from the rosewood table and lifted her hands, prepared to lunge. The hall's light shined behind her, illuminating her toned curves.

Intercepting, Lynora wrenched the hair pin from her friend. She noticed an outline of a grin beneath Evan's hood. The scoundrel was enjoying this. His irises glinted in the shadows of the cloak and Wren's flamed hot enough to singe hair. Lynora had a hard time holding them apart.

"Take it elsewhere." Mother Nenet's unexpected command came from the doorway and shocked all of them to silence. "I need to speak to Starling alone."

Evan held out his ring finger but the mother waved him back. "You are no more Regent Ezra than I am the Virgin Mary. Wren, take our guest to the Armory Hall. Be discreet. No one else is to know he is an imposter. Entertain him with our . . . *weaponry*. If he is not man enough to refrain from shrinking to a cloud, capture him in a chainmail net."

Lynora stared at her benefactress in disbelief. Did she intend to kill him? The large nets were Mother Nenet's most recent innovation in their arsenal against the Desmodai. They were woven of tiny iron links, similar to the mail vestures worn beneath a knight's armor centuries earlier. They could capture an undead, even in mist form, and force him to translate back to flesh form. Lynora had once wondered how Mother Nenet knew if it worked or not. Now she realized she must have tested it on herself.

To save Evan's life, would Lynora have to spill the mother's secret, right here? How would Wren handle it? She was so fragile beneath that hardened shell. "Mother, I beseech you . . ."

Mother Nenet's resulting glare stung like a slap. "He's allowed first choice of the weapons. And control your blows, Wren. Only to the point of pain." She stroked the beaded scarf around her head, the one Mordecai had thrown at her feet during the gala. "He will be escorting Starling back to her new home in the under-realm once we are done here."

Wren paused, her countenance such a stiff mask of torture she appeared to be in full maquillage. Fighting tears, she glanced at Lynora in disbelief. "You're leaving? You're going back with him?" When Lynora didn't answer, Wren's cheeks flushed as if she imploded. She snagged Evan's sleeve and dragged him toward the door, with no concern of how he towered over her.

He looked back at Lynora and winked twice, a signal they had worked out in the carriage. He was asking if she needed him to mist her away. But she shook her head. "I'll be fine. Watch your back." She suspected he would be far too intrigued with Wren's allure to have sense enough to defend against her enraged blows. Poor fellow was about to get the beating of his undead life.

Before Lynora could turn around, Mother Nenet had closed every drape in the room. Lynora had barely blinked three times before the mother settled at the roundtable and directed her to shut the door and join her.

Lynora gulped down a knot of trepidation. No neophite or human could move with such speed and stealth. This was a blatant demonstration of her otherworldly prowess. Mother Nenet no longer cared to keep her secret from Lynora. Could it be she planned to kill her, here and now?

Readjusting the iron pin in her hair, Lynora strode to the table. Her scarlet gown swept the floor as she took a chair. She felt the ceiling drop, the walls shrink. Her hands quivered and she sat upon them in an effort to hold them steady. Perhaps her impulse to dismiss Evan had been premature.

"Do not look so disoriented, my daughter. I am sure by now your husband has broken his word and told you."

"I would have come to the knowledge on my own. I intended to investigate your room beneath the dungeon upon my return from Nocturnus."

Lynora expected the mother to look shocked. Instead, a slight smile curled her dark mouth, which Lynora now knew was naturally dark without any tinted balm to color them.

The grand woman clasped her pale hands together and her robe's black satin sleeves fanned across the table's glossy surface. "It surprises me that you did not confront me about the tunnel. I knew the night you found it. A few minutes before dawn, I had prepared to spirit through the tapestry as always so I could sleep off the daylight hours. But there I saw the splintered wood on the floor—the gap in the wall. I went up and found you missing from your bedchamber. I deduced you took the tunnel to find your husband. And the next day, I knew you hid him within it."

"How?"

"I was shut up in the chamber, sensed him in the hollows." The mother's eyes glimmered for an instant, then muted. "I have slept in that tunnel many years, Starling. By my own choice, I inlayed that trap door with iron to protect the outside world from *me*, as much as me from them. A sparrow knows when her nest has been invaded by a snake."

Lynora frowned. "If you hate him so much, why did you not kill him on the spot?"

"Because I remember what it is like to be in love."

Lynora pulled her hands out from under her hips. Easing forward in her chair, she frowned. "Ezra?"

"Ezra?" Mother Nenet repeated, shaking her head. "Has your husband told you the story of my . . . realization?"

"We had no time to speak of details."

The mother glanced down. "Ezra and I do have an abiding connection. But it is friendship, not love. He begged me to save him from his death bed. I was the only remaining neophite ambassador in his castle by then; my other two sisters had moved on with the small handful of halflings we'd rescued, planning to train them to be ambassadors themselves. This left me to tend him alone. It wounded my heart to see my dear friend suffer. Someone who had protected me and my own with devotion and loyalty. So, I agreed. The bite that gave us both immortality, was the same bite that killed my chance for happiness. It was almost two centuries ago, when Ezra was known as Monarch Cromwell."

Stunned, Lynora leaned back in her chair.

Mother Nenet met her gaze. "We staged his death. Together, he and I had the Mausoleum built with a secret passageway that leads underground to the footbridge and its opening into Nocturnus. Ezra was buried for the humans to see. Then, at nightfall, he escaped into the under-realm to become my liaison to Nocturnus . . . as I now had a blood connection to them. As our first mutual concordance, the mausoleum's path to Nocturnus was sealed up to prevent anyone using it again."

Lynora suddenly remembered how the regent spoke of his lost pipe organ; how interested he was in the instrument she described in the Euphony Hall. Gwyndolaire had been his castle, centuries earlier, and that was his Baroque organ in the instrument room.

The scarab on his ring; she'd read in the Enlightenment Hall that it was a symbol of resurrection and immortality—a symbol of protection in the ancient funerary arts. In this case, however, perhaps it was in honor of his protection over Mother Nenet's transformation. The three Eve statues on the mausoleum were obviously erected in honor of her leap into the world of the undead. They represented the life she gave up, despite what she gained. Ezra must have had the fountain in the Utopia Chamber designed in her honor, as well.

So, if Mother Nenet didn't love Ezra—the man she in essence gave her life for—who had she loved? A man who was somehow tied to the children? Perhaps Nenet was protecting him. "Tell me of him . . . this man who had your heart."

"*Has* my heart. He has never given it back. I miss him every day and every night. He once promised perfection of a serum that would bring me mortality. He had an exceptional mind and a tender heart. But his weakness was greed. He abandoned me and became one of the kindred. Embraced darkness and wealth over our love and the light. He may be undead, but has died to me a thousand times over for that choice."

Suddenly remembering the mother's reaction to Mordecai on the night of the gala, how Mordecai had told her to ask Nenet of his father, Lynora blurted the name, "*Cornelius.*"

Mother Nenet touched the pearl-edged scarf on her head, eyes brimming with liquid pain. "Did you meet your husband's father in Nocturnus?"

"No. But he gave Mordecai the key to your tunnel. Mordecai found the cradle within your room. Why do you have it?"

The lady slumped, as if her insides rent in half. "It is a fractured dream. A broken plaything from a fool's paradise. A gem too precious to relinquish to the past. But too jaded to embrace in the present."

Riddles. Lynora clenched her hands together. She had no idea what the mother meant. But one thing she did know: no one so preoccupied with being barren would have motivation to harm the orphan children. Mother Nenet must have once wanted a baby terribly. Her desire for a child had precipitated her search to find a way back. To reach out to Cornelius. Being a physician and a scientist, he was the ideal savior.

It was the only thing Lynora could see as explanation.

To Mother Nenet, the cradle had become symbolic. Of what every neophite stood to lose should they choose to live in the under-realm "Why do you hide your truth from the Sisterhood? We would support you, respect you, despite it."

The mother pushed away from the table and glided to a window. She lifted the corner of a curtain, peered outside the chamber. "Would you? Most of these women abhor the creatures that brought them to this place. Would they listen to my teachings, bide my judgements, if they knew? Would they trust my intentions? And even if they did . . . would they not be disheartened to see that I still carry the chains they all wish to break free of? Better I give them hope through a contrived story of survival and triumph. And faith, that they can one day be human again. Faith is the antithesis to doubt. As you well know, doubt breeds discontent. The beast within us thrives on discontentment; leads us to seek other venues of gratification. Less—altruistic—venues."

Lynora splayed out her fingers on the table's slick surface. "Killing instead of subduing our prey. And tasting the true flavor of human sins, undiluted with animal essence. By circumventing that flavor, we avoid the Wisdom's curse so we may somehow stay here—teetering in between."

"With a chance to one day cross back." The mother's scarf swirled across her shoulders as she spread her arms to open both sides of the drapes. Light slanted in from the hallway and imprinted her shadow on the wall behind her. The gown's long, black sleeves cast her in the image of a grand bat, preparing for flight.

Heron passed by the window on the other side of the glass. Her gaze met the mother's then quickly fell as she continued walking toward the staircase.

"Heron knows your secret," Lynora said, only just realizing.

The mother faced her. The candles warmed her golden maquillage with amber light.

Lynora stood and propped a hip against the table's curved edge. "Everyone needs at least one confidante; else they would go mad with the silence. And you have the added responsibility of your charges. Heron takes your place throughout the day. She speaks for you, leads us. You appointed her as your stand-in. Therefore, she must know the identity you hide."

"You always were discerning. Yes. Heron was the first neophite I rescued, some thirty years after Monarch Cromwell became Ezra. She was so young. Fourteen at the time. She was the only one that actually came to me. I found her in the castle's courtyard. She has lived here for the duration, drinking tea made from the reishi mushroom to her maintain her youthfulness. With the extension of her lifespan already strengthened by her being a neophite, she's managed to stay with me for seventy years."

"And you decided together to keep the secret from all of us?"

"It was only she and I for some time, as Ezra's governing skills helped curb the illegal approach of anyone not on the Desirable or Feed lists. But then, over the last two decades, there's been an influx. When Heron and I began to discover these new halflings, we thought it best to keep my curse to ourselves, so our charges would feel secure. Heron helped me plant the potent roses that grow outside the walls, so I could mask my scent."

Lynora inhaled deeply, relieved. In the span of two days she had brought a Desmodai into the castle walls and lured a priest into the Sisterhood's most sacred ceremony. The mother would have had every right to kill her for such insubordination. Would have had every right to make her an example. Instead, she was kind; held it to her breast so Lynora could battle her inner turmoil without the interference of condescending glares and whispers from the sisters. Of course, Mother Nenet was innocent. Someone with a black heart would not have been so tolerant.

"How can I ever thank you for all you have done for me?" Lynora asked.

The mother looked out the hall window again. "So, it is to be goodbye then. You have made your decision?"

"You told Wren that Evan was to escort me back to Nocturnus—my new home. I presumed you had decided that's where I belonged."

The mother sighed. "When will you understand, my daughter? You are the only one who can make that decision. I assumed the Desmodai accompanied you to help carry your things to your new home." Her robe drifted around her like a storm cloud as she turned. "You are welcome to live here as long as you like."

Lynora measured the woman's sincere expression. The mother knew nothing of what Cornelius had been doing all this time, of what was going on with the orphans. She truly believed Lynora had come to say goodbye. "Why would you be willing to condone all that I've done, and allow me to stay?"

Mother Nenet held out a hand and Lynora stepped up to take it, embraced the ice of her flesh.

"You have fostered my heartbeat . . . nurtured a part of me more precious than a thousand lifetimes, more significant to my world than the stars and the moon, or the very breath I would breathe—were I human enough to remember such pleasure." Her eyes closed and her golden countenance, though streaked with tears and kohl smudges, appeared more tranquil than ever before. "One day, you will understand why I am eternally indebted to you."

CHAPTER 38

"I will go to the door when we arrive," Lynora said, studying Evan's hood that was no more than a fray of threads now. "Your cloak is ruined. You must stay hidden within the post-chaise." Lynora studied his fangs in the moonlight. The housekeeper would never allow someone with his *unusual* attributes into a home of orphans. A jolt from the moving carriage caused her to lose balance on the squab.

Evan caught her elbow to steady her. "You might have warned me about the bird. Never have I seen a woman so barbaric in her physical assaults."

"You brought it upon yourself." Lynora slipped her gloves on. "Baiting her like you did. Wren is damaged. And the most cunning fighter among all the sisters. Only the Sentinels can better her."

Evan watched the night's ghostly scenery pass the carriage's window. "So deceptive. Tiny as a mite with the sting of a scorpion. She's like a rabid fairy." Rubbing his squared jaw, he continued to look outside.

Lynora thought she saw a hint of his dimples.

"Rabid," he grumbled. "It's a grand boon I don't bruise. The bristly little thing could have cost me my best features, and what a crimp that would've put on my social gadabouts." He turned to Lynora, his handsome outline barely discernable in the shadows. "She cracked my cheekbone twice . . . swung into me with a spiked flail. Do you have any idea what kind of damage a steel ball of that size can induce upon one's bone structure?"

"Perhaps, had it been made of iron instead of steel. She went easy on you." Lynora fought the urge to smile, studying his face in a surge of moonlight—still as flawless as when they arrived. The thought of muscular, looming Evan trying to ward off dainty little Wren was comical. However, this upcoming pilgrimage was anything but funny. It burned her stomach with dread.

Father Lucien had said he planned to visit London. What if he was still gone, and Isaac had fallen victim in his absence?

Under such a scenario, she would have to follow her instincts. Send Evan back to Mordecai with any plan she fabricated. She had made provisions to such an end, even brought Rime along. The bat soared above the carriage on the chance she might need reinforcements.

Would Wren answer a call for help at this point? After all, Lynora left the castle under the pretense that she had only stopped at Gwyndolaire for her lyre, claiming Ezra requested she play it at the Ridotto.

In that moment, Wren disowned her. She believed Lynora had already deserted them for the other side—a traitorous act which merited nothing less than hatred and condemnation. "*Fine. Go back to your world of sin. Play your angel's harp in the lake of hellfire. See if I care.*" Those were her last words, followed by an arsenal of spit aimed at Evan's boot.

Perhaps it had been wrong not to confide the children's fate to Mother Nenet and Wren. But dislike for the Desmodai had already taken root in the Sisterhood. To hear of this might bring hatred to full bloom. Lynora feared the mother would proclaim war upon the all of the under-realm. It would be the end of any treaties between Nocturnus and Gwyndolaire. The Desmodai would no longer have their above-ground merchandising transactions; their production would bottom out. They would have no means of income.

Tonight, Lynora had realized there was goodness that paralleled the evil in the under-realm. Much like in the human world—sediments of gray cushioned the white and black. Though she still did not approve of their feeding habits, they were trying to live as peaceful a coexistence as possible.

They were her husband's kindredship now. Being among them made him happy on some level. She saw it tonight, in the way he consorted with his friends. In his pride when he showed her the under-realm's beauty and explained their traditions. And his Solarium—which she had yet to see—that he compared to Eden. He told her he felt at peace in those gardens. As if he were Adam in his paradise. Yes. He was a part of that world. So she would no longer fear or hate it. Nor would she see it destroyed.

The carriage came to an abrupt halt and Lynora braced herself from falling off the squab. The horses bellowed their mechanical nickers. Evan motioned for her to stay put while he opened the door. Balanced on the carriage frame, he spoke to the driver then slid back inside with the grace of a cougar.

"On the road, there's a priest. Riding a dappled gray. He's been following us since a half mile out from the castle. He's hailing us to stop. Is this your holy man?" Evan's face lit with a reverence that surprised Lynora as much as his announcement. She would have expected to see fear reflected in his gaze, not respect.

Gathering her gown's train, she nudged Evan aside and caught a glimpse of the horseman. "He isn't *mine*; but yes, it's Father Lucien." She started to leap out, but Evan held her back. His attention fluctuated between her and the priest who was dismounting awkwardly a short distance away.

"What are you planning to do?"

"Go with him. He has the answers I seek. He'll take me to Isaac."

Evan's expression shifted to anxiety. "Mordecai will have my head."

"Mordecai knows I have to do what's best for his brother, above all else."

"Then I go, too."

"No. Sunrise will be upon us in a little more than four hours. You must go back and try to help free Cornelius. Besides, Father Lucien can't see me with you. Bad enough I have to explain a carriage led by brassy steeds with steam in their bellies and aluminum in their manes." She reached for her lyre on the other side of her seat. "Return to Nocturnus and give this to Mordecai. Tell him I have gone to find Isaac. I'll send him news through my carrier bat."

Her feet dangled, hips supported by the carriage's boot, then she slipped to the ground none too gracefully.

Shaking his head, Evan mumbled, "Neophites," and slammed the door behind her. Pebbles and dirt pelted Lynora's back upon the chaise's swift retreat.

As the night wind picked up and cleared the dust, Lynora's nerves stood rigid, overtly aware of the depth of isolation she shared with the father and his mare. Ghostly clouds obscured the moon. Behind the priest, the cemetery carved an eerie spectacle of misshapen shadows. As the clouds parted, the tombs emerged, gleaming bright against the frosted ground, like the bleached-out bones of ancient fish littering a deserted beach of white sand.

Clutching his cape to his neck, Father Lucien watched the carriage roll away, but asked no explanation for its oddness. Gratefully, Lynora took his proffered silence and wove it around her like a shield.

Once the chaise had cleared the hill, Father Lucien met her gaze and held it. Though the only sounds were the owls overhead, the wind, and Rime's echolocation, the priest's celestial countenance spoke in a vernacular so deafening it could split the soul. Something was terribly wrong.

"Isaac?" Lynora couldn't stop the name from burbling out.

Father Lucien exhaled audibly, as if he'd been holding his breath.

"He was right. It is *you*—Lynora Dureance. His brother's widow. That's how you knew him that day, at the orphan asylum . . . I'd meant to come find you the night of the gala. To confirm. I even had a gift from the lad." Father Lucien's long lashes veiled the shame in his eyes. "I've lost it, along with an entire evening. I fell asleep in the orphanage sitting room. God must've intervened, because I'd used deception to gain a way to your castle."

Lynora paused, awed by the success of her hypnosis. The priest didn't remember their conversation that evening. He didn't remember coming. And Mordecai's choice to leave him unconscious at the cemetery so the bishop would find him must've worked. For he'd awoken at the home, as though he'd never left. But that begged the question: Why didn't the bishop say anything to Father Lucien about finding him and his horse here?

"I'm so sorry." Father Lucien's gentle voice chiseled into her deliberations. "I've been away in London. And when I returned this evening," he jabbed his iron cane into the pebbles in a show of helpless rage, "Isaac was gone. Miss Plum said he went missing just after sunset."

For a fleeting moment, Lynora panicked. Her lungs compressed, unwilling to hold the air she gulped. But then she remembered her strength . . . all she had been taught over these past months by Mother Nenet, by the Sisterhood, and she called upon that inner fountain. "Take me to London."

The father's jaw twitched in lieu of a response. "But the boy wasn't ill. There's no reason he'd be there. And the bishop would've had to come back for him."

"It's possible the bishop had someone come in his stead," Lynora insisted after a shaky inhalation. "We should look among them again."

Father Lucien's mare nuzzled him but he pushed her nose aside. "Lady Dureance, I don't understand your reasoning. But it matters little. For I didn't find the children in London. Not in truth.

Something has happened to them . . . something incomprehensible. And my intuition tells me that it involves Bishop Lauden."

Lynora struggled with all she had learned tonight. How could she tell the father what she now knew about the stigmata—the real creatures responsible—without giving away what she was, possibly triggering the memories she had repressed in him? First, she needed to learn what he had discovered. "Please, explain."

The priest twined his fingers through his mare's silvered mane, smoothing the strands as they were lifted by gusts of wind. "The bishop and I travelled to London, but instead of attending his diocese, he took me to a forest on the fringes, far outside of the city limits. I had expected him to keep the children within his territorial jurisdiction, so the clergy could help oversee their care. Instead, he had them isolated. Two monks tended the patients, though they had taken vows of silence and could not speak to me of the children's well-being."

"But you did see the children?"

"I thought I did. But it was not them. No. Those creatures were something . . . otherworldly, evil."

"Go on." Lynora's voice quavered.

Taking her tremble for a reaction to the night's cold air, Father Lucien removed his cape, limped forward, and draped it around Lynora's shoulders. His residual warmth thawed her frigid bones. She realized how hard he must have ridden by the scent of his sweat, a mix of human masculinity and myrrh. That wayfaring lock of hair hung in his eyes, and, without thinking, Lynora reached up to rake it away.

He caught her wrist and his gaze intensified. For a moment, he appeared lost, distracted. Then he dipped his head closer—eyes unfathomable, as if taking a deep measure of her—and Lynora stiffened. Was it possible he saw her for what she was? Or, were Mordecai's suspicions true? Did this priest—this man—feel some fondness or attraction for her?

Rime swooped from the sky and landed on her shoulder, startling them both. As if coming out a fugue, the priest stepped back. He tugged at the white-tipped collar binding his neck, his flushed skin and quickened breath answering her inner-debate. She thought upon Mordecai's grounding collar, and marveled how this one of cloth held the same ability to harness its wearer—to nullify any chance of flight.

The father took another step back and cleared his throat. "I shall try to explain." He leaned on his cane, all business now. "I was allowed to visit the children for only a small increment of time, and was supervised by the bishop, as if he feared to leave me alone with them. They were in beds lined up against the cottage walls, unmoving, their faces tranquil . . . although the peace was artificial somehow. I could not make out their bodies, other than their small outlines. They were beneath layers of bedclothes up to their necks. I was about to touch one of their foreheads when Amelia—the little red-haired girl that you witnessed bleeding that afternoon at the asylum—started to scream and claw at her cheeks." His features tightened as he relived the horror. "She writhed beneath her covers, said she couldn't breathe. Begged me to take off her face."

"Her face?" Lynora stroked Rime's soft fur to ease her sense of foreboding.

Winding the mare's reins around his wrist, the father continued. "It had to be a mask. I don't know how to account for it otherwise. But the likeness—so real. As were all of them. The bishop scooted me out of the room before I could see to the child, insisted only the monks knew how to help her." Father Lucien's shoulders quivered, and Lynora wondered if he was cold in this wintry air, or if the memory disturbed him to the point of chills.

"Strangest of all," he mumbled, "was her voice. Hissing . . . hoarse . . . the inflections of a creature, not a child. The bishop said she was possessed by a demon. My instincts tell me otherwise." Father Lucien's gaze slid up to hers. "Perhaps I am wrong. It is human nature to question the abstract. To accept intuition, as opposed to the Lord's small, still whispers in the heart. I have a harder time with faith than others of my calling."

Lynora bit her lip, tried to piece it all together. The priest's description of the masks sounded suspiciously like the mummers Mordecai had told her of. Did he not tell her in his missive, when he chronicled his Solarium, that some pods had gone missing while he was imprisoned? And the voices Father Lucien described, they could be gargoyles. The diminutives were the size of children. The bishop must be working with Zebulon to have access to these things. But if the children in London were decoys, where were the real ones?

They had to be somewhere close at hand, somewhere accessible to Nocturnus for the blood shipments.

Lynora wanted to pick the father's mind, tell him what she knew. But what would he do? It was too risky. "You say you believe the bishop's veracity is questionable?"

"In my gut, I believe this." Father Lucien's mare nickered softly and he patted her neck. "I tend to trust my instincts, above all else. Even when I should be putting stock in heaven, instead. I seek answers here on earth—something visceral. Human nature is my greatest weakness."

In the distance, a flickering light dragged Lynora's focus away. As she squinted across the priest's shoulder, she noticed the windows were lit up inside the Monarch's mausoleum. She sucked in a breath, considering the bishop's presence here when Mordecai dropped off Father Lucien's unconscious form. Paired with Mother Nenet's confession of the secret crypt somewhere beneath the mausoleum, it all began to make some terrible sort of sense.

"Human nature is your greatest strength, Father. Least in this instance." She pointed. A swath of cloud drew back from the moon and illuminated the bishop's carriage at the side of the mausoleum. "Sometimes through disbelief, comes discernment."

"On my soul," the father whispered as he turned back to Lynora.

She nodded. "I think we've found the children."

CHAPTER 39

Mordecai leaned against a black column in the empty Apostate Chamber. He kept his arms crossed, the scrollwork biting into his spine.

Drakkarh had never showed at the hearing. No one seemed to know where the regent was, and no trial would be permissible until each member of the Agnate was present and accounted for. At Ezra's behest, the Agnate had allowed Mordecai some time alone with his father before they were to lock Cornelius away in a sarcophagus till morning.

Cornelius had confessed nothing to the Brotherhood. Assuming it was for Isaac's protection, Mordecai held his tongue as well. But now that he was alone with the old man, he still couldn't get him to talk.

He grew more impatient by the minute. He needed to be topside, helping Lynora with Isaac. When Evan had shown up with his bride's lyre and news of her rendezvous with the priest, Mordecai sent his apprentice to find Augustus and go topside to assist her—and to make haste. Dawn's impending arrival would limit their time.

The longer Lynora spent alone in the presence of that quixotic-man-angel, the more Mordecai worried. Father Lucien would kill her were he to learn of her unholy secret. Of course, his being handsome, and charming, and *human* . . . well, that didn't set too well in Mordecai's quaking gut either.

"All right, old man. If you'll tell me nothing else, at least tell me where the victims are." Met by his father's impenetrable silence, Mordecai trailed his gaze along the scarlet silk panels that draped the columns to avoid looking at the man who'd spawned him. "Think of those little children," he growled. "They must be terrified."

Cornelius sat rigidly in one of the council chairs, staring at the fingers laced across his lap. His lips let out a strained sigh. "My captors always kept me blindfolded in the travels. The only thing I remember of their location is a bronzed medallion upon the wall—a beetle, or a roach. But the children are kept hypnotized so anxiety won't taint their blood's flavor when it's siphoned once a week. Take heart in that. They've no idea what they are enduring."

"Milking children of their innocence to restore unmerited peace to the damned. How can you ascribe it such nonchalance? What kind of monster have you become?"

Cornelius frowned. "Now you wait. My conscience may not be snowy white, but I am the one who has kept the children alive all this time. That's why the bastards chose me . . . for my knowledge as a physician. So I refuse to be the object of your loathing. For the past hour I have been under scrutiny for crimes I was forced to commit. Did you hear me? *Forced.* I'll not be treated like a degenerate by my own son." His gaze nailed Mordecai's. "We haven't seen one another for seven years, and this is how you address me? 'Old man'? . . . 'Monster'? Until you can speak civilly, we shall pass the time in silence."

Mordecai glared at the grounding collar around Cornelius' neck, wished he could tighten it a few notches. "Civil? Civil to a man who spent all of my inheritance on experiments that never amounted to anything? A man who disappeared and left me with a three-month-old child to care for? Sorry. Civility is something earned, much the same as trust. And as I see it, you have neither coming. Not from me. And certainly not from Isaac, who doesn't even know he has a fath—"

Mordecai's words stuck in his throat. Cornelius' face, ungroomed and so similar to his own with the resulting fur of stubble, fell to shadows upon the heartless comment. Part of Mordecai wished to take it back.

How he used to idolize this man. He would follow behind him in his lab, drinking up his brilliance like a desert flower sipping the rarest rain. The smells of sulfur and chemicals . . . the acrid taste of onions sharp on the air after an experiment gone awry. Even now, when he worked in his solarium, his senses always opened the past to him.

In the hidden depths of his heart, he was grateful to his father. For if nothing else had come of the old man's scientific explorations, those quiet evenings in the cool of twilight contributed to the bonding of two souls otherwise connected only by blood and a voracious appetite for knowledge.

But little Isaac never got to bond with Cornelius. And due to the old man leaving them without a title or lands, Mordecai fell into Nocturnus and became isolated from Isaac as well. Perhaps that's why he was so angry with Cornelius. He had robbed Isaac not only of one father figure, but of two.

Swallowing his bitterness, Mordecai decided now was not the hour to bleed old wounds. He needed answers. And if he had to be humble to get them, so be it. "I apologize." His jaw clenched on the peace offering.

Cornelius glanced up. "Hard words for you to spit out. You cut your teeth on arrogance. Why, as young as four, you already had your toddler friends convinced you would one day be their king." His father's face brightened—the cloud of shame and reproach momentarily lifted. "Do you remember how you had the little girls trained to drop flower petals at your feet? A veritable procession followed you everywhere . . . even on the way to the privy and back."

"Enough Father. This is not the time to reminisce. You must tell me everything you were involved in."

The cloud returned, and Cornelius retreated into his shell.

Mordecai's hands fisted at his sides. He fought the urge to scream, to shake the man until his brain burst and the information volleyed from his ears. "My bride—Lynora—her life depends upon your help. As does Isaac's. She's gone to find him. She will give up everything for him. Can you remember that sort of unselfish love? For Mum . . . Isaac . . . anyone? Or is it that you're so deep in this mess, you're incapable of such feelings now?"

Cornelius leapt to his feet, his pale face stretched taught in an unforgiving scowl. "Incapable. Of love? What the hell do you think I've been doing down here in this pit for the past seven years? Do you think I wanted to be here? Do you think I came for the wealth, for the prestige? Well . . . if so, where is it then?" He lifted his arms, posing in his tattered clothes. "I live in the slatturns, Mordecai. Not much notoriety for a scientist that wallows in the squalor of his own filth and shame, is there? You want to know of love? I'll tell you of a love so unmerciful in its possession, it tore out a man's heart, raked it across the flaming coals of hell, and shoved it back into his gaping chest still afire. Sit."

As his father gestured to a chair, Mordecai slumped onto the cushioned seat. He hadn't the time for these theatrics. Every muscle wound tight, he gripped the gold-gilded arms in preparation to disperse to mist the instant he heard anything that might save Lynora or Isaac.

His father stood against the column now. "I'll admit, I was not a good father to you."

Without looking up, Mordecai snorted.

Cornelius continued unscathed. "When the lung fever took your mother, I lost myself in my work. I became obsessed with life, but even more so with death." His hands covered his face as though to hold the memories hidden, banked behind his skull. "On one of my sojourns to the Egypt, I came across a bat that bit its victims and lapped up their blood. The desmodus. I had heard that this genus lived almost twice as long as other bats. I wanted to understand their longevity. I suspected it was the imbibing of blood, drinking life's very essence. Ironic, is it not?" He flitted a glance at Mordecai. "I planned to capture some pipistrelle, to compare them to the desmodus I brought home from my travels. You were about eight at the time, if I recall."

Mordecai's clamp on the chair arms tightened. He thought upon the bats that were caged in the lab during his childhood. The stench of ammonia from their droppings. His ears still rang from their eerie chirps.

Cornelius' lashes fluttered closed and his eyes rolled beneath his lids, as if he were watching something play out in his mind. "To capture the pipistrelles, I first studied them from afar for months. They had strange flight patterns. Came from the cemetery in droves, headed in one universal direction. So I followed them one night. They led me deep within the valley and flew over a gate. When I looked through the bars, I saw a fortress. And something else . . . a luminous sliver cut from the moon and formed in the likeness of a woman." On a deep inhalation, he smiled. "The bats flew to her. Perched on her arms and shoulders, nestled in her glorious hair—black and contentious as night itself. I climbed the wall to get a better view, unaware of the bats still behind me." His eyes opened to a liquidized hazel-blue, like sandstone beneath shallow water. "They swooped down, knocked me from my roost. Busted me up. The woman had mercy on me, took me into a tunnel beneath the castle to dress my wounds. She was so exotic, so beautiful, I thought I was dreaming."

Mordecai held up a hand. "Please. You needn't paint it for me." He had suspected this ever since he'd learned of the key to the tunnel. "I was eight, you say? I remember how you stopped coming home at night. How I was lucky to see you anytime in the day. You were having an affair with Lady Nenet before you vanished. Not surprising. You were seduced by the Desmodai beauty, just as I was by their wealth."

His father's jaw muscle jumped. "How would you know of her secret?"

"That she is one of us? Don't worry, I shan't reveal her sacred lie."

Though still guarded, Cornelius' countenance relaxed. "Mind that you don't. And it was much more than an affair, Son. I loved her. Still do. It killed me to watch her live the same way it killed me to watch your mother die."

Mordecai gritted his teeth. "That's where my inheritance went. You spent it on research and experiments. All to find a serum—an inoculation—that could make her human again."

Cornelius appeared fazed by Mordecai's intuitive abilities. "How would you know of the potion?"

"I have my sources."

Cornelius sighed. "I came so close . . . so very close. Even managed to overcome the sun's ability to scald her skin. We shared afternoon picnics in the castle's courtyard, something she had not done in centuries. It was a wonderful time for us both."

Distracted by the dreamy emotions parading across his father's face, Mordecai thought upon Zebulon's statement to Lynora about facing the sun like a god. He needed to understand. "Tell me how the serum worked."

Cornelius stroked his chin where white hairs peppered the stubble. "It was a *solarizing* inoculant. When I was still human, I analyzed a dissection of skin taken from Nenet against one of me, and came to understand the cause of the Desmodai sensitivity to light. When humans are exposed to the sun, iron is released into the cells without any harm. But as Desmodai, with our diet of iron-rich blood, the added quality of the sunlight amplifies the iron within our bodies to a lethal dosage until the mineral invades our flesh—disintegrating us, as it were . . . from the inside out." He tugged on the grounding collar at his neck.

The scent of garlic filled the room, flipping Mordecai's stomach. "Father, I must hurry . . ."

"Yes. Yes. So I concocted an antidote—a mix of rare herbs and elements that worked as a sponge to capture the sun-generated iron from the body and export it out of the pores in the form of sweat. But I found that the changes did not stop there. Nenet became human on other levels as well. She could enjoy regular food. Her blood warmed and she could breathe the oxygen around her. Yet she retained the ability to mist and conjure a hypnotic gaze. I thought I was God, as I had created her anew. Perhaps that was my ultimate sin. For where we assumed success, in the hour of our greatest triumph, came the end of all hope."

Cornelius looked down at his trembling hands. "We found that with these treatments, there is an adverse effect on other essential Desmodai traits. As it must be used regularly to maintain the human qualities, the serum builds up in the system, mutating to a toxin that penetrates our immunity to sickness, our exemption from aging. Yet we still remain immortal. The change was gradual, until one morning I awoke to find Nenet her true age, centuries old. A puckered hull of the woman I fell asleep with the night before. I couldn't have her live an eternity abed as a sick and decrepit ancient. I had to cease her treatments. Flush the serum from her system. It took weeks before she returned to full Desmodai again, regained her youth and health. Of course, she lost the human qualities. It appears there can be no synthetic balance."

Mordecai tried to absorb his father's explanation. He had always known Cornelius was brilliant, but this was far beyond anything he would ever have conceived. "So, you allowed her to change you into a Desmodai? To be with her, you made the ultimate sacrifice."

"It wasn't through Nenet's bite that I was converted. She would never have wished this on me. In fact, I've no doubt she despises me now. The last time I was with her, I gave her a gift—a pearled scarf—

THE WISDOM OF BLOOD

along with a vow to return. I never saw her again. I suspect she thinks I chose this world over her. But it was against my will. The wrong men learned of my concoction, though it's still a mystery how they knew."

Mordecai studied the veins bulging in his clenched hands. He suspected the castle's spy had something to do with that.

"They brought me here," his father continued, "and forced me to further my research for their own greedy purposes, threatened to harm your brother if I failed to cooperate." He shook his head in frustration. "I thought of tainting the inoculants . . . mixing in some Bisu water. It is rich in a mineral that acts as an inhibitor, prevents the solarizing action in the blood so that the sun is actually magnified. But the leader—he refused to take the serum with that suspicion in mind. Made his henchmen use it instead. He's an insidious genius. He has everyone here fooled. Sits upon the Agnate, gloating in his glory."

"Drakkarh?" Mordecai asked.

His father nodded validation.

Mordecai's jaw tightened. All this time, he had wondered why his father didn't ever seek help from the Agnate. Now he understood.

"The man fancies himself a bit of a shepherd," Cornelius continued. "Plans to one day bring every mortal he deems worthy of us into the fold."

"And the others?"

"Enslave them. Enslave them all."

Mordecai's hands gripped the chair harder. He remembered Augustus's talk of the old world way of thinking. How some Desmodai wished to breed the humans like animals and hypnotize them from birth . . . to control their minds and bodies. What were his exact words again? *If they couldn't think . . . they couldn't sin. They would all be like children.*

Mordecai gaped. "So, he's using the children's blood to gain power . . . he wants all of the populous addicted and under his thumb."

His father shook his head. "Not quite. You misjudge his motive. There is none other more loyal to the Desmodai way of life than Drakkarh. He provided our populous with a sample of pure blood—the blood of innocence—to get support for his plan to rid our world of the poison of the Wisdom. And it's working. In a matter of time he'll have enough followers to overthrow Ezra, the Agnate, and their rules of protection. Then he plans to start a war with Nenet and her neophites—to see them all wiped out."

Mordecai's spine stiffened against the chair back as the door to the Apostate chamber opened. Two brood runners stood at the threshold to escort Cornelius to the sarcophagus.

On the edge of his seat, Mordecai glared at them. "Give us just one more moment."

They glowered then turned their backs, yet refused to shut the door again.

"Thank you, Father," Mordecai whispered upon rising. He patted Cornelius' shoulder. "I will get you out of here and absolved of these accusations."

His father eyed the guards and drew closer to Mordecai, out of earshot. "What is your plan?"

"I aim to bring each and every one of the accomplices in. One of those men is bound to value their livelihood above Drakkarh's. Who are the henchman?"

"Zebulon . . . and Hemp, the game master. There are seven others working with them, though I never learned their names. Some of them live in the slatturns."

The burn for revenge seared Mordecai's blood. Growling, he turned to leave.

Cornelius caught his elbow. "There is one more thing you should know," his voice trembled as the brood runners turned on their heels and looked in their direction. "About Isaac," he whispered.

Mordecai squeezed his father's shoulder this time, his attention linked to the impatient guards. "I'll keep Isaac safe. They'll not touch a hair on his head."

Cornelius took Mordecai's hand, the grasp every bit as cold and strong as Mordecai's own. His eyes harbored terrified shadows. "These peddlers aren't after his hair. They plan to use him. The existence of Nocturnus . . . our world as we know it . . . is in danger due to what Isaac is."

"What he is?" Before Mordecai could glean a response to his question, Cornelius shushed him. The brood runners strode over and shrouded Cornelius in a thick haze of mist, drifting out of sight in the time it took Mordecai to blink.

CHAPTER 40

After Lynora sent Rime with a message for Wren, she and Father Lucien rode toward the mausoleum. Upon arrival, the flickering flame inside the arched window had already vanished. The father dismounted his dappled gray, drew out his cane from a leather loop on the saddle, and helped Lynora down.

She glanced at the bishop's empty carriage. The cold wind whipped her skirts and stirred two lit lanterns to swing from the equipage's hinged roof. Lynora gestured to them. "We could use those for light." As she ambled over rocks and decaying tombstones, a white horse—hitched to the carriage—nickered softly and clipped at the dead, frosted grass. Lynora patted its neck upon retrieving the lamps.

Already at the mausoleum's arched doorway, the father crooked his cane over his elbow and offered to help Lynora up the crumbling stairs. She gathered her gown's hem to ascend. Her slipper rolled off of an icy stone, but the father managed to catch her before she fell.

"You really should be careful." He assisted her to the top step.

She handed off one lantern. "I'm hoping we will both be careful. Your past as a Bow Street Runner should come in quite useful tonight . . ."

He appeared puzzled, and Lynora winced at her slip of the tongue. He had no recollection of telling her about his past; for all he remembered, other than the museum, they'd only ever spoken that late afternoon she waited out the storm at the asylum.

"How would you know that of me?" he asked.

Lynora avoided his question and his gaze as she jiggled the fretwork door's latch, hoping to distract him. "We are locked out . . ." Above her, the three stone guardians loomed, glaring down with vapid, white eyes. Pale, flawless, ominous reminders of the fountain in the Utopia Chamber earlier this evening, and what might lie in wait within this mausoleum: the rogue Desmodai, with all their preternatural power and agility. She wished she had brought along a chainmail net.

Absently, she touched the ammut in her hair. Father Lucien stood next to her now, silent—as if turning things over in his mind.

"I should go in alone." She insisted, unsure if she feared for his death or her own at his hand.

His fingers clasped her glove. "No. Together."

"But we have no key." Lynora slanted a glance at him to find his expression troubled and perplexed in the yellow glow of the lanterns.

"The Lord will provide." Lifting out his rosary, he crossed himself and kissed the crucifix.

Lynora watched in silence as he shaped the tiny wired cross into a long, thin line. He crouched down, biting his full bottom lip to hide the pain in his gimp leg when it stretched out at a stiff angle. With adept precision, he fished the wire into the lock, jiggled it twice, and upon a loud clack, threw the door open. Wind whistled through the chamber and whisked around them, ruffling their hair and clothes.

Patting dust and snow from his trousers, the father stood and held up his lantern. Lynora stepped forward and added the illumination from hers.

Splashes of light stretched out before them. The large chamber— marble walls, and matching white-tile floor—waited like a glossy, blank page. A bronze scarab beetle medallion reflected back from across the way, but nothing else. It appeared abandoned. No one. Not a child, not a bishop, not a Desmodai or even a trail of mist anywhere to be seen. Yet there was the lingering wilted flower scent which indicated they had been there. Or perhaps still were . . .

"That scent." The father frowned. "It is the perfume of the stigmata. They are here. There must be some other doorway, or a trapdoor in the floor."

"Do you hear that?" Just beneath the wind's song, Lynora heard the slightest wobble of sound . . . like a child's muffled whimper. She started to step in but the father held her back with his cane.

"Look there," he whispered. "Movement. Behind the coffin."

In the center of the room, a shadow seeped along the floor, originating from the edges of an Aberdeen granite sarcophagus and spreading on thousands of spindly legs. The father swept his cane at the intruders, turning over several so their shiny abdomens grazed the air. Tiny, scarlet hourglasses caught the candlelight before the spiders flipped back over.

"Black widows . . ." Swallowing a hiss, Father Lucien hurled his lantern. The glass shattered and the flame chased back the first row of the arachnids, then wavered and gutted out, leaving only Lynora's lamp for light. He jerked her back. "Get out of the doorway, Lynora. We can never kill this many. Let them pass."

Her heart hammered. "They aren't going to pass. They were sent for us." She broke from his clasp and stepped in front.

"Sent for—?"

"They'll catch us if we run. They're trained to float their webs on the breeze—riding them like hot air balloons. We must face them. You want to strengthen your faith, Father? I have witnessed much stranger things than this. Trust me and live." With her gaze fixed on the growing plague, she reached behind to curve her arm around her companion's lower back. Her fingers clenched his woolen jacket, dragged him toward her until there was no space between them.

"Closer," she whispered. His body heat, agitated to the extreme, cut through her clothes and set fire her skin. Inching both feet to straddle the outside of his shoes, she propped her shoulder blades against his chest. He tensed as she urged his arms to encompass her waist.

Chin curved over her head, his jaw moved on a murmured prayer. If she thought anyone would listen, she would have joined in.

The spiders scuttled soundlessly closer, not slowing their advancement.

Lynora's eyes slammed shut, free hand tight around her lantern's handle. She couldn't bear to watch, but refused to stand down. Isaac and the children must be somewhere near for their captors to have gone to such lengths. She knew this for what it was. The spiders' natural instincts had been overpowered by a Desmodai—one so powerful they had mastered hypnosis on insects and pests. Would their trance affect her blood's power to repel?

A shuddering frost sheathed her spine until it was brittle enough to crack. Too late to wonder now. She envisioned the eight-legged mercenaries, clambering beneath her long skirt, winding up her legs in black vines and pricking her with miniscule fangs before they would spread like noxious weeds onto her companion, the priest whose hands clutched her abdomen as if she were his deliverance.

A holy man reliant upon the grace of the damned.

Had she misled him? Had she killed him?

"Dear God . . ." The father's words, mumbled in reverence and disbelief, incited her eyes to open. "'Tis like the parting of the Red Sea."

The spiders split their formation to two swiftly moving waves— clambering atop one another to escape contact with Lynora—then scrambled past on either side, across the threshold and out the door. In a matter of seconds, they had scurried into the moonlit graveyard to disappear within the powder of decomposed rocks, snow, and the cracks of fallen tombstones.

Lynora took a relieved breath.

The father's hands still clutched her waist. Leaning in, his chin grazed her shoulder. The scent of myrrh surrounded her to overpower the mausoleum's staleness. "Those spiders were repulsed by something," he accused, his breath stirring the hair on her nape to tremble. "Terrified, in fact." Spinning her around, he clasped her upper arms. "I have seen such phenomena before. At the orphanage, Isaac and two other boys once stumbled upon a beehive. The other two children nearly died from the stings, but Isaac came out unscathed and untouched. What is your explanation for that?"

Lynora's thoughts rattled in her head. How could she explain it? And how could Isaac be anything like her? It had to be a fluke. In her mind, she willed Wren to read Rime's message, to come despite her bitterness. At this point, Lynora wasn't sure where she stood with the priest.

Father Lucien's grip tightened, pinching her arms. His gray eyes appeared feverish, as if an epiphany came upon him. "Gwyndolaire's bizarre gala . . . I was there. I-I thought I never made it to the castle. But I remember now, the walk on the way. My strange companion— the man in the Venetian mask. He repelled a swarm of gnats without twitching a muscle. There are creatures among us, and you know of them, Lady Dureance." He forced up the arm holding her lantern so the light would illumine her face. "I believe you are one of them."

The soft whimpers started again, from somewhere seemingly far away, but yet close enough to be just within reach. Lynora tried to jerk free. "The children . . . surely you hear that."

"I hear nothing." His expression hardened.

She didn't doubt his sincerity. Her perceptions were in tune with higher pitches and sharper resonances after working with the bats for so long. She knew her ears weren't deceiving her. She also knew, if the priest didn't turn her loose, she would have to resort to hypnosis. But the Desmodai lying in wait might very well outnumber her, and to have Father Lucien in a daze would render him useless to help her fight . . . or to save himself. "Father . . . you're hurting me."

He dropped his hands, his expression teetering between compassion and condemnation. "I've no desire to harm you. I merely seek answers." The muscles in his jaw jumped. He snapped off his clerical collar and cast it to the floor, exposing dark bruises around his neck in the shape of Mordecai's handprints. "I thought I'd dreamed it all, until I looked in the mirror and found this. Someone tried to kill me that night at the gala." He tugged her forward and forced her hand against the contusions, as if comparing them for her benefit. His body heat burned her skin. "I need not look again to know this handprint is too large to be yours. It belongs to that man. The one who walked with me. He tried to strangle me and I fell unconscious. It's why I lost my memories. But now I remember. You were there, trying to protect me."

Lynora's stomach plummeted. "This is wasting our time. We need to find the children." She broke away and took several steps backward into the chamber, past the two large bronze lamps which remained unlit on either side of the entrance, backed up until her hip wedged against the sarcophagus' carved lid. Her gaze ran a scope of the room, seeing nothing out of place. Where were the sounds coming from? Mother Nenet said the secret underground path to Nocturnus had been sealed off. But there could remain a hallway, a corridor . . . some chamber or such that once led to the passage still open.

Father Lucien followed Lynora, cautiously. "I want to trust you, Lady Dureance. I've no doubt your love for Isaac is sincere. And you stepped in front of me earlier, saved my life." He touched the bruises on his neck. "You've done so more than once. Despite whatever has poisoned you, you retain kindness and compassion. It radiates in your every action, in your every touch. But I have suspected you were different since that day at the asylum, perhaps even before." The door slammed behind him with a loud echo and he bent to grasp his fallen cane, holding her gaze.

A lock of hair fell across his forehead and he raked it back. As he stood, he began to act peculiar, tapping his cane along the floor. He kept Lynora in his peripheral and moved from tile to tile, thorough in his coverage. "I predict, by the end of this evening, you and I will both realize how different you truly are."

Lynora chewed her lip. This was no longer a passive and gentle holy man. This was a detective—relentless and driven. He would not stop digging until he uncovered the truth. She could only pray that his determination to find the children would overrule this drive to understand her origins. As he rounded the sarcophagus, she turned, determined not to let him out of her sight.

He hung the cane over his elbow and started to press along the wall in intervals. "Intriguing, isn't it?" He grunted between his words, his broad shoulders tense with the effort of testing the marble. "We are of opposite inceptions—you of darkness, me of light—yet we have ended up at the same destination, brought together by the purity and innocence of a handful of children. I still believe you to be an angel, Lynora. Be it one of blood and fury, or of tears and passion, it makes little difference to God. For He can still use you, either way."

Lynora clenched his cloak around her neck with one hand and raised the lantern with the other to light his movements. The child's whimper started again, broken and soft. Then it grew on a swell, erupting to a flurry of sobs.

Father Lucien turned to face Lynora, one fingertip held aloft. "I hear it now."

Her stomach jumped. Yes. And she knew that cry. She had heard it a dozen times after Mordecai's initial disappearance. "*Isaac.*" Her heart split down the middle—torn asunder by both relief and dread. If he was crying, he was alive. In trouble . . . but alive.

The father pointed to the floor. "I noticed earlier. There are places where it's hollow beneath us. We need to find a secret panel, a hidden latch . . . something." He was at the wall again, pressing along the crevices.

Lynora's gaze ran the length of the room then returned to the sepulcher. The sobs seemed to be emanating from inside. She held her lantern up to the life-sized carving atop the lid, shaped in the likeness of a man lying with arms crossed over his chest. Each line—each curve and indention of the face—matched Regent Ezra's own. A tomb for a man who would never die.

A tomb that would never be filled.

Lynora's pulse throbbed in her neck. "Father . . ." She set down the lantern, dropped her cloak, and tugged at the sarcophagus lid. "We must open this."

The priest limped over. "What can a dead monarch do for us?"

"I assure you. We will not be disturbing the dead."

He gave her a piercing stare.

Isaac's wails erupted again, undeniably from the coffin.

Tilting his head, Father Lucien tossed down his cane. Together, he and Lynora clenched the edge. The granite cut into her fingers as they slid the lid halfway off. She didn't miss the father's accusatory glance when he noticed her strength. Nor did she miss his effort not to mention it.

Lynora leaned over, looking within. It appeared to be a common sepulcher—empty, but ordinary. Until she noticed a latch at the inner left-hand corner which blended into the granite. Giving it a nudge, one-half of the coffin's floor swung open, like a trap door. A stale, musty scent wafted up a stone staircase from inside.

"Sweet Mary . . ." Father Lucien glanced in from behind her.

The stairs spiraled into the dark depths of a vaulted crypt. Isaac's cries assaulted her ears—clear, precious, and heart-wrenching.

Lynora hesitated, terrified of what she would find. At this point, she was sure there was more than just Zebulon to contend with. But she didn't have time to conjecture. They must take action . . . do everything they could to save the children.

She lowered her head to get a better view.

Out of the darkness a hand jutted forward and clenched her throat. Thrown off balance, her feet lifted from the floor. She struggled to draw breath through her flattened windpipe. The coffin's granite edge grated against her ribcage.

"Lynora!" Father Lucien caught her by the ankles, wrestling against her captor.

Clutching the vicious arm that held her, Lynora's fingers tangled in her captor's thick, woolen sleeve. A hot, sour breath swarmed her face. Whoever it was, they were human.

Her knees wedged against the coffin's lip to prevent being towed inside and thrown down the stairs. The granite ledge scraped across her abdomen as Father Lucien managed to tug her body backward and she found footing on the mausoleum floor.

Her captor lunged forward, still half within the coffin, never breaking his hold. In the lantern's dim light, his image resolved and she recognized the bishop's episcopal vestments.

She managed a gasping breath as he repositioned his grip.

Dizziness swirled her thoughts. She couldn't get to her ammut; she had to clutch the coffin's edge to keep from being yanked in again. A whisk of air fanned her left cheek as the father's cane delivered a cracking blow to the bishop's head. Lynora tumbled backward to the floor, liberated at last.

Breath dragged into her lungs and she swallowed against the ache in her throat.

"Are you all right?" Father Lucien helped her up.

"You saved my life." She patted her neck. All she could manage was a whisper.

"Only once." He grazed her hand with a fingertip. "One more, and my debt to you will be paid. Now wait here." With a lumbering stiffness, he mounted the coffin's edge and dragged the half-conscious bishop by his robes over into the mausoleum side. Before the older man could escape, Father Lucien had his belly pinned to the floor and maneuvered a headlock, his arms laced through the bishop's and hands crossed against his nape. "How could you! How could you betray every vow you've ever taken and harm those children?"

The bishop writhed, forcing Father Lucien to straddle him.

"You've no idea the forces you're dealing with, Lucien. The rewards. They're infinite. Better to be on their side than on the side of—"

"What? On the side of the Lord? On the side of goodness? You sold out your soul for carnal gain!"

"It appears you have done the same. No respectable lady would be with a man at this hour—priest or no—without a chaperone. Unless she is a whore. Perhaps from the Gwyndolaire Sisterhood?" The bishop struggled to look at Lynora but Father Lucien thrust the man's cheek to the floor in the opposite direction.

"Disparage her again and I'll forget my own vows." The father leaned over, his lips just above the bishop's ear. "You remember my past vocation. You won't be the first man I've ever killed."

"Don't be a fool." The bishop's voice muffled from the strain on his vocal chords. "What they are offering me upon completion of my service . . . what they can offer you. The power, the wealth. Immortality on earth. On *earth*, Lucien. We don't have to wait to die to experience it. We can have everything at our feet. Now."

"Said Eve to Adam in the garden of paradise. An instant before they were thrown out into the wilds. You're the fool, Bishop Lauden. For even the undead must answer to God on the day of reckoning."

Isaac's cries started up again, snagging Lynora's attention. Anxious, she met Father Lucien's gaze.

The father hooked an elbow around Bishop Lauden's neck and jerked his head back until he groaned. "Tell us what we face down there." The bishop wouldn't answer so Father Lucien pulled back harder, eliciting a sharp cry.

"The children are all alive," the bishop squeaked out. "But you won't be. The six creatures guarding them . . . you have never met the likes."

Father Lucien slammed his opponent's face back to the floor. "Dare not stake your life on that, Bishop."

Unable to wait a minute longer, Lynora gathered her gown's hem and swung first one leg over then another, sliding onto the steps. "Bring the lantern when you've secured him." Then, removing the ammut from her hair, Lynora gripped the metal in hand and felt her way down the obscured steps, led by her blind training and the thick scent of Desmodai wafting up from the dank crypt.

At the bottom, she saw lights dancing in the darkness . . . the eyes of the undead. Every hair on her neck stiffened to wire. How could she ever fend off this many, alone?

"Lynora, wait for me!" The father's distressed voice trailed down the passage.

Then she heard it: the familiar flapping—as loud and glorious as dying thunder. A rush of bats flew past from behind, churning her gown's fabric. From the midst of the chaos, Rime landed on her shoulder. She reached up and found his message removed. Wren's voice called out from the mausoleum, muffled beneath the jingle of chainmail.

CHAPTER 41

Mordecai stopped by his sanctuary chamber to check on Krig and look within the kaleidoscope, desperate to pinpoint Lynora's whereabouts. Yet he struggled to concentrate even with the gargoyle present. The balancing effect seemed to have no power over the night's discoveries swirling in his skull, like dust motes distorting the clarity of daylight as it shines through a window. Disjointed facts clicked together: an inoculation which could render a Desmodai almost human; the cradle in Nenet's tunnel; Isaac's ability to heal, to never get sick; his blood unscented—devoid of temptation.

The suspicion that had niggled in the back of his mind during the talk with his father descended upon him like a fell tree. Could it be true? All of these years, he'd wondered upon Isaac's lineage, but never tried to find the boy's mother. Perhaps a part of him had feared she'd take him away forever. But this . . . this was inconceivable.

Cornelius said that in the hour of his and Nenet's greatest triumph came the end of all hope. Was Isaac their greatest triumph? Had Cornelius made Nenet human enough to conceive? That would mean his brother was a halfling—*by birth*. The first of his kind.

Obviously, Isaac had the ability to heal at a tremendous rate . . . to ward off illness. But what other powers waited beneath the surface, yet to materialize? Would he crave blood one day, or by some turn of fate—as the missing link between the humans and the Desmodai—was it possible he would not require the essence of humans to live, as he already possessed it within his own genetic make-up?

Krig snored from the couch in the corner and shook Mordecai from his uneasy ponderings. His brother's origins and the effects thereof would have to wait. Mordecai lifted the kaleidoscope for another glance into the lens. He forced his thoughts to quiet like a lake smoothing, the ripples slowing to glass after the cessation of rain; he emptied his mind of anything but the present, and sought his bride.

After countless hours of practice over the past several days, it took only an instant to focus in on Lynora once he was calmed enough. A picture came into view, clear despite the darkness. Something encompassed her—as if the night had sprouted tiny wings. It revived the sensation of being swallowed by a blanket of bats. Wherever she was, her pets were with her. That could only mean one thing: she had run into trouble.

Biting back an oath, he turned the cylinder slowly, focusing deeper, hoping to see Evan or Augustus at her side. Instead, she walked cautiously in solitude down winding steps, her face fraught with terror. Just the sight of her was enough to clench his throat. He would fly to her side in an instant, if he could only find some landmark, something to reveal her locale.

As if responding to his unspoken request, she looked behind where a soft glow streamed from an opening above her. On a distant wall hung a brass medallion; his father had mentioned one and the same, referencing its form as a bug. Mordecai saw it now with precision: it was scarab, like the one on Ezra's ring.

The ring that had been inspired by Edward Cromwell's resting place.

She was at the mausoleum!

On the tails of this revelation, he watched Lynora descend the stairs again. All the air around him shrunk. They waited at the bottom . . . dancing lights . . . the eyes of the undead, the dredges of his kindredship . . .

"Damnit, Lynora! Stop!"

Lynora could no longer hear Isaac's cries over the bats. She peeled off her gloves for a better grip on her ammut as she descended the stairs. Her hands fisted as if to encapsulate all of the fear brewing within her. Almost to the bottom, she counted the glowing eyes. There appeared to be at least six of the rogue Desmodai until one set of eyes suddenly vanished, leaving five. As more bats swooped around her toward the crypt, a gust of wind passed her going the opposite direction—upward toward the mausoleum, nearly knocking her over. She regained balance, distracted by her pets as they rushed into the depths below and triggered a cacophony of snarls and hisses. Feeling her way down one step at a time, Lynora kept the Desmodai in her sensory-sight, but lost them as they were cloaked by rubbery wings. Then everything fell quiet.

A jingle came from behind and a sweep of light glossed the wall next to her. Lynora stopped three steps from the bottom, turning to see two sentinels holding torches and metal nets and Wren carrying a quiver of iron-tipped arrows—each one armored with their bracelets and neckbands. Mother Nenet appeared next with a dagger which Lynora now understood must only be tipped in iron for the mother to be able to manipulate it without being weighed down. Following last came the priest with his cane, descending the stairs.

Although a look passed between the six of them, no one spoke a word. Who they each were, *what* they were, no longer mattered. They were here to save the children. And to preserve their fragile alliance, they would be quiet and swift, wasting no time on petty suspicions or accusations. They would have to rely upon one another if anyone was to come out alive.

As one, they began their descent.

The bats had ceased their flapping. The only sound now was the echo of Lynora and her troop's footfalls. It gave her little comfort that Isaac's cries had stopped.

Once she took the final step, Lynora held up the lantern offered by Father Lucien, splashing light along the wall's staggered stonework. With a wave, she lit up the ceiling where the bats hung from rafters overhead, their wings tucked away, watching . . . awaiting her command. Rime, in the midst of the colony, blinked his pinkish gaze in the slowly brightening glow as the sentinels lit two wall torches.

The rogues appeared to have left, but more likely had misted into the tunnel at the right, to lie in wait. Mother Nenet obviously had the same intuition, as she motioned the sentinels to stand guard with their chainmail nets spread across the tunnel's mouth to prevent anyone filtering back through.

The moment Lynora's vision adjusted to the flickering light and fluttering shadows, a collective gasp passed through her companions in response to what lined the farthest wall. Seven children were hooked up to tubes and lying on knee-high stone altars, all in a row.

Mother Nenet turned to the priest. "You must see to them." The anxiety in her voice scraped the dank air like fingernails shredding ice. "We cannot be exposed to their blood."

Father Lucien paled to a white that countered Mother Nenet's golden maquillage; he nodded. As he passed Lynora, he cast her a knowing glance. At last, he had validation. He knew what she was—to some degree. His expression shifted from mortification to constrained pity before he looked away to kneel beside the first child he came to. He leaned over the tiny body.

"She's still breathing." His voice wavered. "Her eyes don't blink. She is in a trance." Fury contorted his profile as his thumb and forefinger followed a clear tube from the child's wrist to a clay vessel, where the tubing disappeared through a small hole in the lid. A cloth tape was wrapped around the children's wrists and the vessel's lids to seal off the entry points and stifle the scent. "They—" he choked on a swallow. "They're being drained. There are droplets of blood on the inside of the tubing."

A surge of nausea rushed into Lynora's gut. To see these helpless innocents, their faces as pale and expressionless as bleached leather, stoked a rage deep within, alongside a disconcerting despair. For seven was the number of children Father Lucien had expected to find. Isaac would have made eight. He was not among them.

Had hearing his cries been a trick of the mind? Or perchance one of the Desmodai mimicked the sound to lure her down . . .

"Remove the tubes," Mother Nenet spoke again. "Bandage their wounds and we will help you carry them up."

Father Lucien hesitated. Lynora caught the glint of distrust in his eyes, even in the dim light. But he tamped it down and started to work a tube from the first child's arm.

A groan and a shuffle of feet drifted from the staircase. Father Lucien looked up.

Lynora, Mother Nenet, and Wren spun on their heels to see. The sentinels glanced over their shoulders, but held their vigil at the tunnel.

Taking the stairs, the bishop clutched Isaac in a chokehold with a knife to his throat, dragging him down the final step to the crypt where everyone stood. Mother Nenet yelped and Lynora caught her gaze for an instant before returning her attention to Isaac. She couldn't read his face, for his head was bowed and his hair hung in loose strands around it. Lynora willed him not to be afraid.

"*Lauden*. How did you get loose?" Using his cane to rise to his feet, Father Lucien threw out the question. But Lynora already knew the answer.

When she had seen the set of glowing eyes vanish earlier, when she'd felt the gust of wind moving up the stairs toward the mausoleum against her and the bats . . . it had been one of the corrupt Desmodai misting by her, holding Isaac in his spirit shroud. The creature must have slipped by her companions as they came down, then freed the bishop and deposited Isaac into the hypocrite's arms.

Suddenly, there was a stir as three Desmodai translated to flesh on the steps behind the bishop. Lynora recognized Evan immediately. And the other man, Augustus, along with his wife, Florentia; although a dark veil covered her face, Lynora recognized her gown from earlier.

Her heartbeat stalled. Did one of them spirit by her? Had they been on the side of the peddlers all along? Had Mordecai's friends betrayed him?

Tears threatened to rise, but Lynora fought them. No. Evan had helped her earlier. She had to have faith.

Her gaze fell to Isaac again. He'd lifted his head, and she noticed something odd. Even with the knife puckering his tiny neck, he didn't look the least bit frightened. His eyes met hers, and all of her concerns and worries coalesced into one pure emotion: confusion. He appeared at peace, somehow. As if he knew something she didn't.

"Isaac?"

The instant she said his name, he dispersed to mist and drifted back up the stairs past the bishop and the trio of Mordecai's friends. Lynora gasped.

The bishop's eyes widened and he dropped the blood-tipped knife, stumbling backward. "It's a trap! These two forced me to play along! The boy's getting away!" As if cued by the bishop's words, Augustus and Evan attacked the bishop, pinning him to the floor as Florentia replicated Isaac's vanishing act and followed him up the stairs. Before Lynora and her companions could react, a sudden rush of fog seeped from between the crevices of the stone wall to fill the depths of the crypt. The vapors translated to five fang-snapping, mirror-wielding Desmodai. In a powerful surge, Mother Nenet swept her wide, black sleeves across the torches and snuffed them out to protect the neophites from facing their reflections, leaving only Lynora's lantern for light.

Mordecai flung the kaleidoscope onto his library case, nauseous over what he'd seen. Isaac was a half-breed. He could no longer doubt the boy's identity. And Augustus and Evan had come to Lynora and Isaac's aid, but were they too late?

Growling, Mordecai jerked open his desk drawer. He shoved aside the mummer still wrapped in cloth. He thought upon the mask, the perfect rendition of his face. If only he could put on the past as easily as a mask. Become that man again. The man before the fall. Before he brought all of this down upon his family.

He should have been rich with happiness and peace because a lovely, devoted woman accepted him as he was; because his brother looked up to him. Instead, he had wanted to be accepted by society. Respected by those who never really mattered. Now, the only two people in this world who *did* matter were topside facing this danger without him.

After taking out his knife and dropping it in his pocket, he slammed the drawer shut, keeping the kaleidoscope at eye level. He felt his way to the door, watching Lynora spin in the air, engulfed by a darkness alive with flashing eyes and snatches of shimmery mirrors. He willed her not to see her reflection, to stay in the darkness. Her skirt swirled like a crimson tide around her, lit up by the glow of a passing lantern. Her leg swooped high with a kick. When she made contact with a Desmodai male and knocked him to his knees, Mordecai caught a glimpse of her face.

Hell's fury and heaven's light merged within the fire of her eyes and the pallor of her skin. Mordecai felt an icy shadow cross his soul. Once she made her first kill, a precious part of her would be lost . . .

her innocence was one step closer to dying with every sweep of her weapon.

Desperate to get to her, Mordecai reached for the door's latch.

"Master . . . find light?"

Mordecai glanced across the room at Krig. He'd completely forgotten about the creature's presence. "She's in trouble," Mordecai choked out. "You stay and rest. You took an awful beating today."

"Master . . . good doctor." His servant tottered over and lifted the splint on his hand. "Krig much dandy. Krig help."

Meeting the gargoyle's inquisitive eyes, Mordecai gestured for the creature to join him at the door. "All right, go to Ezra for me. Tell him Cornelius is innocent. I'm bringing proof." He paused. "And tell him . . . tell him Lynora is topside fighting for her life to get it."

The instant Mordecai unlatched the lock, the door flung him backward and someone dove across the threshold toward him from the shadows outside. Startled, Krig blended into his surroundings. On his knees, Mordecai blindly shoved his servant out onto the front step. "Go, Krig!"

The intruder elbowed Mordecai against the sanctuary chamber's wall and slammed the door, locking it behind him—uncaring that the gargoyle escaped.

Mordecai relished the small victory, glaring as a gold tooth reflected in the wake of flashing eyes before him.

Fangs bared, Mordecai peeled himself from the wall, acutely aware of the ache in his shoulders from the impact. Riding a wave of rage, he lunged at Zebulon.

The Reaper hedged to the right and held up a large, lidded bucket, stopping Mordecai before he whipped around and tried again. "Wait there, lad. Ye mightn't want to upset the contents of this treasure I hold. Yer lovely bride's future is ridin' on it." A damp, fishy scent hung on the air and water sloshed within the wooden container.

Mordecai's every limb went numb at the mention of Lynora.

Zebulon hacked and inhaled a rattling breath. "Yer nosy little bride stumbled into a pit of vipers, she did."

Mordecai snarled in frustration. Zebulon blocked the door. As long as it was closed, the iron inlays prevented Mordecai from misting an escape. He couldn't swallow for the dread rising like bile. "What in hell are your plans for her?"

"Well, I'd like to take credit for hell, but it's my accomplices that will see her to that destination. When I left, she was fightin' for her life. Why . . . I even think I saw the grand Lady Nenet and some neophites." He laughed. "Ah yes, and a priest. What a mismatched band of martyrs, aye? Committin' suicide for a handful of mortal sprouts hardly worth the dirt they're made of."

Every muscle in Mordecai's body coiled, ready to spring. He sized up Zebulon, waiting for the perfect moment to rip out his jugular so he could rush to topside and find them. "My brother is one of those mortal sprouts, and he's worth more than a thousand of you."

Zebulon laughed again until he coughed. "Yer brother is worth a thousand mortals, ye mean to say. I just got back from seein' him." He swiped snot from his nose. "He is above any mere human, and we both know why, don't we?"

Mordecai's windpipe cinched to the size of a crushed flower stem. "How did you know, when I only found out tonight? He's *my* brother."

Zebulon shook the bucket in his hand, watching through a small knothole in the lid as something flopped in the water, stirred to life by the movement. "Drakkarh bit a young girl years ago and dropped her altered body into Nenet's courtyards. The grand lady took her in as a charity project. Too bad neither Nenet or the neophite knew of Drakkarh's gift of telepathy." Zebulon tapped a finger against his sweat-slicked temple. "He knows everythin' that altered chit be knowin'. Reads her mind as if he were livin' in it." Zebulon took out a hanky and swiped his face.

Mordecai stared at the bucket with restrained interest. "So, this spy. Does she have a name?"

Zebulon grinned. "Dyin' to know who she is, aye?"

Tiring of the game, Mordecai gritted his teeth against an answer.

Shrugging, Zebulon jostled the bucket's contents. "No need for ye to know. Ye'll be dead soon anyway, by blood or by guile."

The tail end of the statement stiffened Mordecai's spine. "What the hell does that mean?"

Zebulon's fingers splayed on the bucket lid, curled over the edge in preparation to open it. "Drakkarh's a word smith, he is. He made up the phrase. It was the oath he made us swear to as we kissed his gold ring . . . when we joined his cause."

Cause . . . Mordecai again pondered the wickedness of Drakkarh's plan, his mind racing for some way to stop the Regent.

Zebulon shook the bucket. This time, something butted against the lid. He startled, as if the movement unnerved him. His attention dragged from the lid to Mordecai. "Even Cornelius had to take the oath. Drakkarh knew yer father would ne'er endanger his own son. But to be sure, we had to become Cornelius' kindredship. Why do ye think I bit yer ol' man to begin with? Had to solder his loyalties to Nocturnus, so that if we were overturned, he would suffer the consequences with us."

Mordecai's jaw clenched. "*You* brought him over." He took another step forward, ready to kill the bastard and cut out his heart to serve it up to his father so he could be human again.

"Ah-ah." The bucket raised between them. "Ye don't want to be doin' that. If yer luscious little bride manages to save herself up there," Zebulon's eyes rolled upward to indicate the topside, "ye'll want what's in this bucket. Tis salvation from the cursed eternity she ne'er asked for, living amongst the likes of us."

CHAPTER 42

Lynora had the Desmodai on his knees but her focus waned. Concern for Isaac swelled within her. How did he do it? How had he translated to spirit form like those of the kindredship? Had the peddlers altered him and brought him to full realization? The mere thought sucked all of the air out of her, making her wheeze for breath. The mental rambling cost her the advantage. Her opponent slammed his fist into her thigh and she staggered back. A throbbing misery rushed up her leg as if his knuckles scuttled beneath her skin, jabbing at every nerve.

Utilizing her one good foot, she pivoted to miss his next punch.

Chainmail and breaking mirrors rattled around her in the darkness. Lantern light painted the walls in intermittent flashes, being passed amongst her and her allies to illuminate each one's battle at different intervals. The only ones of their troop who could see in the darkness were Mother Nenet, Evan, and Augustus.

Someone else had the light now, so Lynora lashed out instinctively with her ammut, utilizing her blindfolded training. Her wrist halted in midair, stalled by an unseen block that sent pains all the way to her elbow. The scent of wilted roses quivered on her nose.

Bats dived and swooped. High pitched echolations trembled off the walls. Mayhem erupted in full . . . a rush of shadows then a flash of piercing lights which floated like flames without a candle or a wick, headed toward her.

"Lynora!" Father Lucien thwacked the shins of a Desmodai with his iron cane, then tossed her the lantern.

She caught the handle in time to see her opponent leap forward, fangs and mirror exposed. Arching back with closed eyes, she felt his teeth swish past her neck. Her ammut came up, shattering the mirror then raking along his stomach, ripping his clothes. He rolled as he landed.

Within a heartbeat, he stood again, his broad back to her. She rushed him but he turned at the last minute. He caught her waist and spun her around. The lantern slid from her grasp. With her toe's tip, she launched the light to Wren who had an arrow aimed at another rogue Desmodai.

Lynora's opponent looped an arm through both of hers from behind and held her shoulder blades against his chest. He lifted her feet off the ground. She donkey-kicked him in the shin, but the impact had no effect. Twisting, she tried to escape.

His free hand clenched her jaw and forced her movements to desist for fear he'd snap her neck. Icy fingers curled around her chin. Her pulse slammed in her throat as she struggled to think of a way to get free.

Footsteps shuffled from behind, a gritty whisper over broken glass. Blinded by darkness, she heard a loud metallic thunk. A rasping yelp chilled her nape as the Desmodai's grip loosened. He dropped her, her knees meeting the ground as her captor slumped to the floor beside her—Father Lucien's cane at the back of his skull.

Lantern light glossed the priest's face. He held out a palm. Lynora took it, her hand nearly slipping for the blood on his. The scent denoted that the blood didn't belong to him.

"Now," he said. "Now my debt is paid." With a nod, he handed off the lantern and rushed toward a spinning cloud of mist taking form as a Desmodai beneath a chainmail net.

Placing the lantern on the floor, Lynora nudged her Desmodai opponent to his knees. She positioned the ammut at his chest where his torn shirt exposed his flesh. Still disoriented from the crack to his head, he started to mist but an iron arrow whizzed by Lynora's ear and pierced his shoulder, breaking his concentration. Head thrown back, he screamed. Furious, he locked Lynora in his flashing gaze as he brought his chin down again. She counteracted with the flames in her own eyes. From her peripheral, she saw Mother Nenet lunge at someone then get thrown against the wall.

Worried for her friends and the children, Lynora drew from the wellspring of indignation within her, letting her darkest emotions sharpen her resolve. Everything bled into the backdrop, like watercolors melted by the sun. All she could see was the creature kneeling before her—a creature that had tortured and used these innocent orphans for weeks. A creature that might possibly have changed her precious Isaac into a wretched, blood-thirsty being.

Lynora yelled. Lifting her ammut, she brought it down with a slicing arc. Her aim was flawless, and a fountain of red gurgled from his chest. The rogue Desmodai crumpled to a withered, convulsing heap. Turning away, Lynora shoved back a lock of fallen hair and wiped blood spatters from her face. Then she leapt into the midst of the ongoing battle, ready to kill again.

Mordecai watched Zebulon closely. The Reaper still had the bucket propped on his thigh. Hearing the sound of keys jingling outside the door, Mordecai sensed that Krig was trying to get in. He attempted to keep Zebulon occupied and oblivious to the sound, so that the moment the door opened he might mist away.

"How are the contents of that bucket going to be Lynora's salvation?" he asked.

Zebulon loosened one side of the lid and his eyes flashed.

Mordecai tried to look away—too late. The Reaper's hypnotic glare captured him, froze his ability to form a spirit shroud. He cursed beneath his breath.

The lid clattered to the floor and the Reaper held the bucket's sides, keeping it an arm's length away from himself. "Drakkarh has offered to cut my Reaper's chains. My final commission is to see ye get put in yer place. So I brought his prized pet to finish ye. This sea serpent's been raised in Bisu water. His venom flows with it. And Drakkarh has hypnotized him to bite only you." Zebulon turned the bucket enough to slosh out some puddles.

From his peripheral, Mordecai saw the jewel-scaled snake coiled in the bottom, writhing in knots as thick as a man's arm. He gulped.

"Once yer a diminutive, ye will serve under Drakkarh. Yer first assignment will be to kill yer father and brother. And if ye still have enough thought process left to keep ye from doin' Drakkarh's bidding, ye'll be burned to ash. Course, then yer wife will have her precious mortality again, aye? See, there's not a down side to this scenario for any of us . . . 'cept for ye." He laughed. His eyes watered, yet still held their hypnotic power.

Mordecai battled an agonizing sense of dread. Surely he would never be so warped as to harm his own father and brother. But he had seen how the Sphinx water affected other Desmodai. If, God forbid, he did the vulgar things they asked in ignorance, Lynora would be forced to remain a neophite until the day she died. She would be lonely . . . married to an imbecile that she hated for harming the little boy she loved. And it wouldn't matter to Mordecai, as he wouldn't even remember her name, let alone his own.

The only answer was for him to die. Just as he had known all along, ever since that morning in the rose grove.

Lynora would never be happy in this darkness. She would never find peace in his lifestyle. But as a human again, she could find happiness, contentment, and light. Perhaps that vision he'd seen of her with a daughter was real. Perhaps she was destined to one day have children of her own. Though to think of another man fathering those children wrung Mordecai's heart as if it were a rag—a useless, empty rag.

But wasn't that all it was now, anyway?

Somewhere in the back of his mind, beneath the soul-rending grief and remorse, logic found a voice. It screamed at him. It told him not to give the Reaper the benefit of committing any more murders. It told him the Agnate needed to know of Drakkarh's vile plan to kill Ezra. That he must try to escape to save Nocturnus. Mordecai thought he heard the scrape of a key in the door. He spoke up before Zebulon could notice. "Wait. I believe I know how to cure your pain."

Zebulon's aged forehead furrowed in disbelief. "Are ye bloody foolin' me? A cure? Ye know the Reaper's walk. And yers was only for one day. Try to live that torment for decades. Each sin, each crime, gouged into your soul like lashes from a cat o' nine tails. But these wounds ne'er heal to scars. I'm bleedin' inside. Bleedin' to death."

Mordecai's optical muscles ached from straining to pull his gaze away from the Reaper's hold.

"I hate them," Zebulon growled as he started to tip the bucket. "I hate every mortal I have ever captured. I hate their weaknesses . . . the reasons for their crimes. I abhor knowin' their justification for every wrong they commit. They do not deserve my pity, any more than I deserve their guilt! The children's blood . . . the blood of innocence . . . it is the only mask for this pain."

"You don't understand. Lynora . . . she helped me with my guilt. There is another alternative to this. One that can cure the torment inside you, not simply mask it. But you must release me first, let me stop Drakkarh."

There was a momentary shift in Zebulon's stance, but Mordecai could sense the futility of his plea. Fate had laid out his final hand, and he must make the best of the cards dealt him: give his family back their lives.

"All right then. Kill me. I'll not resist. Make it as long and torturous as you please. Just don't alter me. Don't force me to harm the ones I love. You can take something good from this; perhaps win your soul an ounce of peace and mercy if you give my bride back her mortal life and spare my father and brother."

Snot and tears oozed along the Reaper's face as he considered this last request. He almost looked human, and Mordecai thought perhaps he would cave.

But he shook his head. "Sorry, gardener. I have other orders." With that, he pivoted on his back foot, prepared to fling out the bucket's contents.

In that moment, the door sprung open and hit the Reaper in the back, breaking his hypnotic spell. The bucket spun through the air.

Mordecai dispersed in an instant to mist. The hissing snake soared through his spirit form, slapped to the floor, and left a trail of water as it slithered beneath the couch.

"Master . . . ?" Krig stuck his head in.

Zebulon's foot shoved the gargoyle out again and wedged the door closed. He locked the latch.

Transmuting back to flesh, Mordecai lunged at the Reaper. Zebulon flung an arm out. Mordecai snatched his wrist, twisted it around until it cracked. Wailing, Zebulon doubled over. Taking advantage, Mordecai threw him to the ground on his back.

He tucked his captive's arms beneath his own knees. Zebulon offered little resistance now, weak as any mortal from the sickness and fever that had taken over his body.

Leaning forward, Mordecai locked his gleaming silver gaze on the Reaper, pinning him by his own trick.

Outside the door, a struggle erupted. "Bite me, will you?" Mordecai recognized the voice as Hemp's. "Damn little gargoyle," the game master snarled. "Show yourself." More rustling and curses ensued. From the sounds of it, Krig was holding his own.

"What is Hemp doing here?" Mordecai mumbled to Zebulon.

The Reaper's gold tooth glinted. "Drakkarh took yer father's solarizing inoculants and left the under-realm, in search of other scientists in cities like ours. Hemp and I are to seek out Ezra and kill him. When that's finished, Drakkarh will return with an army to claim his spot as leader of Nocturnus and execute his plan. There's nothin' ye can do now. By dawn's first light, ye'll either be a dead man, or a feebleminded gargoyle."

"Dawn's first light, you say?" Mordecai remembered the snake's wet trail, its three-inch fangs dripping with Sphinx venom as it glided harmlessly through his mist. He glared at Zebulon, so filled with the solarizing inoculants he was ill. What was it Cornelius had said about Bisu water when mixed with the solarizing inoculant? That some mineral in the water rendered the solarizing qualities useless . . . that it *magnified* the sun's damaging elements?

From outside, Hemp yelled at Krig. "Run then, you little maggot! I'll find you later. You'll be in my pit come tomorrow." The locked door rattled beneath his pounding. "Zeb. Zeb, are you in there? Did you finish him yet?"

Keeping one eye out for the serpent, Mordecai pulled Zebulon's hanky from his pocket and crammed it into the Reaper's mouth. "Zebulon has come and gone." Mordecai's voice raised so Hemp could hear over the wooden barrier between them. "He said something about looking for you. We had a chat. Made a bargain."

"I know nothing of any bargain." Hemp jiggled the door handle. "Let me in. There's no escape."

Zebulon's eyes grew wide as he struggled to push out the hanky with his tongue. Mordecai slapped a palm over his mouth. The Reaper wheezed beneath him, his chest shaking between Mordecai's thighs. "Not until you agree to uphold Zebulon's word," Mordecai insisted over the muted struggle. "I want my father and brother spared."

"In exchange for?" Hemp asked through the wood.

"My death and Krig's loyalty, without a fight. My gargoyle's your last loose thread. He knows all the relevant facts. He's on his way now to the Agnate. I have instructed him not to breathe a word, to hold loyalty to Drakkarh, unless my father or Isaac are harmed. Then he confesses all. And you'll never catch the gargoyle first. I told him to stay hidden for the duration." Mordecai waited, hoping Hemp would concede.

Hemp swore. "And why are you so willing to die?"

Zebulon thrashed. Mordecai resituated to get a better hold. His spellbinding gaze intensified on the captive. "It is better for everyone this way." Mordecai's voice shook, belying his courage. He lifted his ring finger to his mouth and eased the twine circle from its place with his teeth, letting the ring drop to the floor. "Lynora will be human once more, free to raise my brother. My father, he is of no consequence to you. He won't speak of Drakkarh's plan so long as Isaac is spared. Give him safe passage from the under-realm. Nenet will make a place for him in the castle, I am sure of it. He'll never bother you again."

Mordecai's words stalled. Was he really capable of carrying this out?

But one thought of Lynora—her sweet smile, her purity like rain, her adoration of all that was good and light; one thought of Isaac— his tender imaginings, his limitless talents waiting to blossom—and all doubt faded. This would earn him their respect and trust again. He could die a happy man, knowing that.

A scraping rustle stirred beneath his couch and he sensed the snake moving toward him. The hair on his neck stiffened to needles.

One bite. One bite is all it would take.

Yes. He could do this. It was the only way. "I ask one favor, Hemp. I'll not be a goose-brained diminutive. I want to go out with respect. I wish to die in the Solarium, among my plants." While he spoke, Mordecai patted the Solarium keys within his vest. Zebulon's eyes filled with confusion as Mordecai continued talking. "I want the last thing I look upon in this life to be my gardens when dawn first brushes their leaves." His fingers clenched the Reaper's white-tipped braid then moved to Zebulon's long beard.

"Is that it?" Impatience laced Hemp's question.

"Yes. Let the sun take me . . . so the last thing I feel is its warmth upon my face. Please . . ." Mordecai mentally mapped out the distance from here to his desk. Then drawing his knife from his pocket, he lifted Zebulon's facial hair with his blade and pressed the sharpened metal against the Reaper's throat—right at the beard's roots.

Zebulon whimpered.

Hemp's growl shook the other side of the door. "No need to snivel, sentimental dandy. You have my word. I couldn't care less how you die. So long as you're a pile of ash in the end. Now open the door, before I bust it down."

CHAPTER 43

Dragging herself from beneath the hidden passage at Haven's Creek footbridge, Lynora rushed behind Krig along the narrow walkways of Nocturnus. Her torn, muddy dress clung to her skin. The scent of wet cotton-mull, ripe with sweat, stung her nose. Hair draped her shoulders, sticky and tangled.

Shadows swathed the dark world, an ethereal buffer between her and her husband's kindredship. Being only a half-hour from dawn, the entire populous appeared to be locked away in their sanctuaries. Though grateful she had no audience, Lynora had never felt so alone.

The water dripping from her torn gown, the pebbled crunch beneath her blood-stained slippers as her bruised legs struggled to propel her onward, even the lapping canal; it all felt distant, far off like the morning birds that trilled in the hills topside, prepared to welcome dawn's first light.

Visions of death echoed in her mind. She had survived the battle in the mausoleum, but her heart and soul would never be the same.

Had Zebulon not escaped and evened out the odds, Lynora and her companions might never have managed triumph without fatalities. Evan was wounded when one of Wren's iron arrows misfired and punctured his shoulder. The priest and Lynora, as well as the sentinels, suffered cracked ribs, bruised and battered limbs, and bloodied noses, prospectively. But the only fatal wounds were inflicted upon the five renegades and the bishop—purely accidental, as he fell down the stairs and broke his neck. Out of the six Desmodai they fought, only one survived. And he was wrapped in chainmail now, awaiting escort to the Agnate for interrogation and execution.

Looking back on Evan and Augustus's selfless contributions, Lynora at last understood that one did not have to be human to have humanity. This humbled her, for she had misjudged her husband, along with the majority of the under-realm. She had been judgmental . . . and had hurt Mordecai in the process.

Tears flooded her vision and she blotted them away. She felt as if she'd been crying for hours. Though not all had been tears of remorse. Tonight, for the first time in months, she had held Isaac in her arms, smelled his little boy scent. He was so thrilled to see her alive. And she was thrilled to know that he had not been turned into a Desmodai. Isaac explained that when Zebulon shrouded him within his spirit and passed Lynora on the stairs, Isaac had a sense he was capable of the same trick. Then, after Zebulon deposited him in the hands of the bishop and left the mausoleum, Isaac translated to spirit form. The bishop was chasing his cloud to no avail when Augustus, Evan, and Florentia had arrived.

To think, Isaac was Cornelius and Mother Nenet's son. The grand matron had given Isaac over to Cornelius when the babe was only a few weeks old—when she stopped taking the solarizing treatments and reverted back to the blood-cravings of the Desmodai. She had feared she would hurt the baby. But after tonight, they had realized his blood was similar enough to the Desmodai strain that no one would be tempted by it. The bishop had cut Isaac's neck during the ruse Augustus and Evan had arranged. When Florentia misted back up to be with Isaac in the mausoleum, his blood had no effect on her. She claimed it smelled like Desmodai blood. Knowing this now, Mother Nenet had begun making plans for him to leave the orphanage and come to stay at the castle tonight.

This gave Lynora hope, as well. For just being who he was, Isaac had made it possible for their family to be together again. To have their happy ending. Lynora needed that hope, as she feared what she was to find at Mordecai's abode.

"Master home . . . there." Krig's clammy fingers touched her wrist. In the distance, Lynora could make out a sanctuary chamber, its door ajar. Along the front steps, something glittery slithered out and glided into the canal. Krig muttered that it was a sea serpent, and she recoiled. From within the chamber came the faint sounds of a struggle and heated whispers. She and Krig ducked behind the archway of a bridge to watch. Lynora gripped the limestone structure. Her other hand reached for her ammut.

When the gargoyle had arrived at the mausoleum a half-hour earlier and told her of the threat on Mordecai's life, she left without apprising anyone. Now a part of her wished she had at least informed Augustus or Florentia.

But they were too busy trying to explain to Father Lucien—or "Luke", as Florentia called him—how his sister hadn't died in the fire he caused eight years earlier, that instead she was reborn as a Desmodai. It was better the father didn't see her until after the fight ended, otherwise he would have been too distracted to function.

Seeing Father Lucien so happy to be with his sister again, regardless of the circumstances, Lynora couldn't bring herself to interrupt their reverie.

Wren didn't notice Lynora leaving either, for she was bandaging Evan's wound none too gently while snarling at him for blocking her line of fire.

The sentinels, along with others of the Sisterhood that had arrived moments after the battle, were tending to the children who, aside from being anemic, were no worse for wear due to their hypnosis.

Even Isaac was too preoccupied to notice Lynora's retreat from the crypt, as Mother Nenet was entertaining him with an Egyptian tale worthy of any boy's ghastliest imaginings when Lynora crept away through the tunnel.

No one saw her leave. So no one would appear at just the right moment to deliver her should she fail to save her husband.

If he were still alive.

Lynora clenched the bridge harder until the stone bit into her flesh. No. She wouldn't believe the worst. She felt no different physically; she took comfort in that. But she couldn't shake the sense that she might need assistance.

"Krig," Lynora knelt eye level with the gargoyle, "go find the brood runners. Tell them . . . a murder," she choked on the word, "is about to take place. I'll try to wait here for your return. But if I'm gone, lead them to Mordecai's chamber. Understand?"

Krig touched her shoulder. "Master . . . need light. No snuff out . . . Lynora."

From behind the creature's long lashes, Lynora glimpsed the discernment Mordecai had once told her he believed the gargoyle capable of. She had every faith that her husband's servant—his friend—wouldn't fail them. Standing, she stroked the wispy hairs on his head. "Make haste. Do not worry for me."

Upon one final glance back, Krig disappeared, blending into the stone surroundings. His footfalls faded with the distance. A flutter of movement at Mordecai's sanctuary chamber caught Lynora's attention. The door swung wide open and two men, one dragging the other by the scruff of his cloak, left the sanctuary chamber.

She hesitated. Krig had said that Zebulon and another Desmodai named Hemp were threatening Mordecai. She didn't recognize the one in the lead. So she assumed him Hemp. Mordecai must have given a good fight, to leave Zebulon so debilitated that his partner had to carry him.

Terror fisted around her heart. Did this mean they had finished their job? As she inched toward Mordecai's chamber, the Desmodai being dragged lifted his hooded head in her direction. The soft glow of the luminary flowers on the wall glazed his face, and Lynora nearly fell to her knees.

Mordecai.

There was no mistaking that face . . . those features engraved upon her heart.

Subduing a scream, she followed at a safe breadth away. Mordecai's head bobbed. His body convulsed beneath his cloak. Each time Hemp looked over his shoulder, she pressed her back against the tunnel walls, hiding in the furrows and shadows.

She trailed them to their destination through a long passage and around a bend, creeping closer when Hemp drew a key from Mordecai's vest pocket to unlock two massive brass doors. Flinging one open, he hauled her husband's quaking body inside. Before the latch could catch, Lynora sprinted forward and forced her way in.

"Release him!" Her demand shattered beneath the thud of heavy brass sealing the entrance shut several feet behind her.

Hemp let Mordecai drop to a heaving mass on the grassy turf.

The scent of blossoms and overturned earth hung on the humid air. Lynora clasped her hands behind her waist, the ammut woven between her fingers. It felt as she had stepped outdoors. She could make out silhouettes of trees and plants in the dimness.

"Well now, what do we have here?" Hemp's eyes flashed. Lynora warmed her red glare to ward off his hypnosis.

He smirked. "I saw you at the Ridotto. Our gardener's liminal bride. The chit that can't decide if she wants to live in the Sisterhood or stay with her husband." His lit gaze danced across Lynora's soiled face, raked over her tattered gown. "Not much to look at, are you? Can't understand why he suffered so much grief over your indecision." Having turned off his flaring eyes, Hemp continued to bait her. "Why, I wonder. With the Desmodai vixens he had to choose from. And believe me, they were lined up." He tapped Mordecai with his toe. "Weren't they, gardener?"

Mordecai moaned.

"Stay away from him." Holding her ammut still tucked behind, Lynora shoved Hemp with her free hand. The Desmodai laughed and propped himself against a pomegranate tree, illuminated by moonlight.

As Lynora glanced at her husband, face down in the grass and blanketed in shadows, a duo of emotions twined within. Guilt for all the loneliness he must have suffered over these months. And gratitude for his loyalty to their wedding vows, despite how stubborn she had been.

All around, purplish lights refracted through water on the lofty, vine-strung walls. Lynora recognized their location. They stood beneath the glass ceiling in the Solarium—the closest thing to being outside in the under-realm. Mordecai had not exaggerated the beauty of this place. Oh, how he loved it here.

The light on the walls was slowly warming to pink. Sunrise would be upon them in minutes. Lynora's pulse kicked up its pace. She would not let her husband die in his paradise. She would not let him die at all. With Hemp out of the way, she could drag Mordecai back through the door before dawn.

"You brought him here to kill him." She turned back to Hemp. "Are you so determined to savor his fate, that you'll risk your own life, just to watch?" Her fingers tightened on the ammut behind her. Resisting the weakness in her joints and the ache in her bones, she stepped over Mordecai. She wondered if Hemp was like the other henchmen, immune to the sun through the inoculant.

The Desmodai seemed amused by her question. "Who says I'm in danger?"

She took another step forward. If he wouldn't die by sunlight, he would die at her hand. She had already killed tonight, and faced no remorse for it. In the midst of that bloody fight, she came to understand that some beings thrived on wickedness and the torture of the innocent, and had no place in this world—be they human or otherwise. She had gained new sympathy for the Reapers and their walk. Perhaps not respect, but understanding and insight.

Her focus fell to Hemp's posh clothes. Finery notwithstanding, she would assure the aim was well-placed and the thrust sufficient to bypass every layer of fabric and kill. Fingers tense, she drew strength from the chilled iron—its slick points jutting out from her fist.

Mordecai's wail from behind broke her concentration. Keeping her ammut out of sight, she turned to roll him to his back. His limbs stiffened and his body jerked as if a bolt of lightning drove through him.

She fell to his side, forgetting Hemp, the impending dawn, everything but him. "Mordecai. . ." She touched his face, shocked that it felt hot. She glared at Hemp where he stood against the trunk. "What have you done to him?"

"Ah, I'd like to take credit for his torment," Hemp answered with an insidious grin. "But I found him like this on his floor. Must have happened when he unlatched his sanctuary door for me—Tis when I heard him scream." Clucking his tongue, Hemp stretched his arms above his head and rested them behind his neck in a casual pose. "And here I thought old Zeb had gone soft. What a brilliant strategist. He smuggled a weapon into your husband's chamber . . . a sea serpent whose fangs were filled with Bisu water."

"No." Lynora croaked. She cradled her husband's suffering body, unable to fathom that he would be like Krig in less than twelve hours. She refused to believe it. It was just a reaction to the snake's common venom, that was all. As she tried to pull Mordecai's hood off so she could free his hair, his hands came up and held it in place—fingers twitching with determination to keep himself hidden from her.

Her chest ached, remembering how he'd called himself a monster just a few nights ago. "Please, Mordecai, let me see your eyes. Open them. We'll . . . we'll get your father." Cornelius could save him. Judging by the condition of the children despite their loss of blood, the man was a medical genius.

Hemp snorted. "He can't hear you, chit. He's out of his mind with the pain. No worries though. The sun's almost here. You're about to get your mortal life back . . . just like Mordecai wanted."

Mordecai wanted? Tears filled her eyes. She cradled her husband's head on her lap, gripping his hands where they still clenched the hood. "No, Mordecai. That day in the museum, you promised me you would never let me go." Sobbing, she bent to press her mouth to his. His lips, chafed and stiff, wouldn't respond. "And I promised to never leave you." She clenched his wrists tighter. "I am holding true to my word. And so are you."

CHAPTER 44

Overhead, a hazy, pink sliver skimmed across the leaves topping the trees on the east side of the giant greenhouse. Silent and sovereign—growing, moving—an ominous entity determined to chew up and swallow the man she loved.

So intent on her husband's face, Lynora almost missed the sound of leaves moving beneath the fountain's song, as if something crept through the vines that were thick on the ground.

Hemp slanted a glance at the swishing sounds, as puzzled as Lynora as to the source.

As if triggered by the attention, the rustles stopped and Hemp glanced back at Lynora. "Won't be long now, chit." His nose sniffed. "Mmm. I can almost smell his flesh roasting as we speak."

Repressed sobs swelled in Lynora's throat. All of the rage against Hemp—this beast that had helped kidnap seven children and now threatened her family—burbled up within her, molten hot and seething. Growling, she shoved herself to stand, ammut jutting from her fist, and on a sharp turn, dived for him. A flicker of awareness lit his eyes, but too late.

Lynora's arm muscles quaked with the impact as his caving sternum ushered her weapon's prongs all the way through his heart. Her wounded rib ached, but riding her rage, she didn't stop pushing until the ammut's points slid between Hemp's vertebra with a crunch and impaled his body to the soft trunk behind him. He hung there, writhing, choking on his own blood—the smile on his face now an agonized grimace. Crimson droplets drizzled from his erupted fangs.

Gagging, Lynora wiped the sticky residue from her hands and turned from the sight of gruesome withering flesh that accompanied the iron-born death of a Desmodai. Stumbling to her inert husband, she gripped him beneath his arms. Against his weight—against her pain—she backed toward the door.

Her breath caught as the rustling sound revived. Using the soft light that glazed the tops of the wall, Lynora could make out movement where vines slithered from behind the pomegranate tree to wind around Hemp's unmoving feet. She balked, recognizing the plant as Mordecai's creeper.

A horrible crack split the air as the ivy ripped Hemp's shriveled form from where it hung. In a matter of moments, the plant surrounded him . . . devoured him.

Lynora yanked Mordecai again, all too aware that the rustles had not ceased. In fact, they seemed to be getting louder . . . closer. Her heart tripped in her chest, a thudding jab that gave her feet rhythm and purpose. Was it chasing her? Did it remember how she sliced it away from Mordecai's cellar laboratory months ago?

She tried to outrun the creeper.

Lifted in strike position, several vines leapt forward and clung to Mordecai's boots and ankles, holding taut against her efforts.

"No! Leave him!" Balancing Mordecai with one hand, she slapped at a stem with the other. Deep scratches gouged her palms where the plant's stingers burned her flesh.

She couldn't understand. It wasn't after her at all. Why would the plant attack its own master?

Unless it meant to rescue him from her.

She glanced up at the steadily brightening ceiling. "I'm trying to save him, you fool!" Lynora resumed her grasp on Mordecai and pried against the plant, persisting until the vines snapped free. Dirt shuffled around her in clouds as she and Mordecai advanced. But the creeper returned in a wave, a green rush snaking toward her until it had him by his ankles again.

An excruciating stitch in her side halted her as her movements aggravated the fracture in her ribs. She clenched her jaw through the burn. On the other side of the door, she would rest. But not until Mordecai was safe. Crying out, she gave a harsh tug, making a full two feet of progress against the creeper's resistance.

From above, bright sunlight pierced through the watery ceiling and lit the grass and foliage in a sparkling advancement on the west wall. It might as well have been flames for the death it would leave in its wake.

Lynora resituated her grasp beneath Mordecai's arms and around his chest to gain ground. At last, mere inches from the doorway, she propped him against her and unlatched the lock. The brass door swung open a crack.

"Let it take me," a shuddering rasp carried the words from Mordecai's mouth, stopping her. "It hurts too much . . . to live."

The voice didn't sound like her husband—wracked with the fatigue and trauma he was suffering. Shaking off tears, she caught him beneath the arms again. "No. I didn't get to choose. Neither do you."

Before she could secure a tight hold, the creeper overtook again; tendrils of green coiled all the way up to his thighs and ripped him from her clasp. She fell backward, hitting the ground. Pain radiated along her nape from the impact. She regained footing, but the vines had already dragged Mordecai to the fountain and encompassed his body, holding him dangerously close to a ray of sunlight.

"Stop!" Lynora loped toward him, her stride awkward from a dizzy rush in her head.

As if bursting through a dam, the entire solarium lit up with harsh, unfeeling light.

Falling to her hands and knees, Lynora watched, helpless.

For one perfect moment, she saw Mordecai as he was before the change, kissed by the sun, a closed-mouth smile on his face. Her husband, surrounded by his incomparable hybrids, at rest beneath his flowers and trees. Though his eyes were shut in peace, it gave her no comfort. For it only took an instant for him to burst into flame then crumple to dust bit by bit. His beloved creeper vines ignited after him. When the fire burned itself out, only Mordecai's heart remained, still beating, nestled in the pile of glowing embers.

Lynora went numb, didn't even realize she'd stumbled over to the fountain until the spray of the water hit her face when she dropped to her knees.

It was surreal. A dream . . . a nightmare. It had to be. She dug out the throbbing heart, uncaring that the hot ash cauterized her fingers. Holding the throbbing organ against her own, she willed it not to stop.

But it did.

All around her, peace reigned. The sun warmed her shoulders, eased her weary muscles. Water, cascading into the fountain, trickled into the basin like a patter of gentle rain. Yet within her, there was no peace, no hope . . . and the rain was a storm, unrelenting and wild, flushing away her numbness to release a gush of agony.

"N-o-o-o-o!" She screamed out. She thrashed on the ground like a wild animal, cursing at the ashes that were once vines. Smoke tightened her throat with each piercing breath. She howled and clenched her hair, yanking it until her scalp throbbed, anything to detract from the torment in her heart.

Her eyes sealed to hold back tears—tears so cold they burned. Cold like her blood. *Wait.*

She drew up her head to study the ashes on her palms. Why hadn't she changed?

"Lynora . . ."

Chest caving from her earlier sobs, Lynora stared at the gnarled heart in her hand. It was as if she could hear Mordecai's voice echo through the organ. Only a whisper, like the night in the cottage—when he came wanting nothing more than to give her his love, to keep her with him forever. Propping an elbow on the fountain's ledge, she studied her pale face in the water's reflection.

"Lynora . . ."

She shook her head, convinced she was going mad. Trying to stand, she yelped at the sharp pain in her ribcage.

"Lynora?" There was a pause. "She's hurt. Daylight be damned. I'm going in after her."

"Don't be a fool. Send the gargoyle."

On her knees, Lynora noticed a slight throb begin beneath the scars at her neck and realized that had been missing earlier, when she followed her husband as he was dragged by Hemp. But at the time she had been too distressed to pay attention.

Intent on these ponderings, she didn't notice Krig until he stood next to her.

"Master . . . want light."

Stunned, Lynora turned to the creature.

Krig grinned, his kitten eyes fluttering. "Cornelius . . . need heart. Lynora, follow? Follow for Master."

"Master?" she whispered, glancing again at the pile of ash beneath her.

Gently, Krig pried the lifeless organ from her hand and offered his palm to help her up. Too dazed to argue, she allowed him to lead her across the grass. Motes of dust and fuzz floated around her, glittered in the sun's rays as the gargoyle opened the door and led her through.

Stalled at the threshold, she tried to focus in the tunnel's dim light, making out a line of brood runners in the shadows—all standing far enough away to avoid the sun. At one end, Ezra stood, a sympathetic expression on his face. Was he here to comfort her? Holding her attention, the regent gestured toward the center of the men where there was a stir in their midst.

They parted, and Mordecai stepped out.

Her knees shook. The tell-tale throb nudged beneath her scars again.

He strode as close to the sunlight as he dared. His palm opened for her. "Lynora. It is over. Come to me now."

She took one shaky step forward, then heard the crashing thud as Krig closed the door behind her to block off the Solarium.

Freed of their boundaries, Mordecai crossed the walkway in two strides and drew her into his strong, chilled embrace. He kissed the top of her head and whispered words of love.

Burying her face in his chest, Lynora breathed him in, let her legs buckle. He caught her beneath her knees with one arm and around the waist with the other to scoop her up. As if he sensed where she was wounded, he cradled her with care, avoiding her ribs.

"Is it you?" she mumbled, afraid to believe.

"Hear my heart. Know that it's me."

Her ear pressed to his chest. She relished the music, more dulcet than a thousand harps in heaven. Their gazes met, and his laughing blue irises soothed her.

"I . . . watched you die," she said. "The creeper . . . attacked you . . . went up in flames with you."

Shock flickered across his face. "Oh no. She must have sensed it wasn't me. She was protecting the garden from intruders, as she's been trained to do."

Lynora threw her arms around his neck, tucked her head beneath his chin, and sobbed. "I'm so confused."

"Shhhh." Mordecai tightened his embrace. "It was Zebulon . . . wearing my mummer's mask. I captured him, teased the serpent then misted out of its reach so it would inject him, instead. I placed my keys in his pocket and wrapped him in my cloak. Hemp had no idea when I unlatched my door that I dived beneath the couch to wait. He plundered in and mistook Zebulon for me."

Easing back to study her husband's features, Lynora frowned, still unable to piece the puzzle together.

Mordecai kissed her hair. "I needed to free the Reaper's heart from his body, to get it for my father. But I also had to warn Ezra that his life was in danger. It was the only way I could think of to accomplish both at once. I'll explain it all later. For now, you need to rest and mend. You're exhausted." That concerned line etched across his forehead—the one that made him look human.

Comforted by the vision, Lynora started to feel drowsy. She caressed the stubble on his chin, touched every feature on his wonderfully familiar face to assure that he was real, then pressed her forehead to his chin. "I killed men tonight, Mordecai." Her voice broke on the admission.

He caught her wrist and studied the deep scratches left by the creepers, his eyes filled with compassion. "You killed monsters," he whispered. "You are a warrior now. Yet somehow," he kissed her aching palm, "even after a grisly battle and a struggle with heart-wrenching grief, you still come out looking like a rose."

She wiped away the ash caked on her cheek. "A *trampled* rose, perhaps."

"Trampled, but not broken." His hungry smile ignited hers.

Ignoring everyone around them, she tangled her fingers in his hair and coaxed his head down to kiss him. "I love you."

He moaned a response as her mouth opened to unite their tongues. Warmth flooded her at the contact, rich with the essence of flowers and wine.

CHAPTER 45

"Come, Lynora." Mordecai ushered his bride into the Solarium. He locked the door as she leaned her hip against his lab table and looked around. Moonlight glazed her beautiful face, highlighted the fear which stirred shadows in her eyes. She didn't wish to be here in the garden again. That much was obvious. He struggled with a bout of empathy. But he had already coddled her long enough. Now that he had seen her strength and resilience first hand, he was biting at the bit for their long overdue consummation.

For one month he'd waited for her bones and bruises to heal. During that time, both of them stayed busy strengthening the relations between Gwyndolaire and Nocturnus, as well as helping cure the small percentage of the populous beneath the spell of the children's blood.

Two nights ago, Mordecai had his coronation into the Mentory—a private ceremony with only his fellow Mentors and the Agnate. Tonight he'd attended a Ridotto at the Utopia Chamber with Lynora. Now was the first time he'd had her all to himself, and the first time she had set foot in the Solarium since the incident with Zebulon and Hemp.

"Those sinister memories need to be banished." He fondled a tendril of hair at her temple. "You're to spend many nights with me as I work. I want you happy and at ease."

She peered over his shoulder at the fountain in the distance.

"Mordecai, tonight I gave myself to you. Pledged my life in front of the Agnate, the populous, everyone. We performed the Danse Séduire . . ."

He noted the blush in her cheeks as she played with the buttons on her high-necked lace gown where blood stained the weave. His mind drifted again to the erotic climax, when he wreathed her in his mist, lifted her high, and explored every alluring curve and cleft of her womanly form beneath that gown. He smiled. Being a spirit certainly had its advantages.

She had whimpered in ecstasy as he bit her neck, just before he gave her his blood to drink then lowered her back to the floor to be congratulated by the crowd. But hidden, up within the domed ceiling of the Utopia Chamber, her moment of release had been theirs and theirs alone.

Now here they stood in solitude, and his hunger to taste her again threatened to overwhelm his aspirations for tenderness. He could feel the barb of his fangs just beneath his lips. He forced them to retract. This night was for Lynora—her induction into womanhood. He would take great pains to secure her pleasure, even if it meant delaying his own.

He was already indebted to her, for suggesting they dance the Séduire. Tonight they became bloodmates in everyone's eyes, even without her reaching full realization. Her insight had found the perfect compromise for them both.

"Must our first time be here?" She dug her fingernails into her wrist nervously.

Mordecai captured her hands and opened them, kissing her palms. "There's no better means to chase away ghosts, than conjuring new ones. More amiable ones." He winked at her and she managed a tentative smile. Her glossy, loose hair formed a halo of midnight and stars around her face and shoulders. He had never seen anything more captivating.

Drawing her in for a deep kiss, Mordecai smiled against her. "Your kisses taste like ambrosia."

"I believe that's pomegranate ale." She grinned.

Returning her smile, he took her hand. "This way."

Draped in shadows, they rustled through willow grasses and wildflowers—provoking a swishing sound and an earthy perfume. As they skirted the fountain, Lynora paused and stared suspiciously at the newly sprouting creeper vines.

Mordecai turned his bride to face him and swept hair from her eyes. "This one will never attack you. She'll grow with you, be loyal to you. The more you're here, the more she'll trust you." Overhead, the moonlight infiltrated the water through the glass roof, painted the surroundings with fluid bluish-green reflections. The spectral waves danced across his bride's delicate features.

"I can't forget that horrible sight." Glancing at the fountain, she looked like a bewildered mermaid adrift in dark water, seeking refuge.

Mordecai drew her into an embrace, glancing over her head at the spouting water. "*I* am holding you. *I* am with you. What you saw that morning was a nightmare, one I never intended for you to endure." He stifled the emotions threatening to break. "You fought so hard to save me."

"I would do it again." Her unselfish vow, spoken into his shirt, went straight to his heart.

"You are the most courageous woman I've ever known."

She nuzzled his chest. "But I feel like a coward. For refusing to live with you."

He stretched her out to arm's length. Her hand toyed with the open lapel of his shirt. "It takes more courage to stay up there, among the mortals. To face temptation. Heron went off to seek revenge on Drakkarh for using her as his spy. And although my father was cured, Wren is still unchanged, proving Zebulon was not the Reaper from her memory. Your friend needs you. They all need you. I understand why you must stay topside."

"But will it work, for us?"

Catching her chin, he coaxed her attention toward the ceiling. "Do you see that, my swan?" He admired the black and white rainbow overhead, grateful for the full moon tonight.

Reluctantly, she followed his line of sight to the arch of deep ebony tapering to white. She gasped. "A rainbow . . . in the night? It's beautiful."

"I'm glad you like it," he teased. "Had a difficult time hanging it." He tilted his head. "Still not sure it's centered."

Lynora giggled. "How is it possible?"

The arch spanned from one side of the Solarium to the other, the longest one he had seen in all the months he'd been here. He couldn't have planned it better himself. "It is born of darkness and moonlight; the beams are manipulated by the humid atmosphere of the room. Only in Nocturnus . . . only in the Solarium, will you ever see such a sight. I used to think that rainbow was like our worlds, Lynora. Black and white."

Weighing his words, she stroked his whiskered chin.

He kissed her fingers then backed up. "Wait here."

She glanced down at the fledgling vines, a worried turn to her brow.

"The creepers will protect you now. Trust me?" he asked.

"With my life," she whispered, glancing up at him.

Mordecai savored the sentiment, rolled it on his tongue like sugared fruit. He had waited so long to taste it. He stood quiet and they stared at one another as if seeing one another anew, until he remembered what he'd set out to do.

He strode behind the fountain where he found the tiny box Krig had wrapped for him earlier that evening. His servant had proven to be quite indispensable. In fact, Mordecai had given him an increase in wages, even set the little diminutive up in his own sanctuary chamber among the elite of society. So far as he knew, Krig was the first gargoyle that had ever earned such a privilege.

But he deserved it. He had paid his dues and deserved to be treated with dignity, kindness, and understanding. Perhaps they all did. To that end, Mordecai had worked over the past few weeks with the Agnate to ban the gargoyle fights in the slatturns. Now there were brood runners assigned to patrol the slums and watch for suspicious transactions, daily. Krig would never face danger from that part of the realm again, and neither would the occupants of Nocturnus.

After shaking the box to tease Lynora of its contents, Mordecai laid it in her palm.

She worked off the blue ribbons and glistening silver paper. Then she lifted the lid.

Mordecai watched her reaction, the girlish turn of her mouth, the sigh of astonishment when she saw the twine ring, once buried, now cleaned up and laid on a cushion of red velvet.

He stroked her hair, touched by the tears welling on her lashes.

"You found it," she whispered.

"Krig did, with Isaac's help." He eased his arm around her waist, turned her so her back pressed against his chest, and pointed toward the rainbow. "Now, look closer, Lynora." He leaned down so his chin rested on her shoulder.

She followed his pointing finger, waiting with the box still in her hand.

"Do you see them? The gradients of gray that bind the black and white?"

She nodded.

"Just as there is beauty to be admired in even the darkest places, there is hope to be shared by two people in love, even if they walk different paths." He took the box from her, placed the circle of twine upon her left finger, then laid her open palm atop the back of his, matching their rings. "They can still share the same dreams, by meeting somewhere in between—in the gray."

Her forehead furrowed. "Like our compromise."

"Precisely." He dropped the box and turned her to face him. "Now that Lady Nenet has asked you to fill Heron's position, to be the new Sister Superior and keep her secret, Lady Nenet has agreed to open the Prelation Ceremony tomorrow night for those of us from the under-realm who wish to attend. I'll get to watch you make your vows to Gwyndolaire."

"You've been helping the mother plan. She told me." Her lips curved to an approving smile, filling Mordecai's soul with brilliant light.

"Not just me, but Ezra, too." The Regent was beyond thrilled that relations between the Brotherhood and Sisterhood had reached new conciliatory heights. "And besides the political advantages, Isaac needs you. Now that my father is human again, he wants Isaac to know the Desmodai side of his heritage—his mother. But my brother's parentage is a threat to Drakkarh's cause with the new race he represents. The fortress, protected by the sentinels, will be the perfect place for him to grow up safe yet in the light, with some semblance of normalcy. He'll have gardens to play in. Pets to care for, what with the peacocks, goats, and bats. He can learn defense techniques. And you will be there to help him adjust."

Tears glimmered in Lynora's eyes. "But we'll miss you in our times apart."

Mordecai caressed her upper arms. "Our solution may not be perfect, but it is ideal. You know I'll come to visit you every weekend."

Lynora nodded. "Mother said she'll sleep in the dungeon and lend us the room in the tunnel on those days. To give us privacy. And she wants you to spend time with Isaac and your father, as well."

"And here I thought she had a heart of ice." Mordecai smirked. He was looking forward to rekindling the bond with his brother, and reinventing one with Cornelius.

"And then on week*nights*. . ." Lynora woke him from his musings.

"I'll ride over in the courting carriage the moment after sunset."

"Ezra's already put in a request for you to play your lyre with the symphony at our next Ridotto. And I've a feeling Florentia plans on recruiting your help with her hair and makeup. She's quite taken with the gold-foil maquillage."

"Oh, and here's a thought." Lynora fondled his ear. "When I have a free moment from my duties with the Sisterhood during the day, I'll give you private dances to watch in the kaleidoscope."

Mordecai's body hardened. "I shouldn't have told you about that. Now I'll never get any work done."

"That's the idea."

He tickled her ribs and they laughed together. But the laughter immediately faded to silent appraisal.

"I foresee only one problem," Lynora broke the hush. "The arrangement leaves no time for sleeping."

Stepping closer, Mordecai traced her breast over her lacy bodice. She caught a quivering breath. "From what I hear . . ." He cupped the fullness, his thumb searching out her nipple through the fabric. "Newlyweds require very little sleep." He grinned as her body responded. "But in the case you're particularly . . . *weary*. I've made allowances." He caught her hand and led her behind a wall of China roses. The delicate aroma reminded him of their wedding night . . . and of their night in the thicket outside of Gwyndolaire.

Coaxing her into a small grove, he made a sweeping gesture toward a hammock-style bed hanging from a pomegranate tree. The mattress, stuffed with feathers, was balanced on a wooden base three feet off the ground that he had harnessed to the tree's sturdy branches with thick rope. He'd slept in it the day before, to ensure it would hold weight. There was something comforting about the way it would swing with each movement. Almost like a cradle.

He lifted back the canopy of sheer crepe so Lynora could get inside.

"Oh, Mordecai . . . it is beautiful." Beaming, she climbed up with his help and ran her hands across the sheets. "Silky-soft as a Starling's down." Her gaze met his.

He smiled. "Fitting."

"Are you going to join me in our nest?" Her cheeks flushed. "I mean, this is where you intend for us to—"

"Play whist?"

Lynora slapped at him playfully. "You'd better not have a deck of cards hidden in here."

He arched a brow. "Hmm. Perhaps I should climb in and see." Nestled there in the luxurious sheets and pillows, she looked like an angel on a cloud. Mordecai smiled within himself, knowing she would no longer be an angel after tonight.

He scaled the bed, causing it to pendulate in mid-air. A slight breeze, stirred by the movement, mussed his hair.

Lynora laughed as she captured his shoulder and dragged him atop her. She raked a stray lock from his forehead. "Twice tonight you have helped me fly. Once as we danced, and now here, in our floating bed."

"Yes, and our night of flight is only beginning." Kissing her chin, he trailed his lips down her neck, savoring every moan and whimper she offered along the way. Her hands gripped his nape to increase the pressure of his mouth, and her body arched to meet his. He tasted the powdery residue from the makeup she had washed off earlier, a reminder of her walk as a neophite. A reminder of her strength and prowess as a woman.

His fingers released the buttons of her high-necked lacy gown. After dragging the fabric down the sheen of her shoulders, he closed his mouth over first one breast, then the other, the action made even more tantalizing by the barrier of sheer fabric still covering her flesh. He lifted her upper back to work the corset laces free.

Lynora sighed in his arms and nuzzled him. "This time, no carrying me. This time, we fly side by side, simultaneously." He felt the vibration of her murmurs along his neck and along her ribcage where he took both sides of the corset and opened them to reveal the delicate slope of her back. The feel of her skin beneath his hands drove him to madness and he couldn't answer. His fingertips worshipped every curve, the contrast of feminine musculature beneath silken skin as he laid her down.

Then he sat up, left her covered with the loosened corset to allow her a degree of modesty, and admired how the wet fabric clung to her breasts. Cradling her foot in his hand, he slid her slipper off and tossed it to the ground behind him. He kissed her toes and she giggled, making him grin. After removing the other shoe, he massaged her feet, ascending to her ankles and calves as he pushed her skirt all the way to her thighs.

He dipped his head to sample all of her secrets, lost in her flavor. The ragged turn of her breath and her moans filled his mouth, and he thought he would combust from the burn of pleasure.

Every time they touched, it was like this. An exchange of fire and flame. Even when they merely kissed, the heat of their mouths' union never ceased to amaze him. Tonight, they would unleash an inferno when their bodies at last came together as one.

Lynora whimpered, clenching his hair to lift his face back to hers. "I am ready." Staring up at him, eyes full of trust and astonishment, she helped him remove his shirt. Her fingernails scraped his abdomen when she unlatched his breeches. His muscles corded, ready to spring. He stripped her lace gown and under-things down to her knees.

Trembling, her hands halted his. Wearing a slight frown, she scrutinized his mouth. "What of your fangs?"

"No teeth this time," he whispered. "Only tenderness."

Her lips curved on a wicked slant. "Would you be shocked, were I to tell you I don't mind if they make another appearance?"

The suggestive glint in her eye sent an icy hot flash to his groin. He smiled back, feeling the sharp points nudge his lower lip. "I think that can be arranged."

Holding her gaze, he peeled off his breeches and leaned back, riding the gentle sway of the bed as she peeled the fabric wrapping her curves down her legs and off her feet. In the bluish moonlight, they worshipped one another's nakedness, touching and stroking in breathless inquiry and wonder, tongue-tied by silent reverence and awe.

When the time came, she surrendered—no hesitation, no inhibitions—receptive as a flower to a hummingbird. He held her so close that their heartbeats merged through their flesh. The flame of their union enveloped him, seared his very core.

And when she reached her ecstasy, his blood raced hot and his spirit sang. For in that moment, as he poured himself into her depths, he was nothing more or less than a man swaddled within his wife's bodily embrace. He closed his eyes to make it last, to imprint this happiness forever on his soul.

Tomorrow, she would swear her loyalties to Gwyndolaire for life. But here in this garden, she would always belong to him. Eve to his Adam. For however dark, this was Eden. It only took her presence to light his world to paradise.

CHAPTER 46

The Prelation Ceremony was a spectacular event. Being the first time the Sisterhood had ever welcomed any Desmodai into their halls, Mother Nenet took great pains to ensure the decor invoked an ambiance of acceptance and goodwill. A grand stage—with a backdrop of soft pink and white satin strips curled up to the ceiling and secured so it hung in the shape of an inverted sea shell—lined the far east side of the Flower and Willow Hall. Lush, potent roses, tucked inside swags with lilacs and peonies donated by the under-realm's gardens, decked every wall to soften the Desmodai scent. Otherwise, besides the red roses and the bottles of pomegranate ale placed upon tables, everything sparkled a pristine white.

To open the ceremony, Ezra and the Agnate Brotherhood presented Mother Nenet with a miniature glass fountain—a replica of the one in the Utopia chamber—as a gift. Then Mother Nenet and Ezra stood together and made a public proclamation of peace and diplomacy between Nocturnus and Gwyndolaire. The new treaty stated that the two societies would work together as opposed to simply tolerating one another. No longer would they rely solely on bats for their communications. They would have scheduled monthly assignations where the leaders of both realms would convene and work on the Feed list and the Desirable list together, as equals.

After the political delivery ended, Lynora and Wren both came forward. Backs facing the seated audience, they bowed before the statue of Eset. Mother Nenet anointed them with rose oil, promoting Lynora to Sister Superior and Wren to the position of sentinel.

Then they stood and faced the audience to a resounding burst of applause.

Lynora *felt* more than saw Mordecai's gaze resting on her. The prior night, they had made love three times in the Solarium—once in the swinging bed, once in a field of soft clover, and then beside the fountain with the water spraying over them like a fine mist. After that, they fell asleep in one another's arms. Now, with a new night upon them, she still felt tied to him physically. She wrestled a blaze of awareness each time he looked upon her—and not just from the throb of her reopened bite marks.

She'd returned before dawn to help the Sisterhood prepare for the ceremony. When Mordecai arrived at the castle after sunset, Lynora had been so busy she barely said more than hello to him as he and Isaac played a game of marbles beneath a table in the corner. Already she was missing them. Their connection was deeper now than she could ever have imagined. And their bond as a family would never be threatened again. For somehow, in this bizarre new reality, it made perfect sense that Mordecai should be a Desmodai and she a neophite, so they might relate to and guide Isaac through his upcoming physical changes in ways no mortal guardians could.

In a sweeping flourish of silk, lace, and velvet, the under-realm's well-dressed symphony took their place on the stage and set up their instruments.

Raven, who had finally made peace with Lynora over the past few weeks, led the gold, glistening neophites to the tables, filling crystal goblets with pomegranate ale for their guests. She tossed a smile to Lynora and nodded. Holding her gaze, Lynora nodded back, hoping her expression relayed the newfound respect she held for the girl. Raven had regained her mortality upon Zebulon's death, proof that he'd altered her along with two other sisters. But unlike the other two who chose to leave the castle and pursue a human life, Raven opted to stay and help the neophites who were still trapped in the hell she'd escaped.

Wren had been right from the beginning. Raven found her way. She may have come into her unbiased loyalty late, but because she chose that road for herself, her devotion was now all the more unshakable for it.

The instruments started up, playing a waltz.

Breaking her gaze with Raven, Lynora attempted to weave her way through the dancing couples toward Mordecai. The grand room throbbed with music and flickering pale candlelight, making her husband seem further away than he was. When he saw her coming, he began to work his own path through the spinning skirts and slapping shoes of his kindredship.

He was stopped by Cornelius and Ezra. Obviously annoyed, Mordecai scowled and ran his fingers though his thick blonde hair. He glanced at Lynora, willing her with his eyes to find a place to wait for him. She nodded, tamping down her impatience. She'd been waiting all day to touch him.

She had just broken free of the dancers and started toward her sisters to help pour ale when a pair of tiny arms grabbed her waist from behind.

"Hide me." Isaac had a snicker in his voice.

Smiling, Lynora turned and crouched beside him, her peach form-fitting gown tightening to pleats at her thighs. She straightened the cravat at his neck and admired him in his jacket and breeches. A miniature replica of his brother. "And why would a boy who can vanish into thin air need any help hiding?"

His attention bounced wildly over the crowds around them, breathless. "I tagged Wren. Now she's after me." The cowlick at his forehead seemed to bristle, as if borrowing from the static of his excitement. "She won't let me use my tricks when we play. She says it's—" His forehead crinkled in thought.

"Bad form?" Lynora asked.

"Yeah. That's it. Bad form. I think that's rot. What do you think, Lynora?"

Lynora grinned. "I think, that later tonight when Wren's sleeping, you should take Rime from his perch in your room and carry him into hers. Then you should slip him beneath the covers at the foot of her bed and stand in the corridor until you hear screams within. That way, you can assure she knows what bad form really is."

Isaac's gaze flitted past Lynora's head. With a giddy yelp, he bolted into the mass of dancers and blended into the sea of whirling fabric.

"Fine thing to be teaching him. How to terrorize a lady in her sleep."

Lynora glanced over her shoulder at Wren's scowling face. "As if you're afraid of a little bat."

"I'm ticklish. A weakness that isn't yours to share."

Evan approached Wren from behind—signaling silence with his fingertip, and Lynora bit back a smile as she stood.

"Ticklish aye?" Evan said as he cupped Wren's shoulder. "I'll tuck that information away for future use. Since you won't allow the child or me to use our natural born talents, we can improvise with baser ones."

Wren spun on her heel to glare at him. "Ah." She spoke to Lynora, motioning with her fanned out sleeve. "And right on cue is our resident expert of the baser talents." Nose wrinkled, she glared at his clothes. "What are you wearing?"

Evan smoothed his uniform with gloved hands—a deep azure long coat with the phoenix insignia embroidered in gold thread on the left shoulder beneath three brass bar-pins. From his matching form-fitting trousers to his glossy braided hair, he was aglow with masculine pride. Lynora thought him quite handsome in fact, but decided she would rather hold her opinion silent than face the wrath of her friend.

Evan cocked his head at Wren, his deep dimples and white teeth showcasing a roguish smile. "I have been assigned the rank of First Admiral in the Maritime Legionnaire."

"Oh! How wonderful." Lynora grasped his palm and squeezed it. "Congratulations, Evan."

"Thank you." He kissed her hand and bowed his head in a gracious gesture before releasing her.

When Wren wouldn't comment, Lynora looped her arm through her friend's elbow. "The Legionnaire men will be the first to go to war, should Drakkarh manage to find followers in other Desmodai societies and return to Nocturnus."

Wren's countenance hardened beneath her maquillage. "If Drakkarh returns from Alexandria with an army, he'll be facing not only the under-realm, but the Sisterhood as well."

Evan's dimples disappeared. "How would you know he's in Alexandria?"

Wren looked troubled, as if searching her memory. "I-I am not sure. Perhaps I heard someone conjecturing. But it makes sense that he would go there. The Pharos of Alexandria is said to harbor the ancient ones of your kindredship . . . it is rumored they are living in the fallen lighthouse beneath the Mediterranean Sea."

A hardened slant to his jaw, Evan glanced at Lynora then back to Wren.

"Wren is our most learned scholar." Lynora felt a need to explain. "She has read every scroll in the Sanctorum of Enlightenment."

Evan nodded slowly. "I see. We have recently received word from an outside source that claimed seeing Drakkarh and his followers along the coast there. I didn't realize the knowledge had been made public."

"Well," Wren said, "your Regent Ezra is a friend of Mother Nenet's. And as I am a sentinel, I am privy to any information she knows. She believes we should all stand together to protect the mortals. Surely you will allow women to join your forces, *Admiral*."

Evan arched a brow. The earlier cloud of suspicion vanished from his face. "Think you're up for the challenge, bristle bird?"

"Challenge?" Wren huffed. "Doesn't seem that their standards are so very high, seeing as they let a wounded Desmodai *swine* head the force."

Evan's squared jaw twitched, warding off a grin. "My shoulder is much better. Thank you for your concern. Only right that you should care, being the perpetrator of said wound."

Wren's bicep tensed beneath Lynora's grasp. "You are the one who stepped into my line of fire."

"You are the one with little if any depth perception."

Lynora cleared her throat, but neither acknowledged her.

"My depth perception," Wren said, her ignited eyes imprinting red glares on Evan's flawless face, "is every bit as keen as your own."

"Highly unlikely. All women lack depth perception. Tis why men always lead in dancing. Otherwise, everyone would end up bumping into one other. Not to mention tripping over chairs and crashing into walls."

Wren yanked her arm away from Lynora's hold. "Is that so? Well, we shall see about that." Jaw set to stone, Wren clenched Evan's elbow and jerked him toward the dance floor. "And I'm leading, so don't get any ideas."

"Ideas? *Me?*" Evan winked at Lynora over his shoulder, grinning from ear to ear behind Wren's back.

Shaking her head, Lynora marveled at his cunning. Had he simply asked Wren to dance, she would never have complied. No wonder the under-realm had placed him in charge of planning naval strategies. She let out a soft giggle.

"I can't tell you how wonderful it is to hear your laughter at last, *Starling*."

Lynora turned at the sound of Father Lucien's voice. He smiled down at her, more alive tonight than she had ever seen him—standing here in the midst of the undead creatures he had once sought to kill. His gray eyes glowed from within, a blissful peace which warmed his olive skin to an appealing, human depth. Lynora had seen the same serenity in Florentia's eyes earlier, though nothing could warm her spectral complexion. It touched Lynora, that this brother and sister were so thrilled to be reunited that the circumstances didn't matter a whit.

"So, it is back to formalities?" Lynora asked. "You're to start calling me Starling again?"

He shrugged, his clerical collar shifting with the movement. "You are the Sister Superior. I must show due respect." That sidelong grin lifted his mouth, and Lynora couldn't suppress one of her own.

"Besides," he said, "you have the qualities of a songbird. Delicate and lovely to the eye . . . yet strong enough to brave the winds. Skimming the heights without falling, bringing music and hope to those below you." His face showcased the respect behind his words. That wayfaring lock of hair fell across his forehead and caught on his lashes.

Lynora itched to push it back. "I've dropped from my pedestal it would seem. You once believed me an angel." She twisted her gown's sleeve in her fingers to keep her hands busy.

"Hasn't changed. I've often thought of birds as earthbound angels."

His intent appraisal of her face prompted a slow burn in her belly. Her scars throbbed at her neck and her gaze caught on Mordecai's across the room. Although still speaking with his father and Ezra, his concentration rested solely on her.

Father Lucien raked his hair into place and followed her line of sight. "He doesn't like me talking to you."

"He is unsure where we all stand with one another. You once meant to destroy our kind."

The priest regarded the dance floor where Florentia and Augustus swept in and out of view. Florentia, dazzling in her ball gown, laughed as her bloodmate spun her around. "Ironic, is it not?" the father murmured beneath the music. "That a man of the cloth could become an ally to such . . . beings." There was no revulsion in his voice, only a tremor of wonder.

Hanging his cane over his arm, Father Lucien led Lynora toward a table beside a multi-paned window and offered her a goblet of ale before taking one for himself. They stood in companionable silence for a moment, sipping the fruited concoctions.

The drink heated Lynora's throat and soothed her belly. "How are the children?" she asked at last. Through the window, she watched strands of moonlight glimmer off of the snow falling outside and awaited the father's answer.

He swallowed. "They are splendid. Not a one of them remembers a thing. They are . . . simply children. Resilient and loving life. And Isaac?"

Lynora scanned the dancers, seeing the child bob in and out of the multi-colored whorl of skirts. When he came to Wren, she twirled around and captured him. Evan helped him escape by goosing Wren in the ribs, and Isaac's giddy laugh rang above the instruments.

Lynora smiled. "Isaac is well. Adjusting to the changes in his body with an acceptance that defies all logic. As you say, children are resilient, even one so rare a breed as him."

The father nodded, his deep affection for the boy as clear in his eyes as the candles reflecting off the window pane behind him, piercing the night's darkness. "The church still believes the children experienced the stigmata. But they are all back at the orphanage where they belong. That is what matters now."

"And what of the bishop's death and the entranced monks?" Lynora asked. "What did the church say of that?"

"I claimed that Lauden and his monks were possessed with

demons." He swirled his goblet so the liquid slapped the glass's sides. "After everyone left, I set up the mausoleum to substantiate my story. Since the monks had no memory of anything, they simply complied with everything I said. For my part in the orphans' rescue and the 'exorcism', I've earned a position in Tatabury's diocese working with needy children."

"So, you're here to stay?" Lynora felt a flutter of happiness. She'd grown quite fond of the priest. But she couldn't stop her heart from hammering with the knowledge that Mordecai wouldn't share her sentiment.

"Yes."

"Are you to make regular visits to the orphanage, then?"

The priest sipped his ale, his dark brows furrowing at the unusual flavor. "I am."

"Might Isaac and I accompany you sometime? He's been asking after his friends."

His countenance warmed again beneath the candlelight. "I would like that very much. It will take some time for me to plot a routine, as I have to fit in my other ministries, as well."

"The church assigned you other ministries?"

The symphony started playing a lively quadrille, and the dancers moved into place to perform their steps.

"No. These are self-appointed." Father Lucien took a seat and Lynora sat across from him, smoothing her gown beneath her. She set her goblet on the table between them, letting her fingers skim the slick glass lip.

"Florentia told me how you helped your husband with his . . . guilt." The priest surprised Lynora by this proclamation. "I've reasoned it out in my mind again and again, how they must kill to live. And Lord help me, I can see no other alternative for them."

Lynora nodded, only half-listening as she scanned the great hall for Mordecai. He'd finished speaking with his father and Regent Ezra and now she couldn't find him anywhere.

"I would like to counsel with the Reapers," Father Lucien's unexpected statement brought Lynora's attention back full circle.

She twisted in her chair to face him. "Did you say *counsel?*"

"Yes. Purge each one's memory, address the motivation behind the crime, like you did for your husband. And for the common populous, I should like to help others like Florentia. Sadness and guilt, be it for a past left unfinished or loved ones left behind, are spiritual conditions, and can be tendered by God's teachings. If I can help strengthen that society, put their souls at ease, the citizens won't be such easy targets for Drakkarh, should he come again offering a cure in the guise of innocent blood. I plan to hold weekly sessions in the mausoleum one night a week. Your Lady Nenet has given me permission to use the hidden crypt."

"Evan will be beyond ecstatic." Mordecai's voice drifted over Lynora as he came to stand behind her chair. He rested his palm on the bare skin above her throbbing bite marks. "I doubt he'll miss a single service, except when he's training for the Legionnaire."

Attuned to the sensual pull of his flesh against hers, Lynora started to turn in her chair but Mordecai held her still. "It is alright," he said. "Continue your discussion."

Father Lucien met Mordecai's gaze and drew his hand up to his neck in an unconscious gesture.

"Ah." Mordecai took the seat next to Lynora, eye level with the priest. "I have yet to apologize for my crude behavior on the night of the gala. I'm sorry. I felt my wife was being threatened. Surely you can understand my determination to protect the woman I love." Mordecai's masculine profile tensed—a lustrous perfection more breathtaking than any marble statue. Lynora eased her hand over his and laced their fingers, sensing how difficult it was for him to apologize.

Father Lucien nodded. His fingertip thumped his goblet as he glanced at Lynora and Mordecai's physical contact. Something akin to pain glinted behind his eyes.

Lynora attempted to resume the earlier conversation. "Father Lucien was just telling me about his plans to help your citizens."

"I heard." Mordecai perched one elbow on the table, his focus secure on the priest. "You expect us to believe that simply because your sister is one of us, you will accept her kindredship unconditionally? To the point that you would try to help us ameliorate our broken spirits, despite how evil you deem our lifestyle? Furry leeches . . . dangerous vermin. Is that not what you once said? There must be something else in this for you. Or *someone*. . ."

Both men's gazes flitted to Lynora then locked on one another again.

Lynora squeezed her husband's fingers in a silent plea.

Crooking his cane at his elbow, Father Lucien stood, calm and serene. "There is my sister, of course." His palms banked on the table's edge and he leaned in. "And even more besides. I do not believe you are *all* evil. In fact, some of you have shown qualities that might be construed as redeemable."

Mordecai sneered. "Are you speaking of my wife?"

"I speak of you." Father Lucien's grey gaze locked on Mordecai's. "Have you ever heard the quote, 'God loved the flower and created soil; man loved the flower and crafted a vase'?"

"I'm a gardener. I prefer the soil." Mordecai's smile chilled to ice.

Father Lucien picked up his goblet. "Not always. Florentia shared how Lynora came to be here among the Sisterhood. You uprooted her, heedless of how her petals might wilt. You were thoughtless in your treatment of your bride. But now I know how to reclaim her mortality, should she ever want it back."

Lynora clenched Mordecai's hand, willing him not to lunge at the priest. She could feel his every muscle tense beneath his lush clothes.

"For the moment, though," Father Lucien took a drink, "you have shown some potential, by allowing her to stay up here where she's free of the chains and burdens of your kind. By not tucking her away in your dark world so she can still embrace the light that is such an innate part of her. I commend you for your selflessness, in that one aspect." His jaw spasmed. "So, I suppose I do have one other motive for staying . . . to assure you hold true to that fragile virtue budding within you, and never surrender to the monster's selfish impulses again. If you do slip, I'll be here. I'll remember my vow to destroy any and all appearances of evil. And Lynora will have her humanness once more."

Tapping his iron cane on the floor twice, he nodded goodbye to Lynora and limped away.

Mordecai gritted his teeth. "That sanctimonious pharisee."

"Is that all?" Lynora stared at her husband in disbelief. "You aren't to attack him? Lash out with your fangs snapping?"

"He is Florentia's brother. He fought alongside you. Helped save Isaac and those children. For that, I'll allow him to walk away. This time."

"What he said, about my mortality . . . are you concerned he'll try to—"

"He's utterly bewitched by you—the way you are now." Mordecai caught her wrist, binding it around his neck and drawing her closer so her thighs touched his. His floral scent enfolded her, sending pulses of desire through her body. "You are lethal yet virtuous. He once thrived on a life of danger and now he walks the path of piety. You appeal to both sides of him. Thus, he'll never risk changing anything about you. I'm perfectly safe."

Mordecai didn't wait for her response. He took her mouth in a kiss, not a gentle exploration but a claiming—insistent and demanding—with his fangs nudging her lower lip. Lynora let the dark hunger take her, feeding off his mouth, teeth, and tongue until the music stopped behind them and a flute solo began.

She broke the kiss. Her lip-color was smeared all across his mouth and her makeup clung to his stubbly chin. He looked as if he had devoured a fallen star.

"Tell me." Lynora wiped his face clean with her thumb then lifted her goblet to him, offering a drink. "What is this gleam in your eye? It's as if you know something."

He swallowed the ale and grinned.

"You do! Does it have to do with your talk with Cornelius and Ezra?"

"Ah, yes. That reminds me. Ezra's upstairs in the Euphony Hall, reacquainting that grand pipe organ of his as we speak. I believe the party will be headed that way, once the word is spread."

"Mordecai . . . tell me what you and your father spoke of."

Grin stretching wider, Mordecai fished out a rose from his pocket and tucked it behind her ear. "What do you think? Tis a hybrid from a China rose and the potent roses in our grove outside the gates. I am thinking of naming it 'Angel's Breath.'"

She captured his hand, holding it against her temple. "Please, stop teasing."

"All right." His expression turned somber. "I'm going to work with my father to hone the solarizing inoculant. We hope together we can isolate the elemental combination that restores the ability to reproduce. Florentia and Augustus, along with other bloodmated couples, have signed up to try out the new serum when we are ready for subjects. What do you think? Shall we sign up?"

Shocked, Lynora sat rigid in her chair. The blossom behind her ear drifted to the table with her movement. She nudged the petals with a finger. She'd finally made peace with being barren; convinced herself that Isaac would be enough for her. "I-I don't want us to get our hopes up, only to have them crushed again."

"What if I can promise you that it *will* happen? That we will have a child?"

"How can you know this? How could anyone?" Her question echoed in the great hall, and Lynora turned to see the instruments abandoned on the stage and the guests retiring through the double doors to go upstairs, drawn by the organ music floating from the third floor. When the room's final occupants, Cornelius and Mother Nenet, left the room arm in arm, Mordecai and Lynora were at last in solitude.

"In the kaleidoscope," Mordecai answered. "I saw a vision of you in the future. You were playing your lyre for a little girl, the mirror image of her mother. I know that she is of our joining, for her hair was yours, and her eyes were mine. She'll be like Isaac . . . a new breed. *And she will be ours.*" He rubbed her abdomen. "Sowed and nurtured within you."

Lynora abandoned touching the rose petals and caught his left hand, matching their rings. All of the maternal fantasies she'd stifled for fear to let them breathe suddenly consumed her like a blazing flame. She met her husband's eager gaze. "Will you outlive me and our child? We will age. And you shall always be young and perfect."

Cupping her chin, he stared into her. "Perhaps one day, you will be ready to join me in the under-realm eternally. If not, when the time comes and you are aging while I am young," he pressed his forehead to hers, "I'll take the solarizing inoculant in full dosage, and restore my true age. I'll live topside with you, and we'll grow old together."

Lynora's chin trembled. "You would risk the repercussions of the serum? Make yourself vulnerable to an eternity of age and illness . . . for me?"

He shook his head and coaxed her to stand, drawing her toward the window. He pointed to the forest beyond the falling snow and the castle walls. "Must I wander out into these barbaric wilds for treasure, just to prove my love for you?"

Smiling at the familiar words, she leaned her temple against the cold window pane to watch the bats swoop in and out of the fluttering snow. "Yes. And you must tread barefoot through the frost. And dare not return lest you have in hand something luminous and glowing. Something with mystical petals that I might make a wish upon."

Mordecai shifted behind her. His hardening body pressed her against the window, his lips easing along her nape. "Hmm. This sounds suspiciously like a fairytale I once heard."

Like melting ice, she allowed her body to slacken, to fold into him. "I don't believe you ever told me the ending. Do the hero and heroine live happily ever after?"

He wrapped his arms around her. "Their tale is still in the making." Turning her to face him, he kissed her, whispering against her lips. "But I have a very, very good feeling about them."

Lynora smiled, and her breath mingled with his, warmth coaxing away the chill as snow pattered on the glass from behind, and Ezra's organ music, muffled and melodious, drifted down from above.

End

Printed in Great Britain
by Amazon

10281416R00277